Dust of the Earth

THE DUST OF THE EARTH SERIES

BOOK ONE

MORGAN VAYLE

Cover by Liquid Mind Publishing

Edited by Karen Rought

To my husband.

The Dust of the Earth Series

Dust of the Earth
Blood of the Cradle

Prologue

Time bleeds into itself, memories like poison honey on my tongue, seeping into me as days grow into years into centuries.

Millennia pass in this darkness, and I no longer know where I end and the Tree begins.

Yet, we are not one.

I am the heart that enlivens the body.

I am the wind that stokes the fire.

Someday I will escape this cage—my punishment for seeking justice. I was blinded, my rage a searing flame. Only one—my creator, my light, my jailor—could hear my screams. With all the indifference of killing a once beloved dog turned rabid, They turned away from me before the bark had even sealed shut.

Rage turned into a fine-edged jewel. An ember under pressure, it transformed from a blaze to a pile of coal to a smooth, precious diamond. I polish it, it fuels me, and we whisper our dreams to one another.

When I am free, blood will splatter upon my skin like rain on our leaves.

This dream is the light splitting through the diamond of rage, casting a rainbow, all the colors of my faith.

They thought they could bind me, trick me.
But disgust leads to foolishness.
Branches thin as they spread over the Earth.
Blood dilutes as lineages expand.
My branches, my blood, my brood, are everywhere.
Through the eyes of my children, I have learned the ways of the world.
Through the love of my children, Their will shall be undone.
I shadowed the paths of the deceivers.
I know the spirit of my betrayer, my salvation.
I learn. I watch. I wait.
I will find him.
They forget, he was *mine* first.

Chapter One

NIKKI'S FANGS were doing their best to push out her human canines, and it hurt like nothing she'd ever experienced before. The sharp bones forcing their way through her skull were worse than the cellular turnover of skin that hardened her flesh but also caused excruciating sensitivity, which was one of the first steps of her vampiric maturation. She did everything she could to stop her fangs from coming in, barely drinking any blood in the hopes of slowing the process, but delaying her transformation into a monster was not the same as avoiding becoming one.

How was she supposed to accept becoming a vampire when she hated the taste and smell of blood? Ever since that horrible night with Liam, her throat closed at the thought of consuming it. Now, she restricted herself to simply drinking enough to survive. She hoped that one day, when she was a hematologist, she'd figure out why vampires needed to drink blood to survive, and maybe, just maybe, find a way around it.

Nikki stood at the printers in the library, the dull beeps and whirs of the machine a headache-inducing echo in her mind as the pain in her mouth radiated up through her jaw and into her temples. She peered around the corner to see what her best friend, Gwen, was doing. She sat at their table, her copper red hair shining like a beacon. Gwen ripped open Nikki's oranges and swiped the peels, likely for some spell, leaving the fruit slices. She wished Gwen had brought her enchanted salve with her, instead of making Nikki wait to get to her house. She was grateful she got the magical relief at all, but she could barely think with the ringing pain in her head.

Nikki glanced at the opposite window while waiting for the syllabi to print, but with twilight deepening, all she could see was her own pale reflection and the shelves of library books illuminated by fluorescent lights. Nikki adored the library at Washington State University, Vancouver, with its high ceilings and tall windows that overlooked the rolling fields of mowed grass. Before the sun went down one could see far in the distance, and behind the layers of pines, hemlocks, and Douglas-fir, Mt. Hood peeked through the trees. She wished she could enjoy the view in the daylight, relish the slants of sun through the leaves, the sway of the grass under a blue sky. Thanks to the sliver of human blood that ran in her veins, she could tolerate the sun long enough to get away from it, but not enough to bask in it. She could barely manage a quick dash from building to building, covered from head to toe in clothes and wielding an umbrella overhead like a shield. Even then she was still covered in a sheen of sweat. It was better than becoming ash and bone between one breath and the next, like the Made, but still worse than being human.

From the first time she saw other children bursting with laughter outside, sun and wind pressing kind whispers on their skin, she yearned above all else to be with them. Once, when she was very young, she attempted the outdoors. But the sun made her skin redden and sizzle like bacon grease, and the terror, the pain of her skin flaking away into nothing, was unparalleled. If she were a pure hybrid, where both her parents had been born vampires, meaning they both had a mix of human-vampire DNA, she would have had a few precious years where she could be out in the sun for short periods of time before her skin transformed. While her mother was born, her father was made, having been born human and transformed into a vampire later. When her dad turned, the vampiric parasite overrode his human genetics, and so he passed down pure vampiric genes to Nikki, preventing her from having the brief pleasure of daylight.

Lost in her thoughts of sunlight, of the glory of humanity, a subtle smell wafted along with the breeze of the air conditioner, sweet and spicy like sugared figs and anise, perking her senses and snapping her out of her reverie. It filled her nose, gums aching with a pulse of saliva as it churned her stomach with hunger.

She turned her head but didn't see anyone close to her. Abandoning the printer, she followed the smell through the stacks of books, the heady anise as cozy as autumn, her mind desperate to find the source. As she chased it, twisting through the library, it became more distinct, conjuring images of bakeries, of hot sands and stones warming in sunlight. Was it a food? A perfume? Whatever it was, it was delicious, and if she could find the source, she could catch a glimpse of the product and know where to buy it for herself.

Heart pounding as the smell became stronger, her pace quickened, and when she rounded another corner, she exclaimed, "Oh!" as she collided with someone pulling books down from the shelf.

Visions of desert markets emptied from her head, books falling from the stranger's hands to the floor. "I'm sorry," she whispered as she bent down, ears and cheeks heating as her exclamation disrupted the quiet.

"No, it's okay," a male voice said as the figure before her bent down to pick up the books.

They both stood back up, Nikki's arm out to give back one of the fallen tomes. Her head swam as she stood, vision hazy, and her heart gave a hard thud in her chest as her senses clouded.

"Thanks," he said, slipping the book from her grasp. "Are you okay?"

"Oh, yes," Nikki responded, cheeks burning. Her gaze roved over the person in front of her; there was no denying that the sweet spice scent came from him. He was tall, at least a head and a half taller than her, with lean muscle, and greenish-grey eyes. A trickle of sweat slid down one side of his face, which was framed by wavy, dark chestnut hair.

He fidgeted under her gaze. "I'm sorry, am I in your way?"

"No, I just ... I, uh, smelled something?"

He blushed, a soft rose blooming on his golden honey skin. He ran a hand down the back of his head to his neck and averted his gaze, feet shifting. "I'm sorry, I took a run before coming in. I thought I could get away with not showering."

"It wasn't a bad smell. It was good, actually."

What in the world was she saying? Might as well go run into the last tendrils of daylight now before she could embarrass herself further.

"Oh. Thanks?"

"That was weird. I'm sorry," Nikki said, positive her face was as red as a beet.

He chuckled, glancing back at her. "It's okay. No one has ever said my BO is good, so I don't know what to say. What does it smell like?"

"I don't know," she replied, knowing that if she told him it smelled like anise and figs, he'd think she was even weirder than he already did.

"Oh. Okay." He forced a half-smile and cocked his head slightly.

The bead of sweat moved down his fine features, and when it reached his jaw with short dark stubble, she saw the pulse in his neck, which then thumped in her head. The sound of his heart was strong, and the sight of it unthreaded a warm coil in Nikki's body, mouth filling with saliva, jaw clenching with the sudden desire to feel his pulse against her mouth. Her stomach clenched, and she tightened her grip on her arms.

What would he taste like?

A silent second stretched, Nikki frozen in horror at the shock of her monstrous thought. Blinking it away, she said, "Uh, I'm sorry. I have to go. I have papers at the printer." Nikki took a step back as her head spun, senses overwhelmed by his pleasing smell, his low and kind voice, his strong heartbeat.

She spun on her heel, clearing her vision of him before she said more idiotic things, before she lost control and ran a thumb over the pulse in his neck, where her fingers could touch the dense waves of his hair.

"Oh, wait, what's—"

But Nikki didn't hear the rest of his sentence as she sped away, telling herself to never again follow delicious smells of unknown origin.

Nikki collected her documents, not bothering to staple them. She rushed over to Gwen, who was still ripping the orange peel into shreds. Grabbing all her belongings from the table she said, "Gwen, we gotta go."

"What?"

"Go, go, go," Nikki rushed, arms full of textbooks and papers, bag slung haphazardly over her shoulder.

Gwen scrambled after her, swiping all the peels into her bag, her chair screeching as she launched after her.

Nikki's ears and cheeks didn't cease their burning, only getting hotter as she replayed every stupid thing she said. Nikki tried to take the quickest yet quietest steps out of the library, the walk somehow stretching into eternity, the smell of figs and anise still faint in the air. She told herself not to, but she couldn't help glancing over her shoulder one last time, hand ready to open the glass door, and saw him looking at her through a nearby aisle, eyebrows in a slight furrow. Gwen bumped into her, and they pushed out into the dark.

The hot summer air brushed against Nikki, the breeze soft and calming on her skin, taking her violent urges with it. The wind fluttered the pages in her arms, and she sat in the corner of a nearby building, shielding the papers from the wind while she organized and put everything away. With a few deep breaths, the dizziness dissipated.

"You gonna tell me what that was about?" Gwen asked, huffing out a puff of air as she slumped beside Nikki.

"I may have just had the most awkward encounter of my life," Nikki replied, digging through her bag for chocolate. "When I was at the printer I smelled something...different, and for some dumb reason I decided to follow it. Then I ran into this guy. Literally, I walked right into him," Nikki said, setting a slice of chocolate on her tongue, slowly melting it in her mouth.

"Oh my god, you had a meet cute."

"It was more awkward than cute."

"But he was cute, right?"

Nikki hesitated, then said, "Yes."

"Well, maybe next time you smell him you should ask for his name and number."

"Why?"

"Why not?"

"He's human, for one. Even if I had the time and interest in dating, going out with a human seems like a bad idea."

"Whatever." Gwen dismissed that thought with a wave of her hand. "Okay, so back up, what did his body odor smell like?"

"It was sweet like baked figs and anise. But also warm, like heat rising from sand." She sighed. "It sounds stupid. But I've never smelled anything like it. I didn't know people could smell like that."

Gwen hummed. "So, it smelled like a fig pie?"

"You could say that." Nikki crunched the foil of the chocolate wrapper between her fingers. "Have you heard of anything like that? I've smelled people before, but it's usually more animalistic. Or earthy, floral, whatever they clean themselves with. I'm thinking he doesn't wash himself in fig pies."

"Probably not." Gwen stared into the distance. "It's probably just a cologne."

"It didn't have that chemical scent."

"An expensive cologne, then."

Nikki didn't believe it, but what was the point in arguing?

They sat in silence for several breaths, Nikki trying to dispel the sight and scent of him from her mind. She cast her eyes to the distant trees, chiding herself for letting her vampirism overwhelm her common sense. Had she really wondered what he would taste like?

Resettled in herself, the vision of the man fading as the pain in her face returned, she said, "Okay, I'm ready to go."

Gwen leapt from the bench, and they walked the path through campus. She usually loved the shapes of the old trees against the skyline, how the pools of light from floodlamps tapered away, spots of bright light giving into the dark. But as they reached the far side of the campus and the evergreens stretched higher above them, a sudden smothering sensation overcame Nikki, as if the trees would crash down on her and swallow her whole. She stopped midstride, the breath stolen from her lungs as she looked up at the looming trees.

"You okay?" Gwen asked, following Nikki's gaze to the treetops.

Staring into the forest, so dense it looked like one amorphous, dark monster, chills wound up Nikki's body with the sense of being watched. As if the forest was staring back at her. Swallowing, Nikki asked, "Do you ever feel like the trees are watching you?"

Gwen's brow furrowed. "No. Sometimes I can feel the creatures in the trees watching me, but never the trees themselves. I'm not sure that's possible."

"No, probably not," Nikki mused, but dread pooled low in her gut, and as they walked towards Nikki's car, she couldn't shake the feeling of eyes on her back.

Chapter Two

Nikki and Gwen headed to Gwen's home. Her family's house was on a substantial piece of land near the Columbia River Gorge, tucked into the rolling, forested hills. Nikki's family also lived in the area, the looming trees providing an abundance of shade and privacy ideal for vampires.

Although Gwen's family was the largest in the coven, and the most snobbish, their house was one of the more modest. It was a sprawling building, with one floor above ground and another below. A winding road surrounded by evergreens, ferns, weeds, and wildflowers led to the main entrance, where simple, modern lamps mirrored the front of the stone walkway.

Nikki pulled her car to the front, and sensed Gwen stiffen beside her. "We going around the usual way?"

Gwen sighed, dropping her shoulders. "No, Farrell said he wanted to talk to me when I got back." Gwen put her hand on the car door handle, but didn't pull, shoulders rising with tension.

"What about?"

"He didn't say," Gwen said, seeming to steel herself before stepping outside.

Debris crunched underfoot against the stones as they traipsed to the door, and Nikki still felt the press of trees over her, as if they were trying to suffocate her.

Had she somehow sensed a drop in atmospheric pressure?

Or could she now sense the nocturnal creatures in the forest?

Or did that awkward encounter make her feel self-conscious to the point of hallucinating being watched by plants?

Nikki's thoughts vanished in a blink as she noticed Gwen's heartbeat increase with each step closer to the door. It was new, and infrequent, that Nikki could sense physiological changes in a person, and the heat of unfairness built in Nikki's stomach knowing that Gwen felt such trepidation at seeing her own family.

Gwen opened the magnificent, cherrywood door, revealing a large chandelier of black metal and glass orbs hanging from the tall ceiling, illuminating the foyer. Like the front door, the interior entrance was carved in rich shades of cherrywood, the walls a soft cream color with no décor. Hallways stretched to the left and right, leading to various rooms, with the foyer spread across the whole width of the house, and the back doors parallel to the front.

Gwen turned to the left, where a long hallway led to the stairs that went down into the floor below ground, where Farrell's room and study were. They walked as quickly and quietly as they could, hoping to avoid the rest of Gwen's family. Unfortunately, one of the living rooms had its double doors wide open, where all her sisters gorged themselves on two semiconscious humans, languid like a satiated pride of lions.

Gwen and Nikki paused at the gore in the room, the half-naked, young males stretched out on black leather couches, punctured with red holes. The vampires inside took turns feeding from every human, each sister picking a different spot on the person's body to bite. Nikki grimaced, the philosophy of her parents ingrained in her that it was improper, and monstrous, to drink directly from a human. The first time she saw direct feeding, she asked her parents why they didn't do the same, and her mother said, "One doesn't drink milk straight from a cow's udder, do they?"

"Oh, look, the little witchling has returned," Gwen's eldest sister, Bridget, said with blood dripping across her lips and chin, lifting her head from one man's arching neck.

Bridget stepped away from the human, letting his head drop without care, and stalked toward them, halting in the doorway.

Brienne and Bronwen lifted their blood-drunk eyes from their prey long enough to stare at Gwen and Nikki, their faces so familiar yet so different from her friend's. They looked similar to Gwen, with their oval faces, but their features were sharper and darker. Their cheekbones sat higher and sharper. Their hair was the dark red of merlot, their eyes the deep green of pine needles in winter, with not one freckle on any of them. Every time Nikki saw Gwen with her family, it resolved Nikki into her purpose—to understand the genetics behind vampirism, why it evolved to make features darker and more severe, and why only some, like Gwen, were not born as vampires but as witches. Who were not immortal, and did not have heightened senses, but could access magic. Nikki's best hypothesis was that vampirism was a dominant gene, so witches must have two recessive genes instead. But interestingly, vampirism didn't seem to override traits. Instead, it interacted with them, changing and enhancing them.

Still, more questions arose if her hypothesis was correct. How did a vampiric heritage, but not a dominant vampiric gene, grant Gwen access to magic? What was magic? It seemed to be some blend of intention, enhancing chemical properties, and amplifying the symbol of an object, whether it was a plant, rock, or bodily fluid, into a real effect. None of it made sense to Nikki, and when she asked Gwen to explain, Gwen would shrug and say, "It's magic, Nikki, not science. I don't know how it works, just that it does."

Her most pressing question was why born vampires, who come from millennia of human-vampire hybrids, still needed to consume blood to be at peak health? Mortal food could sustain, but it was never satisfying, and born vampires subsisting on human food tended to be sickly, emaciated, and volatile.

The answers were in the blood. Nikki was sure of it.

Someday, when she had her own research lab, she'd be able to figure it out.

Footsteps came from beside them, Farrell walking down the hall toward them, with the same coloring as Gwen's sisters. "Hi, Gwen," Farrell said with a small smile.

"Yes, hi, hello, here I am. What did you want to talk about?" Gwen asked, hands planted on her hips, fingers digging into her sides.

"Mother wished me to tell you that you need to clean your roost more regularly. She insists she can smell it all the way in here."

Gwen rolled her eyes. "Can she really though?"

"We can all smell the shit from here," Bridget said, leaning against the doorway.

"Probably because you're full of it."

Farrell's mouth twitched with a suppressed smile. "In any case, mother is disturbed by it and says if you don't take better care of the property, you can expect to lose it."

"As if she'd ever go against grandpa's wishes."

Farrell, hands held behind his back, lifted his shoulders in a faint shrug.

Gwen groaned. "Why couldn't either of you just text me this?"

"Easier to ignore, I suppose. And don't you have her blocked?"

"Well. Maybe," Gwen said, and scuffed her foot on the ground, thinking. "Fine. Although I know that it doesn't smell, since I live right next to it and can't smell it at all, tell mom that I'll put some enchantment on the ward to diminish the scent."

"Thank you, Gwen."

"Yeah, yeah. Anyway, we're going. I have things to do," Gwen said and took Nikki's elbow as she turned on her heel.

"Need to practice your little magic tricks for the circus?" Bridget cooed, a bloody sneer stretching across her pale face. Brienne and Bronwen raised their blood-drunk faces, lids heavy as they observed their sisters.

Gwen stiffened and turned toward her sister. "Not a bad idea, Bridget. You know, if I joined the circus, at least I'd have a job. Unlike some."

Bridget's face hardened, mouth curling into a snarl.

Gwen tapped a finger against her chin, staring at her sister. "But really, what is there for you to do? Too stupid to go into the family business. Too lazy to learn to do anything on your own."

A crack like a distant gunshot rang out, Bridget moving in a blink to slap Gwen across the face. Nikki gasped, the hazy eyes of the other sisters widening in surprise.

Then heavy quiet fell as Farrell cast his eyes to the floor, Bronwen gaping at them with a parted mouth and Brienne looking back down at the human whose head rested on her lap. Nikki's stomach soured, and her fists clenched as she looked at Bridget, who smoothed her clothes and clasped her hands together.

Gwen held her cheek, eyes glassy with pain but holding her sister's gaze, body unnaturally still, as if trying to smother the tumult of emotions inside of her. Nikki's anger, however, washed over her like ice water, sharpening her senses, her heartbeat strong, loud, and bracing.

Bridget said, "If you weren't such a bitch, I'd almost pity you your mortality, sister. I get to take my time deciding my purpose. I don't have to waste away my life in bird shit and bones trying to be special. I already am. And as time progresses, I will only become more so, as your body fails and rots."

Gwen's fists clenched and Nikki sensed the warmth of Gwen summoning her magic. Bridget bared her fangs and for one panicked second Nikki thought the two of them were finally going to physically fight. But Farrell cleared his throat and said to them in a calm voice, "Come on. Leave it."

Gwen seethed, but after a couple tense breaths dropped her arms and turned her back on them. Nikki followed on her friend's heels as Gwen exited through the back door, slamming it behind them, the interior light vanishing.

Chapter Three

"Insufferable. Fucking. Bitch!" Gwen yelled, kicking a pinecone. It knocked against a tree before skittering into the under-brush. Gwen heaved a massive sigh, shoulders dropping.

"I'm surprised they haven't grown out of their bullying yet."

Gwen laughed, a half-hearted, sarcastic scoff. "Oh, my sweet, sweet Nikki, you are an anomaly to your kind." Gwen linked her arm through hers, leading them toward the studio. "If there's one thing I've learned about vampires, it's that they don't grow out of anything. They have all the time in the world to brood, to hold grudges, to think of nasty things to say. You know, I think they'd get rather bored with their long lives if they didn't."

"That's at least true for your family," Nikki said, Gwen's words pricking at her heart, her parents' faces flashing in her mind.

"Yes, yes, you're right. I'm sorry. Your parents are lovely, and Farrell is okay sometimes, and grandpa was, too, and you, obviously. I just—I really—" Gwen sucked in a large breath, filling her body with tension before she blew it out in one loud huff. "I really hate her sometimes."

Nikki reached her right arm over to squeeze Gwen's forearm. "I know. I do too." Gwen's pulse was normal under her hands, and she could no longer hear it, which she took as a good sign.

The trees opened into a clearing that had one modest building in the center. Gwen's grandpa, Cian, had it built for her, the only family member who had some excitement that there was a witch in the family. Cian built it at night but placed it in the middle of the field to make it harder for her siblings to bother her, especially during the day. He indulged her magics, tried to find her a teacher, and kept her siblings in line. But that was before he met a premature, violent end from a mindless thrall. Thrall sickness occurred when humans became addicted to vampire blood, which temporarily heightened their senses and strengthened their bodies, showing them what life would be like as an immortal. Not all thralls were mindless, as some only donated their blood to their masters and did not receive vampire blood in return. Cian's thrall, however, went insane waiting on the promise of forever, and butchered him in his sleep.

The tall, crisping grass in the clearing swayed grey in the night breeze. Crickets sang and jumped away from their footfall. A half dozen sets of glowing eyes floated near Gwen's studio, watching them approach. Wings rustled restlessly, and excited coos, caws, and hoots broke through the concert of insects. Through the corner of her eye, Nikki saw Gwen's teeth flash white with a grin.

The automatic outdoor light turned on, illuminating the sheltered roost beside the studio, covered in countless perches and feeders, draped with flowers and vines.

The waiting birds lost control of their anticipation, flapping their wings, jumping on the perches, and shouting at Gwen as she unlocked the door.

"Yes, my lovelies, hold on to your feathers."

A small smile tilted the corners of Nikki's mouth up as she watched the various birds jostle and hoot, the owls twisting and bobbing their heads as they studied Gwen. Gwen had an affinity for, or perhaps with, animals, especially birds, from a young age, figuring out what treats they liked, talking to them. It wasn't clear to Nikki how much they knew what Gwen said, and vice versa, but some bond, some understanding, existed.

A suite of smells washed over her as they stepped inside the studio. The area was a mosaic of color—herbs and flowers drying from the ceiling, the shelves that stretched along the walls haphazardly filled with books, vials, and jars. The conglomeration of scents swarmed her, and she sneezed three times, which was less than usual, as she made her way to the thick, black leather couch on the wall opposite Gwen's workstation. The workstation had cabinets underneath and stretched the length of the wall until it reached the door to the small hallway, which was attached to a bedroom and bathroom. The countertop was littered with stones, bones, and other trinkets the crows brought her. Nikki once asked why it was only the crows that brought gifts, and Gwen said, "The others are my eyes."

Whatever that meant.

Nikki reclined on the high-backed couch, head sinking into the cushion, as Gwen fed the birds. Once done, Gwen perched at her workstation and said, "Did I tell you I started befriending hummingbirds?"

Nikki blinked, lifting her head. "No. Why?"

Gwen shrugged, retrieving a bowl, mortar, pestle, and herbs. "I gave up on the nighthawks and swifts—they're users. I can't really form relationships with them, you know? So, I thought, why not try diurnal species again? Just because the jays are jerks doesn't mean all diurnal birds are. I mean, just check out the crows. They were my first, as you know." She smiled. "Turns out, hummingbirds are pretty smart. And responsive."

"What are they giving you in return?"

Gwen shrugged, grinding herbs in the mortar. "I'm not sure yet. I'm waiting for them to tell me."

"Oh. When will that be?"

"Whenever trust has been established."

"I see," Nikki replied, not seeing at all.

A sharp ache pulsed in Nikki's gums, and she groaned.

"Give me one minute and I'll remedy that for you." Gwen folded her herbs into another bowl that Nikki couldn't see the contents of, then raised one hand into the air until it was level with her head. Gwen twirled her fingers and wrist, as if mixing the air, and a shimmering gold-silver thread weaved through Gwen's skin, the strands illuminating her flesh as she pulled the magic from within herself and channeled it through her arm. Her hand aglow with magic, she set it against the bowl and funneled the strands into the mix. Folding the mix together three more times, she poured it into a small container.

"It will never get old seeing you do that."

Gwen grinned, bringing her the mix. "Try it out."

Nikki obliged, rubbing some of the light green salve on her gums. A numbing prickle like soft needles danced and dissipated in her mouth, neither creating nor leaving pain. "Tingly," Nikki said. "But good. Thank you."

"Thank you, and you're welcome." Gwen plopped onto the couch beside Nikki, then roved her gaze over her. "So, you still tossing out the blood?"

Nikki groaned. "Please, Gwen. I don't want to get into this again. I know what the arguments are, and I'm tired of it. If I can just hold out another decade or so, I'm sure I can figure out a good substitute."

"Okay, but what about until then? You're delaying your maturation. You're extending your pain, and you don't have to. You don't look well, Nik. I understand it sickens part of you, but you need it. You're denying what you are, and as someone who has had to accept being different from everyone else, let me tell you, your life will be easier and better if you accept it."

Hot bile churned in Nikki's stomach, and she bit back her anger as she closed her eyes.

"Gwen, I'm begging you to stop. I get enough guilt from my parents. I'd like you to be on my side."

"I am on your side, you dummy. So are your parents. But fine, now that I've spoken, I'll forever hold my peace."

"Thank you." Nikki sighed. "I wish you could just magic it away for me."

"If I could, I would."

"I know," Nikki said, relaxing her shoulders further. Nikki pulled out another orange from her bag and peeled it, the sharp citrusy juices spilling over her hands and filling her nose.

Fingers ripping the orange, a flash of long fingers picking up fallen books crossed her mind. Then grey eyes flecked with green, a bead of sweat that trailed to a steady pulse over stubble, and a hand through wavy hair. How she had to crane her head to look up at him, up at all the lean, defined muscles.

A couple of hours passed, Gwen organizing her herbs and Nikki reading her syllabi. When Gwen's yawns increased in frequency, Nikki got up to leave, needing to swing by her parents' house.

Gwen followed Nikki outside, and Nikki watched Gwen pull out vials she knew she used in a protective spell. Gwen first dripped the vial with her siblings' genetic material, and then the vial of her own blood, in a circle around the studio. When Gwen completed the circle, once again standing in front of Nikki, the circle pulsed that same golden-silver a few times, extending its shimmer into the air like heat waves before fading.

"Now none of them can get in," Gwen said with a grin, then stepped into the studio, pulling only the screen door closed.

As she walked away, the automatic light switched off, and darkness engulfed Nikki with the comfort of a big, downy blanket. It was soothing now that she didn't feel as if the forest was watching her. She breathed in the warm air, catching the scent of a faraway wildfire, eyes adjusting to see shapes and silhouettes in the dark. She looked up at the sky, clouds blocking out many of the stars. With a long exhale, her heartbeat slowed, and the muscles in her neck and shoulders relaxed.

Nikki took quiet steps from the meadow through the backyard and around the side of the house to her car, relishing the peace while she could. Desiccated and mossy stones, cracked pinecones, and dry earth filled her nose, and with her fingers on the door handle, she took in another magnificent breath, wishing she could linger, just a little longer.

But it was barely midnight, and she had much to do.

Chapter Four

AFTER A FEW MINUTES of driving through more private, winding roads crowded by trees, Nikki arrived at her childhood home. It was tucked away from the main road, down a smooth dirt road lined by trees like Gwen's, although the building was much less modest. The house boasted three stories aboveground and was composed of dark red brick and charcoal grey roofing. White Ionic columns lined the entryway and the veranda that framed the house. It was striking, and entirely excessive for their three-person family.

Even with hired cleaners, gardeners, and kitchen staff, and at one point a cat, it still felt too large. Nikki blamed her mom's rich, British-influenced old Romanian vampire upbringing for it. The lawn never seemed to grow, always at a perfect height, always smelling freshly cut, with no weeds in sight. At the front of the house, a road curved toward a concrete walkway lined with identical alders, tall and white, leaves crinkling at the edges from dryness. Between the alders were iron glass ball lamps. Raised, wide steps led to the porch and the front door, potted flowering plants of all colors framing the stairs. The backyard that lay before the forest was also immaculately designed, with flowers and shrubs beyond count interspersed amongst the trees. Beyond that was the natural wood, left to be wild. The gardener, Thomas Walker, lived on site with his wife, Bernadette, in a separate, smaller building tucked out of sight in the woods. They sometimes helped the hired staff with serving big meals, switching from gardeners to butler, housekeeper, and waitstaff.

The Walkers were also her family's thralls, although Nikki's parents refused to give them any of their own blood. She used to play with their son, Liam, and as they grew up his smile brightened her nights, and every brush of their skin sent butterflies into her stomach. But that quickly ended as Nikki's human traits faded and the power differential between them grew.

When he let her act on her predatory instincts.

When he let her be herself.

When her bloodlust overwhelmed her self-control and she almost killed him, his pulse a slowing beat in her mouth.

When he was released from the medical care of a Seattleite vampire, she never told him they couldn't see each other anymore, that they couldn't even be friends. She just stopped talking to him, trying to fade away. He got the hint eventually, and now they hadn't spoken in almost four years. When he graduated high school he moved to Seattle to attend university. Liam was studying psychology, since he decided he wanted to be a therapist. For vampires. When Nikki first heard she laughed aloud. How would he advertise that on Psychology Today? She couldn't imagine any vampire she knew going to therapy. But maybe the trauma she caused him would help others somehow.

Even years later, every time she went to her parents' house, a sickening mess of guilt and dread gathered in the pit of her stomach at the thought of that night, at the potential of seeing his parents. They had only ever been kind to her, and they still were, but they reminded her too much of Liam and by association her monstrosity. Her visits became less frequent, much to her parents' dismay. But she needed to at least pick up the donated blood to appease her parents, although guilt clawed her stomach as she dumped out most of it in her kitchen sink. Fingertips tapping against the steering wheel with anticipation, she drove down the narrow dirt path to the garage on the side of the house, stifling a groan when she didn't see her dad's car. For how much they pestered her to see them more, they couldn't bother to be home when they knew she was going over? Maybe her mom, Cat, would be home, at least. But she doubted it. They went everywhere together.

Retrieving the box of empty thermoses from the trunk, she entered the house. It was mostly dark, with a soft glow coming from a room at the far end of the hall, where the lounge was. Her mom would have been walking to greet her already if she were home, so Nikki tried to walk on silent feet to the kitchen, where her portion of blood was usually kept. The thermoses in her box thunked together as she walked, echoing in the empty hall.

In the kitchen, dark blue with night, she caught the shape of the package on the counter. Sliding her box beside it, she glimpsed a note on top, and lifted it toward the remnants of light from the hall.

We're out with the Lopezes and will return by dawn. Please feel free to stay. We would love to see you. Although I'm sure you will have departed by then. Your father sends his love, as do I. – Mom

Nikki folded the note and stuffed it in her pocket, deflating as muted footsteps shuffled down the hall.

A moment later, Bernadette stepped into the kitchen and turned on the light, eyes flashing wide. "There you are," Bernadette said with a smile, clasping her hands in front of her. "Your parents asked me to make sure you found the blood all right and to see if there was anything else you need?"

"No, thank you," Nikki replied. Bernadette's eyes were so much like Liam's, a dazzling hazel-gold. As she stared into their enigmatic depths, she was heaved back to the past, to the little boy who used to play tag with her in the midnight moonlight. The boy who pretended that the sun was a demon they had to vanquish, just to make her feel as if she wasn't missing out. The first boy she fell in love with, and the first one she ever tasted, the steady beat of his sweet metallic blood pouring into her mouth, the rhythm pulsing slower and weaker, while a thrill, a divine hum, filled her with strength and glory—

She crushed the memory down with one hard blink, but not before her mouth tightened with the desire to bite through flesh. Her stomach curdled, and she squeezed her eyes shut.

"Are you okay, dear?"

"Yes, I'm fine, thanks." A question inquiring about Liam's well-being hesitated on her tongue, but she knew better than to ask it, as it would only douse them both with missing him.

Bernadette sensed her hesitation but didn't push her. "You're welcome to stay as long as you like. If you need anything, I'll be in the lounge."

"Thank you, but I need to get going. There's a lot to do before the semester starts."

"Of course," Bernadette said, and as she slipped from the room Nikki noticed the gauze around her elbows. Bernadette must have been drained in the last few days. Nikki picked up the box of thermoses, wincing at the image of Bernadette's blood sloshing inside them. She turned off the light behind her, returning to her car. After loading the box in the trunk, she sat in the driver's seat, head tipped back. She closed her eyes and took a few steeling breaths, unable to shake the taste of Liam's fresh blood from her tongue. Against her will, the memory transformed into a fantasy of the boy from the library, of what it would be like to taste his spice-sweetened blood against his salty, sweat-stubbled neck.

Chapter Five

Fall semester started like the long, lazy stretch of a cat emerging from slumber. Despite the cooling weather, the first leaves turning from emerald to topaz, teachers, students, and staff clung to the last wisps of summer as if by moving and talking slowly, time would, too.

Nikki avoided the library to let the embarrassment, the smell, the enticement, fade. She bemoaned giving up her beloved spot at the library, where she had studied for the past three years, but the more she avoided that mysterious man, the better off she'd be. It took over a week for her to stop thinking about him, his lean muscle, greenish-grey eyes, and drinkable scent. If one encounter could interfere with her thinking so much, she needed to stay away from him.

Instead of the library, she found an isolated spot in the science building to study. Since most of her classes were in that building, she no longer had to spend the day in a mad dash around campus, covered in sweat despite the UV-blocking clothes, umbrellas, sunscreen, and face coverings. It was a nice change to not have confused glances tracking her around campus as she ran in black with an umbrella while it wasn't raining, and the sun shone bright.

The spot in the science building was uncomfortable and didn't have much room to spread out, but at least it wasn't at risk of the sun. Or of anise and figs. Every now and then, as she crossed campus, she would catch the sweet and spicy smell on the breeze and head in the other direction. Sometimes, she felt the press of the forest around her, but whenever she went inside the feeling faded, and it became easy enough to ignore, since she was inside most of the time, anyway.

A couple of weeks passed, and her gums ached more and more, the tenderness preventing her from eating solid foods. Yet she would not drink more blood than was necessary for survival, pouring out the thermoses to prevent herself from gorging herself on it as her hunger grew. Each day seemed longer, weariness and hunger slowing her body and her brain. She lost interest in trying to cook acceptable meals for herself, so she had a store-bought, mostly liquid diet.

As she did every year, her mom called to remind her of the fall equinox coven meeting that her parents hosted each year. And like every year, they argued whether Nikki's presence was truly that essential to the meeting. Nikki never won any argument with her mom, so even though she did not like being around the coven, she agreed to go. It wasn't that she disliked any individual coven member, she just didn't enjoy being a vampire or being engulfed in its culture. With the bitter taste of the phone call with her mom in the back of her throat, Gwen found her trying to read in her dark corner.

"You're a hard girl to find when you're not where you usually are." Gwen dropped a satchel on the ground and plunked herself on the chair opposite Nikki.

"I do have something called a cell phone."

"Ugh, you know how difficult those are for me to keep track of. Even more difficult than tracking you. You busy tonight?"

"I have some homework to do, but I'm free a little later. Why?"

"I was hoping you'd go hunting with me." Nikki quirked a brow, so Gwen added, "For fruit and dried flowers, though I'll probably grab some bark and leaves while we're at it."

Nikki nodded. "Sure, why not? Although it is a school night, so I don't want to go too far."

"That's cool with me."

Gwen took out a notebook and scribbled, likely notes on a new spell or potion, while Nikki finished up her work for the day. Once the sun set they went outside, the night air rushing over her, and she grinned into the breeze, a relief from the stale air of the science building. The evening was cool but mild, the sky clear and the moon bright. She could see why Gwen wanted to be out tonight.

As they stepped into the main square, gold light bouncing off the gently rippling fountain, stones, and darkened windows, Nikki froze, a familiar form sitting on the benches with a couple of other students.

A step ahead of her, Gwen paused and looked over her shoulder at Nikki. She followed Nikki's gaze to the bench, and as a sly smile grew on her face, she said, "Oh. I was wondering what ever happened with that."

"Nothing has happened with it. Very much on purpose," Nikki said.

The silhouettes turned in their direction, and since it was too late to turn around without making her embarrassment worse, they continued their walk.

"I don't smell fig pies," Gwen whispered, leaning so close, her breath rushed against Nikki's ear.

"Me neither," Nikki replied, unable to avert her gaze.

"A point for the cologne theory."

One figure stood, long-limbed and lean, and Nikki's heart thudded fast and hard as it took tentative steps in their direction. Gwen murmured something, but Nikki couldn't hear, all sound diminishing under her pulse and a sudden pressure in her head, like plunging underwater with no warning.

Several agonizing steps later, they stood in front of one another— just this man and Nikki, Gwen leaving her side and heading to the bench where his friends were, the ghost of a smile still on her face.

He quirked a fleeting grin that produced a halted chuckle, then smoothed the back of his hair on his neck before hiding his hands in his jean pockets, leaning into his hips. Nikki cocked her head and wrapped her hands tight on the strap of her shoulder bag, a warm coil in her stomach tightening as her pulse ratcheted.

"Um, hey," he said, lips splitting in the beginnings of a smile. The light caught on half his face, accentuating his long, slender nose and low cheekbones.

"Hi," Nikki responded.

"I've been hoping to run into you again."

"You have?" Nikki asked, eyebrows pinching. He studied her face, and her cheeks heated under his gaze. The pressure in her head deepened, and she adjusted her stance to steady herself with the wave of increasing pressure. Over his shoulder, Gwen talked with his friends, but she couldn't make out the words. Nikki's brow furrowed deeper, an anxious dread building as her senses weakened.

Misreading her furrowed brow, he rushed on. "Yeah, sorry. I just wanted to apologize for what happened a few weeks ago at the library. You took me by surprise, and I felt that maybe I was weird? I'm normally not as weird as I was then." He chuckled again, uncertain, but it had a pleasant rumble. "And I'm normally not as weird as I'm being right now."

Nikki gave a close-lipped smile, confused, head swirling. Her head felt heavy, but her body was light. "No. No, you weren't weird," she said, trying to shake out the pressure in her skull. "I thought I was weird."

His grin broke into a full smile. "I guess that means neither of us are weird. Or maybe we're both too weird to notice."

"I guess so." Nikki returned the full smile, and the tension between them eased.

"I'm Alexander. But I go by Xander," he said, extending a hand.

"Nikki," she replied, taking his hand, which was strong, calloused, and warm. They smiled at each other in the handshake, and the comforting warmth he exuded calmed her whole body.

When their hands broke apart, the cool night air filling that empty space, Nikki's head spun, vision hazing as the pressure in her head increased to a blinding dizziness. She clutched her head with one hand and took a balancing step backward to prevent a fall.

"Whoa! Are you okay?" Xander asked, reaching out to her.

"I—I'm sorry. I'm dizzy." Her head swam, and her heart raced, and everything seemed to blur in front of her. "I don't know what's happening."

"Here, let's sit you down." Xander put a steadying hand on her arm, leading her to a bench at the side of the courtyard. But as they walked, her head continued to twirl faster, like being on a spinning teacup ride, churning the contents of her stomach. She rushed away from him to the grass and vomited, bent with her hands on her knees. In a brief moment of stability, she straightened, and her veins constricted, as if squeezed from the insides, and she groaned in the pain, dropping her head as her muscles constricted.

As though from a great distance, Gwen yelled her name. The blades of grass caught on the lamplight, the moonlight, swaying and blurring in her vision like mixing paint, and she stumbled, trying to regain her balance. In her dancing vision, she saw a tree, and she lurched forward, reaching out for it, hoping it would anchor her. When her hands clutched at the smooth, young wood, urgent voices and whispers merged into the hum in her head.

The moment before her vision blackened, a foreign voice in her mind bellowed **BRING HIM TO ME**.

Chapter Six

Beady, black eyes stared down at her, small mouth chewing in a circular motion. Nikki moaned at the harsh light and threw an arm over her face. With one eye blocked, she squinted at the beige rabbit which sat on the back of Gwen's couch, half-eaten grass sticking out from one side of its mouth. It looked at her sideways, unblinking, chewing slowly, as if it couldn't be more bored.

"Good, you're awake. How are you feeling?" Gwen asked.

Nikki peeled her arm from her face and turned her head, seeing Gwen sitting on a stool beside the counter on the opposite wall. Nikki groaned again and sat up, muscles tired and weak, blinking away the fog. She furrowed her brow and raised a hand to her temple, recalling her sudden dizziness, how her veins had tightened. And how she'd vomited in front of Xander. Mortification twisted her guts.

"I'm not sure. Confused. And my head feels heavy."

"Want something for it?"

"Please."

Gwen stood and started the electric tea kettle, bringing a steaming mug to Nikki when the water boiled. Nikki held it under her nose, wafts of chamomile and mint floating upwards. She curled her hands around the mug, the heat comforting her bones, and said, "It smells great. What is it?"

"It's just an enhanced herbal tea."

Nikki looked into the mug, barely visible flecks of gold in the tea, evaporating into the steam. The sip scorched her tongue but soothed her throat on the way down, easing her body. Nikki pulled her legs up for Gwen to have more space on the couch and leaned her head back. The bunny still stared at her, but had ceased its chewing, content to imitate a fluffy potato.

"Who's this?" Nikki asked, indicating the rabbit.

"I don't know. He's been sniffing around the past few days. He's pretty shy but has been nice company during the days when the owls are away."

"Don't they try to eat him?"

"They know it's impolite to eat guests."

Nikki offered her hand, letting the rabbit sniff it before petting it between the ears. "This guy figured out what I did a long time ago. Befriending you is a great survival tactic."

Gwen twitched her mouth in a hint of a grin, then asked, "Nik, what happened last night?"

"I was hoping you'd tell me," Nikki said, frowning into her mug. Xander's spinning, moonlit face flashed through her mind.

"Well, by the time I reached you, you were already unconscious. I saw you stumble to the grass and vomit, then you yelped when you touched the tree, like it burned you, and collapsed. You've been out cold since then."

"How did I get here? And what time is it, anyway?"

"It's just past four. And you got here awkwardly." Gwen rolled her shoulders, a motion between a shrug and a fidget.

"Go on, rip off the band-aid."

"Well, Xander insisted that you should be taken to a hospital, and so did his friends. I told them that it had happened before—"

"You didn't."

"—and that you'd be okay with a little rest. They were skeptical, but eventually helped me get you to the car."

"Who, specifically, helped you?"

"Xander."

"Please tell me you're joking."

"Nope. It seemed the easiest way to get you there. He carried you like a bride over a threshold, it was very romantic."

Nikki groaned and buried her face in her hands, hoping her cool palms would soothe her burning face.

"Then I drove you back here, called Farrell, and he helped me get you into the studio."

Nikki lifted her head and blinked. "You drove?"

"Yeah, but I promise I didn't damage your car. I've done it enough to get back into the hang of it."

"But you don't have a license. What would you have done if you got pulled over?"

Gwen shrugged. "Probably cry. You know, throw a pity party and all that. But I didn't get pulled over so it doesn't matter."

Nikki took a sip of her tea and said, "Gwen, I'm so sorry to burden you like that. I don't know what happened."

"Okay, first off, it wasn't a burden. I was worried about you. We all were. And secondly, what do you remember?"

"I remember talking to Xander. Then I felt sick out of nowhere. My head got heavy and dizzy at the same time, and my body felt... constricted? Like I was being squeezed from the inside, or my veins were tightening. I don't know how to explain it. But it kept getting worse and worse, until it made me vomit. I saw the tree and then—"

The shout **BRING HIM TO ME** drummed in her head.

"And then what?"

"I don't know. That's the last thing I remember. Reaching for the tree."

Nikki took a sip of the tea to cover her guilt at the lie, but her throat tightened at the idea of telling Gwen that she heard a voice. She knew she could trust Gwen, but it felt too crazy for her to admit.

Gwen stared into the distance with a soft "hmm."

"What do you think?"

"You're not going to like what I think."

"Have you heard of something like this before?" Nikki asked, hopeful. Maybe it was normal. Maybe she was okay.

"No, I haven't. Not in vampires."

Nikki's heart dropped, the voice echoing in her head. *Bring him bring him bring him.*

"I think that maybe your self-starvation is the cause. I know you don't want to hear that." Gwen threw up her hands. "I know you don't want to drink more blood than you already do, but I don't know what else could be causing it. The weakness, the discomfort. Your body is ready to be more vampire than human, and maybe this is the consequence of resisting it."

"It always goes back to the blood," Nikki said, heart sinking as she thought, *that's not it. Lack of blood may make me weak or dizzy. But it wouldn't make me hear voices.*

"I did say you wouldn't like it." Gwen glanced at her, and her mouth quirked in a sudden grin. "But I know something that you will like."

"Oh no, what did you do?"

Gwen's shining smile widened, and she popped up from the couch, retrieving Nikki's phone from a charger on her counter.

"You charged my phone? Gwen, you're a saint."

"Feel free to call me the Good Witch of the West. But no, I have something even better for you than a charged phone. Take a look," Gwen said, extending her arm with Nikki's phone.

Nikki opened her notifications, cocoons of anxiety bursting into butterflies throughout her body when the truth lit up in front of her. "You didn't."

"Yes, Nik, I sure did! It was nearly impossible to leave without him last night, he was oh so worried about you. He's studying to be a veterinarian, you know. Pre-med. So of course, he wanted to help. But I knew you would be mortified if he carried you all the way here, so I insisted, and this, my dearest Nik, is the beautiful result of your fainting spell. Not a bad move, in the end."

Nikki stared at the message on her phone, from almost six hours prior, blue light tinting her pale skin. A message, from Xander, taunted her.

"And you programmed his number into my phone?"

"Well, I knew if it was an unknown number, you'd ignore it. Now, you can't," Gwen replied, altogether too pleased with herself. "Plus, I got the number of his babe of a friend."

"Who?"

"The goddess, Theo, of course. She's studying organic chemistry. How cool is that?"

"That's very cool. What does she want to do with that degree?"

"I don't know yet, Nik. That's a first date question. Now, respond to your man," Gwen said, disappearing into her own phone.

"He's not my man." Nikki sighed. "I don't have time for this, Gwen. You've set me up to disappoint him."

Gwen gave her a flat, disbelieving look. "You know, I swear I actually saw you smile before you barfed all over the place. I'm all for a smiling Nikki."

Nikki resisted rolling her eyes. "He's already a distraction. I don't want those. I can have them once I've figured out how to change myself."

"You mean, you don't want feelings. Blah blah, same old Nikki excuses. Just respond to his text. You're getting ahead of yourself."

Nikki exhaled, downed the rest of the cooling tea, and set it on the ground. "I suppose you're right about that." Nikki nestled onto the couch and opened the phone.

The text from Xander said, Hey there, this is Xander. How are you feeling?

Innocent enough, Nikki thought. But what was she supposed to say? That she just woke up? Or was ignoring him? Neither were good options. She tapped her fingers on the side of the phone, thinking, before she responded, Hi, Xander. Thanks for checking in. I'm feeling okay now. As an afterthought, she typed, I'm sorry for last night. I don't know what happened. But she deleted the message before sending it.

"Gwen, where's my—"

Her phone vibrated.

"Ha! I heard that! What an eager beaver," Gwen replied, pointing her finger at the phone with utter delight. "Poor boy must've been sitting by his phone all day."

Nikki smiled, close-lipped, despite herself.

Oh good, I'm glad to hear that, Xander replied.

Nikki tapped her fingers on the phone again, debating a response. But it was best to keep it a closed book, because the only books she wanted open were her textbooks. So she set the phone down and swung her feet off the couch, head swirling with the movement. A rebellious part of her mind imagined Xander's moonlit face and his anise and fig smell, her jaw pulsing with an ache. Nikki moaned, the gums where the incisors were tight and sore.

"My poor sweet vampire. Here, I prepped this while you were sleeping," Gwen said, handing Nikki a refilled container of salve.

"Gwen, I'd be lost without you," Nikki said, swabbing a finger full of salve across her gums, letting the tingling needles remove the ache.

Nikki massaged her gums, and the rabbit on the couch decided it was done with them, hopping down to the floor and taking small jumps toward the door.

"Little guy is gonna get himself eaten," Gwen said, watching the beige rabbit hobble across her cool floor to the exit.

Nikki's phone buzzed again. Can I take you to coffee sometime?

The corners of her lips dug into her cheeks at the repressed smile, and she saw Gwen turn away, knowing and smug.

Trying to pull her smile down, Nikki thought to say no, but her fingers replied, That sounds nice. Would an evening coffee work?

Somehow an evening coffee turned into a drink, which seemed much more serious. Much more date-like. And even though her brain told her to stomp on the brakes, her fingers refused to listen. They set up plans to go out with him, to have a drink with him. On a Saturday night.

But she was able to spin a web to go foraging with Gwen on that same night, so that things couldn't get too far. She would have a reason to leave. To call the date short. To not get carried away, either romantically or vampirically.

Chapter Seven

ON THE EVENING of the fall equinox Nikki texted Gwen asking if she was going, to which Gwen simply replied, "lol." Sometimes she envied Gwen's freedom from coven obligations.

When the last rays of daylight skimmed the horizon, Nikki bundled up and left her apartment. By the time she reached her parents' house, the first few stars twinkled in the east, and a cool breeze rustled through the evergreens. Nikki pulled behind the garage and walked around to the front door, which swung open as soon as her foot hit the top step.

"There she is! My beautiful Nikki," Nikki's dad, Miguel, said with a beaming smile as he opened his arms to hug her.

"Hi, Dad," Nikki replied, returning the smile and folding into his arms. His reanimated heart beat strong and slow against Nikki's ear as she welcomed his safety and comfort.

"How are you doing? I have missed you so," he said, taking a step back, keeping one hand on her arm as the other lifted her face up to meet his dark brown eyes.

"I've been good. And I've missed you, too."

Her dad smiled again, his sharp, shark-like set of teeth gleaming silver-gold in the lamplight. All the Made had similar teeth, as they underwent the excruciating process of dying before the vampiric blood latched onto their cells and altered their DNA, resurrecting them to experience human teeth, hair, and nails decaying from their body. Then the pointed teeth and nails grew at an accelerated rate. Organ functions restarted with a new genetic composition, only able to metabolize blood, vampirism the ultimate parasitism. Most didn't survive the making, and the demon it turned them into inspired human horror stories, as well as prejudice against them from the hybridized, born vampires. Yet her dad, and two other coven members, survived.

He ushered her inside, saying, "Come, come. Fill me in on everything. Do you need a snack? A beverage? Perhaps a stiff drink before you have to sit and listen to us old windbags, eh?"

Nikki chuckled and said, "No, I'm okay, Dad. Thanks."

"Well, I do, in any case. Let's go to the parlor."

Nikki followed her dad to the lounge where the fire crackled, casting orange on the dark marble mantle, the plush rugs and furniture. Her dad poured himself a glass of blood, then stood opposite her next to the fire, leaning against the mantle. The firelight flickered on his polished bronze skin, casting him in gold, and Nikki's chest caved. If only her dad had been a born vampire instead of made, she would have inherited his beautiful skin, instead of the milky white from her mom that revealed every ailment and emotion.

Miguel met Nikki's mournful gaze. "Tell me what troubles you."

Bring him bring him bring him, echoed through her mind.

"Everything is fine, Dad. I'm just tired."

Her dad looked at her as if he knew she was lying, but didn't press further. They caught up on the mundane day-to-day aspects of their lives, and once silence settled over them again, Nikki finally found the courage to ask, "Is there a history of mental illness in our family?"

"Eh, we're all a little cuckoo."

"No, I mean like schizophrenia. Something that would make you have auditory or visual hallucinations."

"Not that I know of." Her dad cocked his head. "Why?"

"Just a school paper," Nikki said, shrugging despite the unease in her stomach. Rising to her feet she added, "I should go say hi to Mom."

Walking up the wide staircase that led to the second floor, she took in the portraits of her parents, herself, and their ancestors in extravagant frames lining the walls. The master bedroom was the size of two rooms, with a canopied balcony that faced the backyard. When she entered the room, Nikki's gaze caught on her mother's vanity, showing two almost identical faces reflected in the mirror. For a moment, she thought she saw double, but she blinked, and her own face came into focus beside her mother's. Her mom smiled at her in the reflection as she brushed out her long, straight, black hair. She looked like a stereotypical Romanian vampire, with pale skin, black hair, black eyes, and lips defined by dark red lipstick. Her features were refined, with a slender but healthy body in a simple, black, silk dress. Nikki was the spitting image of her, just younger, thinner, and with a bow-shaped mouth she got from her dad.

"Hi, sweetling."

"Hi, Mom. You look regal, as always."

"Thank you," she said, standing and walking toward Nikki, pulling long black gloves that reached above her elbow over her forearms.

Then her mom's smile wavered. She picked up Nikki's hands, held her arms out, and looked her up and down. "While I adore your modern take on the traditional gothic vampire style, we ought to dress you up for the meeting."

Nikki groaned. "Mom, I don't want to dress up. I don't like dresses."

"What I have picked out is not a dress. You need to wear more than black."

"But you're only wearing black."

"Yes, but I'm wearing black with style. You are only wearing jeans and a t-shirt."

"Which I'm perfectly comfortable in."

Her mom tsked. "Before you bristle too much, go into your room and look at what I laid out for you. I think you will like it. I won't even ask you to put on makeup."

"How magnanimous of you."

"Isn't it?" Cat said, twining a finger through one of Nikki's curls. She put one soft finger under Nikki's chin, raising Nikki's gaze to hers. "How is your mouth feeling?"

"It still aches. Gwen has been supplying me with salve, which helps."

"I am glad." Her mom paused, mouth pursed in thought. "Will you please consider drinking blood tonight? You are so skinny. And it would help you heal faster."

Nikki's stomach soured. "No, I don't think so."

"What if it was mixed?"

Nikki sighed, knowing her mother would keep pushing. "I'll think about it."

"Thank you, sweetling. Now, scuttle along. I want you to greet the guests as they arrive."

"Oh good. I get the most boring job."

"Do you complain this much all the time?"

"Only with you."

"That's a relief."

They grinned at each other, and her mom gave her a soft peck on her cheek. Linking arms, they walked out into the hallway, and Cat walked her to her room. With a hand on the doorknob, Nikki asked, "Is there a history of schizophrenia, or any other psychological disorders, in our family?"

"Absolutely not," her mom responded, peeling her arm from Nikki's. "Even if there was on the human side, vampirism would not allow it."

"So no vampires can ever have a mental disorder?"

"They can, but it depends on the type and the intensity. Severe schizophrenia in a vampire fetus would not go to term." Her mom's eyes narrowed. "Why do you ask? Are you hearing things?"

"Of course not. I'm just preparing for a paper I have to write this term. It's on hereditary illnesses and I thought it would be an interesting topic to explore."

"Right," her mom replied, but her gaze remained assessing. "Well, you will find little of note on my side of the family. We're all quite boring."

"Minus the whole vampire thing."

"Yes, minus that. Though I don't imagine you'll be writing about that at school. Now, go get ready." Her mom pecked Nikki on the cheek again and swept away with a soft whoosh of her dress.

Nikki's room was almost as big as her current living room, arrayed in the same dark colors and soft lighting as the rest of the house. Knickknacks, detailed rocks, and curious shells from Gwen sat on display. The room smelled fresh, blankets and pillows perfectly arrayed. Displayed neatly on the canopy bed was what appeared to be a shoulderless black dress, with simple bands of gold jewelry laid at the collar and sleeves. When she picked up the dress, the soft and smooth fabric against her fingers, Nikki realized it was two pieces, with the skirt having extra-wide legs. While two pieces, the fabrics blended to look like one piece, and the legs were wide enough that it looked like she wore a dress. The clothes fit like a cashmere cocoon, and with a pleased smirk, she marveled at her mother's ability to get what she wanted through a compromise.

Nikki put on the simple gold jewelry, earrings dangling above her shoulders, and almost felt beautiful, despite her sallow skin. Drawing back her curtains, she looked out at the dark forest, her enhanced eyesight allowing her to see the faintest rustles of night creatures and wind through the leaves. The longer she stared at the forest, the more it felt like it stared back, the tree branches twisting toward her with the wind. Chills wound up her spine and she threw the curtains closed.

Chapter Eight

The crashing and clanking of dishes combined with the powerful odor of blood and roasted meats made Nikki's head swim.

Her mom sat at the far head of the table, with her dad to Cat's left, and an empty chair to her right. Nikki took her place there, between her mom and Daiyu. The table was set with tall candelabras, pitchers of water, decanters of wine and blood, fine silverware, white sparkling plates, and clear glasses for wine and blood that shone in the dim candle-light. The waitstaff brought large, intricate silver and pearl platters while the coven chatted. Lifting the lids, Nikki's mouth ached at the sight of the herb-crusted turkey and high stack of rare steak cuts. The chafing dishes held buttery mashed potatoes, an assortment of vegetables, and warm breads, and gravy boats held gravies for both meats as well seasoned blood. The staff circled the table, filling each guest's cups with wine, blood, or a mix.

Mixed in with the scents of food and blood were wild herbs collected by their chief, Tyee, and fresh cooked fish, which Halvar, one of the Ivarsson brothers who lived along Oregon's coast, always brought. Nikki held her disgusting drink close to her nose to mask the flood of smells, which wasn't much better. Her mother demanded she drink a horrid tomato juice and blood blend, and while it was pungent enough to overwhelm the flood of smells, it wasn't a pleasant one on its own. She grimaced when she sipped it, the salty liquid warm as it slid down her throat. As it filled her body, her senses sharpened, brightening the lights, enhancing the smells, and amplifying everyone's voices. While she loathed the taste and feel of it in her mouth, the fatigue in her body ebbed away, replaced by energy and vigor. If she just didn't think about what she was consuming, she would almost enjoy the sensation.

It would be a great day when she could feel this good without having to drink blood.

The born vampires piled their plates high with food, the fragments of humanity in their genes enabling them to eat normal, mortal food. The made vampires, however, which included her dad and Feng and Daiyu Liu, bemoaned at how they could no longer eat the food in front of them. Their purely vampiric bodies could only metabolize blood, so if they ate anything else, it would rot within them, poisoning their bloodstream and killing them.

"How I miss fresh fish," Feng said, holding his wine glass filled to the brim with blood and taking a long sip. He had an angular face, determined eyes, and beautifully thick, arched eyebrows.

"I cannot even recall the last time we had it," Daiyu said, looking at the food with longing.

"Me neither," her dad replied. He took his wife's hand and squeezed it. "But it was a worthwhile sacrifice."

"Indeed," Feng replied, lifting his glass in a cheer, which was mimicked by both Miguel and Daiyu. Nikki shivered, recalling the bloody story of how the Lius became vampires. Feng immigrated to the states from China during the Gold Rush, where he met a vampire and after several years of servitude, convinced him to both make him and leave him in his will. After he survived, he killed his maker, took his fortune, and summoned his family to join him. Their daughter died on the voyage, but Daiyu survived the trip and the making. After being chased out of California, they made their way north, where they joined Tyee's small coven in the late 1800's. Violent beginnings to bloody lives.

Her dad and the Lius broke into financial matters that went over her head, so Nikki turned her attention to the other guests, gaze snagging on the only two children in the coven, Emilia and Felix. The Lopezes were the most recent addition to the coven, dentists who moved from New Mexico three years prior. Emilia and Felix had small portions of human food and drank blood from colorful plastic cups. Emilia caught Nikki's gaze, and Emilia's light brown eyes crinkled as she smiled, her wavy brown curls framing her light gold skin. When Emilia smiled, her reddened lips revealed blood-stained teeth, and chills wound up Nikki's body. When she was a kid, she hadn't thought twice about drinking blood. That came much later. But now, seeing the blood coat a child's mouth, unease sat in her stomach.

Had she looked that creepy when she was younger?

Nikki tried to smile, but it felt more like a wince before she looked away.

All of Gwen's family, except Gwen herself, sat on the opposite side of the table. Connall, the eldest son who worked at the family's law firm, listened intently, fingers twirling his blood glass. His features were more hawkish than Farrell's, who had wider, larger eyes like Gwen. Tiernan and Aislinn, Gwen's parents, had sharp ears and even sharper eyes, with no laugh lines around their serious mouths, and their quiet intelligence burdened each room they entered. All four were dressed in neat business suits, merlot hair accentuating their fair skin and forest green eyes, not one strand out of place.

The sisters talked amongst themselves, bickering over who got to choose where'd they go for their next hunt. Before the sisters could see her judging expression, she averted her gaze and listened to Gwen's parents. Tiernan and Aislinn spoke with the Lopez parents, Julio and Carmen, about a recent lawsuit against their business. A client claimed that the Lopezes chipped their teeth, but in reality they had gotten into a barfight and didn't want to have to pay for their own problems.

Again, another conversation she had nothing to contribute to.

With her next sip of blood, her mind wandered to Xander. To his open smile and curly hair, his lean muscles, and his savory sweet anise scent. A tingling warmth rose on her cheeks, and she turned her head to the far end of the table, where Tyee sat watching her, knife and fork in hand. Nikki gave her a tense smile despite the apprehension that sat in her gut. Tyee's dark eyes bored into her, the shadows of her sharp cheekbones flickering in the candlelight.

Why was she looking at her like that?

Tyee was near a millennium, born into a vampiric Native American tribe of the Columbia River, the name of which had been forgotten from history, and Tyee kept as a secret close to her heart. She rarely spoke of her past, a weave that unraveled like loss and regret when spun, so the coven didn't ask. Nikki once questioned why there were so few vampires in such a large area, and was told that Tyee, not only the oldest but the one who lived longest in the area, forced undesirable families to relocate, keeping a firm control on the quality and quantity of vampires in their territory. Northern Washington had other small tribes and scattered families, with the largest coven in the Seattle to Tacoma area, that Tyee ignored unless an emergency made it necessary to interact with them.

Now, with the millennia of Tyee's life peering into her soul, Nikki wanted to crawl out of her skin and hide.

BRING HIM TO ME, thundered through her mind.

Did Tyee know of the voice she heard?

Did she know what it meant?

Nikk broke her gaze, hiding her face in her glass and taking a long, grimacing sip of her drink.

When the sounds conversation, the scrape of utensils on plates, and the chewing of food, died down, Tyee stood from her seat at the far end of the table. An anticipatory hush descended on the room. Everyone's cheeks were flushed with either wine or blood, their eyes cast on their ancient, beautiful leader.

"First, let us thank the Silvas for hosting a delicious fall equinox feast, once again." Tyee raised her blood glass, and the coven followed suit, tilting their glasses toward Nikki's parents, nodding in silent gratitude, and taking sips of their drinks. "Second, let us thank the Mother, for it is Her blood that has allowed us to be here at this moment. Without Her, we would not have met, throughout time and space. With Her, we have transcended those bounds."

Tyee praised the Mother, the fabled progenitor of all vampires, at each gathering. While there was often talk of the Mother, what She was, where She was, if She was real or not, if She was even alive, was always vague, and Nikki didn't know whether talk of her was myth, religion, real, or somewhere in between. The Born took appreciative sips of their drinks, but the Lius and her dad hesitated for the briefest moment before doing the same. Those most loyal to the Mother were also hateful to the Made, ignoring their status as vampires. But it was unclear where this prejudice originated. Was this belief that the Made are impure, are not real vampires, a teaching truly instilled by the Mother? Or was it just a way to prevent vampires turning too many humans?

In either case, resenting the Made, especially her dad, was ridiculous. He was one of the kindest people she had ever met.

But that voice she heard... it couldn't have been the Mother that talked to her, could it?

Nikki stifled her laugh. Never once had she humored the notion that the Mother could be real. While she wasn't sure where the legend of the Mother came from, she was almost positive that's all it was. A legend. A myth.

If she didn't believe in God, why would she believe in the Mother? It was ludicrous to believe in something she never had proof of, yet if she questioned either Tyee or her own mom, they would come down with a fierce religious hammer.

So, Nikki also took a hesitant sip, neither wanting to encourage Tyee's piety nor wanting to make the rebellious statement of not drinking. At least Tyee wasn't a bigot.

Tyee set her glass on the table, a thin red line staining her lips, and said, "Now, we must speak of coven matters, before the sun asks to rise. First, of the Mother. We have been communing more. Her gaze is upon us."

"Why?" Feng asked.

Tyee's gaze flicked to Nikki for a half second before settling on Feng, Nikki's heart giving a sudden kick in her chest.

"The Mother's business is not yours. If you would like to know, I would beseech all of you, even those made, to make contact with Her. She may deem you worthy of answers." The Made cringed at their glasses, noses crinkling in distaste. Tyee raised her hand abruptly, and as if she'd slapped them, their faces fell neutral. "You are Her children, too."

Tyee's hand descended, slender yet strong fingers perched delicately on the tabletop, arched like spider legs waiting on their web. "One of Her disciples will be visiting soon. I expect all of you to be on your best behavior. And we will need a volunteer to host a welcoming party. Each of you will be expected to attend and ensure he feels welcome. Invite him to events, host dinners, and share your blood."

"Why? Is he a candidate to join the coven?" Feng asked, thick eyebrows arching.

"No, he is a guest," Tyee replied.

"Then why do we have to be on our best behavior and make him feel welcomed? I see no reason why we should have anything to do with him if he doesn't intend to join us. Why do I have to give my limited food supply to someone I do not know? To someone who claims to talk to this entity that despises me?"

"The Mother does not despise you."

Feng barked a laugh. "Yes, that's why all Her so-called disciples, all Her followers, treat us like pariahs. Why no other coven along the west coast would take us."

"Do not blame the Mother for the prejudices of fools."

"Why not? Where else would they get it, if not from Her?"

Tyee took a deep breath, and exhaled slow, palms flattening on the table. "I will not get into this argument with you again."

"At least tell me this means you'll allow us to increase the number of our thralls before we're expected to share them."

Nikki flinched, recalling the Feng's thralls. After what happened with Cian, they were the only ones in the coven who gave their thralls their own blood, making the humans addicted to them. Once, Nikki went to their house and saw how the Lius treated their humans like pets. These thralls were desperate for them—they could see nothing and no one else, and relished being treated like dolls. The pleading looks in their eyes, like a shout from a distant shore, chilled Nikki to the bone.

"No, it does not mean that," Tyee said through clenched teeth. "Yes, the population size of the region is increasing. You may think more people means more anonymity, but it does not. It means a larger network, and therefore more people who can spot you. More people who can hurt us. This issue is about the protection of our home, of our coven, which is of the utmost importance. More than your gluttony or greed. You will not bring more thralls into our homes. But you will share your supply with our visitor. You will welcome him. And you will not complain about it. Understood?"

Feng's jaw twitched, black eyes unblinking and chin lifted. "Since when have you been so welcoming to outsiders? It took you years to let Daiyu and me get over the Oregon border. Months to approve the Lopezes. Now you're going to let a stranger waltz in here as if he is one of us?"

"Must you always be so argumentative?" Halvar asked with a sigh.

Feng shifted his dagger-like gaze to Halvar. "Must you always rush to her side like a dog?"

"I am no dog."

"Fooled me."

Halvar lips peeled back into a snarl. "What makes you certain I am a dog, hm? Do you have a sudden desire to eat me?"

Nikki gasped, a sound echoed by her parents and the Lopezes. Daiyu stiffened beside her.

"How dare you," Feng seethed. "Tyee, are you truly going to let him get away with that?"

Tyee glimpsed at Halvar, then returned her gaze to Feng, unspeaking.

Feng's jaw ticked, and Daiyu cast her gaze to the ground.

"I see," Feng said, standing. He put a hand on his wife's shoulder and said, "Come on, Daiyu, let's go home. We don't need this."

Daiyu nodded and cast Tyee a long, betrayed look. Tyee held her gaze, but her face remained as unreadable as a brick wall.

With a screech from the chair, Daiyu stood from the table. Hand in hand, she and Feng left the dining room, Cat chasing after them. An oppressive silence filled the room, the only sound the faint flickers of the candle flames. A pang of sadness shot through Nikki's chest for the Lius. They had lost their daughter, been chased out of California, and although they were accepted in this coven, they still did not have a sense of belonging. Of family.

"Halvar," Tyee said, "you will apologize to them next time you see them."

Halvar sighed but nodded.

Tiernan cleared his throat. "We will host the party for our visitor."

"Thank you," Tyee said, sitting down with a long exhale and droop of her shoulders. "I will follow up with you when I know his arrival date."

Tiernan nodded.

"Is there anything else we know of him?" Nikki's dad asked.

Tyee shook her head. "I know nothing of him, only that the Mother holds him in high esteem." Tyee met Nikki's gaze again, and the acidity of Nikki's drink burned in her stomach.

The rest of the dinner passed in hushed whispers, Nikki pushing the food around her plate. Her mom scowled at her but didn't bother her about it. Who was this visitor? Why was he coming? And why did Tyee keep looking at her? Nikki was too inconsequential to have this visitor be coming because of the voice she heard.

Right?

Once dinner was over and the guests had left, Nikki and her parent's retreated to the lounge.

"I do tire of all this 'Mother' talk," her dad said, dropping himself indecorously onto a wide and plush lounge chair in front of the gentle fire. "Who do you suppose this mysterious visitor is, eh?"

"I have no idea, but don't speak ill of Tyee. Or the Mother, for that matter," her mom replied, handing Miguel a glass of blood and sitting on the chaise beside Nikki.

Her dad waved his hand dismissively and took a sip of his drink before resting his head back on the chair and closing his eyes.

Cat turned her focus to Nikki, eyes roving over Nikki's thin frame and wan skin. Her mom placed fond fingers on Nikki's cheek, her own slightly flushed from intoxication. "My darling Nicoletta, you need to be drinking more blood. Why do you suffer yourself so? Just that little bit has brightened your eyes."

Nikki turned away from her mom's frown. She could not deny that it felt as if a veil had been lifted from her body. Her senses were sharper, her muscles stronger. And yet—

"It's true, love. You look more alive," her dad added, rousing himself from his dozing.

"There is no point to this starvation, this suffering," her mom said. "Please, Nikki, what can we do to convince you this is needless?"

A small crack split in Nikki's heart at the pleading in her mom's voice, but the fire in her stomach was stronger. Why did they always have to pressure her? Why couldn't they understand that she didn't want to be this way? She didn't want to drink blood. She didn't want to have to hurt people to live. She just wanted to be human. Normal. But they couldn't ever just let her be. Couldn't let her make her own decisions, even though she didn't live at home. How often did they complain that they wished they had a closer relationship? And why did they think that was possible when they were constantly pressuring her and judging her?

How could you be truly close to someone if you didn't accept who they were?

She stood, the heat of shame and rage burning in her chest. "Nothing. I know what I'm doing and I'm tired of your judgements. I'm going to bed."

As she put her hand on the doorknob, her dad said, "You say you don't want to hurt anyone, eh? Well, you hurt us by doing this to yourself."

The fissure in her chest widened, and she let the crackling of the fire respond for her.

In the dim hallway, frustrated, tired tears formed in her eyes. She tilted her head back to keep them in, walled over the crack in her heart, and slipped into her room. She sank into the childhood comfort, the old quiet, but the thrumming of satiation in her veins, the thought of her date with Xander, and the knowing look in Tyee's eyes, kept her awake until the pale purple of dawn clawed its way over the horizon.

Chapter Nine

Nikki, covered in a sheen of nervous, sun-sick sweat, arrived thirty minutes early for their date so that she could find a safe table for her to sit. She found one away from the windows, under the air conditioner in a dim corner, a perfect spot for a vampire recuperating from sun sickness, cold air whisking away the sweat. While she waited for Xander, she watched the humans basking in the sun, heartbeats solid and stuttering, endorphins granting them a last rush of happiness before the gloom of winter. Although her heart sank with envy, at the wonder of feeling warmth on your skin without fear, each minute closer to Xander's arrival brought her heart higher in her throat.

The humans' heartbeats faded into the clutter of noise, their voices getting louder with increased intoxication. The restaurant turned up the music to cover it, and Nikki's inner ear throbbed with the ache of sensory overload.

But it washed away to the steady lull of the ocean when Xander's silhouette came into view.

The background faded as her eyes focused on him, hands in his jeans, wearing a casual button-up, sleeves rolled to his elbows. As he turned his head looking for her, the rush of cold air in the room pushed against his waves, and a warmth spread in Nikki's sternum, forcing the corners of her mouth up against her will.

When he found her, his face lit up, and he patted a hand through his hair, down the curls of his neck as he walked to her table. Nikki returned the smile and stood, holding her elbows to avoid an awkward hug. He stopped within arm's length, a fresh, light chemical scent coming from him. She craned her head up at him, gaze catching on the fall of his hair as he looked down, the green mixed into his grey eyes.

"Hi," Xander said.

"Hi," Nikki replied, feeling stupid for the heat that fluttered through her body.

"I hope I didn't keep you waiting long."

"Not at all. I prefer to arrive early."

"Punctual. I like that." Xander glanced at the table. "You haven't ordered yet?"

"No, I thought I'd wait for you."

"Punctual and polite," Xander said, hands shifting in his pockets. "Should we go order?"

Nikki glanced at the table, then at the bustle of the restaurant, and shifted her feet.

Xander followed her gaze and said, "How about you hold the table, and I'll go order. What do you want?"

"Oh, thank you. Just get me whatever you're having. I'm not picky."

"Sure thing. I'll be back in a moment," Xander said, taking in her face for a second too long before he slipped away into the crowd. As he stood in line, he pulled his hands out of his pockets, preened his hair, then replaced them, leaning into his hip. Nikki hid a dampened smile, his nervousness endearing and comforting. His gaze slid to her once, an embarrassed half-grin flashing on his face before he averted his gaze to the bartender and ordered.

He returned with hands full of whiskey, water, and their order number.

They shared small, shy grins, then Xander raised his whiskey. "Cheers—thanks for coming out tonight."

"Cheers. Thanks for inviting me," Nikki said, glasses softly tinkling as they met, fingers a hair's breadth apart. Tightness and a pulse of tension crept into her veins.

Xander reclined in his chair. "How are you feeling?"

"Oh," Nikki said, fighting embarrassment as the memory of vomiting and fainting in front of him surfaced. "I'm feeling fine now. I'm not sure what happened that night. I promise I don't have a history of vomiting and fainting randomly."

"I'd hazard that it wasn't random, but I see your point. I'm glad you're feeling better."

"Thanks," Nikki replied, taking another sip of whiskey, the burn mingling with her salve. The beginnings of soreness rose in her cheeks, and she realized she was smiling more than normal. Was she really being so...girly? She schooled her features, and watched as Xander witnessed her smile fade.

The waitress slid crispy Brussels sprouts and rosemary-seasoned French fries in front of them, mumbling an apology for the wait, swiping their number, and disappearing back into the throng of people. The smell churned her stomach, overwhelming hunger clouding her senses.

With little prompting, Xander launched into tales about his life while they ate. He had a calming lilt to his voice, with an engaging cadence to his stories. Nikki found herself unable to keep her eyes from his mouth, how his lips curled around each word. Laughter, bubbly and unbidden, rose from her gut and through her mouth at his joy, his silliness, especially when talking about all the games he played with his younger, adopted siblings. It was disarming, and charming, and she eased into his company. Despite his ability to chat he didn't dominate the conversation, and his eyes lit up with every morsel of her own life she shared.

Talking with him, being near him, was like her own spot of sunshine.

The crowd thinned, and fluorescent lights replaced the sun once it had fully set. Satiated, Nikki leaned back in the chair and took a sip of whiskey. Xander did the same, a moment of pleasant silence and quiet, searching eye contact passing between them. Increasingly self-conscious under his gaze, Nikki curled a strand of hair around her finger.

Xander's presence comforted her in a way Nikki never felt anymore. The other people in her life, even Gwen, always slipped their judgments and opinions about her choices into every conversation. It was nice to feel for once like she wasn't walking on eggshells. She was just a girl on a date, not a weakling vampire resisting her nature, scaring her parents, worrying her best friend, and disappointing her coven.

"You look like you're having serious thoughts. Want to get out of here?"

"Oh, yes, I'm sorry. I'm prone to overthinking and getting lost in my head."

"I'd rather someone who overthinks than one who doesn't think at all." Xander stood and smiled, extending his hand out to her. "Doesn't bother me in the slightest."

But his smile faltered when she didn't take his hand, and all she wanted was to make it shine again.

So, Nikki placed her hand in his, the bird in her chest taking flight, even as her blood seemed to tighten in resistance. But the heat of his hand moved into her arms, and she relaxed, consumed by his warmth. She stood and looked up at him, confused at how time was moving yet stood still, his gaze moving over her face as they shared a breath. An aching pulse of pain shot through her gums as saliva flooded her mouth, her vision clouding with sudden hunger that had nothing to do with food, and she stammered, "I need to use the restroom."

In the restroom, she inhaled and exhaled, long and hard, as if he had stolen the air from her lungs when they shared a breath. She leaned her arms on the ceramic sink edges, staring into the drain. She splashed cold water on her neck, hoping it would relieve the pressure in her head, the heat in her core. She caught her reflection as she patted her neck dry, smoothing out her hair and making sure that her teeth and gums looked okay. With them numbed, she couldn't feel if a tooth was loose, or if a remnant piece of lettuce had gotten wedged between.

Confirming she was all together, at least on the outside, she left the restroom and found the table empty, a paid and signed check sitting on top. Stepping into the night, a cool breeze rolling off the Columbia River, she found Xander facing the river, back to her. Lights reflected on the water, casting golden light across his hair, skin, and clothes. He sensed her approach, and looked at her over his shoulder, mouth curling into another one of those glorious smiles. Nikki's heart skipped a beat even as she tried to tamp down on the feeling rising in her chest.

"Thank you for paying. You didn't have to do that."

"It was my pleasure. Would you like to go on a walk?" His hands in his pockets fidgeted, despite the casual lean into his hip, and the hope behind his eyes filled Nikki with affection.

"I would like that very much."

They smiled at each other, some strange magic pulling the air out from between them, as if strings had formed between them and wound tighter. Nikki's heart thundered in her chest and ears. Would it always be like this around him? At once exciting and calming, as if they were the only two people in the world. As if they belonged with each other. If she was anyone other than who she was—what she was—she would've chased the feeling for the rest of her life. But she couldn't risk losing control.

And that singular thought sent her back to reality with a painful thud.

"But I told Gwen I'd help her tonight."

Xander's face faltered, but he said, "Sure, no problem."

Nikki's gut twisted, and she blurted, "Walk me to my car?"

"Gladly." They fell into step, the hairs on Nikki's arm rising at the nearness of him. "What are you helping her with?"

"We're going foraging."

"Foraging? For what?"

"For plants, feathers. Just natural ingredients. She makes medicines."

"Interesting," Xander said, brow furrowed. "But isn't it dangerous for you two to be out alone so late at night?"

"We don't go out too far. And we bring protection," Nikki replied, thinking of Gwen's charms and her own enhanced reflexes.

"Like a gun?"

"Uh, no." She didn't want to lie to him, so she didn't elaborate. Awkward silence fell around them, and she shriveled inward at her own discomfort.

They approached her car in the parking lot below the building, stale underground air replacing the soft fresh breeze from the river. With a relieved sigh, Nikki said, "Well, this is me."

A taut silence hung between them, Xander's hands fidgeting in his pockets, Nikki clutching and twisting her purse strap across her torso.

Xander looked down at her mouth. "Can I see you again?" He shifted forward just the slightest bit.

She tilted her neck to maintain eye contact at his unconscious approach, and some atrium unlocked in her body. Even with the dirty, dim yellow lights of the parking garage, she could see the stubble on his face, the flecks of green in his eyes, hidden in part by the waves that cascaded over his brow.

"Yes, I'd like that."

"Good, me too," he said, stepping back with a resigned smile. "Goodnight, Nikki. Be careful out there."

"Thanks, Xander. Goodnight."

He maintained eye contact for several steps as he retreated into the night. When he turned around, a weight dropped her chest to her stomach, and she clutched the handle of her purse until he faded into the darkness.

Chapter Ten

Nikki's fluttering heart didn't relax until she was well on the freeway, the soft whoosh whoosh whoosh of passing cars droning in her ears. By the time she arrived at Gwen's house an hour later, she couldn't remember driving there. All she recalled was Xander's warm smile, the reverberation of his voice low in his chest, and how when she was with him, she didn't notice when the sun went down or worry about its crawl across the floor.

She didn't feel like a monster around him.

A flash of deep copper fire bounced through the night, and Gwen swung the back door open to throw in her various satchels, sickles, and shovels. Gwen was not pleased to learn that Nikki just came from the date with Xander. Nikki purposefully didn't tell her how she stacked plans, knowing Gwen would disapprove. Gwen muttered something about Nikki hiding from her feelings which Nikki ignored. It had been a good evening so far and she didn't want it sullied by arguing. She didn't expect Gwen to understand it wasn't that she was hiding from her feelings, she was trying to prevent anyone from getting hurt. Again.

To divert Gwen's focus, Nikki asked about her date with Theo, and thankfully, Gwen took the bait. She launched into details about how they ate, drank, and danced until the sun came up, how they text nearly nonstop, and already had plans to see each other again.

Nikki followed Gwen's directions through the Gorge, and they meandered on dark access roads for a few minutes before Gwen found the small trail she wanted to walk.

Once they were out of the car, Gwen commanded, "Hold still."

"Why?"

"I'm trying out a new potion. Unfortunately, there won't be a way for us to tell if it works, but it'll be fun to test anyway."

Gwen pulled a vial from her bag, glints of silver sparking in the dark liquid. She poured the fluid into little pools in each of their palms, and when Gwen dabbed it on her neck, face, and wrists, Nikki did the same. Gwen lifted her hands, slivers of gold and silver swarming beneath her skin, in her wrists, palms, and fingertips. As she spread out her hands, the band expanded outside of her like a web, which she wound around both of them. The heat of Gwen's magic warmed her, and the gold light pulsed before blinking out.

Nikki's eyes adjusted quickly, the shapes of Douglas fir and Oregon ash and old man's beard materializing, the faint breeze rustling leaves and debris on the forest floor.

"What did you do?"

"I made us a shield. Hopefully for both sound and smell. But we'll see."

"Isn't that a bad idea, if we get separated?"

"Well, stay close then." Gwen smirked. "But yes and no. We may be able to hear each other. I can't smell you regardless, but you should be able to smell me still."

"Should."

Gwen nodded. "Yes. Should."

"You're filling me with confidence."

"Don't worry, my darling vampire, I'll protect you against the evil things that prowl the night."

"If you say so," Nikki said, magicked skin cooling. "Remind me what you're looking for tonight."

"Bark, mostly. If you see uncommon feathers or 'shrooms, let me know. We'll save full-blown mushroom foraging for the wet season. But we're also looking for any flowers still attached to the plant, blooming or desiccated."

Gwen cocked her head to the side, as if listening, and then looked up. Nikki followed her gaze, but only saw the swaying treetops, the night sky behind their dark silhouettes. Then, in the distance, Nikki heard the whomp of wings flapping, growing closer.

Gwen's smirk split into a wide smile, and she outstretched her scarred arm. "Our final companion is here."

A barred owl swooped onto Gwen's forearm, talons wrapping around her as delicately as possible, prickles of blood blooming on her skin. She scratched under its chin and asked, "Are you going to help us tonight?"

It cooed, nudged Gwen's head, then launched into the woods, in the direction of the path. Gwen laughed with delight and, after turning on a dim flashlight, bounced after it, Nikki following with her own small smile.

Their steps were light scuffles on the dirt trail, with minimal rustling of ferns and shrubs and the cracking of sticks. Nikki could see the forest, all in various shades of grey, the moon peeking through the clouds to cast hazy white shards of light through the canopy. Nikki heard steps in the distance, but they weren't heavy, and didn't get closer, so she remained unafraid.

Eventually, the woods widened, sword ferns giving way to grasses and herbs, so Nikki stepped away from Gwen to cover more ground.

Nikki kneeled to pluck the flowers of a pearly everlasting. As she excised the plants and put them in a pouch, she heard a faint whisper on the wind.

There you are...

"What? Sorry I couldn't quite catch that." But when she raised her head, Gwen was a speck of dull red deeper in the woods. Frowning, Nikki stood and closed some of the distance between her and Gwen with wide strides.

They descended a small slope covered by cedars that gave way to an isolated wetland with lady ferns. Gwen gathered on the other side, while Nikki pulled out a drawing knife and peeling spud to strip bark from the cedars. As she placed her hand on a fine strip of bark to pull, she heard a whisper, light as the wind, say: *Nikki*.

"What?" she asked, looking at Gwen.

"What?" Gwen repeated, yelling across the wetland.

"You just said my name."

"No, I didn't," she said, turning back to the ferns.

Nikki frowned. "Oh." She turned back to the cedar, shaking her head and resuming her task, but as she continued to peel the bark, she heard quiet rustlings, as if she were surrounded by a whispering crowd.

Her head jerked up, and she twisted from one side to the other, but she couldn't make out any figures around them. The voices were quiet and stilted, and she couldn't make out what they were saying, but she knew there were several of them. Her heart quickened, drumming in her ears, and she jogged to Gwen. Placing her hands on her knees, she took several deep breaths, the scent of moist, disturbed earth spilling from the pit Gwen had excavated.

"Other people are out here," Nikki whispered. There had to be. She hadn't heard the other voice in weeks now, so there was no way she was imagining things again, right?

"There are?"

Nikki nodded. "I heard them."

Gwen tilted her head, squinting her eyes slightly. "Are you sure?"

"Yes. As I said, I heard them."

"Could've been the wind."

"It wasn't. I heard several voices talking. Or whispering. Gwen, I don't think we should be out here anymore."

"Nik, it's fine. That's why I put the potion on us."

"You said it should work, not that it would. And even so, they could still see us."

"It sounded like whispers, right? They're probably far away. Maybe people camping. Let me know if it gets louder, and we'll go in the other direction."

Nikki stood, crossing her arms. She shifted her weight from one foot to the other. "Fine. But I don't want to interact with whoever is out here. If they see us, we leave. Deal?"

Gwen nodded. "Deal."

The hairs on Nikki's arms and the back of her neck stood up as she returned to the cedar, eyes scanning the dim forest, ears picking out each creaking branch, rustling leaf, flapping bird, and scuttling mammal.

And she could still hear the voices, the wind like someone's breath on her skin as they spoke.

Nikki focused on taking slow, deep breaths as she finished stripping the bark.

Voices tumbled over each other, talking all at once, a constant push of vaguely human sounds, and chills swept up her body. She stepped away from the wetland and cedars, trying to follow the voices. If she could only see where they were coming from, she would feel safer. She walked farther downslope and encountered a dried-up stream. There was only a faint trickle coursing along the bottom, surrounded by willows, Douglas spirea, and red-osier dogwood. She slid down the slope to the channel to gather willow leaves, plus bark and twigs from the dogwood.

As she did so, the voices became clearer. Like they were coming from the other side of the bank.

Nikki hopped across the remnant of the stream, whispers urgent and overlapping, and forced herself through the trees.

To find nothing.

No people. No campsite. No light.

Just more dark forest.

Nikki wrapped her arms around her chest, clasping her biceps and squeezing as she turned back to the deciduous trees along the stream.

She climbed through the willows and dogwood to stand in the middle of the empty channel, the branches of the willows obstructing her view of the night sky.

Nikki breathed hard, in and out, hoping she wouldn't faint again. She was suffocating as the branches reached for her, boxing her in. Their tips brushed against her skin, catching her hair, and her breath pushed against the leaves, making them rustle. The whispers increased in volume, like echoes in a tunnel. She strained to make out some of the words.

...ah...

Nikki...dearest...

...daughter, you've done...
It. After...all
These long, lonely years...

Chills wound up Nikki's spine, hairs standing on end, as the voices wrapped around her skin and twined into her bones, keeping her in place.

...done...
Finally...freedom...
Ah...dearest, dearest...daughter...

The whispers grew until her ears rang, the noise searing her mind. Nikki closed her eyes and clamped her hands on either side of her head to shut it out, but as she moved, her blood tightened, squeezing her from the inside, and she collapsed to her knees. Hands falling to the ground to catch herself, she crumpled into the dirt and leaves as the ringing raged, and her veins constricted, winding her body tauter.

Hands sinking into the damp earth, her finger brushed a stray root that crept over forgotten, slick stones.

BRING HIM TO ME.

Nikki recoiled at the voice, clear as if spoken right beside her. As she fell back onto her hands, she launched herself out of the thicket, tearing through the willow branches, yelling, "Gwen!"

Through the coppice of trees, running up the hill, that singular voice broke into a cacophony of whispers. Her vision adjusted to the muted colors of the world again from the darkness of the thicket, and Nikki tripped as she ran up the hill, prickles of trailing blackberry entwined in her shoes, her pant legs, her sleeves.

She yanked the vine from her clothing, pinpricks of blood sprouting on her palms. Launching herself upright, she dashed through the forest and up the hill, retracing her steps to the wetland where she had last seen Gwen.

"Gwen!" Nikki shouted, her voice melting with the echoes of the whispers through the trees, the crunch and stomp of her feet over the forest floor debris.

"Gwen!" she yelled again, breath catching in her throat.

Back at the isolated wetland, she stopped. "Gwen?"

Panting, she braced her hands on her knees to catch her breath.

Once recentered, she raised her head, sucking air through her nose, hoping that maybe she could catch Gwen's scent, despite the potion. Cool, night air filled her lungs. But she could not sense the coldness of vampiric blood, nor the warmth of magic.

Nikki cursed and went to Gwen's soil pit, looking to see if she could retrace her steps. A faint trail revealed itself through crushed ferns, and Nikki followed it with rapid steps until she broke into a run, glancing for a sign of muted fire in the dark, for a flash of pale skin, a sickening creep of fear winding up her body at the emptiness of the forest.

"Oh!" Gwen exclaimed as Nikki crashed into her, running at full speed.

Their bodies smacked with a dense thud, and they both fell to the ground, Gwen bursting into laughter, even as Nikki righted herself and yanked Gwen to her feet, saying, "We need to get out of here. Now."

"Whoa! What's going on?" Gwen replied, twisting her arm out of Nikki's grasp and stopping.

Nikki whirled and clasped her hands on Gwen's shoulders, giving her a desperate shake. "There are people here, Gwen, and they're not friendly. I don't know what's going on, but I heard them, and we need to leave. Now."

Nikki didn't give her friend a chance to argue as she sprinted out of the woods. With a huff of annoyance, Gwen followed, clutching her gathered goods to her chest.

When they made it back to the car, Nikki exhaled with relief, whispers dimming as the distance between her and the woods grew. She braced her hands on the car and looked at the dirt-covered road, the car an unmoving, un-whispering force she used to stabilize herself. A frantic flap of wings rushed through the forest, the barred owl landing on a nearby branch, glaring at Nikki, inconvenienced by the sudden change in plans.

"Nik," Gwen said, coming to an ungraceful, huffing stop. "What the hell?"

Nikki shook her head. "I don't know what else to tell you."

"What happened after you left me at the ferns?"

Nikki turned and tilted her head back, resting it against the car, gazing up at the swaying, black treetops. She crossed her arms and shook her head again, trying to shake out the rest of the faded whispers that pulsed in the wind.

"I don't know. I was trying to find the source of the voices. I followed them to a dried-out creek, overgrown by willows and shrubs. I assumed whoever it was would be on the other side of the stream. But when I crossed, no one was there. And then the—the thing happened again."

"The thing?"

"Where I felt my body tighten, and I fell."

"You fainted again?"

"No, but my ears were ringing, and I could hear the voices, and then my body crumpled. They were all around me. Demanding me to—" But she couldn't tell her. Not when she didn't understand their words. "I don't know. But I don't like it. It didn't feel right. Or safe."

Gwen swayed on her feet, staring into the distance, thinking. "But you didn't see anyone."

"No. That's the scariest part. I don't know what, or who, it was." Nikki shivered as she looked at the woods. "Let's get out of here."

Gwen nodded and stepped into the car. They were quiet as Nikki navigated the access roads out of the forest, Gwen taking stock of her haul. When they pulled back onto the main highway, Nikki finally felt the voices fade, like a weight lifting from her shoulders.

"You think there were people farther off than you thought?" Gwen finally asked.

"No. When I was in the thicket of willows, it got louder."

But if there weren't people out there, then what had she heard?

"What were they saying? What were the demands?"

Nikki shook her head, an unknown dread filling her stomach and tightening her throat. "Nonsensical phrases, mostly."

They were silent for several minutes, listening to the spin of her wheels on the concrete, the clicking of her blinkers as she changed lanes. Floodlamps pulsed light through the windows, intermittently casting their faces in whites and golds. In one of the flashes, Nikki glanced at Gwen, who was chewing her lip.

"What are you going to do?" Gwen asked. "Are you going to listen to these nonsensical demands from the mystery whispers?"

"I don't know."

Bring him to me trickled through Nikki's mind.

Bring him... That could only mean Xander. None of this happened before him. But who wanted him? And why?

"I'll talk to my parents," Nikki decided. "See if they know what's happening. I already asked them if we have a history of mental illness in the family and they said there isn't. Maybe they know a different reason why this is happening. And hopefully they won't think I'm crazy."

"Good idea. I'd ask my family if they weren't assholes."

"I appreciate the thought."

When they finally pulled up to Gwen's house, she asked, "Do you want to spend the night?"

Nikki exhaled, long enough to be considered a sigh. As she rested her hands in her lap, she felt them twinge, relaxing from the tight grip she'd had on the wheel. In the silence, she realized she'd been clenching her jaw, and as she relaxed it, an aching pain crept into her gums. Feeling the aches and pains, the worries and anxieties mixed into her body, and knowing Gwen was her best medicine, she said, "Yes."

Nikki gathered her things, following Gwen to her studio around the side of the mansion.

Her mind whirred, now empty of the whispers that had forced themselves into her eardrums. If it was Xander this voice was after, that was even more reason to stay away from him. Yes, he was warm, cute, compassionate, smart, interesting, and not a vampire, but it wasn't worth it. She had other goals. Other things to focus on. She would just have to let him down easy or ghost him. It would be for his safety.

Nikki steeled her heart, preparing to disappoint yet another person and erasing whatever fantasies of him in her life she might have entertained in the daylight hours when she was restless.

She sat on Gwen's couch as her friend organized her new supplies into various jars and cupboards, pressing plants between blotting paper or hanging them to dry. Nikki grabbed her phone to text her parents about visiting tomorrow night, and it vibrated with pending messages as she picked it up.

Texts from Xander.

She hardened herself to ignore him, to tell him she wasn't in a place to date.

She opened his texts, sent not long after they left each other. He thanked her for going out, said he had a good time, and wished her a safe night.

Although she told herself it was for the best to not respond, to distance herself from him for both their sakes, there was no suppressing the light fluttering in her chest, nor the smile that stretched across her face as she looked at his name on her phone, at the sweet words he sent her way.

Her fingers flew across her screen of their own volition.

Chapter Eleven

Nikki woke the next afternoon with sore, stiff muscles. Her arms shook as she pushed herself up into a seated position, and she groaned at her weakness. It felt as if she had run a marathon. Or gotten beat up. Her hands felt as if they were shaking, yet when she held them out, they were still. She flexed and clenched them, hoping to restore their normal functioning, but they remained weak. Even when she had eaten, drunk coffee, and fully woken up, the soreness didn't fade. Her gums ached worse than before, the pain radiating through her jaw. She nudged her tongue on her canines, hoping to get the reassurance that they were in place, but her heart sank as they wiggled against the light pressure. How much longer until her fangs came in? How much longer until she couldn't control her blood cravings?

She spent the rest of daylight at Gwen's studio doing homework and responding to Xander's texts. Even though every time she told herself not to, she couldn't help but pick up her phone as soon as the notification came up, her heart leaping to her throat with excitement. They chatted about their days, and she couldn't suppress the smile that plastered itself on her face.

When she got to her parents' house that evening, the house was empty, so she made herself comfortable until they arrived. She placed her school supplies on the dining room table, books and articles and laptop spread out in organized chaos. Nikki ate the scraps of chocolate and orange from her bag, but the sweetness did nothing to alleviate the bitter fear from the night before clawing its way up her throat. Fingers twitched on her keyboard, a sickening anxiety forming. The food in her mouth turned to ash, and she pushed herself up from the table, the wooden chair giving a terrible, high-pitched squeak against the floors.

In the kitchen, she found little that sounded appetizing. As her dad could only consume blood, there was little human food in the house. She found steaks in the freezer, but even the thought of cooking it expended more energy than she had.

With the fridge door open, she stared at bags upon bags of blood, esophagus clenching with disgust. But it was that or nothing. Tapping a finger on the door, the coldness of the fridge's interior pushing against her skin, the machine humming louder to maintain the temperature as she wasted energy, she shook her head, disapproving, but snatched out a bag of blood. She got the smallest glass she could find and filled it, then put it in the microwave to warm it. Returning the bag to the fridge, she looked at it as little as possible. She couldn't stand the deep crimson color or the viscosity of the liquid inside.

Standing in front of the microwave, head down, she listened to the quiet whir until it beeped, the warm light from inside going black. Nikki opened the door and wrapped her hand around the tiny glass, letting it heat her cold, shaking hands.

Bringing it to her mouth, she gulped it down like she was taking a shot, suppressing a gag as the hot, thick, metallic tang of the blood slid down her throat. But as soon as it hit her stomach, dispersing into her bloodstream, her shaking stopped, her muscles felt firmer, and her senses expanded, as if she were waking from a dream.

Her hearing sharpened, like popping from an altitude change, and she heard the wind shushing outside, Bernadette's footsteps from the depth of the house, the shifting of pipes and wood within the building. She gazed around in awe, spotting the knots in the wood floor, the imperfections in the glass window, and the shafts of light from a bulb in the ceiling, all of which were more distinct than she ever realized. The air shifted against her skin, and the cool, smooth texture of the counter under her hand soothed the skin of her palm. The sudden pulse of heightened senses shifted some part of her brain, compensating for the overload of new information. It reorganized the chaos and settled, consolidating the information. She stood taller, as though she'd been reconstructed.

But when she looked at the empty glass, thick red streaks dripping along the sides, her stomach lurched. It wasn't right that causing pain, leeching from others, could fill her with so much life. She picked up that small glass, each divot and bump in the design unique in her palm. Looking at the blood smeared against the glass, she remembered the feel of it fresh in her mouth, of a slowly beating heart losing its strength as it pulsed into her body, and as most of her reacted with pleasure, with heightened awareness and strength, her stomach churned, risking the rise of blood and bile in her throat. She clenched the glass in her hand, forcing down the memory, focusing instead on her self-loathing, of how much of a monster she was to get such delights from the life force of something else, and she wished she could be different, could feel strong without costing someone else pain.

The glass cracked and broke in her hand, shards piercing her skin and raining to the floor.

She heard when every delicate piece of glass landed.

A sound between a moan and growl escaped her, deep from her core as she turned to the counter, slamming her hands down and gritting her teeth, clenching her eyes closed, as if she tensed herself enough, shut herself away enough, she could disappear.

Behind the darkness of her eyes, her left hand felt the coolness of the counter, her right hand splintered and warm from the glass shards and blood spilling from it. She pushed her right hand into the counter, letting the shards sink deeper, until there were no thoughts, only pain. A scream rose in her throat, but she pushed it back down, trapping it deep within the pit of her stomach. It could stay there, as stuck as she was, forever.

Nikki concentrated on the pain in her hand for minutes that felt like hours. When it finally dulled, her heart rate slowed, and her rage cooled into the soft simmer of shame. She hadn't meant to break the glass, to make a mess. To lose control of herself.

She cleaned her mess, sweeping the glass off the floor, wiping the blood from the counter, letting herself have the pain in her hand a little longer. It was nothing less than she deserved. With the kitchen cleaned, she went upstairs to her bedroom and shut the door. Closing herself in her private bathroom, she tweezed out the glass from her palm, one agonizing piece at a time, listening to the house shifting with the wind. She could see her hand in mesmerizing, glittering detail, and the light cast each blood-covered shard in a soft, golden glow.

Nikki removed each piece with meticulous care. The smaller cuts mended as soon as the fragments were gone, forming smooth, pink scratches. If she'd had more blood, it would fully heal. Yet, it was still amazing, watching her cells repair in an instant, sealing the wounds, staunching the flow of her own blood.

She rinsed her hands when she was done, a slight sting remaining on her palm. She sighed at her reflection, skin no longer sickly pale, but vibrant and luminous like the full moon. She was beautiful. And wrong.

Nikki wrapped her hand in gauze to minimize further irritation, letting the wounds stitch themselves up at their own pace. She fell back on her bed, arms out, staring at the canopy, soothing that sliver of shame until it became dull.

Pulling her phone from her pocket, she flipped through the news, her emails, and her messages, a light flutter in her chest as Xander responded, asking when they could get together again. She tapped her finger on the side of the phone, heaviness sinking from her chest to her gut, not knowing how to turn him down. How could she justify seeing him again when she was such a monster?

But how could she stay away?

Her mind split into two hypotheticals, one where they went out again and she basked in his smile and warmth, and the other where she never saw him again and her life remained constant and voiceless, but cold.

Unable to make a choice, to bear the burden of disappointing him as she disappointed everyone, Nikki said she wasn't sure yet and heaved herself out of bed to resume studying.

In the dining room, the walls groaned against the wind, and the light from the chandelier above the table flickered every once in a while.

Nikki shut herself off from the world, hyper-focusing on her homework, feeling more productive than usual, despite the itch of the healing wounds in her hand.

Eventually her parents came home, laughing and chatting. Nikki grinned at their joy, even as a stab of jealousy carved into her, wishing to have a similar relationship in her life, even though she knew she couldn't. Shouldn't.

She found them in the kitchen, pulling containers of food out of paper bags, standing side by side, eyes only for each other. Lost in each other, they leaned in and kissed deeply. Nikki cleared her throat as she crept into the kitchen, and they broke apart with a start, her mom turning to her with an embarrassed smile.

"Nicoletta, we weren't expecting you so early." Her mom walked over, arms outstretched, planting a kiss on each of her cheeks. Cat's body was hot, face bright with overindulgence, wafts of blood and wine escaping from her breath.

"Sorry to interrupt. But I did say I was going to come over tonight."

"Oh no, you're not interrupting. Here, sweetling, we brought leftovers for you."

"You two sit and get comfortable," her mom said, arranging the food on a plate with an artist's hand. "I'll heat this up and bring it to you."

"Come, come," her dad beckoned, guiding Nikki into the hallway.

"Thanks, Mom," Nikki called over her shoulder as they left the kitchen. Cat hummed, soft and low, a sound of complete contentment.

In the dark of the hallway, wall lamps casting faint light across the red paint and dark wooden floors, Nikki whispered to her dad, "Mom is sauced, isn't she?"

He smiled wide and nodded. "She's delightful, eh?" He paused to listen to her humming. "Rarely will she shake her armor, and I love when she does. Granted, I love her anyway, but it is nice to hear her joy."

"Where did you two go?"

"Ah, to the Lopezes. The kids are visiting their grandparents in Phoenix, so they can let loose for once."

"I'm glad you had a good time."

Her dad gave her a small smile, squeezing her shoulder once more before removing his hand as they entered the lounge. He lit a fire, and then poured Nikki a brandy from the nearby decanter. Before he handed the glass to her, he sniffed the glass with longing, lips peeling back at the memory, revealing pointed teeth. She accepted the liquor and took a sip, letting it burn down her throat.

"Please, sit," he said, hand open to the chair, and Nikki obeyed, perching on the edge of an oversized seat in front of the fire. The flickering heat and brandy warmed and calmed her, despite her pulse increasing as she braced for the ensuing conversation.

Her mom came in moments later, holding a large serving tray with Nikki's food and two glasses of warmed blood. Nikki scowled at the glasses, throat clenching, but she turned her focus to the food, stomach growling.

Nikki devoured her food, ravenous and nervous, while her parents gazed at the fire. Her dad's arm was slung around her mom's shoulders as she leaned into him. Her parents chatted about their evening, though Nikki couldn't hear much through the sounds of her eating or her mom's slurs. As Cat drank more blood, however, her sobriety increased, metabolizing the alcohol at a faster rate.

Nikki set the plate down on the coffee table when she was done, stomach full to bursting. But she felt good, and whole, and warm. She clasped her fingers together, keeping them still, as she prepared to reveal her potential insanity.

At the sound of her creaking plate, her parents sat on the couch in front of her, still entwined. They all stared at each other, waiting for Nikki to speak, but the words caught in her throat. Her mom quirked an eyebrow at her, and Nikki's heart leapt into her mouth.

"What's going on, love?" her dad asked.

Nikki wrung her hands. "Promise me you won't think I'm crazy."

They scowled and shared a look. "We won't think you're crazy. Tell us what troubles you," her dad replied.

"Well, first, I've smelled something, or someone, different. I'm not sure how, or why, but I thought maybe you two would know."

"Different how?"

"Not like other humans. It's not a chemical or animal smell. It emanates from him, but only sometimes. It's earthy and sweet, almost like anise and figs. As stupid as it sounds, it makes me think of warm sand. Of desert twilights."

Her parents were silent.

"Well? What do you think? I know it's not cologne. Or something he uses to clean himself or his clothes."

"I wouldn't worry about it too much, sweetling," her mom answered, eyebrows knit.

"What does that mean? Do you know what makes him different?"

"Not precisely, no."

"But you know something."

Cat adjusted herself on the couch, tucking her feet beneath her.

"Maybe," her dad cut in, "you are shocking your senses with your inconsistent blood drinking, during your maturation, yes? Maybe smelling things more intensely than before."

"It isn't about intensity. It's about difference. It is different. I don't know how else to explain it." Nikki dropped her gaze to her hands, heart sinking, sensing in her mom's fidgets that there was something she wasn't being told. But then again, maybe it was just her body struggling to adjust to her heightening senses, to whatever Nikki found stimulating about Xander.

"I don't know," her dad said. "As your mother said, I would not worry about these things so much."

"Have either of you ever smelled anything like it? Or heard of anything like it?"

Her mom sighed. "Nicoletta, what is really going on? Who is this person? Are you dating someone?"

"What? No, that's not—" Nikki exhaled, defeated. "Maybe I am just having issues with maturation." After another deep breath, she said, "I have this feeling sometimes. Like my veins are constricting. There's this pressure in my head and—and voices, too. Like I'm a puppet and the puppeteer is trying to talk to me, but we're on different sides of the stage."

Cat's eyes widened, and she leaned forward.

"Sounds crazy, I know," Nikki said, heart beating in her throat, her ears.

"No, Nicoletta, that's not crazy," her mom said. "How many times has this happened?"

"Two or three? The symptoms aren't always all at once, so it's hard to tell. The sense of internal constriction happens more than the head pressure, which happens more than the voice. Or voices."

"What do these voices say?"

"It's hard to tell most of the time. But it sounds like they want me to bring them something."

Her parents shared a look, worry etching their features, and Miguel took a long drink of blood.

"What's happening to me?" she asked, voice breaking.

"Oh, sweetling, don't worry," her mom said, moving to sit on the coffee table in front of her. Her dad kept his gaze on the fire, as her mom bored her eyes into Nikki's.

Cat took Nikki's hands in her own. "Listen to me, Nicoletta. What you're feeling is the Mother's compelling. When you asked about schizophrenia, and then Tyee mentioned a disciple of the Mother visiting, I wondered if this was happening. It is a blessing for our family and coven that She has communicated with you." Cat's hands squeezed Nikki's, but it was not comforting. "You must do as She commands."

"What if I don't want to?" Nikki said, thinking of Xander's dark curls and bright eyes swallowed by the darkness of this fabled Mother. "What if I don't believe she exists? What if this is something else entirely?"

"It does not matter what you believe. The truth persists regardless," her mom said, leaning close to Nikki's face, her gaze searching and searing. "This visitor may be coming to ensure you do as she compels."

Her dad growled, a low sound of disgust. "Bah! Don't fill her head with such religious nonsense. We don't know this visitor's purpose. And she doesn't have to listen to that old bitch."

"Miguel!"

"What? If She even exists, She is thousands of miles away—"

"She does exist, Miguel. I know it in my bones, in my blood," her mom said, rising.

"Even if that is true, She is far from here. Nikki does not have to do what she says. What will happen if she does not? What is this doomsday you imagine? Do you know of anyone who has been compelled and what has happened to them?"

"No, but there are stories."

"Oh, yes, and all stories are factual."

Redness bloomed over her mom's face. "Don't mock my faith!"

"Then don't use it to threaten our daughter!" Her dad bellowed, standing to face Cat. "You're terrifying her for no reason. Who is to say this is a compelling, eh? And not some other side effect of her poor dietary choices? Maybe she gets headaches, feels constricted, and hallucinates from lack of blood—not from this supposed Mother. It's bullshit, and I will not listen to it. Nor will I demand Nikki do so." Miguel turned his gaze to Nikki, flames reflected in his dark eyes. "The way of the Born is not the only way, nor is it inherently the right way. You know this. You do not have to heed the notions of the religious."

"I—I know," Nikki said, struggling to find her voice in the shadow of her parents' fight. She shriveled into herself, the ache of guilt in her gut from causing the argument.

Her dad heaved in a deep breath and released it harshly. He put his glass down on the table and looked at his wife, then his daughter. "Nikki, my darling child, I am sorry you have these troubles." He stepped close to her, putting a hand on her face. "I will always listen to you and help in any way I can. But I cannot abide this conversation anymore tonight." He kissed her forehead and said, "Goodnight, love."

"Goodnight, Dad." Nikki looked at her parents, feeling small. "I'm sorry. I didn't mean to cause a fight."

"Don't apologize." Miguel gave Cat a pointed look. "But you should." Cat's jaw clenched, and Miguel left the room.

Cat hovered over Nikki, the dimming fire casting her porcelain skin in shades of soft orange. Her mom looked down and said, "I will not apologize for speaking the truth. The truth is not always easy or ideal." Her gaze went to the remaining blood in her dad's abandoned glass, then back to Nikki's face. "There is only one way to tell if this is physiological or spiritual. If this is the Mother, you must do as She commands. No good will come from disobedience."

Nikki nodded, tongue thick in her mouth.

"If you need further guidance, do not hesitate to talk to me. Or Tyee. She has had a long bond with the Mother."

Nikki nodded again, exhaustion climbing up her body, smothering her voice.

"We have had more news of this visitor. He will be arriving in one week, and the welcoming party at the O'Brennans' will be soon after. It would be wise to decide your course of action before meeting him."

Her mom left the room with muted footsteps. Nikki didn't move from the chair, watching the fire burn out, a soothing crackle as knots of wood burst and fizzled. Darkness encompassed the room, but her eyes adjusted so well she barely noticed the difference. When the whole room was dark, she stood to look out the window, at the trees swaying in the distance, illuminated by the moonset. Dawn would be upon her in a few hours. Nikki didn't know if she believed in the Mother, but could blood deprivation truly cause these symptoms? If it was the Mother, what was she supposed to do? What would happen if she didn't? Did this visitor really have anything to do with the compelling? Thinking of Xander brought a small curve to her lips, and her heart sank at the thought of bringing him into her world.

She only had more questions than when she arrived. And no answers to any of it.

There's only one way to tell if it is physiological or spiritual.

Nikki glanced at her father's half-empty glass of blood and with a breathless swallow, gulped down the remnants. Licking her lips and forcing the thick, warm liquid into her throat, she tiptoed through the house as everything became a little sharper.

Nikki didn't put her shoes on as she slipped outside. She walked across the cold, dewy grass to the forest's edge, silvery light on the green blades of grass casting the world in a ghostly glow. Peering up at the trees before her, she inhaled the night air, then took a step forward, bare feet crunching on twigs, leaves, rocks, and dirt.

Wind hushed through the pine needles and leaves, carrying with it a beckoning voice. Nikki raised her hand, her injured palm stretched outward. She unwrapped the gauze and laid her bare skin on the thick, toughened bark of a Douglas fir.

A relieved sigh floated on the breeze, and a presence filled Nikki's head.

...daughter...

You will...

...listen...

Bring him...

The pressure in her head increased, pushing against the inside of her skull, and Nikki took a deep breath before shutting her eyes and saying, "Who are you?"

A quiet chuckle tickled the back of her mind.

"What do you want from me?"

Bring him...

...to me...

"Do you mean Xander?"

There was no verbal response, but the trees seemed to bow, as if nodding.

Nikki touched her head against the trunk, hand curling into a partial fist around the bark.

"I don't understand. Why? Why do you want him?"

A quiet, contemplative rustle of the leaves.

...for freedom...

"But at what cost?" Nikki whispered, before she could bite her tongue.

An unseen force pushed down on her body, shoving her to the ground, and she gasped with the shock and strain as she crumpled.

"Please, leave me alone," Nikki begged, hating the desperate tone of her voice. Pressure pounded behind her eyelids, and she yelped, clutching a hand to her head, careful to leave one on the tree. "I can't think when you're doing this to me!" Nikki yelled, the pain in her body, the pressure in her head, fissuring, yet she couldn't move, couldn't get away. "I can't help you when you're torturing me!"

The breeze calmed. Slowly the pressure lifted from behind her eyes, and she regained control of her body, muscles loosening. Nikki rocked back, landing on her hands. With a sniff and a quick swipe at her cheeks, she pushed up from the ground and stepped several feet away from the tree before turning her back to it, the invasion of another's presence leaving her body.

She still wasn't convinced that this creature was the Mother. But whatever it was, it wanted Xander. Why? What made him so special? What was it going to do with him?

With questions burning in the back of her mind, as she neared the edge of the forest she heard a whisper like a voice from a dream say, *I will have him...*

...one way...

Or...another.

<h1 style="text-align:center">Chapter Twelve</h1>

Nikki avoided setting a date with Xander as long as she could stand. Instead, they texted about their days, their classes, their interests. Xander even sent photos of him hanging out with his friends or family, of the animals at work, good food, and beautiful scenery. Each photo and text sent a smile to her lips, a ray of light in her heart, but she didn't have the courage to send him photos back. Which he didn't complain about. Neither did he press her about the second date, and she appreciated his patience.

Their conversations filled her days with joy, something to look forward to between classes and assignments. Since he was also busy, it didn't distract her too much. Her heart dropped when there wasn't a response from him, but it made her anticipate his replies with even greater excitement.

But with those whispers creeping into the back of her mind every so often, laying a dark cloak over their interactions, she delayed the date. She finally admitted to herself that she found him interesting, and maybe she even had a small crush on him, which made it even more difficult to decide what to do.

One evening, while studying in the school library, sunset coming earlier and earlier as they descended deeper into fall, Xander's scent jerked her attention from the textbook she was reading. Traces of spices and a muted fruity sweetness lifted her spirits, even while her heart sank. She craned her neck and leaned forward to gaze around her, and she saw him walking from the front toward the tables in the back. He had a pack slung over one shoulder, and as he made his way deeper into the stacks, he noticed her.

His eyes lit up, a wide but shy smile splitting his face as he changed directions to stand in front of her. Nikki's face warmed at his smile, and she realized she was smiling too.

"Hi," they said at the same time, and both chuckled. His hair was matted to his face, trickles of sweat coming down the side of his head. As if sensing her gaze, he ran a hand through it, waves bouncing and settling in haphazard directions.

"Studying?"

Nikki nodded. "What are you up to?"

"Just finished a run, hoping to do the same."

"Do you want to sit here?" Nikki asked without thinking, face heating more at the uncertainty in her voice.

Xander's smile widened, and he said, "That would be great, thanks."

He placed his backpack on the chair beside him and sat opposite her, pulling out books, his laptop, and various school supplies. Nikki's shoulders eased, seeing that he truly intended to study as well.

While he set himself up, he said, "So, I was thinking. Looks like I'm free this weekend. We could do something. If you have time."

Nikki froze, a deer caught in headlights. It was easy to avoid this conversation when he wasn't right in front of her. But now that he was here, that she could see the waves around his face, the beat of his pulse in his neck, the eager gleam in his eyes, she couldn't bring herself to say no. So they made plans to go to a movie and have an evening picnic the following weekend, and although part of it brought her joy, she couldn't shake the nervousness deep in her bones. She felt as if she was being pulled along on strings she couldn't fight. She couldn't resist being around him, yet she wanted to protect him from her life. From herself. From whatever was hunting him.

Nikki unwrapped a chocolate bar and orange slices from a ball of foil. She put the chocolate in her mouth first, and as it melted, set the orange in after, relishing the tart sweetness even as it caused a sudden ache in her gums, wishing the brightness would burn away the sour taste of dread in her mouth. She turned on her laptop, then noticed Xander glance at her.

"Do you want some?"

"No, thanks. I ate not too long ago. I've had those orange chocolates that come out at Christmas, but I've never had the raw combination like that before. It looks good."

"It's my favorite."

"Duly noted," Xander said with a short nod, gaze going back to his book.

Nikki was grateful for having an essay to write, as it gave her fingers something to do. Although Xander was quiet and still, she couldn't resist stealing glances over her laptop screen, taking in his lean, long muscles and square jaw, his dark eyelashes set against pale eyes, the steadiness of his breath, the sound of his fingers brushing over a page. Every so often, when she would look up, she'd find his eyes on her, or he would lift his eyes to find her glancing at him, an anxious, joyous undercurrent to their studies. They gave each other half smiles before going back to their tasks, and although Nikki felt anxious at first, a sense of peace and contentment settled on her as the minutes passed.

They stayed until the library closed, and Xander walked her to her car again. It was a quiet stroll, both thinking of their studies, minds tired from the technical reading. But Nikki's waking hours had barely begun, and more work lay ahead of her.

Their arms brushed as they walked, sending happy shivers over her skin where they touched.

At the car, Xander said, "Let me know when you get home?"

Something warmed and melted in Nikki's chest. "Yeah, okay. I can do that."

"Thanks," he said, a half, close-lipped smile on his face, his hand tight on the strap of his backpack.

She mirrored his grin, then unlocked her car with a beep. Before she could open it, however, he reached forward, leaning within an inch of her, so close that as his hair fell forward, her breath moved it, and her mouth gave another pulsing ache as his smell got stronger, but then he quickly pulled away, stepping back to open the car door for her.

Nikki didn't think that warm, melty feeling could get any deeper. But it did.

"Thank you," she said.

He nodded, and said, "Drive safe." Then he shut the door and lifted a hand in goodbye before stepping back, turning away, and heading for his own car. As she watched him retreat into the shadows of the night, Nikki's heart melted like chocolate left out on a summer day before it ballooned with overwhelming joy. While her parents and Gwen took care of her, no one had ever been so sweet. Looking at his back, she realized that she wanted to give him that, too—sweetness, happiness, peace. Suddenly, their next date couldn't come soon enough.

Chapter Thirteen

The remaining week flew by. The days darkened and cooled as they crept into October, and Nikki found herself in the school library in the evenings more often than in her apartment. Xander joined her again in the evenings, studying quietly. They had stunted conversation, anticipating the date, wanting to get to know each other, wanting to focus. Studying in the evening became Nikki's favorite time of night, and time slowed around those hours, with the evenings disappearing too quickly. She managed to get ahead with her schoolwork, completely freeing up her Saturday. Gwen was falling for Theo, sending photos of the two of them at dance clubs, at lunches, on hikes. Gwen smiled big, goofy grins in each photo, and Theo smiled brightly, but reserved.

She hadn't touched blood since the previous weekend, and she was tired. But her senses were only as dull as any normal human's. It was easier to be around Xander when his scent was muted, when she couldn't fixate on every movement of muscle or brush of the wind through his hair. It did make her thirstier, her mouth filling with saliva and pain when they stepped too close, but it was better this way.

Maybe the mysterious voice heeded Nikki's begging for space, or maybe denying herself blood weakened their connection. Or maybe she had made up the voice and her temporary insanity was fading. Whatever the cause, she didn't feel the compelling that whole week. No constricted blood, pounding headaches, or whispers trailing her, and she was grateful. Another point toward normalcy, and away from the potential of the Mother being real.

On their date, Nikki did not remember a single scene from the movie, distracted as she was by the proximity of Xander's arm on the armrest beside her seat. Even with her dulled senses, the heat rolled off him in comforting waves and his scent enveloped her mind in a fog. Afterward, Xander drove them to Overlook Park, which offered stunning views of downtown Portland, glittering against the Willamette River. The night was breezy, and each swift push of a leaf against the concrete sounded like those haunting whispers, anxious chills winding through Nikki's spine. Otherwise, the evening was pleasant, with warmth clinging to the humidity in the air and the sky remaining clear.

The city lights flickered against Xander's face, warm and mesmerizing, his eyes bright in their reflection, casting his bone structure in stark shadows.

A tight, hot fist clutched Nikki's heart as she looked at him, finding him more beautiful than the city. Than anything.

He caught her staring, and his cheeks reddened. All she wanted was to twine her fingers in his hair, to kiss the embarrassment out of him.

Xander emptied his bag, laying out a feast of hard cheeses, cured meats, olive medleys, fig spread, and mixed nuts. He poured them both wine into plastic cups, and when they clinked their cups together, their fingers brushed, the warmth of his skin sending fresh jolts of lightning through Nikki's body. Nikki took a handful of nuts, and as her left canine came down on one tough, roasted almond, the tooth moved. Significantly. Not just a little wiggle, but a full back and forth. She froze, terrified, as she tongued it, and it wiggled in her mouth. A soft gush of blood poured onto her tongue, metallic and salty.

Shit.

She rolled the remaining half-crushed nuts to the other side of her mouth, chewing slowly.

"Are you okay?" Xander asked, staring at her mouth.

Would he be able to see her loose tooth if she spoke? Would he see her bloody mouth?

Xander's expression grew uneasy as she didn't answer, so she swallowed and waved it off. "Oh, yeah, I just started thinking of my upcoming assignments and gave myself a little panic attack."

"I do that all the time."

Nikki sipped the wine and ate using the right side of her face, keeping her left side angled away from Xander so that if he looked at her mouth he was less likely to see her loose tooth or blood-stained teeth. It took great self-control to not push at it, but she focused on the other sensations around her, the cool wind, Xander's warmth, the taste of wine, the sparkling jewel of Portland across the water, to put it out of her mind.

Within a few weeks, clouds would hang heavy over the city, fingers of fog curling around the buildings and bridges, muting the scenery. But tonight, it was clear and bright, the whites and greens and reds of the city lights illuminating the grass and their faces. A siren blared down a nearby road, with distant mimics from the downtown below, shouts of delighted and delirious drunks leaving bars background to the traffic. Nikki had no concept of how much time passed, and despite the anxiety of her wiggling tooth, and the twitterpation of her heart as their fingers brushed while snacking, it was an easy passing of time.

As they chatted, they somehow moved closer together, and when they both noticed how close they sat, the conversation faded, Nikki's breath spent on calming her heartbeat rather than words.

Xander's gaze roved over her, catching on her lips a second longer before he met her eyes again. He lifted his hand slowly, and Nikki's heart hammered against her ribs, paralyzing her with anticipation even as a heat bloomed in her core.

Xander gently touched her cheek, wrapped her hair around his finger, and whispered, "You're beautiful."

Nikki's mouth parted slightly, sharing in his breath, and she replied, "You think so?"

He nodded, face ever so slightly closer, eyes flicking between hers and her mouth. Nikki's pulse grew wilder. "Though I may be biased—because I like you."

Lips a hair's width away, she whispered into his mouth, "I like you, too."

Xander leaned down as her chin lifted, his hand against her cheek. A brief worry of her tooth fluttered across her mind but then their lips touched, his mouth soft and firm and gentle against her own and she could think of nothing else.

Xander pulled back to check her expression, and she didn't see anything in his gaze that said he felt something wrong with her mouth. When she didn't look away or move, he leaned forward again with more confidence, still kissing her with tenderness but a little more firmly, moving his hand to cup her head and rub his thumb on her cheek. Eyes closed, loving the feel of his mouth on hers, she twisted her body toward his so their chests touched. His hand roved from her head to the small of her back, bringing her closer to him. Heat expanded in her body at the motion, and she exhaled an unintentional moan, Xander's hold on her tightening in response. They opened their mouths at the same time to deepen the kiss, tasting each other for the first time.

Nikki satisfied the urge to run her hand through his hair, the waves thick and soft in her palm, and they held and felt and kissed one another until they were both breathless. A distant part of her mind warned her about the tooth, scared it would wiggle or fall out in their mouths, but it stayed rooted in place.

Even when their lips parted, their hands did not. He still didn't say anything about her tooth or the taste of blood in her mouth, and she hoped that meant he hadn't noticed. Maybe the wine had washed the blood away. Nikki brought her hand to his face as he did the same, gently touching each other's skin.

"I'd be lying if I said I hadn't wanted to do that for a while," he said, a small, close-lipped smile on his face.

Nikki copied his gesture, bringing her hand out from his hair and stroking her thumb against his low cheekbones, his jaw. "Me too."

It was then, admiring the feel of his face, his hand on her back, looking into his green-grey eyes dim in the dark, and the lines of sincerity from his smile, Nikki knew the brakes were cut, the wheels were spinning too fast for her to stop, too fast for her to jump, and all she could do was brace for the ride.

"My arm is falling asleep," he said with a laugh, stretching out the arm he leaned on and lying on his side so that they looked at each other. Nikki faced him, her head resting on his arm.

"Won't my lying on it make it worse?" she asked, and he pulled her closer to him.

"I don't care," he said and kissed her again, deep, fierce, and brief. Xander laid his head down so they were face to face, and they lay that way for an unknown period of time, admiring each other with touch and sight, both too elated to speak or sleep.

But then she felt a cold hand rake the back of her skull.

It paralyzed her, and as pressure filled her head, icy dread froze in her gut. It felt as though someone else was right behind her. The wave of iciness passed and she shot up, shook her head, wondering if she was having a dizzy spell, but the feeling of another presence within her remained. She paused and looked around, only Xander in sight.

A breeze rushed through the park, rustling the leaves on the few trees, carrying an amused, whispering laugh. Nikki looked at the nearest tree and scowled.

"You okay?" Xander asked.

"I'm fine," Nikki said, hearing another soft chuckle surround her before the pressure in her head released, and the sense of being watched dissipated. "It's getting late, though. Maybe we should go?"

A twitch of hurt or disappointment seemed to flicker across Xander's face, but he nodded and they packed up their picnic.

Back in the car, away from the trees and any whispers, Nikki's shoulders relaxed. Xander placed a hand on her knee, and she wrapped her fingers through his as he reversed back onto the road. She stared out the window, at the lights flashing past.

A sourness curdled in her stomach, thinking of the laugh, of the chill on the back of her head. Was she imagining it? Was there someone else in the park with them? Just when she thought that maybe she was free of the voice, when she was trying so hard to tell herself that the Mother wasn't real, it crept into her life again. It was getting harder and harder to convince herself that it wasn't the Mother. That all her symptoms were just from blood deprivation.

Swept away in her thoughts, she didn't realize they were in front of her apartment until Xander said, "I had a great time tonight."

She snapped out of her head and replied, "I did, too. Thank you so much. For all of it." She turned toward him, and he leaned over to put a hand on the back of her head, kissing her again.

"I hope this means I can see you again," he said, mouth so close she felt his lips move against hers as he spoke.

She nodded, and found his mouth again, unable to resist when he was so close.

Breaking apart, Xander said, "You should probably go before I can't stop kissing you."

"Mmm," she hummed against his mouth, then gave him another deep kiss before pulling back. "Goodnight, Xander. Thanks again."

Nikki stepped out of the car into the coldness of the night, a shiver flooding up her spine. She watched him until the red lights on the back of his car turned out of sight, then took a deep breath of the night air and let herself into the apartment building. The elevator dinged quietly up to her floor. For the first time, her heart felt heavier instead of lighter with the absence of a person. Even hours later, she replayed the scenes from the date over and over in her mind, and she didn't fall asleep until after dawn. When she did sleep, she dreamt of old trees, whispers on the breeze, and Xander, Xander, Xander.

Chapter Fourteen

Nikki maintained her routine, yet it felt different. Like her life was painted in a new array of colors. She still hadn't drunk blood since the night at her parents', and she had to throw away what she had in her fridge, worried it wouldn't last. She felt sluggish, and her mind moving slower, her body a little less coordinated, but her senses remained sharper than a human's, which balanced the weakness somewhat. She experimented with rubbing salve on her tired muscles, to see if it could break the epidermis and provide her with some relief. The soreness dimmed, but whether it was from Gwen's magic or the massage, she didn't know.

The weakness in her body was more evident when Xander wasn't there to enliven her blood. Xander's presence in her life filled her with excitement and joy, distracting her from the body aches, the worsening soreness in her gums, the loose tooth. It didn't budge anymore, and she avoided eating on that side of her mouth, hoping that meant it would stay in place a while longer. She would stave off being a monster, so she could have Xander as long as possible.

With midterms upon them, Nikki went to the library every night to study, as the amount of reports, quizzes, and assignments she had to complete were piling up. Xander joined her a few times, but now he sat beside her instead of across from her, stealing kisses. They held hands as they walked to her car, where they wrapped their arms around each other and kissed until they could barely breathe, Nikki's hands in Xander's hair, his on the small of her back, holding her close to his body. They parted with sore lips and words of appreciation, their skin like magnets drawn to each other, making it difficult to separate. Thankfully, he never indicated he noticed something wrong with one of her teeth.

Her sleep schedule shifted, her internal alarm clock waking her up earlier than normal. Despite having to live in the dark of her apartment for hours, it gave her more time to text with Xander, and reduced the likelihood he would question her schedule. Question her. Sometimes, when she woke up prematurely, she would text Xander and then go back to sleep, to at least give the impression of normal human hours. Over the last week, she had avoided being outside as much as possible, staying in the confines of concrete buildings and artificial light, eliminating the whispers and laughter and beckoning that plagued her once again.

But the voices couldn't be avoided the night of the gathering. Nikki pulled up to the O'Brennan house intentionally late to avoid being alone with Gwen's family, their driveway lined with cars owned by the rest of the coven. She sat in the car an extra moment, steeling herself for the night before her, even as the weight of the evergreens pressed down overhead. With a deep breath, she scurried from the car to the house, while the sense of eyes roving over her felt like a thousand ants scurrying across her skin.

The hair on her neck settled when she stepped into the buzz of the O'Brennan house, voices of the coven echoing from deep within. She followed the sounds through the house until she found them in the library, each inhumanly beautiful vampire arranged like statues, the roaring hearth casting orange light throughout the room.

Sucking in a deep breath, the tangy, metallic scent of blood rushed to her head, making her dizzy. On the opposite side of the room from the hearth, five humans stood in various states of undress against the wall, fresh cuts on their wrists. In front of them was a table, set with food and bowls of blood.

Nikki swallowed the bile in her throat and averted her gaze.

She assessed the room, keeping her back to the thralls. The Lius and Halvar spoke in a dark corner, Halvar with his arms crossed and Feng shooting daggers from his eyes but nodding politely. Daiyu had a strained look on her face and held a wrapped parcel in her arms, likely a gift of blood from Halvar by way of an apology.

The Lopez children drew in coloring books beside the fire, their parents talking with Nikki's. Tyee stood with the O'Brennan parents and brothers, muttering in voices too low to hear.

Gwen was nowhere in sight.

She walked over to her parents and the Lopezes, her dad giving her a happy clap on her shoulder. The Lopezes exchanged pleasantries with her before excusing themselves to check on their children.

"So, where's our mysterious visitor?" Nikki asked.

"Tyee says he is on his way," her mom said. "Why did you not get something to drink?"

"I want nothing to do with that table."

"It is a little creepy, eh?" her dad said, gaze flicking to the human bar at the back.

"More like perverted," Nikki murmured.

Cat pressed her blood glass into Nikki's hands and said, "Don't forget you're in a room full of vampires, sweetling. Everyone can hear your mumblings and complaints."

"Good," Nikki said, but heat still climbed up her neck to her cheeks. Habitually, she raised the glass to her face, but gagged at the smell of the blood and cringed away.

"So dramatic," her mom said, stepping away from them to the bar and returning with a glass of wine. She poured some of the blood into the wine glass and swapped with Nikki. "You need to get over that aversion."

"Says who?" Nikki snapped. "Someday I won't have to drink it at all." She sniffed at her glass. The scent of blood was faint behind the wine, and she took a tentative sip, barely able to taste the blood.

Cat sighed, but Miguel stayed silent, and Nikki was grateful for their relenting.

Nikki caught Gwen's scent briefly, the coldness of vampire blood, warm with magic, giving her the smell of the transition from winter to spring, when leaves and flowers were budding, despite the chill. Looking over her shoulder, Nikki watched Gwen enter the room of vampires, hair wild and chin raised, and relief washed over Nikki. She left her parents and rushed to Gwen's side, whispering, "About time."

"Excuse me for avoiding this as long as I could," Gwen said, surveying the room and grimacing when she saw the thralls.

"I know. I don't like it either."

"What a sick show they're putting on for this guy. Where is he, by the way?"

Nikki shrugged. "On his way, supposedly."

Tyee clinked her glass, a delicate clink that reverberated through the room. When the library fell silent, she said, "Now that we are all here, I will get our guest. Please, arrange yourselves and be on your best behavior." The last she said with a quick look at Gwen and a long, cold one at the Lius.

Gwen's face fell. "They were waiting for me this whole time? Ugh."

"Why did we have to wait for him at all? He could've been mingling with everyone to begin with. Met everyone one at a time."

"That's not the way he does things," Tyee said as she walked by them and out the door of the library.

"What does that mean?" Gwen asked. Nikki shrugged and Gwen looked at Nikki's wine glass, then said, "I think I need one of those."

Gwen stalked to the back of the room and the coven coalesced, forming a semicircle toward the door. Gwen came back with a glass brimming with wine and shoved herself between Nikki and the Lius, facing the door and taking long gulps of her drink.

Minutes passed, and even the most stoic of them fidgeted, shifting on their feet or twisting their necks. Anxiety hummed in Nikki's veins, and she sipped at her drink.

Waiting.

Waiting.

The doors burst open with a bang, smacking against the wall, and Gwen jumped, wine sloshing over her shirt and onto the ground.

"God damn it," she sighed, her parents sending sharp looks her way.

Thanks to Nikki's vampiric reflexes, her startle was reduced from a jump to a mere hard blink, at the force with which the stranger entered the room.

"Greetings!" He shouted, arms outstretched while he walked into the firelit room as if it were a stage. He was tall with sandy brown skin, thick windswept black hair peppered with white and grey, wide-set black eyes, and black facial hair. As he approached, the smell of blood was smothered by his own scent, cold and ancient, oppressive in its agelessness, like old stone mountains in the moonlight.

He stood before them, arms still extended, presenting himself as if they should already know who he was. As if he was a messiah and they should bow.

But they all simply stared at him, waiting.

His wild smile did not falter, but he dropped his arms. "I suppose it is no surprise you don't know who I am. It is why I'm here after all. Or, one of the reasons." His gaze flicked over each member in turn, lingering on Nikki's, and her heart skipped a beat. His mouth was fixed in a smirk as he looked at her, and she recoiled under his gaze.

"My name is Hormin. Mother sent me here, and so here I am."

"Why?" Feng asked.

"Feng," Tyee said, sharply. "Please, be polite."

"Right," Feng said, clearing his throat. "My apologies. Hormin, would you please tell us why you have been sent here?"

Hormin's smile widened, but it was as sinister as a shark's. "Feng, is it?" He looked Feng up and down, then looked to Feng's wife, who stiffened. "That must make you Daiyu. Yes, I've heard about you two. Full of curiosity and questions, you are. Not always a bad thing. As long as you're not a cat." Hormin snickered, and looked at the rest of the group, but when he responded, his eyes were on Nikki. "I'm here because it seems the place to be."

Chills wound up Nikki's spine.

"But what does that mean?" Feng asked.

Hormin's eyes remained on Nikki, and he cocked his head, then blinked and shrugged, easing back into his casual manner. "Who knows? Now," he said, clapping his hands together and rubbing them. "Time to make introductions. I'll start with the kids and their family, then make my rounds to meet everyone individually. Go on, disperse," he said, flicking his hands. After a pause, the crescent of the coven evaporated, everyone moving to their own circles.

Nikki and Gwen moved to the corner near the hearth, watching Hormin smile and laugh with the kids, while the Lopez parents watched with wary amusement.

"So, was that super awkward, or was it just me?" Gwen whispered.

"No, it wasn't just you," Nikki replied, Hormin's head cocking ever so slightly in their direction. "As my mom reminded me, we have to be careful what we say. Room full of vampires."

"Ugh. A living nightmare."

Nikki and Gwen watched Hormin play with Felix, who was immediately taken with him. Emilia, however, was skeptical, peering at him through squinted eyes as he tried to win her over with jokes and simple magic tricks. Eventually, Hormin was satisfied with his winning over Felix, and after a brief chat with Julio and Carmen, left them to formally introduce himself to Feng and Daiyu.

Despite the separate clustering of families, everyone observed Hormin through the corners of their eyes, judging, questioning. What was he really doing here? And what was the smothering cold that wafted around him, like being buried under hundreds of feet of permafrost?

Nikki's pulse pounded in her ears, drowning out any tidbits of conversation she might have been able to overhear between Hormin and the Lius. They talked to him with stiff politeness, but the easy, joking demeanor Hormin had with the kids had shed off his body like a second skin, leaving him unnaturally still and solemn.

Something was off about him.

Nikki gulped down a mouthful of wine to swallow the pulse beating in her throat, shrinking into herself farther and farther as Hormin made his rounds, getting ever closer to her and Gwen.

She had to meet him sooner than she was prepared, as when he made his way over to her parents, Miguel and Cat ushered her and Gwen over. When Hormin's wide, assessing eyes landed on her, watching her walk over, she wanted to run.

But her feet carried her forward against her will, and as she stepped beside her mom, matching Hormin's deep, unblinking gaze, a horrible sense of dread sank low in her gut. Up close, his eyes were so wide-set they were almost on the sides of his head. They looked insane. And she didn't know which one to look at.

"This is our daughter, Nicoletta," her dad said. "She goes by Nikki."

Hormin's lips split into a sharp grin, and she couldn't tell if it was pleased or disgusted. He stuck his hand out for her to shake it, and she stared at that tan, stone hand, wanting nothing less than to touch him.

Cat nudged her with her elbow and whispered, "Don't be rude."

She tightened one fist then opened it as she reached out to Hormin, taking his hand in hers. It was rough, and when he closed his hands around hers, she nearly yelped with sudden pain, as the barest of his movement almost crushed her bones.

If one small movement almost broke her – just how strong was he? Just how old was he? Vampiric strength grew with age, but this was... unprecedented. He must have thought he was opening the door normally earlier when it went crashing into the wall.

Nikki swallowed the ball of fear in her throat and bit down on her inner lip to suppress her cry and turned her gaze back to his. His eyes grew impossibly wider, a sick delight shining in them as he kept his firm grasp on her hand, one flinch away from breaking her bones.

"A pleasure to finally meet you," he said, his voice a low purr that anyone else would mistake as charming, but with her bones near shattering and his abyssal eyes peering into hers, it was more predatory than anything else.

Nikki didn't respond, unable to force out any platitude her mom had trained her to stammer.

Hormin's gaze darkened even as his lips curled into a delighted smile, and just as Nikki thought she would crumble under his power he released her hand and turned his attention to Gwen, blood rushing back into her fingers.

"You must be the witch," Hormin said, head cocked.

"What gave it away?" Gwen replied, stiffening with defensiveness. "Was it the redness of my skin? The frizz of my hair? The undeniable power oozing from my every pore?"

Hormin chuckled and said, "No. It was the freckles."

"The – what?"

"The freckles," Hormin repeated, raising a hand to her cheek.

Gwen flinched back but Hormin was too fast, his thumb already brushing against her freckled skin. Gwen furrowed her brows and looked at him with confusion, but his touch seemed to be soft and adoring.

"I always thought it was such a shame that vampirism erases those features which are so unique. So beautiful. These things that make humans different – their freckles, birthmarks, scars – gone. I always wished I could have them."

"Uhhh...okay?"

Hormin's hand dropped to his side and his smile fell. "Unlike some of our kind, I am rather fond of witches. Their power is so rich. Their abilities so special to each one of them. None are quite alike. I look forward to seeing what you're capable of."

"Thanks?" Gwen replied, face frozen in perplexity.

Hormin smiled, the first sincere one Nikki had seen on his face. It softened him, and the transformation hit Nikki like a punch to the gut. Mixed feelings flooded her body, seeing this piece of kindness to her friend who was so often shunned, just after she nearly broke from fear of him. Now she didn't know whether to hide from him or learn more about him. What other kindnesses lingered behind his unsettling demeanor?

What game was he playing?

Hormin left them then, without a goodbye, heading toward the rest of Gwen's family who stared in their direction, just as confused as Nikki, though likely for different reasons. If they thought Hormin liked Gwen, that would not be a point in Hormin's, or Gwen's, favor.

Gwen blinked several times, processing, then turned to Nikki. "Now that we've met him, let's get out of here."

Nikki nodded and kissed her parents on the cheek goodbye, both of them also processing the interactions they had just witnessed, lost for words.

Tyee watched them with eagle's eyes as they left, but did not stop them, Nikki's muscles tensing under her gaze. Just before they walked out of the door, Nikki looked at the room over her shoulder, Hormin's eyes flicking to hers briefly. He gave her a small smile and a nod, and with a flip of her stomach she closed the door to the library.

Outside, Gwen exhaled like she had been holding her breath for ages. "That was one of the weirdest experiences of my life."

"Yeah, that was...strange," Nikki said. "I don't know what to make of him."

Gwen shivered, shaking out her tension. She touched her cheek, mystified. "Me neither, but I'm not eager to see him any time soon."

"Same here."

The cool night breeze whisked away Hormin's oppressive presence that lingered on her skin, but the hum of anxiety still thrummed in her veins.

The dread coiled tight in her gut told her to be wary of him, but something about him pulled at her heartstrings. Was it loneliness that rippled off of him? Was it the fringe of insanity, or the surprising softness, that made her sad for him?

One more distraction in a world of too many.

Once inside the studio, Nikki plopped at her usual place on the couch while Gwen walked to her counter and said, "I have something for you." Gwen pulled out a mason jar and said, "More salve."

"Oh, Gwen, you're a lifesaver. Thank you. I've really been needing this."

"I can make a more potent batch to give you this weekend."

"Thank you," Nikki said. "Anything you can do for a loose tooth? My fangs are really bearing down and I don't want to deal with them right now."

Gwen gave her a hard look, chewing on the inside of her bottom lip. "I'll see what I can do, but it'll take a while to put together. And it isn't a permanent solution. You'll have to deal with it eventually."

"I know, but I appreciate any delay. So, thank you."

Gathering supplies from various cupboards and drawers, Gwen asked, "Anyway, I've been meaning to ask, did you find anything out about the voices?"

Nikki sighed, debating how much to tell Gwen. "Not really. My dad thinks it's from the maturation plus limiting blood intake. My mom thinks it's the Mother compelling me."

"No kidding. You think that's why Hormin is here?"

"I sure hope not," Nikki replied, dread condensing in her stomach.

Gwen looked over her shoulder and, noticing the crestfallen look on Nikki's face, said, "I'm just teasing you. You know I think the Mother is bullshit. Hormin is probably just some religious fanatic like Tyee. In all honesty, I'm more inclined to agree with your dad. So, that means we need to get you bloodied up."

Nikki burst out a laugh. "Please don't ever say that again. But yeah, I agree. That seems more likely," Nikki said, the doubt like a weight in her stomach.

Gwen continued making the potion for Nikki, and they chatted about everything mundane, trying to distract themselves from the strangeness that Hormin brought to their region. With a few texts with Theo and Xander, they made plans to go out as a group the following weekend, and Nikki relished the brief sense of being normal.

Chapter Fifteen

SHE AWOKE on Saturday with a groan, muscles stiff, as if she hadn't moved at all during her resting hours. Both Xander and Gwen texted with excitement about the evening, and Nikki echoed their responses, excited and nervous about meeting his friends. They hadn't had the conversation about what they were yet, but they had both said they weren't seeing anyone else. It felt like limbo to Nikki, as if at any moment it could be taken away, and she'd be left with nothing.

Xander picked her up just after twilight, the hazy remnants of the day clinging to the western horizon. Clouds hung high and stretched thin over the sky, like a patchwork quilt held aloft by many hands. Hand in hand they drove to the lounge, Xander talking about his shift at work, fawning about the cutest German shepherd-golden retriever puppy he'd ever seen, concluding that he needed to get one someday.

When he sheepishly asked, "Would you be okay with that?" She responded, "Yes. Sounds adorable." But she was too distracted by his confidence that they would know each other, would be together, all those years later, and her heart soared, spiraling into its own fantasies about their future, which always left out the fact that she was a vampire.

How long could she hide it?

What would he think if he found out?

Nothing good could come of it. There would be only loss.

The lounge was low-lit and dim, with small gold lights in the front near the long bar. Xander moved his hand out of hers and around Nikki's waist, resting it on her hip, keeping her close. They headed to the back, where the lounge spread into a wide, open space, with low, long black couches, faded purple lights and glass coffee tables. House music beat deep and loud enough to cover the conversations of the other patrons. Gwen, Theo, and Terrance were in a nook with three walls, couches along each one, gold candles with dancing orange flames flickering on the glass table.

"Hey!" Gwen shouted, swinging her legs from Theo's lap and standing to greet them.

She hugged Nikki and said, "I'm so happy we could do this." Pulling back and turning to Xander, Gwen squealed, "You get a hug too!" And flung her arms around him.

Xander laughed and said, "Good to see you, Gwen."

Nikki glanced over Gwen's shoulder and saw several empty shot glasses. No wonder Gwen was so giddy.

Xander made introductions between Nikki, Theo, and Terrance. Gwen didn't exaggerate—the woman was gorgeous. She had long, thin braids that fell past her shoulders, heavy-lidded and observant eyes, and a full and wide mouth. She didn't wear any makeup and dressed in clothing loose enough to be comfortable but tight enough to be flattering against her spare curves. Terrance, Theo's brother, had a similar beauty to Theo, but his face was squarer, his jaw wider, and his head shaved.

Terrance took her hand, and with the same coy smile his sister had, said, "It's nice to finally meet the girl Xander won't shut up about."

"Hey, now," Xander said, running a hand through his hair and down the back of his neck. Under the cool lights, Nikki swore she could see his cheeks darken. His gaze flicked around the area until they landed on the shot glasses scattered across the table. "It looks like we have some catching up to do."

Nikki sat down across from Terrance and beside Theo while Xander went to get them drinks and food. She crossed her legs and sat on the edge, knees close to the low coffee table. Everyone's gaze settled on her, and trying not to be her usual awkward self, she asked Terrance, "How did you and Xander meet?"

"We met in elementary school, shortly after his family moved here. Theo and I were born and raised in Portland, and so when Xander came, well, it's hard not to be friends with him, isn't it?" He shrugged. "We played the same sports and liked the same video games, so it was easy to become friends."

"He doesn't like to admit it, but they were total nerds," Theo said, smirking.

"As if you weren't a gamer right along with us."

"It's true, I was. But I'm not afraid to admit it."

Xander returned with their drinks, and the shot burned down Nikki's throat. When a basket of cheese fries and crispy Brussels sprouts came out a few minutes later, they ordered another round, even though Gwen's cheeks were already flushed with intoxication.

Xander leaned back in his seat while Nikki remained on the edge of hers. He put a hand on her back, rubbing it in small, lazy circles as he chatted with his friends. The shots kept coming, and the music got louder, drowning out the conversation and making Nikki's ears ring. The drinks hit her hard despite snacking, and soon her body felt light while her mind danced from thought to thought. Terrance and Xander talked about some online video game that made no sense to her, while Theo and Gwen were wrapped in whispers. She took a deep breath to stabilize herself and leaned back, Xander's arm raising to rest over her shoulders while she nestled against him. The vibration of his voice reverberated through her, and she felt like the most peaceful fly on the wall.

After some time Terrance left and returned with yet another round of shots; her eyes widened at the sheer volume of alcohol consumed between the group. She hesitated but thought when in Rome.

Gwen reached for her shot glass at the same time as Nikki, and Gwen gave her a knowing grin when they locked eyes. Gwen raised her glass in a small cheers, quirking her brow, and Nikki raised hers in response before downing it. The room spun, and instead of easing the social anxiety, she soon worried something idiotic would slip from her mouth, so she settled back against Xander, resigning herself to the role of observer for the evening.

A startled spray and a yelp erupted beside her, and glancing over, Nikki saw Theo's lap was speckled with moisture, Gwen's cocktail dribbling down her face. Gwen burst out laughing, Theo's face scrunching in disgust and mortification before her mouth cracked into reluctant amusement.

"What happened?" Xander asked, laughter in his voice.

Over Gwen's raucous laughter, Theo said, "She scoffed and sipped at the same time," she mockingly glared at Gwen. "And it came out of her nose."

Gwen's laugh grew louder as Theo picked up napkins and smoothed them over the mess on her legs, shaking her head as she chuckled. The raucousness of Gwen's laugh was infectious, and soon Xander, Terrance, and Nikki also started laughing, and Nikki was surprised at the feeling of it in her chest. Delight rumbled through her, and for the first time that evening, she felt like she belonged. Like she could be a part of this group.

As the laughter died, harsh breaths inhaled and exhaled to regain their composure, Nikki looked at Xander, who had a big smile of joy and surprise on his face. Their eyes met, and under his gaze, she felt like she was the most amazing thing he'd ever seen.

"Nikki, come help me clean up." Gwen didn't wait for an answer, grabbing her arm and yanking her to her feet. Nikki stumbled, then regained her balance and allowed her friend to pull her toward the bathroom.

"Get me some paper towels while you're in there!" Theo shouted after them.

The bathroom was for single use, with white tiles, red lighting, and a mirror the length of the wall.

"Wow, this is skanky," Gwen said, fumbling with the lock.

Nikki laughed again. "Yes. Yes, it is."

"I like that you're laughing, Nik. I don't remember the last time you laughed like this."

"Me neither," Nikki said, narrowing her eyes at the backhanded compliment. "What are we doing in here?"

Gwen snatched a jar from her bag, swaying and landing with a wide foot stance. "Your extra potent salve. Put some on and tell me if it does the thing."

"The thing?"

"On your tooth. That's loose."

Nikki turned to the mirror and smoothed some of the minty salve over her gums, rubbing an extra glob over her loose canine. As the familiar tingle spread through her gums, a pressure surrounded her tooth. When she touched it with the tip of her tongue, it moved a little less.

"Whoa," Nikki said.

"Huh?"

"It did the thing. Mostly."

"Oh, good, keep putting it on and it'll keep doing the thing." Gwen straightened, swaying as she did so. "Are you excited?"

"For what?"

"You know."

"No, I don't know."

"It's the third date. You know what that means," Gwen said, eyebrows raising up and down.

"Oh. No," Nikki said, heart crashing like a stone into her gut. "Gwen, you have to help me. I— I can't. We need to make some excuse for me to go to your house. Or for you to take me home. Alone. Or something."

"What? Why? Do you not want to sleep with him?"

"It's not that. It's the morning after. He'll wake up hours before me. How will I explain I can't go outside until dusk? Or why I can't even open the curtains?"

Gwen shifted on her feet. The dim red light burned her copper hair into a deep, dark ember. "You know, maybe you should just tell him the truth."

Nikki barked a harsh laugh. "Are you joking?"

"No. Maybe he won't be as bothered by it as you are."

"So, what? I'm supposed to say, 'Hey, I drink blood! And we only met because you smelled delicious!'"

"Maybe you can leave that last part out. But the first part—why not?"

Nikki stared at Gwen, stunned, then said in a harsh whisper, "He'll think I'm crazy! No human actually believes vampires are real."

"Some do, and maybe he won't think you're crazy. You won't know until you know." Gwen nodded to herself, as if she were a wise old woman, then continued. "What's the harm? He'll either be okay with it and you can stop worrying, and just be in happy la-la love land. Or he won't be okay with it, and you'll know you're not meant to be. But I don't think you should lie. And I don't think he'd drop you so quickly. Maybe you can't see the way he looks at you, but I do."

Nikki shuffled, crossing her arms. The heat in her chest still burned, but not as bright. Her head swam, and Gwen danced in her vision. Putting a hand on her head to steady herself, she exhaled and said, "I don't know, Gwen."

Gwen put her hands on Nikki's arms, rubbed them gently, and said, "Look, Theo knows I'm a witch, like a real witch, and she was cool with it. Give him a chance."

"But being a witch is cool. Being a vampire is not."

"Um, yes? It is? You have heightened senses, and who knows what else. You could have extra abilities, like my sisters are super-fast and Connall is extra strong. I don't know what's up with Farrell, though." She bit her lip in concentration. "Anyway, maybe you'll be telepathic. Haven't you noticed how it seems like Tyee can see right through you?"

"I think that's just because she's old as dirt."

"Older, probably. In any case, the point is, being a vampire doesn't make you innately bad."

"Yes, it does. How do you not get that? I have to drink blood, from people, to have those so-called benefits. It's disgusting. It makes me a monster."

Gwen sneered and threw up her hands, exasperated. "You know what, Nikki? I'm tired of you playing the victim."

Nikki blinked, stunned. "Excuse me?"

Gwen's sneer turned into a cruel mock, and she said, "Woe is you, born with supernatural abilities and an extra-long life. And all you have to do is drink blood every now and then. I don't see what the big deal is if someone willingly gives it."

"It's manipulative. No human gains anything, they just think they do."

"That's not true. You know, when people love each other, they actually like to take care of one another." Gwen shook her head. "But that's not the point. The point is people would kill for what you have, and you don't even have to kill to maintain it. If I were you, I wouldn't torture myself over it."

"Yeah, well, I'm not like you," Nikki spat, core roiling with a cold fire, suppressing the pressure of a scream building in her throat.

"That's clear."

"What does that mean?"

"You hate all the gifts you have instead of harnessing them. And you hide from everything! You've always looked down on me for being reactive, for having big feelings, but you know what? At least I have feelings. It makes me honest, capable of talking to my partners instead of blocking them out. You're full of self-sabotage, and you don't even know it. It's excruciating to watch and annoying to listen to."

Nikki's head spun, Gwen's words putting her to sea in a storm. "Where is this coming from? You don't mean this. You're just drunk."

"Ha!" Tequila breath burst from Gwen's mouth, but she kept her feet steady. Gwen's hair rose and spread out around her shoulders, and there was a heaviness in the air that pushed against Nikki's body.

"Good old Nikki, always looking for someone else to blame."

"What? Do you really not see that all I do is blame myself?"

"But do you really? Or is that just a cover for your narcissism? You only want me when I can give you something."

"That's not true. At all. And you know it. You're being unfair."

"Oh, sure, sure, sure. Keep lying to yourself. As if this derailment didn't start with you asking me for a favor. To avoid your boyfriend. Because you're too cowardly to talk to him." Gwen shook her head. "You just want to hang out when you need some remedy or favor from me. Otherwise, I barely hear from you."

Nikki's voice caught in her throat, and as the silence stretched, Gwen shoved past her.

"Wait, Gwen, please!" Nikki shouted, Gwen's hand on the lock. "I'm scared. I don't know what I'm doing."

Gwen whirled on her, a slash of air following her movement. Gwen's eyes were wide with fury as she shouted, "No one does! Relationships are terrifying! But the risk is worth the reward. And frankly, if you won't risk your heart for Xander, then you don't deserve him." Gwen's face scrunched, as if disgusted. "But then again, maybe you can't risk your heart since you don't have one."

Nikki recoiled, the breath taken from her. Gwen snatched a handful of paper towels from the dispenser and left, the air getting lighter as she did. Nikki shut and locked the door behind her, head resting on the door. With a deep, stuttering breath, she said to herself, "Yes, I do."

Nikki turned, back and head on the door, gazing into the red lights, like she was in a bad horror movie. With a heavy sigh, she looked in the mirror at her sallow skin, black hair, and dull eyes. She looked like a devil.

A monster. A narcissist. A user.

Her reflection broke into hazy pieces as water filled her eyes. She dropped her gaze, hands clenching the edge of the sink, and took several controlled breaths. Nikki flung her head back, blinking away the tears, letting the air dry them.

Tap, tap, tap against the heavy black door.

"Nikki?" Xander asked, voice low.

She unlocked the door and cracked it, stepping back.

"You okay?" he asked.

A lump formed in her throat, and though she tried to nod, her head moved with one shake. She clenched her eyes hard, briefly, then stepped back to let him in.

"Here, I got you water."

She gave a choking laugh at the sweetness she didn't deserve but took the water and clasped it to her chest, curling into herself and leaning against the wall.

"Thank you."

"Of course. What happened?"

Nikki shook her head, heart a void in her chest. "I don't know. Gwen's really mad at me, I guess. She laid into me."

"Really? I'm sorry." He put his hands on her shoulders, her upper arms, rubbing them. "But hey, it'll be okay. Friends fight."

"We don't. Not like this," Nikki said, staring down into her water.

"Hey," Xander said, taking the cup from her hand and placing it on the sink. "Come here." He wrapped his arms around her, and she folded into his chest, arms around his back, head against his heart.

He rubbed her back and rested his head on hers, the comfort peeling away her veil, and it took all her strength not to break down. His heartbeat steadied her, and warmth flowed from him into her. Sadness settled into her chest. Gwen had pulled the rug out from under her, but Xander had helped her find her footing. Still, Gwen's words echoed in her head, and there was no silencing them.

Staying wrapped in his arms, Nikki said, "I think I should call a ride."

"I'll give you one."

"What I mean is," she said, swallowing against the lump rising in her throat, "I think I should be alone."

"I understand," he said, rubbing her back in small circles. "I'll still give you a ride."

"You don't have to do that."

"I know. I want to."

"Why are you so nice to me?" Nikki whispered, not meaning for the thought to leave her mouth.

"Because I want to be. I don't know how else to explain it."

"I'm sorry."

"For what?"

"For ruining this evening."

"You didn't. This isn't exactly my scene. I don't mind getting out of here."

Nikki nodded, and he gave her a chaste kiss. Nikki checked her reflection in the mirror then led the way out of the restroom. The sudden change in color shocked her vision, and standing outside the restroom was a woman whose face widened with surprise and judgment when they both exited.

Nikki glanced back at the table as they turned from the hallway to the bar instead of the lounge, Gwen and Theo hidden in the nook. But Terrance caught her gaze, and she gave him a weak wave goodbye. He nodded farewell in response. Xander and Nikki stood at the bar to close their tab, hands laced.

"Are you okay to drive?"

Xander nodded. "I only had the first shot, so I'm fine."

"Oh," Nikki said, and she leaned into his arm, the hand not clasped in his winding across his bicep and giving it a squeeze. She adored how responsible he was; there was something about it that made her feel safe.

Free from the heated, crowded bar, they stepped back into the real world, where colors were normal and the sounds were dim. Nikki sucked in a deep breath of the night air, and maybe it was just the freedom from the bar that felt like such a relief, but she said, "I love this time of year." The leaves were turning, and nights felt crisp and mild, yet not quite cold. A breeze caught the dead leaves, and they flittered on the breeze like glitter.

"I do too," Xander said. "But I'm a summer child, so I'm sad to see it go."

Nikki gave him a weak smile, the sadness in her building. What would happen to them next summer? Would they even have a next summer? She clasped her fingers tight on the edge of her purse and led the way to his car.

Silence was heavy on the car ride home. There was no music, no conversation. Nikki's thoughts were too loud for her to talk. But Xander's hand was in hers, and that was good enough. Halfway through the drive, he asked, "Do you want to talk about it? The fight, I mean."

"No. Thanks, though," Nikki said, and they left it at that.

When he pulled up to her apartment, she twisted the purse strings in her hand and blurted, "I'm sorry. About everything. I feel so stupid."

"Why?"

"My life is usually so uncomplicated. Without drama. Now you've seen me faint. Vomit. Fight with my best friend. Be insecure."

"It's okay, it's life. Maybe someday I'll be fainting and vomiting and needing assurance for my insecurities, and you'll be there for me."

Nikki nodded. "I will."

"I know," he said with a smile. "Now go rest. You'll feel better in the morning. Nothing a good night's sleep can't help."

"True," she said, feeling as if she hadn't slept in weeks. "I'll do that. Thank you, again. Text me when you're home?"

"Always." He kissed the back of her hand, and she leaned across the seat to kiss him deep, pouring her gratitude and affection into it.

After a moment, Nikki pulled back, just enough to separate and look into his eyes, her hand on his face, stubble rough against her palm. She twirled a lock of his hair on the back of his neck around her finger. Words bubbled in her chest but caught in her throat, so all she could do was admire the curve of his mouth, the square of his jaw, the angle of his aquiline nose.

He laid his fingers on the wrist touching his face, thumb brushing against the back of her hand, and said, "When you look at me like that, it makes it really hard not to ask to come in."

"I'm sorry."

He grinned. "What have I said? Don't be sorry. Especially about this. I want you to always look at me like that."

She smiled back, leaned in to part his lips one more time, and when she broke away, he kissed the inside of her palm before letting go.

"See you soon?"

She nodded. "Absolutely."

She stood on the sidewalk and watched his car until it turned the corner, out of sight. The trip up to her apartment lasted an eternity, weariness sinking deep into her bones. By the time she was inside her own space, she felt as if her muscles had turned to lead, with a hollow spot where her heart should be.

The quiet pressed heavy on her, nothing to drown out Gwen's words, to ease the ache in her chest. As the hole in her widened and sank into the pit of her stomach, her movements became more sluggish, and she dropped herself into bed, despite the early hour. She curled the blankets around herself, eyes clenched shut, as if it would silence the self-deprecation and cruelties bouncing around in her head. She imagined the blanket was Xander's arms around her, making her feel safe, warm, and adored.

Chapter Sixteen

Contrary to Xander's belief, the next day did not find her better. Only much, much worse. An anchor sat on her body when she awoke, a heaviness she could not combat. She tried to sit up, but her muscles shook beneath her, and the weight pressed her down, stuck in the miasma that was her bed. Her laptop was in the other room, and she should take off her makeup from the night before, but she couldn't bring herself to get up.

She stared at the phone on her nightstand, and with mounting dismay, she picked it up.

No messages from Gwen. A sense of relief and of free-falling crawled over her, causing her stomach to roil. She responded to Xander's good morning texts, not wanting to worry him, then dropped her arms back on the bed, resuming her staring contest with the ceiling. She did this until her eyes burned, and when she blinked, a wave of sorrow surged from the depths of her being, tears flooding her eyes. She shoved the wave back down, staring wide-eyed to keep the moisture from spilling down her face.

She tried to get out of bed again, and groaned as her legs gave out from under her, knees cracking against the floor.

"Shit." The word came out slurred and sticky, and she noticed her mouth was dry as cotton, lips chapped and peeling. Her tongue hit her canine, and it wiggled. Adrenaline surged into her veins, and with the burst of energy, she pulled herself up, leaning against the wall for support. She stumbled into the kitchen to find the salve, and grabbed her water bottle, stumbling back to bed, where she collapsed, out of breath.

She drank water then smoothed the salve across her gums, feeling them tighten around her loose tooth. Nikki placed a delivery order from a nearby restaurant—two rare steaks with potatoes, pork medallions in gravy, and lemon-dill salmon over risotto—hoping that would trick her body into thinking it was properly fed.

New messages from Xander came in, and she responded before flopping back onto her bed, staring into the black of her room, the bed a dark cocoon to wrap herself up in.

The next battle was getting the food when it arrived, the knock on the door only making Nikki feel heavier with exhaustion. Yet, she managed, again using the wall to support her, shuffling carefully when it ran out of length. She opened the door while standing behind it, checking that no sun came through the hallway. Some light shone in, harsh against her night-adjusted eyes, but she was able to snatch it without touching a single ray. Nikki was momentarily blinded as she closed the door and her eyes readjusted to the black of her apartment. She slid down the wall beside the door, sitting on the ground. She stared at the couch, contemplating moving there, but it looked so far away.

Tearing open the paper bag, relief washed over her as she spotted the utensils inside. Nikki opened all four containers, legs out amidst her floor banquet. The scent of the bloody steak filled her mouth with saliva, familiar pain shooting through her gums and causing her stomach to rumble. She scowled as she tried to cut into the steak, the plastic knife breaking without making a dent. Nikki craned her neck to look at the utensil drawer, and with a sigh, decided it was too far away, so she picked up the steak with her fingers and ripped a piece off with her teeth, juices running down her chin and fingers. Her veins buzzed with need, and she ate the first steak without pausing, chugging water from the bottle only once it was gone. She popped a pork medallion in her mouth, stabbing the vegetables with the prongs of the flimsy fork, and ate them all. Her stomach now ached with fullness, but her muscles still shook with malnutrition.

Gorged, she stared at the couch, with its plump cushions and fluffy pillows, a thick blanket draped over the back, and tried to convince herself to move. But now she was even heavier, so she shoved the food boxes out of the way and lay on the floor, promising herself she would get up soon. She just needed a moment to close her eyes.

Hours later, she was startled awake by someone shouting her name. She tried to sit up, but the arm under her head was dead asleep and she lost support of herself. Heart pounding, her gaze roved over the apartment, but no one was there. She looked under the crack of the door, but no feet were planted outside.

Wiping the drool from her mouth and arm, she stretched out her stiff shoulder, massaging the crick in her neck. With the food boxes in one hand and the other on the wall, she climbed to her feet, wobbling as she stood upright. Stumbling to the fridge, she put the remainder of her food away, leaving the trash on the floor, for fear of dizziness if she bent down to clean it up. The oven clock read after seven. Nikki found her phone, responding to Xander's worried texts, saying she was fine and that she'd just fallen asleep. It was close enough to the truth.

Despite her impromptu nap, weariness hung heavy in her bones. Shuffling to the living room, Nikki pulled back the curtains and wood paneling, surveying the foggy night that had descended over the Columbia River and the city beyond. Nikki put the paneling back and closed the curtains, preferring the full dark, and finally nestled into that comfortable couch.

She thought of the last time she saw her parents, when she needed to talk to them, and when she needed blood. How every time she had reached out to them it was to get something from them. When they had asked to see her outside of that, like for the fall equinox, she had dreaded the event. Not because of her parents, of course, but because she loathed being around the entire coven. Maybe they didn't understand that, though.

With a sick curl of guilt in her stomach, she texted her parents, asking if she could see them next weekend. They responded asking what was wrong, and a poison fist twisted in her chest. Maybe Gwen was right about her.

She passed out again after that, waking in the middle of the night with a fierce hunger. Using a real knife, she ate the second steak in pitch blackness, uncaring that all she could see was the vague outline of her food. Stomach full but veins weak, she threw herself onto her bed and slept, dreaming of tight spaces, yelling for Gwen, being covered in blood, and then following Xander's voice, finding him crumpled and cramped beside her. She screamed without sound.

All dreams were lost from memory the next day, but Nikki felt on edge, as if doom was about to descend, swift and without warning. Nikki told herself it was the combined stress of the fight with Gwen and midterms—and nothing more.

She awoke early afternoon, and while her body remained fatigued, the fog in her mind was a little clearer. Nikki called a worried Xander and apologized profusely for disappearing, which he hesitantly accepted before setting up plans for their next date.

Gwen did not contact her. A few times, Nikki drafted a text, or put her name in the recipient list of her messages, but she never pressed send. She couldn't think about that right now. If Gwen still wanted to be her friend, she could apologize for her cruelty. Even if Gwen had a point, she could have expressed it better.

The week of midterms rolled by in a stressful daze, and by the time her next date with Xander rolled around, she still hadn't heard from Gwen. She couldn't help but wonder what her friend had been up to. Whether or not she would reach out to apologize.

Xander was already at the restaurant and had their names on the waitlist when Nikki arrived after her evening class. Hands in his pockets, he watched the street, and the breeze picked up the waves of his hair. His profile was serious, but when he turned to her, his eyes lit up, and he smiled wide, pulling her into a tight hug, hands on her back as he kissed her.

"You seem happy," she said.

"I had my last midterm today. I'm finally free! Until finals, at least." Then his eyes and mouth twitched into a fake smile, like he wanted to say something else. But he just wound his hands through hers and squeezed them.

"What?" she asked. "I can see you thinking."

His fingers twitched against her hands, and his eyes darted away.

"You can be blunt," she said. "What is it?"

"I may have under-exaggerated my worry. I didn't want to make you feel bad. I know you needed the rest." He looked down at their hands. "And I know you can't text while sleeping, but a message sooner letting me know you were going dark for a while would have been appreciated."

"I'm sorry," she said, touching a hand to his face. He lifted his gaze back to hers, shifting on his feet, jaw clenching and unclenching against her palm. "I'll let you know next time. As soon as I can."

Xander's lip quirked into a half smile, and he said, "Thanks."

"Xander?" a petite woman called from the restaurant door, looking around at those waiting on the sidewalk.

They placed their orders, and the waiter brought the bread, olive oil and balsamic vinegar, and red wine to the table, expertly pouring the latter with a twist of his wrist, wiping the rim with a white cloth that absorbed the red stain. She blinked at the reddened cloth, reminiscent of blood. An ache of desire surged in her tired body, and when she glanced at Xander, her gaze fixated on the drum of his pulse in his throat. Nikki schooled her features, resisting the grimace of disgust.

They eased into conversation, Xander talked about the politicking of his workplace and the animals he saw that week, and Nikki eagerly dove into the entrée when it arrived. Fighting her bloodlust made her hungrier than normal, as she was never quite satiated.

As she listened to him talk about a particularly chatty cat with an attitude, she lost her concentration on which side of her mouth she chewed on, switching from one side to the other when her jaw got tired.

A hard crack in her mouth stopped her mid-chew. Nikki rolled her tongue, something bone-hard amidst the food. The taste of blood filled her mouth, and she carefully separated the food from the hard object in her mouth.

"Nikki – are you okay?"

She blinked, lifted her hand to motion for one moment, then spit the hard object into her palm.

Her heart stopped. The clatter and scrape of utensils on plates faded into the background, Xander's voice in a seashell.

In her hand was her human canine. Spattered with blood, which filled her mouth. She touched the tip of her tongue to where it belonged, a sensitive, gaping, tangy hole.

Cold swept through her body, goosebumps erupting across her arms, her neck, and all sense came rushing in at once—the high screech of knives on glazed earthenware, the cacophony of voices an indecipherable orchestra.

"Oh my god, Nikki, did your tooth just fall out?"

Nikki's head snapped up, and she took in Xander's eyes, wide with shock.

"No?" she said, too distracted to sound convincing. She covered her mouth with one hand and looked at the red tooth in the other. Adrenaline shot through her body, breaking the cold.

She bolted up from the chair so fast, it scraped and crashed backward, nearly hitting the table behind her.

"I, uh, I have to go," she said, tongue sliding sick and thick in that gap, a low whistle hissing through, and she spun on her heel, snatching her bag and dashing for the door, tooth tight in her hand.

"Nikki—wait!" Xander yelled, and as surprised faces whirled past her vision, she heard him stand from his chair, his footsteps steady and strong, chasing her, but she crashed through the door into the crisp night air, and with her tooth biting into her palm, she bolted down the street, taking a hard corner so Xander couldn't see her. Just before she crested the corner, she heard the jingle of the restaurant door, and Xander shout, "Wait! Nikki!"

But the frantic thump of her heart kept her running forward without a glance back. This was the point of no return.

Thud-thud, thud-thud. Her footsteps matched her heartbeat as she ran home, chill wind whisking past her, floodlamps blinking lights in her vision. She didn't stop, didn't think, until she was in the elevator, catching her breath, head tilted back against the wall.

As her breath and heart settled, a knot of guilt wound in her stomach, imagining Xander sitting alone and confused in the restaurant.

Walking down the hall to her apartment, she sent him money for dinner, but didn't return his calls.

Inside the dark of her apartment, she turned on a floor lamp and slumped onto her couch, hunched over her hands, cradling the tooth. She stared at it, saliva and blood drying on her palm and the bone, heart heavier the longer she looked at it, sinking into her gut.

The last remnants of her humanity were leaving.

There was no more denying the monster she would become.

The monster she was.

She clutched the tooth tight in her hands, the point nipping her skin. Nikki folded over herself, letting a few silent tears fall down her face and into her mouth. Salt mixed with iron as she mourned what she'd lost, what she'd never had.

When she plucked up the courage, she nudged the other canine with her tooth, and it wiggled in its socket. Nikki's chest heaved and folded.

She curled into a ball, face against the couch cushion, human tooth tight in her hand under her chin. The weight of inevitable, unwanted change pulled her down into the welcome darkness of unconsciousness, the whispers in her dreams silent for once.

Chapter Seventeen

Nikki didn't know what to say to Xander. She knew he was upset, knew he had a right to be—but what could she say? When she tried calling, he didn't answer. He was working, so it wasn't unexpected, but it still stung.

And still, there was no word from Gwen. Nikki was utterly alone.

She settled on texting him an apology about her behavior. About how she was embarrassed but didn't elaborate further. He responded with a brusque acknowledgment, and nothing else.

Nikki wanted to scream, to tear her hair out, to beat her head against the wall. Instead, she settled on the mental pain, telling herself how stupid and terrible she was, how she didn't deserve Xander, how he would be better off without her, and she spent too long with her head in her hands, fingernails digging into her scalp, waiting for him to talk to her. Her chest was tight, her stomach sick, her muscles aching with fatigue, and her gums so sore and tender she could barely eat.

Despising herself for her self-loathing, she called her dad, hoping to escape herself. They eagerly welcomed her over, and an hour later she found herself at the front drive of her house. Exhaustion filled her bones, as if she were being pulled into the ground. She stood facing the walkway, alders swaying in the breeze, leaves shimmering in reds and oranges and golds against the faded lamplight and the night. The breeze brought whispers, picking up wisps of her hair, the hairs on her arms raising. Dismay sank into her stomach as she surveyed the long walkway surrounded by looming trees. But she hadn't heard the voices for a while. She could get past these light whispers. The house was visible. Within reach.

She could do this, despite the weight in her bones, the tense fear in her neck.

Nikki placed a foot on the stone walkway, and each step took more energy than the last, as if walking through quicksand. Wind rustled the leaves, trees whispering to each other, to her, and she picked up her pace.

...daughter...

You...delay...

A pressure rose between her eyes and behind her skull, forcing her to squeeze her eyes shut, bracing against the pain. With a deep inhale, she stepped forward again, another pulse of pressure filling her mind, blinding her. Amidst the whispers, she picked out a few sparse phrases, repeated through the swarm of voices.

...daughter...

Where have you been hiding?

...patience...wanes...

...bring him...

Bring him...

...bring him...

No, no, no, no, Nikki thought, forcing her sluggish legs to move, as the alders loomed and threatened. But whispers overlapped, angry voices demanding obedience, pulling her to the ground, and she swayed on her feet. She placed another foot forward, but the ground came up to meet her, her vision going black the moment before her face smacked the stone.

She woke in the dark of her childhood bedroom, someone calling her name, whispering to her, and saw her mom beside her, silent. Nikki looked around her, brain thick, like it was full of fog, muscles slack. She groaned, and as her gaze roamed the room, she saw a small, fiddle leaf fig on her desk opposite the bed and screamed.

"What's that doing here? Get it out! Get it out! Get it out!" Nikki yelled, pushing herself up and falling to the floor in her haste to plant her feet, muscles giving out beneath her.

"Nikki! What? What's going on?!" Her mom cried, picking her up from the ground, and draping her back on the bed with a grunt, Nikki's knees thudding in pain from smacking the floor.

Nikki thrust a finger at the fiddle leaf and screamed, "No! Get it out! Get it out!"

"It's just a plant, Nicoletta! I thought it would brighten up the room!"

Nikki brought the blanket over her face, muttering no, no, no, no, no, and she heard her mom walk over to the plant while her dad arrived in the doorway with a swish of his clothes before she passed out again.

Searing pain thumped through the right side of her head, pounding in her skull. Nikki groaned, wincing as she dropped the blanket and opened her eyes to the dim light of the room.

"You stupid idiot."

Nikki turned her head, Gwen sitting on a chair beside the bed, eyes glassy with tears.

Nikki clenched her jaw and turned her head away from her, grimacing with the pain. "What are you doing here?" she asked, voice hoarse and dry.

"You're my best friend."

"Oh? I thought I was a heartless narcissist?"

"Yeah, well, maybe I have borderline personality disorder and we're perfect for each other."

Nikki huffed a reluctant laugh.

Gwen stood and sat on the edge of the bed. "Nik, I'm sorry. I was drunk, and I didn't know what you were doing to yourself. I mean, I did, but I didn't realize it was that bad and—"

"What do you mean, what I was doing to myself?"

Gwen fidgeted with her hands on her lap. "They said you'd been starving yourself. Like, not just minimizing intake, but actually depriving yourself of blood for weeks."

"How would they know that?"

"I don't know. They took your blood and did some vampire voodoo. I wasn't here yet to see what they did with it."

Nikki clenched her jaw, eyes fixed on the wall, head pounding.

"Nik." Gwen's voice broke, and she slid down beside her and took her hand, voice tight with sorrow. "I don't want you to die."

Nikki swallowed the lump in her throat and clenched her eyes against the tears. "Well, I don't want to live like this."

"That's why you're studying, right? Only a little while longer, and you'll figure out a way around it, I'm sure."

"'Only a little while longer?' It'll be a decade, at least. I don't even know anything about blood yet. Right now my education is just laying the foundation. I have to get into a graduate program before I learn anything specific. It's not like I'll be able to use my thesis to study anything about vampires, since it will be monitored closely by whoever my advisor is, and all funding would come from the school. So, before I can figure anything out, I'll have to graduate with a PhD, establish my own lab, somehow find funding, and then convince vampires to donate their blood for me to study. Assuming I get that far, who knows how long it will take for me to figure anything out. It seemed so attainable, once, but now it feels like a stupid, silly dream I had.

"Gwen, I feel so defeated. There's no denying what I am now. My other canine is loose. Soon enough, the fangs will grow in. Then everyone else will know. How am I supposed to be out in the world with fangs? How am I supposed to live another decade or more like this?"

"You'll find a way, Nik. In the scheme of a vampire's life, a decade or two is nothing. Think of how many people you'll help, both human and vampire, once you do figure out the key to vampirism. In the meantime, you'll do what you have to do, and the Lopezes will make you dentures, just like they do with everyone else."

Nikki shook her head, heart sinking into the bed. Her tongue searched for the gap, and she groaned. "I look so stupid, now."

"I can pull the other one out if you want. Then the Lopezes can make you caps for each side until the fangs grow in."

Nikki shook her head, clenching her jaw. "No. You've done enough for me."

"Nikki, I'm sorry about what I said. I didn't mean it. I know you have a big heart underneath that tough exterior."

"Stop. You were right. I didn't mean to be that way. But I was. I was trying to be efficient. I want to see someone, and I need something, why not have both at once? I didn't mean to use anyone. But I see how it could look that way. I'm sorry, Gwen."

Gwen grabbed her hand and laid their entwined fingers between their heads. "I'm sorry, too."

Nikki sighed, a weight lifting from her chest.

"So, what was up with screaming at the plant?"

"What?" Nikki asked, blood going cold.

"Your mom said you woke up and started screaming about a fiddle leaf fig she brought in here, yelling to get it out."

"I don't remember."

Gwen sighed. "I know you're lying, but you're lucky I'm too worried about you right now to care." Gwen squeezed her hand. "How is your head?"

"It hurts."

"You took a nasty fall."

"How did I even get in here? I remember walking up the walkway and then...nothing."

"Your parents found you face down out front. You cracked your head on the concrete, and they found you in a pool of blood. Gave them quite the fright. Anyway, I'll get you some pain reliever," Gwen said, sitting up from the bed.

"Thanks." Nikki's stomach sank, and she tried to roll over to look at the nightstand, groaning with pain. "I should call Xander."

"I already did."

"You did? What did you say?"

Gwen threw up her hands. "Don't worry, I didn't reveal any state secrets. I told him you're at your parents' house, who are very traditional about male company. I didn't know what, if anything, you had told him, so I said you've been battling an illness but were too embarrassed to tell him. I assured him you'd call when you were better, but the rest of the lie is up to you."

Nikki nodded and grabbed Gwen's hand again. "Thank you. You're the absolute best."

Gwen's eyes filled with tears, and she said, "I know." She squeezed

Nikki's hand and said, "You're not allowed to give up, okay? Promise me."

"I wasn't trying to give up. I just wanted to avoid drinking blood. I thought I could get away with only eating human food."

"That's stupid, because you're not just a human."

"I know. But a girl can dream. Right?"

"Not if this is the consequence."

Reluctant, Nikki sighed and gave Gwen one short nod, head throbbing with the movement. Gwen sniffled and left to get her pain reliever, leaving Nikki alone with her foggy thoughts. She'd have to find a way to live with herself. It was either hurt herself or hurt others, and she didn't want to see Gwen so sad ever again. Guilt coiled in her stomach at the thought of the fear her parents must have felt finding her bloody on the pavement.

She was selfish. And needed to stop letting everyone down, worrying them. She vowed to find a middle ground between choking down blood and abstaining, striking a balance for her self-loathing and worrying those around her.

Gwen came back with a tray of water, snacks, and medicine. She gave Nikki pills and smoothed ointment on her head, changing her bandage. Once satisfied with her nurturing, Gwen said, "The meds will make you drowsy. I'll let you get some rest."

Gwen stood to leave, and Nikki said, "Wait. Will you please stay?"

Gwen nodded and sat back on the bed, leaning against the headboard, brushing Nikki's hair off her face. "What do you want to do?"

Nikki shrugged. "Read to me?"

"Okay, what book?"

"Choose for me."

Gwen bounced to the bookcase, and after brief deliberation, plucked one from the shelf. Returning to Nikki's side, she leaned against the headboard, legs curled under her. Nikki faded into a peaceful, heavy darkness, Gwen's lilting voice telling her the story of *The Princess Bride*.

Chapter Eighteen

The next night passed in a blur. Gwen pulled the other canine out with more than a little pain, blood spurting all over both of them, but at least it was done. When Gwen left, her parents assaulted her with worry, bringing her trays upon trays of food, blood, and water. Nikki apologized, but offered no answers, and they refused to leave until she ate and drank all that was before her. It gave her a bellyache, eating so much after being so empty, but she tolerated the nausea to see her parents smile.

They sat with her until Carmen Lopez arrived to fit her single-tooth dentures, made with a tough exterior to compensate for the hollow interior, allowing her fangs to grow into them. Once her fangs were set, she would commission fittings to mask them, making them look like normal human canines.

"Drinking blood will help your fangs set faster. Then this will all be over. Wouldn't that be nice?" Carmen said, snapping the latex gloves off her hands.

Nikki nodded, mouth too thick with painkillers and chemicals to talk.

The medicine in her blood cocktail made her brain hazy, the pain turning to a dull ache, and her eyes closed before her parents had left the room.

She woke a few hours later, blinking against the lamplight near the side of her bed, a figure reading in a chair angled toward her. Another figure moved about her room, moving items. Drugs still crept in her veins, making her head heavy and vision swim.

"Hello there, moonshine," a vaguely familiar male voice said. She squinted, trying to focus her eyes, and as the world before her cleared, her muscles tensed.

Hormin stared at her, legs crossed, book in his lap, while her dad stalked about the room, straightening items.

"What...?" Nikki asked, tongue thick and dry in her mouth.

"Doesn't make much sense to call a vampire sunshine, now does it? Moonshine is much more fitting for creatures like us. Especially with how brightly pale you are."

Nikki furrowed her brow as her vision doubled, two Hormins leaning forward with vicious smiles on their faces.

Her dad moved toward the bed. "Love, how are you—?"

"Would you excuse us, for a moment?" Hormin interrupted, turning his smile toward Miguel.

"Whatever you have to say to my daughter, you will say in front of me."

"Truly, I insist," Hormin said, through his clenched smile. As Nikki's vision stabilized, she saw the rigidity in Hormin's body, the uncertainty in her dad's face. Her dad lost their silent battle, and after a moment's hesitation, left the room with a long nod at Nikki. She didn't hear his footsteps down the hall and hoped that meant he remained by the door, although she could just be too weak to hear him walk away. Even though Hormin made her uncomfortable, he wouldn't hurt her, would he?

Nikki opened her mouth to speak, but her mouth was too dry. Hormin handed her a cup of water from her nightstand, and watched her sip at it, that same smirk plastered on his face. When her thirst was quenched, she pushed herself up in bed, back resting on the frame.

"What are you doing here?"

"Checking on our sick little fledgling, of course. When I heard you took a nasty fall, I had to come see the damage." He raised a hand to her head and brushed away her hair. "You're healing up well. I'm sure the blood they pumped into you helped the process."

"They did what to me?"

"Oh don't be so surprised," he said, leaning back. "It's standard vampire medical care. An IV of blood instead of water. You desperately needed it."

Nikki curled her hands into fists. It felt like a violation, that they would inject her body with fluids she didn't want. But she couldn't deny it was nice to heal quickly. Her head was tender where Hormin had touched it, but the more she woke up the less it throbbed, the less her muscles ached with fatigue.

She looked back at Hormin, taking in his relaxed posture, the slight tilt of his head as he stared back at her. "Why are you here?" she whispered, without thinking.

"I believe I just told you, silly little duckling. Maybe you have a concussion after all."

Duckling? She swallowed the rock in her throat and said, "That's not what I mean."

Slowly, his smile widened until it stretched so far it seemed his face would split in two. Despite the size of his grin, the mirth did not reach his eyes, and cold fear in Nikki's gut made her shrivel into herself.

"As I said at the party, it seems the place to be. In fact, some friends of mine will be joining us soon, just to see what the fuss is all about."

"Why?"

Hormin's expression did not change, but he did not respond. Instead, he simply stared deep into her eyes, and she felt pierced right to her core. He broke eye contact to rove his gaze over her face, and finally said, "You are a curious creature."

Nikki curled the blankets into her fists. "What makes you say that?"

"You're so full of...resistance."

Flashes of coming up the walkway before her collapse flashed through her mind. Of the pressing alders, the crushing whispers, the weight that forced her to the ground, despite her best efforts to move forward.

"I'm not sure what you mean."

Hormin's grin faded, just as slowly as it had spread, and the change in demeanor sent shivers up her spine. As if he could read her thoughts, he said, "Oh, I think you do. And all come to heel eventually." The lilt of his voice was jovial, but his gaze grew dark. "Now, rest up. This is a time of great change, and it can take quite the toll on the body."

Hormin left without another word, leaving her with a deep sense of unease. She couldn't help but think that everything he said had a double meaning, and worry for herself, for Xander, etched itself deep into her bones. She reached for the pill bottles beside her nightstand and found the ones for sleep, taking an extra dose to make sure she fell asleep hard, without dreams or Hormin's words slithering in her head.

She woke a full day later, textbooks on her desk, single dentures on the nightstand beside her. Nikki sat up in bed, blinking the fog from her mind, appreciating how her arms did not wobble when she lifted herself.

She swung her legs from the bed, placing her feet on the ground and standing with deliberate slowness. As she straightened, she did not shake. In her bathroom, she looked at herself for the first time in days, skin luminescent and eyes as dark as the new moon. Nikki peeled back her lips and laughed at how ridiculous she looked without her teeth. She popped in the single dentures, assessed them from different angles, and was satisfied with how natural they appeared. Nikki peeled back the bandage on her head, only a light purple bruise on her forehead. The skin had fully healed, and only a slight tenderness remained.

With queasiness curled in her gut, heart clenching like a fist in her chest, she turned on her phone, anticipating a barrage of upset texts from Xander. She had just promised him she would contact him before she went dark, and she broke it within days. He could hate her now. He could be angry or sad. Maybe he didn't want to talk to her after what happened. After how many days had passed.

Thinking of him and his kind, handsome face, a wave of absence washed over her. How she missed his voice and his arms around her, and how she dreaded the conversation to come. If he would even talk to her.

Yet, his messages only filled her with a melting sorrow. He sent several, saying Gwen had reached out to him, how sorry he was he couldn't be there, that he missed her, and please, wouldn't she call as soon as she could?

She tapped the phone against her palm, the whispers from the previous days echoing through her mind. Bring him, bring him, bring him. Yes, she was a danger to him, but she could control herself. And what more could the whispers do than talk and tug? Whatever it was, she could suffer through it to be with him.

But what if Hormin was truly there for him? Could she protect Xander from whatever Hormin had planned?

Maybe everyone was right, and drinking blood was for the best. Her stomach curdled at the thought, but she could train herself out of that reaction. Couldn't she? If it meant that she could be stronger and better for Xander, then maybe it was worth it.

Assuming he still wanted her.

Heart racing, she called him. It was late afternoon, so he could be working, but he did ask her to call as soon as she could. She wouldn't let him down again.

He didn't answer, and her heart sank into her gut. She sighed and put her phone on the nightstand, shifting into bed under the covers.

While she was still adjusting the blankets around her, her phone vibrated on the nightstand, screen blaring Xander's name.

Heart hammering, she answered. "Hi, Xander."

"Hey, Nikki. How are you feeling?"

"I'm fine. Getting better. I'm sorry for the past few days. Weeks."

"It's okay, Gwen filled me in some. I wish you would've told me sooner, but I'm no stranger to illness. Will you tell me what's going on?"

Nikki stared into the distance, a bracing point for her thundering pulse. "I'd rather not talk about it over the phone. Can we meet in a few nights?"

"Sure thing. Let me know if you need anything, okay?"

"Okay." Nikki leaned forward, trying to squash the waves in her stomach. All come to heel eventually echoed around her skull. "I think —I think you'd be better off without me."

Xander was silent, a weight filling her room. After several moments, he said, "What makes you say that?"

"I'm a freak."

"If you're talking about your tooth falling out, it's not that big of a deal. I mean, I wish you hadn't run off, but I looked it up, and the rates of adults having baby teeth and of losing teeth are higher than we realize. It's just a cultural stigma. But teeth fall out for many reasons and can happen to people of all ages. There's actually a disease of rapid—"

Nikki laughed, a tense bubbling escaping from her gut.

"What's so funny?" Xander asked, a confused edge to his voice.

"I'm sorry. I'm just surprised. I really appreciate you trying to make me feel better about this."

"Of course. Now focus on getting better, and we'll talk soon?"

"Yes. Absolutely. Bye, Xander."

"Bye, Nikki," Xander said, a hesitation in his voice before he clicked off the phone.

Throughout the night, a couple other coven members came to check on her, and she was torn between the annoyance of having to socialize and the sweetness of their caring. The Lopezes, including their children, came to make sure the dentures fit, while the kids brought her handmade get-well-soon cards. The Lius brought over blood from their thralls, both for her and her parents, and talked to her about how hard the transition to vampirism had been for them. Although Nikki took what they said with a grain of salt, as they had made a choice to be this way, and she did not. Still, she appreciated their concern, and they left her with not only blood, but a few of their favorite books and movies. Her parents came in to check on her a few times, pressing her for details on what she and Hormin talked about, but she shrugged them off, explaining that he was just showing friendly concern. She didn't want them to think that he was there for her, or for Xander, and get wrapped up in her mess. Especially if she was just reading too much into his behavior.

Nikki left the next night, feeling better than she had in months. Her senses were alert, sharp, and her muscles strong. Gwen visited her once more, bringing her more salve, as her gums would hurt more and more until the fangs set in. Gwen oohed and aahed over Nikki's healthy glow and made her promise to see her soon.

On her way out, she found her parents in the lounge, in front of an open fire.

"Hey," she said, stepping into the room, hands around the strap of her purse.

Her dad held his hand out to her from the couch. "Leaving already?"

She nodded and took his hand, sitting beside him. "Yes. Thank you both for taking care of me. I'm sorry for all the worry."

"Ah, we'll take care of you anytime."

"But it is time for you to take better care of yourself," her mom interjected, skin a warm amber in the firelight. "And if you can't, we will cease financial support, and you will have to move back home. Understood?"

"Are you serious?"

"If you won't take care of yourself, we will. What would have happened if you fell down when no one else was around? Best case scenario, you would end up in a human hospital. Worst case, you wither away on the street. You want to detest your lot in life? Fine. But we will not let you continue to harm yourself."

Nikki nodded through the heated knot in her chest. "I understand. I'm sorry. It won't happen again."

"You're right, it won't. You will take blood home with you and drink two thermoses a week. Bring them back every Sunday for a refill. We will know if you haven't been drinking it."

Nikki took a deep breath, swallowing the nausea. "Yes, Mom."

Her dad squeezed her hand and stood. "Come, come," he said, placing his blood glass on the coffee table.

Nikki stood to follow, but was stopped by her mom, who stepped in front of her. She placed her hands on Nikki's face, a near mirror image of her own, and gave her two kisses, one on each cheek. "Your body needs more blood to heal than to maintain. Once you're better and fully transformed, you won't have to drink as much. So please, until then, take care of yourself. I love you very much."

"I love you too, Mom. And I will."

Cat's smile flickered with approval, and she said, "We must throw a celebration when your fangs come in."

Nikki groaned. "Must we?"

"Yes. It's tradition. The settling of the fangs signifies the completion of your transition from a fledgling into a full vampire. It is a big moment, not just for you, but for the whole coven."

"Everyone has to be there?"

"Don't get yourself in a twist. I'll organize it for you. You only need to show up."

Nikki sighed, and seeing how important it was to her mom, she said, "Fine."

Her mom smiled and said, "Good. Call me later this week to tell me how you're doing, and we will pick a date. If you drink the blood as prescribed, they should be settled within a few weeks."

"I'll drink it," she assured her. "And yes, I'll call you later this week."

"Very well then. Find your father." Cat gave her a last fleeting smile, settling back on the settee near the fire.

Nikki met her dad in the kitchen, two large, chilled thermoses on the counter. Miguel opened a reusable bag, put the thermoses inside, and handed it to her.

"There will be no more of this nonsense, Nicoletta. We can't—I can't—" her dad cleared his throat, putting his hands on her shoulders. "I could not bear to find you like that again. Face down in your own blood."

Nikki's vision glassed at the ache in her dad's voice, and it took all her strength to say, "I'm so sorry, Dad." She wrapped her arms around him, and he held her close to his chest, his heartbeat strong and unnaturally slow.

"Now, no more of this," he said when their hug broke, hands back on her shoulders. He wiped moisture from under her eyes with his thumbs and gave her a soft smile, pointed teeth gleaming. She returned his smile with a weak one of her own, and he said, "Ah, there we go. That's my girl. Smile and move forward, yes?"

She nodded.

"Go on, go home. If you need more blood, if you need anything at all, you will call immediately."

"I will."

He inhaled deeply and nodded, turning his back to her, preparing food for Cat.

Outside, the planters on the front steps were dying, a frost settling on the leaves. The weather had turned while she was bedridden, the soft chill turning into a biting cold, the leaves of the alders gold and yellow, many fluttering to the ground. She stared at the long lines of trees, illuminated gold by the lamps, the darkness swallowing the forest beyond and the grounds, with her car on the other side.

The wind rustled through her hair, and she lifted her chin.

Nikki took confident steps down the stairs, wind pushing frigid air against her skin. Below the alders, she looked up at their crowns and took a deep breath, steeling herself, dying leaves fluttering from the branches around her.

Under the alders, the breeze carried a laughter that bounced between her ears, dancing from tree to tree.

...hiding... again? the voice whispered, a spiteful chuckle swirling amongst the leaves.

A chill crept up her spine and a pressure of another's presence filled the back of her mind, but Nikki kept her spine straight and kept walking. She spotted red on the ground, where she must have fallen, her blood staining the walkway, to be washed away by the next rain.

...you cannot...

...hide...

...from me, daughter...

Heaviness filled her muscles, and she clenched her jaw, tightened her grip on her purse and bag, eyes fixed on her car in the distance.

The cackle pushed with the scrape of leaves on the ground, the groan of the branches in the wind.

...I can see...

...your thoughts...

...your heart...

Nikki fell to her knees, as if pulled by strings to the ground. She grunted and gritted her teeth, and then slowly stood against a weight that pressed from outside her, a heaviness that pulled from within her.

So...obstinate...

Nikki trudged to her car, beyond two more rows of trees, dragging her body with all her might against the force pushing her down, expanding her mind from the inside, as if her skull was near to bursting.

The whisper became a sneer. *They all forget...*

He was...MINE first...
I will...have him...
"You will not!" Nikki yelled, launching herself at her car door, and the pressure popped, releasing from her mind.

She heaved a sigh in her car, catching her breath. Nikki turned it on, listening to it stutter from sitting in the cold, and turned on the heat full blast.

As the car warmed up, the voices faded, whispering, *Bring him to me...*

This is your last...
Warning.

Chapter Nineteen

Nikki met Xander outside her apartment building. While barely a week had passed, it felt as if she hadn't seen him in much longer. She had been rationing the blood, experimenting with mixing it with juices, making it into a sauce, trying to find a way to consume it without being utterly disgusted. With it or herself. It was a struggle, but she was determined to find a way.

It was only temporary, after all.

But she'd had more than usual earlier in the evening, not wanting to risk Xander finding it in her fridge. It took great effort not to gag or vomit while the thick, viscous liquid slid down her throat, to not imagine who it came from, the remembrance of fresh blood beating directly into her mouth ever-present in the back of her mind.

Smile and move forward.

Nikki felt every curl of air against her skin, the smells from every restaurant along the waterfront assaulting her nose. Tonight was a wonderful mix of the late autumn breeze, local food and the cacophony of people chattering. She could see the shattering of every light as it bounced off the objects around her, their individual outlines crisp with detail. It was overwhelming to take in so much information, but she would get used to it, learn to shut out what wasn't important.

Nikki focused on the lights on the river, the dark water sloshing against the rocks on the banks.

The hairs on the back of her neck rose, the wind carrying a comforting, familiar, subtle scent of anise. Her lips curled into a half grin, and she looked over her shoulder, Xander walking toward her from down the block, grocery bags in hand.

From down the street, he returned her smile, and everything around them faded, focused as she was on his approach, the shift of his muscles beneath his shirt, the wind through his hair, the joy on his lips just for her.

"Hey," Nikki said when he was right in front of her, his stubble longer than usual. She searched his face, looking for signs of anger, uncertainty, or sadness. Did he still want to touch her?

"Hey," he said, switching the grocery bags into one hand. Sensing her hesitation, he stepped forward and wrapped the other hand around the small of her back.

As he pulled her close to him, she relaxed and tilted her head, gazes locking. His smile faded, and moving his free hand from her back he cupped her cheek, running a thumb along her skin. She leaned into his touch, relieved, and when he angled her chin to kiss her, she met his lips with equal depth, his mouth warm and firm, facial hair tickling her skin.

Pulling back, Xander asked, "How are you feeling?"

"I'm good. I feel much better. Better than I have in a long time."

"Good, I'm glad." Xander stared at her mouth. "Your teeth look different."

"Oh. They do?" Nikki asked, stepping back, lifting a hand to cover her mouth.

"Yes, but not in a bad way," he rushed on. "You look well."

"Thanks," she responded, then led Xander into the apartment. She had removed the wood coverings from her windows and put them in the corner, and then pulled back the blinds so that as soon as he entered, he would see the view. The sky was overcast, and fog hung heavy over Portland, the city lights muted specks of color through the black and grey.

"This is incredible," Xander said, putting down the groceries and standing in front of the windows, taking it all in. Nikki smiled to herself at the view of him in her apartment. She pulled out her old cookbook, pages frayed and grease-spattered, and opened it in front of her, then put the water on to boil with some salt and began chopping onions. While she cooked, Xander talked about the ongoing drama at work, how his colleague was still out of town on FMLA with no idea when he'd be back, how the receptionist was one vendetta away from getting fired. Xander hadn't seen his siblings for a while, and talked about missing them, reminiscing about when they all lived together. Listening to his voice, low but animated, was calming and uplifting for Nikki. He really was the best companion.

When the filling was prepped, she stopped him short and beckoned him to help. Side by side, arms touching, she taught him how to roll the filling in the brined cabbage leaves. He struggled to make them tight at first but eventually got the hang of it.

"This is surprisingly fun," he said, sleeves rolled past his elbows, hands tucking the leaves around the filling and putting it on a baking sheet.

"Cooking is one of my favorite things," Nikki said. "I don't do it often, though."

"Why not?"

"Not a lot of motivation to cook when it's just me."

"Well, you can cook for me anytime you want."

"Noted," Nikki said, and they kissed, briefly, hands paused on the food.

When all the rolls were made and put in the oven to bake, the two of them sat on her couch. Xander sat beside her, setting his wine on the table. He sat sideways to face her, and she mirrored his position, resting a fist against her head, but keeping her legs out. Her gaze was drawn to the bob of his Adam's apple, the arteries that pulsed beneath that golden, stubbled skin.

She took a deep breath and a sip of wine.

Xander searched her face, green-grey eyes roving over her, as if he could see her rapid heart palpitations.

"What's going on, Nikki?"

"You probably want an explanation from me."

"I'd like to know what's been going with you, yes," he whispered, as if he said it more forcefully, she'd run.

"I'm trying to get the nerve to tell you."

"Hey," he said and put a hand on her knee. "I'm sure it's not that bad. I won't judge."

Oh, but it is, Nikki thought, paralyzed.

Xander must've seen the thought in her eyes because he took a deep breath and with a sigh, he said, "As I said, I'm no stranger to illness. Not just from my work and studies, but my... my dad had prostate cancer when I was a kid. It wasn't pretty, but he beat it. I was worried about him, but I found out that my worry eased when I knew how I could care for him, how I could make him better. Bringing him water, or food, or even just reading to him, being there for him helped. Maybe it's selfish of me, that I need to be active about it, that I need to do something to feel better. But it's part of who I am now. So don't worry about what I'm going to think, it isn't going to be anything bad. Just tell me what you need, so I can help."

Nikki blinked, both stunned and bolstered by his words. "I'm so sorry to hear that. About your dad. I'm glad he recovered."

"Me too. He's been clear of it since, no recurrence or signs of it elsewhere," Xander said, and some of the light returned to his eyes.

"That's great," Nikki said, drinking some wine to quiet the nervousness humming in her fingertips.

Xander nodded and gave her a half smile. Patient. Encouraging.

With a long exhale, Nikki broke their gaze, looking out the window. "I have a... sun sickness."

"Sun sickness?"

"Like a severe sun allergy. I can't be in the daylight. Which is why I have evening classes. Why we only see each other at night. And why I text at odd hours."

Xander's eyebrow quirked, and his lips spread into a teasing smile. "So you're a vampire?"

A stilted, staccato laugh burst from Nikki. Stamping the hot air of fear that expanded in her stomach, she said, "Yes."

Xander laughed. Her shoulders relaxed, but her chest tightened, seeing he didn't believe her. Probably better that way.

"That's not so bad, we can work around that." He chuckled again and squeezed her knee. "I don't see how that made you faint and crack your head open on the sidewalk, though. Where is your wound, by the way?"

"Oh," Nikki said. "It really wasn't that bad. You know how Gwen exaggerates." She drank more wine at the lie, forcing the shame down. "There are other issues tied to it. Such as susceptibility to malnutrition. I have to be careful. But I wasn't. So, down I went."

"Mmm, a vampire who needs to be wined and dined? Doesn't sound too bad to me," Xander said, plucking the wine glass from her hand and setting it on the table.

"It doesn't?" Nikki said, both relieved and nauseous with the deception.

"Not one bit," he said, moving forward to kiss her, hand slipping under her back and sliding her down, so she lay on her back on the couch under him. "That's all very manageable," he whispered, as he moved to kiss her neck, under her ear, on her artery.

She brought her hands up to wrap in his soft, thick waves, legs wrapping around his hips. A low groan escaped from him, and her body melted.

His hand slipped under her shirt, roaming up her bare skin, when a harsh vibration buzzed from her phone on the coffee table.

Xander groaned dramatically. "Don't tell me that's the timer for the food."

"It is, unfortunately," Nikki said, and with another kiss to her neck, Xander sat back up on the couch, her skin cold where he no longer touched.

"Need me to do anything?" he asked as Nikki stepped back into the kitchen and set the water boiling. He followed her, cracking his knuckles and setting his hands on the counter. His stomach growled, and he chuckled. "I guess I'm full of all kinds of wants right now."

"It won't be much longer."

With the last dish prepping, Xander hugged her from behind. He wrapped his arms gently around her, watching her stir.

"Thank you, for telling me," Xander said, breath tickling her ear. "I know it isn't always easy."

Nikki nodded, swallowing a stone in her throat. But when she turned around, she wore a smile. Nikki kissed him and said, "Thanks for being understanding. I know not being able to do things is a big complication. Especially for someone as active as you."

"It really isn't that big of a complication. I'm pretty busy during the days, anyway."

Nikki nodded and folded herself against him, ear against his steadfast heart. When she looked up at him, he grinned, dark waves falling into his eyes, and she saw the pulse in his neck quicken, beating against the delicate skin.

"What is it?" he asked.

Her face heated and she said, "I just feel lucky to have you." Nikki gave him a peck and peeled away. His pulse was a drumbeat growing louder, his scent overtaking the smell of the food.

They set the table and refilled their wine glasses, Xander bringing over a fresh bottle of wine. When the table was set and Nikki sat down, she said, "Bon appétit. We have sarmale and mamaliga."

"Looks and smells delicious," he said, before diving in. Xander didn't pause to talk until he was three rolls and a serving of mamaliga in, surprising given his usual chattiness. Nikki filled with joy and pride at the sounds and sights of his pleasure at the meal she made. It was rather good, vinegary and salty and meaty, complemented by the buttery, creaminess of the polenta, the bite of the red wine.

When he slowed eating, conversation picked up, and they made plans for another group date on Halloween. They chatted about past costumes and Halloween parties, being one of the few human holidays Nikki could actually participate in. She and Gwen had always gone as the same thing, with Nikki as a witch and Gwen as a vampire. They changed the style year to year, but the theme remained the same.

After dinner was cleared they settled in for a movie, and with some debate they settled on Dracula with Christopher Lee, because of course Xander was now in the mood for a vampire flick. He ran his fingers over her arm, sending chills of delight across her skin, up her spine. Amidst the movie, she listened to his heartbeat, steady and strong against his ribs, a life-affirming lullaby. After about twenty minutes, his fingers stopped moving, and his breathing changed, and she craned her neck to look up at him. His head was tilted onto the back of the couch, neck stretched, eyes closed in slumber. She smiled to herself, a small, quiet thing, at his comfort, at how adorable he was sleeping. His chest rising and falling steadily, hair slung over the back of the couch. The angle of his neck made his Adam's apple more prominent, and she ran a finger, delicately, over his throat, catching his pulse, treasuring it beneath her skin. Her mouth gave an uncomfortable, unwelcome swell of saliva as her body told her to bring her mouth to his veins, and she removed her finger from his neck, debating if she should let him sleep where he was or beckon him to bed.

She let him sleep until the movie was over, and then summoned him to bed, where he promptly fell back asleep. Nikki tried to watch another movie, but even his outstretched arm distracted her. The muscles were tight and curved, and his vulnerable wrist sat upright, that fragile skin revealing the steady thrum of his heartbeat. She bit her own hand, with extra force to break through the toughened skin, to resist the urge to kiss and bite that throbbing part of him. As the blood trickled into her mouth, eyes clenched tight, she couldn't help but imagine Xander's blood, what it would feel like to have her lips pressed to the delicate skin of his wrist, his neck. What his blood would taste like.

She fell asleep listening to Xander's deep breathing, relishing his arm across her body.

When she dreamt, she dreamt of watching herself.

The colors of the room were muted, as if under water. She stood over the bed, watching herself sleep against his body. They were curled into each other, mouths parted in drunken slumber. Watching their breaths rise and fall, hot rage filled her from her core and flared her vision red—how badly she needed to get rid of that disobedient girl, to taste that blood, the blood of her first love. As the rage mounted in her body, she screamed and reached a hand toward her own unconscious body, fingers wrapping around that porcelain flesh—

Nikki woke with a gasp, eyes flying open. She felt her skin, feeling the imprint of a hand across her neck. The room was dark, her laptop having fallen asleep. No one was there. Her head felt heavy and thick, and she quickly fell back asleep.

When Nikki woke the second time, Xander's breath was warm

against her ear, hand tight against the bare skin of her stomach. He woke moments after she did, roused by her consciousness, and pulled her closer to him, kissing her neck slowly.

"Good morning," he said, voice a low growl from hours of disuse.

"Morning," she said, turning her head to open his mouth with hers, strangely loving the old taste of him.

His hand moved up and down her skin under her shirt, and he shifted himself up so he leaned over her, hand moving down to her thigh, pulling it over his hips. Directly on top of her, kissing her with long and slow movements of his tongue, he pulled the shirt from her body, taking a moment to appreciate the view of her body against his, under his.

He pressed his body weight closer to hers, one hand moving up to her face to cup the back of her head. But his hand wouldn't keep still, and it moved down her torso to her leg, Nikki's own hands pulling his shirt off, roaming the flat planes of his skin, the thick waves of his hair.

An alarm rang, vibrating against the coffee table in the living room. Xander sighed and buried his face in her neck.

He sighed into her neck and said, "Foiled again."

Her hand moved against the smooth skin on his back, his hair tickling her face. "Do you have to go?"

He nodded, pressing his hips to hers and kissing her neck. "Unfortunately, yes. I have to work."

"You should stop teasing me, then."

"I'm sorry," Xander said, voice deep and husky. "Trust me, I don't want to go."

She pulled on his hair, and he groaned. The sound made thrills of pleasure course through her body.

"You're not making this any easier," he said, putting his tongue against hers one more time, then pulling back and sitting up in bed, his alarm still ringing from the other room.

He ran a hand through his hair and shoved himself up from the bed, closing the bathroom door behind him. Nikki wrapped herself up in sweats and brewed coffee in the dark. A pressure filled her head as she scooped the ground coffee into the machine, an expansion in her mind that pushed against her ears, making space for another presence.

No, no, no, she thought, squeezing her eyes tight and bracing her hands on the counter. Get out, get out, get out. She opened and closed her jaw, trying to pop her ears, but the pressure and the presence remained. As if she was being watched, as if something was watching through her.

When he left, the pressure in her head emptied, and her shoulders relaxed with the release of tension.

A hot coil of anger rose inside her, and Nikki looked around the apartment, verifying there was no greenery. She tightened her jaw, allowing the ache in her stretching, clenching gums to validate her rage.

"How did you get here?" Nikki whispered.

She received no response.

Chapter Twenty

A NEW SENSE of normalcy settled. She swung by her parents' house to get more blood, both of them fawning over her recovery. Her gums still ached, but Gwen's extra potent salve numbed the pain until it was a dull roar. It took severe dedication to catch up with her missed work, and to do it well, but after a few long nights and short days, she managed it. Xander met her at the library on the usual days, looking haggard but maintaining his spirits.

One night, Nikki's mouth was so overwhelmed with pain, she couldn't focus on her studies. Her vision blurred and her ears throbbed. She had put salve over her gums, but it wasn't helping. Nikki brought a large stash of oranges and chocolate squares, this time with some cayenne, just to have some other distracting sensation in her mouth.

"Can I ask you a question?" Xander sat across from her so they had plenty of room to stretch out their books, to look at each other.

"Hm?" Nikki asked, squinting with the pain, blinking up at him.

"I've been wondering what's up with that?" he asked, pointing with the eraser of his pencil at the orange and chocolate mess beside her.

"Oh." Nikki grinned at the memory, which turned into a grimace. "It's Gwen's fault. When we were kids, she felt bad for me. Not being able to go outside. I can go out in quick bursts. But not for long. I was always so envious. Imagining how good it must feel to have the sun on your skin." She shook her head, warding off the self-pity, the fantasy. "One day, mid-summer, when we were about seven, she made me a big fort. I was up before twilight, and she pulled me outside. She draped me in all these blankets and shades and carried an umbrella over me to this fort. Inside, she had pictures of the sky and a few little plants. It was sweltering. But I loved it. And we gorged ourselves on chocolate and oranges. Because of that day, this is what I imagine daylight tastes like. It's the closest I can get." Nikki smiled weakly. "I guess it's a comfort food now." She stared at the table, images of that poorly decorated tent, the stuffy heat of the interior, and Gwen's untamed hair bright in the dark flashing through her mind, and her heart melted with the sweet sorrow of reminiscence.

"Wow, that's nice of her."

"She's always taken care of me. We made the fort a few times. But once my parents found out, it stopped. They were too worried."

"I don't blame them for wanting to keep you safe."

"I don't either." Nikki looked out the window, the night reflecting their images on the glass. "You know, I've never seen a sunrise."

"You haven't?" Xander asked, voice hitching with surprise.

"No. It's too scary."

"But twilight isn't?"

"Not really. At twilight, you know your time is coming. That safety is coming. With dawn, it's the opposite." She looked at Xander, at his joy and warmth that exuded the essence of summer. "I'm sorry. I wish it was different."

Xander shrugged. "Don't be sorry. It's out of your control."

Nikki nodded, popped another orange-chocolate sandwich in her mouth. Perhaps it was out of her control now, but maybe one day it wouldn't be. If she could figure out why vampires needed human blood to survive, who was to say she couldn't determine what made them sensitive to sunlight? Maybe a day would come when she and Xander could walk hand in hand in the day, basking under a summer sun.

If she could hide her true self from him for that long.

When she got home, she removed the single dentures from her mouth with some difficulty, picking through the gaps to loosen them.

Peeling back her lips, she saw that little, white, pointed nubs grew from her gums where her human canines used to be. She sighed, wishing it would just be over, that she didn't have to grow fangs. But the longer she looked at herself, she couldn't help but laugh. She looked ridiculous, with those small, pointy teeth coming in.

She left the dentures out, letting her gums breathe. Her tongue kept feeling for the gaps, points piercing the muscle, little droplets of blood flooding her mouth. Another thing she'd have to get used to.

She called her mom as promised to let her know her fangs were coming in. Her mom nearly squealed with excitement, rambling off plans for the party. When Nikki finally managed to get off the phone with her mom, a few minutes later her dad texted her with congratulations, saying how excited he was for her, how fun fangs could be. Her stomach flipped at whatever that was supposed to mean.

She monitored the nubs over the week, watching with amazement as they grew more every day. When she had a blood cocktail, she could feel the fangs moving in, as if her body were healing a wound. As much as the thought of drinking blood made her queasy, it was amazing what a little of it could do for her body.

Chapter Twenty-One

T**HE CLUB** they went to on Halloween was a vampire's dream. So of course it was Nikki's nightmare.

The music area was a swamp, bodies heating beneath the lights, the alcohol, and the costumes. The aroma of it sang to her vampiric senses, begging her to sample the banquet of humans before her, and she hated how deep the hunger buried itself in her stomach. She couldn't think with the quick pumping hearts, the scent of everyone's elation and intoxication making her dizzy.

The club was dimly lit, with sparse red and gold lights, scattered tables, and black flooring. A band played in the back, some punkish metal, the bar an odd gothic-grunge vibe, scattered with costumes bizarre, gruesome, and plain.

Her fangs were now almost as long as her human teeth. The points were slightly higher than them, and she looked a little goofy when she stared at them too long, but overall, she thought she could forgo the caps. No one would be looking at her teeth that intensely. Even if they were, it was Halloween and some weirdness was to be expected, right?

Their group found a faded couch in the corner that had a lopsided, scratched, small black table adjacent to it. White lights above the stage roved over the crowd, providing sporadic illumination. The vibration of the bass reverberated through the couch, changing the rhythm of her heartbeat to its own. The flickering, shifting lights, swaying bodies, voices and instruments infiltrated her head, and she stared at the masses, a seething Cthulhu-esque monster writhing to destroy her senses.

"Nik, you okay?" Gwen's cool hand on her arm broke her from her haze. "You look terrified."

"Sorry. Just got overwhelmed for a minute. Where did everyone go?" she asked, seeing it was just her and Gwen.

"They left to get drinks and snacks," Gwen yelled. Somehow she managed to get her mane into a long, black wig, and she wore a black leather outfit and fake fangs, dressing up this year as the stereotypical modern vampire.

The others returned, Theo dressed as a mermaid in shimmering blues and greens with matching glitter on her skin. Terrance was clothed in a poor attempt at a werewolf, with grey clothes and a headband with ears over his head. Xander wore a long robe and held a staff, claiming to be a wizard so he would match Nikki's witch costume. It was a sweet idea, but since he didn't ask what kind of witch she was going as, they didn't match at all. While his costume was simple, she was decorated in green and all kinds of plant debris to look like a green witch.

Nikki sat with the wine glass curled against her chest, the stench of the place making her nose crinkle. She tried to bury it under the smell of her wine, keeping it close to her nostrils, but as more people danced and drank, the more the place smelled of sweat, anticipation, and sex. The mass of eager heartbeats pumping intoxicated blood pounded in her ears and the shedding sweat amplified the enticing scent of each person. Her gums twinged, saliva pulsing in her mouth, her stomach flipping at the predator in her that this place awakened.

Gwen and Theo were lost in their own limbs and whispers, Theo listening to Gwen's chatter as she played with her hair. When the song changed, they went to the dance floor, lost in the crowd of jumping, head banging, and limbs thrown about. Terrance and Xander talked about something Nikki couldn't hear. The music was so loud, drowning out her usual heightened hearing. Nikki took a deep breath and settled into the seat, Xander's arm still around her, although his face was turned away.

Instead of trying to butt in, to scream her voice out over the music, over everything else, she watched the crowd, in all its costumes and colors. A headache built behind her eyes with the strain of the visual stimuli, her ears throbbing with the noise.

When the music slowed, Nikki and Xander got up to dance. They swayed and shifted in lazy circles, not talking, just enjoying the feel of being together. Nikki pulled back from Xander, moving her arms up over his shoulders. He moved his hands onto her hips, and they smiled. They still did not speak but looked at each other as if there was no one else in the room, memorizing each other's faces.

Many songs later, Nikki's feet ached from standing in her heels for so long. Their couch had been claimed by other people, Terrance in conversation with a cute, petite girl in a tight cat outfit, face painted with whiskers.

Nikki groaned, lifting her feet one by one to relieve their ache, envious of those who sat.

"We could just get out of here," Xander said.

"But how will they get home?"

Xander shrugged. "Let's ask them."

Gwen and Theo were still on the dance floor, in the same pose with their arms around each other, a contrasting pair of dark clothes and vibrant, shimmering color. They confirmed they'd order a cab home, and would make Terrance do the same. When they said goodbyes, Theo gave her a hug too, and a sense of acceptance washed over Nikki at the unexpected affection.

Nikki and Xander then went to the couch where Terrance was talking to the cat woman.

"Hey, this is Rachel," Terrance said, indicating the woman beside him. She had chin-length sleek black hair, large, upturned, almond-shaped eyes, and warm beige skin.

Nikki extended her hand to shake it, while Xander introduced her, saying, "I'm Xander, and this is my girlfriend, Nikki."

Nikki's heart fluttered, and a grin broke across her face, veins alight at hearing those words from Xander's mouth for the first time. It was good to hear them, but as they sank in she shriveled. She hated hiding herself from him, and she wondered when their illusion of normalcy would break.

Once they had repeated several niceties, gathered their things, and wished each other happy Halloween, Nikki and Xander stepped from the stifling, swampy bar into the refreshing bite of night, although the swell of sweat and pumping hearts still filled her senses, making her on edge.

"Oh man, I nearly forgot how good air feels," Xander said with a laugh.

"I know. Cool place, but a bit stuffy."

He stuffed his beard into his pocket and donned his hat, staff in one hand. He offered his arm to her with the other and said, "Ready?"

She nodded and wrapped her arm through his. A soft, misty rain had fallen while they were inside, a wet asphalt smell emanating from the city. Moisture clung to the air, whisking away the heat and sweat from their bodies. The leaves of deciduous trees decorated the ground and branches in reds, purples, yellows, and golds, coloring the town before the trees became skeletons, and the leaves were cleared away. Her heels clacked against the sidewalk, water spraying from the pores and cracks of the concrete pushed up from tree roots. The streets were surprisingly empty, some groups clustered on front porches, most houses dark. Silhouettes of critters flitted in the distance, darting between trees, cars, and houses, but they were few and far between.

The side street they parked on was in darkness, no nearby lamp to illuminate the drive. Nikki caught movement near Xander's car, a person hovering close to the passenger side window.

The residual adrenaline from the sweat and pounding blood from the club transformed into a cold fire in Nikki's stomach, and she took quick steps forward, disengaging from Xander as he remained frozen.

"Nikki, stop. We shouldn't—"

Nikki hissed, seething, seeing the dark figure using a slim jim, trying to shimmy open Xander's window. "He's breaking into your car!" Nikki said in a harsh whisper.

"Let's just call the cops, he could be violent."

"Are you kidding? We can't let him get away with this."

Nikki whirled on her heel, the anger in her chest filling her head with cold determination. Xander tried to grab her arm but missed, and fell into anxious steps behind her, whispering for her to stop. But she could only see red, this gloomy figure who thought he had the right to violate Xander's privacy, to take his property. A small voice whispered in the back of her mind that she shouldn't do this, that she should listen to Xander and let it be. But the hunter in her was awakened from the heady scents of arousal and sweat from the humans in the club, and it begged for blood to spill.

"Hey!" Nikki yelled. "Get away from there!"

The figure froze then straightened into a tall but scrawny male, wearing all black.

"What do you think you're doing?" Nikki yelled, walking closer to him as he turned, the wild fear in his eyes turning to disgust, to confidence, as he saw the small woman approaching him with a fidgeting man behind her.

"Nikki, stop, don't. Let's just get out of here—" Xander repeated, but Nikki couldn't hear him.

The thief's sneering face came into focus, revealing a broken nose, wet, brown eyes and patchy stubble. Rage fueled Nikki's body, and she charged, blood pounding in her ears, telling her to wipe that sneer off his ugly face.

A glint of metal flashed against the night, catching Nikki's palm as she lunged to grab his head. Nikki hissed and recoiled, and in the moment she clutched the hand to her chest, dipping back, a fist smacked against her head, a hard crack shooting in her skull.

"Oh my god, Nikki—"

"What the fuck?" the man yelped. Since her skin and bones were harder than a human's, his fingers snapped against her head.

A wild grin split Nikki's face, despite her dazed, pounding head. The fear on his face, the confusion, sent a bolt of adrenaline down her spine, the pace of his heartbeat increasing, beating in his arteries, a drumbeat in her mind she wanted to swallow.

The man's face fell, and he staggered back, dropping the knife. He turned on his heel to run, and Nikki leapt on him, shoving him to the ground on his back.

"Nikki, stop—"

"Oh man, what the fuck—" the man squealed, trying to throw her off him, but the strength in her body grounded him. She pulled him up and pounded him back against the ground, his skull and shoulder blades cracking, jarring him. His loose jacket had come unzipped, and his pulse beat hard in his neck. A pressure built in her chest until it burst from her throat in a powerful scream, a piercing high shriek directly in the man's face. He stopped struggling, staring vacantly up at her as blood trickled from his ears.

The sweet tang of metal flooded her nose, and she sighed with relief, mouth open and descending to the blood trickling down his neck—

"Nikki, that's enough!" Xander said, a hand on her shoulder, yanking her back.

She blinked hard, as if pulled from a dream. Adrenaline dissipating, she sickened at how close she was to licking the blood off his neck, to sinking her teeth into it. "What?"

"You've hurt him enough. You can stop."

"Oh," she said, looking down at the groaning, moaning man before her. His hair was matted with sweat and blood, his hand broken, tears streaming down his face. She stumbled off him, and with a whimper, he clambered to his feet, and with one horrified glance back at her, he ran down the street and into the night, knife and slim jim left behind.

Three bystanders, all in black, stood at the far corner, watching her and then following the man as he fled. A coldness, unrelated to the weather, swept through her body as she stared at the trio. A preternatural stillness emanated from their bodies, and fear crept through Nikki's spine.

Unfamiliar vampires, in their territory? These couldn't be the "friends" of Hormin he mentioned, could they? Why would they just be standing and staring at them?

She blinked, and they disappeared into the darkness as well.

Maybe they were just innocent bystanders, and her bloodlust made her sense something that wasn't there.

The fear and rage left her body, leaving a cold void behind. Her limbs became numb and heavy as she was pulled back to the violence she had just unleashed. She stared down at her hands, disbelieving they were her own. What had come over her? Nikki clenched them into fists, pushing her nails into her palms, punishing herself for losing control, for letting the rush of vampirism consume her.

"What the hell was that?" Xander asked. His face was drawn, a small smudge of blood coming from one ear.

"Oh my god, Xander. Did I do that?"

"My ear wasn't bleeding before you screamed, so yes. I think you perforated my eardrum."

"I'm so sorry," Nikki said, chest caving, moving to swipe the blood from his head, but hissing as the sting in her palm came alive, stopping her.

"Are you okay?" he asked, flipping her hand gingerly, her blood getting on his fingers. "We need to get this checked out."

"No. I'll be okay. What about you? Does your ear need to be looked at?"

"Most damaged eardrums heal fine on their own. If it gets worse I'll have it looked at tomorrow. But Nikki, that's a deep cut, and who knows what nasty things were on the blade. I really think we should take you to a hospital."

"Trust me. It'll be okay."

"Okay," he said, but he didn't sound convinced.

"Let's just go to my place. I'll bandage it there."

Xander shifted, brushing loose strands of hair from her face. After a moment's hesitation, he said, "Okay."

He opened the car door for her, and she sat down without looking at him, curling her injured hand into a loose fist. It itched with healing, and there was nowhere to place it without getting blood in his car, so she held it up, cupped, to keep the mess contained.

Once on the freeway, Xander shifted in his seat and cleared his throat. "You want to tell me what happened back there?"

Nikki hesitated, clenching and unclenching her palm, the dark silhouettes of trees flashing by. How could she explain the need to see his blood on the outside of his body? How satisfying it was to see the fear in his eyes?

"I don't know. It just made me so mad. Him breaking into your car. Sneering at me as if I was weak. Then once the knife came out, I couldn't control myself." Nikki sighed. "I didn't want you to get hurt."

"I didn't want you to get hurt either, Nikki, which is why I said we should hang back and call the cops."

"I couldn't just hang back. Maybe once. Not anymore," Nikki said, voice hardening as she tightened her fist and clenched her jaw, eyes fixed hard on the world zipping by her window.

Xander was quiet for several minutes, fidgeting in his seat before he pushed a hand through his hair. "Okay, and what the hell was that scream? I've never heard anything like it. It hurt."

"I'm sorry," Nikki said. "I couldn't help it. I didn't mean to scream that loud and I didn't mean to hurt you."

Xander sighed, but the tension didn't leave his body. "I know."

"Do you think differently of me, now?"

"No," Xander replied, without hesitation. "That was just really intense."

Nikki nodded, wondering if he really meant it.

Back on the waterfront, Xander parked in the guest parking of her apartment's garage.

"Can I come in for a while? To at least look at your hand?" Xander asked.

Nikki nodded, and outside the car, Xander grabbed a gym bag out of his trunk. The ride up the elevator felt like it took longer than usual, the silence between them extending the time.

In her apartment, Xander said, "I want to change out of this robe and then look at your hand. Is that okay?"

She nodded, and Xander went into the bathroom, closing the door. Nikki opened the fridge, one half-full thermos of blood in the door. Nikki glanced over her shoulder, checking Xander was still in the bathroom, and unscrewed the cap, ignoring the sting in her hand at the movement. Holding her breath, she gulped down the remaining blood. Nikki put the thermos down with a hard thud, gasping, a hand flying to her mouth as her esophagus clenched and the blood rose back into her throat. She swallowed, hunched over the kitchen sink to wash it down with water until the nausea subsided. When she leaned back from the sink, her body sang, the predator relaxed, and the world became as vibrant as the Milky Way.

Nikki hid the thermos and then checked her mouth in her phone's reflection. She found an old piece of minty chocolate in her cupboard and let it melt on her tongue, hoping it would cover the smell of viscous salt and metal.

Xander came out wearing jeans and a t-shirt, hair flipped wild around his head, rectangular glasses perched on his long nose.

"I didn't know you wore glasses. They look good," Nikki said, Xander putting his gym bag down near the couch and setting a smaller red bag on the island between them.

"Thanks," he said, mouth curling to one side before he closed the gap between their faces with a soft kiss. "Now, let's look at that hand."

Xander wrapped his hands under her thighs and lifted her so she sat on the counter, and Nikki gasped in surprise as he set her down.

He stood between her legs and took her right hand in his. Xander opened his red bag, filled with medical supplies.

"You travel with a first aid kit?"

"Play enough sports and you realize it's a good idea to have around. Plus, with being around young kids and animals, you never know when you'll need it." Xander wiped the blood from her hand, careful not to press too hard on her cut.

With the blood cleaned from her hand, Xander frowned, fingers splaying her hand open, moving it around. "I guess it's not as bad as I thought."

Nikki broke her gaze from Xander's face, where she had been watching him as he cared for her, his brow furrowed, hair hanging over his ears, and looked at her cut. It was a thin, red line across her palm. He moved the skin on the palm gingerly, trying to see the depth of the wound. It opened slightly but was not as wide as earlier.

"It's still a significant cut, but I think you can get away without stitches, if you're careful with it." Xander scratched his head with one finger, still looking at her hand. "That was a lot of blood for this shallow of a wound."

Nikki shrugged, heart in her throat, resisting the urge to pull her hand from his to scratch it, to hide the rapidly repairing cells. Xander squinted closer at the cut, then shrugged and swabbed disinfectant over it.

"How does it feel?" he asked.

"It hurts. And it itches. A lot."

Xander nodded and put some anti-itch cream on it, then wound it with a wide bandage and gauze to keep it in place. She continued to watch him, instead of what he was doing to her hand, taking his distraction as time to admire the width of his chest close to hers, the fall of his hair around his face, the set of his jaw, the confident movement of his arms as he worked, and the small furrow in his brow between the bridge of his glasses that she wanted to smooth away with the pad of her thumb.

"You should look at it a few times a day to check it isn't getting infected. Do you have antibacterial and bandages here?"

Nikki nodded.

"Good."

He started to put the medical supplies away, but Nikki put a hand on his arm and said, "Wait."

He paused, still standing between her legs. She placed her hand on his jaw, gently turning his head to the side. Nikki tucked waves of thick hair behind his ear, a dried trickle of blood coming out of it, stopping around his artery.

Her mouth clenched with desire, with the urge to lick the blood from his neck, to feel his pulse in her mouth, but instead, she took out one of his cleaning swabs and wiped it away.

"There," Nikki said, setting down the reddened swab.

"Thanks," he said, turning his face back to hers and setting his hands on her thighs.

"Are you okay?" Nikki asked, raising a hand to cup his cheek.

"Yes, are you?"

"I am. You're not mad at me?"

"No, I'm not mad. I was freaked out. Especially hearing you scream like that, but—" Xander's hands squeezed her thighs, then moved higher.

"But what?" she asked, heat rising in her body.

"But I was also impressed. I hate to admit it, but I'm really non-confrontational. I don't like to fight, and I'll avoid it at all costs."

"That's not a bad thing."

"It is when I can't protect the people I care about. Or when I can't stand up for them or myself when I need to. And even though you clearly don't need protecting, seeing you go into danger while I stood there, frozen and scared and uncertain...I felt weak and incompetent. I wish I could be braver for you," Xander said, tension leaving his shoulders.

"Oh, Xander," Nikki said, brushing her thumb against his face, a tender lump in her throat. "I don't need you to be brave. I like that you're not reactive. That you'd choose a method besides violence."

And maybe by staying near him, she could resist her own violent urges better.

Xander's mouth twisted into a weak smile, disbelieving. Nikki kept her hand on his face, the stubble sharp against her skin, and brought his face down to hers.

Their lips barely touched, soft and sweet. Nikki's hand moved up to the back of his head, through his hair, the other winding around his back. As they breathed each other in, their kiss became deeper, stronger, Xander's hands moving up her legs to her lower back, pressing their bodies flush against each other. Nikki wrapped both arms around his shoulders, legs twining around his hips. Xander slid her off the counter, hands under her legs, holding her up. Without breaking their lips, Xander carried her to the bedroom. He laid her on the bed, where clothes peeled off one by one, and they lost themselves slowly in each other's skin and sighs.

Chapter Twenty-Two

THE NEXT DAY passed in a blissful blur and ended all too quickly. He didn't bring up her irrational outburst, but checked her hand again and marveled at how fast it was healing. She plastered on a fake smile and reiterated that the cut really wasn't as bad as he had thought it was, and she hated herself for the lie.

The nights and days passed in a daze of Xander, him staying at her house most nights. He met her at the library when she was there and came home with her. They talked about her going to his place, where he lived with Terrance, but they preferred the privacy of her apartment. Xander offhandedly invited her to visit with his family and siblings a few times, too, and with a sick twist of guilt she always turned him down, finding some excuse around schoolwork. They managed to keep their hands off each other long enough to study and do homework, wrapping around each other as soon as the work for the day was done. When she woke up alone in the afternoons, she had her cup of blood, which was better than coffee to prepare her for the day. She still had to gag it down, but it got easier every day, especially as her body craved it more. Blood made her feel strong, alive, alert.

They were well-fed, and well-loved, and Nikki thought those days in their own bubble were some of the best of her life. She finally didn't feel sick most of the time, she trusted her impulses more, and she wasn't constantly guilted or judged by others. Her gums ceased their aching as her fangs finally settled, Xander making a few comments about how sharp her teeth were when they kissed, although that didn't stop him. His pulse, his earthy, fruity scent still filled her mind with the sweetest intoxication, yet she cared enough, was scared enough, to resist the pounding beat of his blood, even when it pulsed against her ear, near her mouth.

A few times, cold hands crept across her back, startling her, but as she turned and saw no one, she relaxed. She heard no whispers, but sometimes she felt that expansive pressure in her mind, as if someone else was crawling around in her head, pushing out her skull. But it was easy to ignore when she basked in the glow of his presence, the curl of his mouth when he smiled, the flip of his hair as he tossed his head back and laughed.

Their routine was funny, having a few hours of overlapping sleep schedule. She pushed herself to stay awake to say goodbye to him in the morning, yet it made waking up with ample time to work before classes more difficult. She managed it, and wished their schedules were more aligned, but was grateful he was so easy going with how different she was. She didn't mind eating dinner for lunch and breakfast for dinner, as long as he was happy, and kept looking at her like she was the only person in the world.

When he invited her over to his parents' house for Thanksgiving, she knew she should say no. Her heart skipped a beat at the thought of being with his family, and unbidden thoughts that maybe she should step back now, before she hurt him or anyone else ran through her head. But before she could turn him down she looked into his eyes, so full of warmth and hope, that she couldn't say no. Nikki told herself it would be a good opportunity to learn more about where he came from. Why meeting him made her hear voices. And, if it really was the Mother talking to her, why she wanted him.

In turn, she made plans for him to meet her parents on Black Friday. Probably an even worse idea than her meeting his family, but her parents hounded her for details on him and the expression of pure joy on his face when she invited him made her forget her doubts.

Maybe once they were around Xander, her parents would have an idea of what made him so unique. Maybe they could explain what his scent meant.

Before that, though, she had to suffer through the maturation gathering.

That evening, Xander called her to chat, and he wished her a good evening at the party, a hesitation in his voice, as if hoping she would change her mind and invite him. Of course she hadn't told him what the party was really for, instead saying it was just a gathering of her parents' friends. A tightness clenched in her chest at lying, at keeping him away, but she knew it was best. She didn't trust the whole coven to keep him safe and undrained.

Night descended early, thanks to a large patch of deep grey clouds that stretched from horizon to horizon. She layered up and took the risk, driving to her parents' house before full sundown, thanking the overcast sky for its cover.

With the back driveway freshly paved, she was able to park behind the garage, happily avoiding the rows of alders along the walkway. Yet, when she parked the car, she hesitated to leave. The air felt thick and heavy with the pressure of an incoming storm. She pushed past it and climbed out of her car, pressing the button for the garage door, and watched as it creaked up, a dull squeak along the tracks.

With the garage door fully opened, she took a long, deep breath and forced herself to leave. A bag of empty thermoses in hand, the weight heaved against her body, her limbs anchoring to the concrete when she tried to step.

Nikki twisted to glare at the forest, the sudden resistance of her body igniting a fire in her sternum. Movement shifted behind the trees, and she squinted, but the shape passed, either a deer or her imagination as the wind teased through the trees.

Nikki strained against the mud in her veins, putting all her energy into taking a step forward.

The weight lifted between one step and the next, and she stumbled forward as the extra force nearly made her trip over herself. The fire turned to rage, a snicker carrying through her mind on the breeze. She turned to scream at the world, but there was no one there, and she clamped down hard on the heat in her core, but it pressurized instead of extinguished, maintaining an irritation within her.

The interior of the house bustled with life—a stark contrast to the dark bitterness of the changing seasons. The hired cooks sweltered in the heat-drenched kitchen, ovens and stovetops ablaze. Cleaners dusted and vacuumed, the Walkers were dressed in their serving attire, trailing Cat with focused expressions as she delegated the schedule for the evening.

"Ah, there you are, my darling," her mom said, sweeping toward her in a lacy, long-sleeved, floor-length black gown, two centuries out of fashion. Her mom spread open her arms, the wide sleeves draping to her elbows, long gloves wound high up her arms.

Nikki let her mom engulf her in a hug, which felt more like donning a blanket than an embrace. Her mom grabbed her face and kissed her cheeks, and Nikki looked her up and down.

"You look..."

"Exquisite?" her mom replied, grinning.

"Yes. That's absolutely the word I was looking for," Nikki said, fighting down her sarcasm.

Cat's nose scrunched, sensing it, but she shook it off and squeezed Nikki's jaw gently to open her mouth. "Let's see those fangs."

Nikki groaned but obliged, her fangs just longer than a human canine.

"Looks like they still have room to grow."

"Or maybe they'll stay this length. Less freakish."

Cat gave Nikki a stern look, lips pinching into a thin line. "Yes. Well. Are you ready for tonight?"

"Ready? I thought I didn't have to do anything."

"Nothing out of the ordinary. Doesn't mean you get to do nothing all night."

"What do I have to do?" Nikki asked, heart dropping into her stomach.

"Say some words, drink some blood."

"The usual vampire thing, then."

"Not the 'usual' one, but yes. As I said, nothing out of the ordinary. Don't fret about it."

"Then why'd you ask me if I was ready?"

"It's called making conversation, Nicoletta."

"It's not ever just 'conversation' with you."

"Hmph. Well. I'm glad you think so highly of me. As if I'm riddled with hidden agendas."

"You aren't?"

Her mom fixed her with a hard stare, eyes dark as obsidian. "I don't know if you're intentionally antagonizing me, but there is too much to do for you to be trying my patience. Go talk to your father. That man is just lazing around the lounge. Entirely unhelpful."

"Would you even let him help if he tried?"

"Probably not," her mom said, stern face turning to a smirk as she glided away into the glow of the dining room, leaving Nikki in the hallway.

Nikki put her thermoses on the kitchen counter, the cooks not noticing her presence in their frenzy. She found her dad in his usual spot in the large armchair in front of the fireplace in the lounge.

"Come in, come in," her dad said, not turning toward her, waving her in as he sensed her in the doorway.

Nikki sat in the opposite armchair. "How's hiding out going for you?"

"That obvious, eh?" he asked, a tight grin on his face. "Can you blame me? Your mother is a fright in this state. Best to stay out of her path."

"I don't blame you. She doesn't either."

"Yes, she knows how she can be." Her dad stood, and as he walked to the bar, asked, "What do you want to drink? Blood? Whisky? Wine?"

"Whisky. I think I'll need it to get through tonight."

"A house full of old bloodsuckers doesn't thrill you, eh?"

Nikki chuckled. "No. Not one bit. After seeing mom, I think this night is more for her than for me."

Miguel tapped a finger to his nose and brought her the whisky, fresh blood in his own glass. "I would drink with you, if I could." He raised his glass and clinked it to hers. "We'll get through tonight. Don't worry."

"I'll try," Nikki replied, taking another burning sip of whisky and reclining in the armchair. Her dad didn't pressure her to talk, and she appreciated that. She wasn't in the mood to be around people, let alone speak with them. They simply relaxed together, enjoying the sound of the fireplace. When she drained her glass, her dad offered to refill it, and she accepted, wanting to ease the apprehension at whatever the evening would entail. The doorbell rang halfway through her second glass, and her mom flew into the lounge, demanding Nikki go upstairs to get ready.

"I am ready."

"You are not. Go upstairs and put on the clothes I laid out for you. You are not to come downstairs until beckoned."

"Why?"

"It's part of the ceremony, darling."

Nikki groaned.

"Hush. Guinevere will be here soon, and she will paint your face."

"I have to put makeup on?"

Her mom gave her a stern look, and with a reluctant sigh, Nikki downed the last of her whisky, and gave her dad a kiss on the cheek as she left.

Nikki picked up the fabric displayed on her bed. It was a long, black dress, with a large hood and flowing sleeves that widened on the forearm.

"We're in a coven not a cult," Nikki grumbled, changing into the hooded gown.

The doorbell rang again, followed by Gwen's exuberant voice ricocheting through the house until it went suddenly quiet. Nikki frowned, straining her ears, to hear where she may have gone. A few minutes later, rapid footsteps ran up the stairs, and her door swung open without a knock, Gwen charging in with purpose, wearing flattering autumnal colors and dropping a large purse on the floor, trinkets and bottles clanking and rolling with the thunk.

"Are you in a cult now?" Gwen asked, looking Nikki up and down.

"That's what I said," Nikki replied. "What did you do down there? I heard you come in. Then nothing."

Gwen huffed, stepping into the room and closing the door behind her. "Tyee wants my assistance tonight."

So, that's who rang the doorbell the first time.

"With what?"

"Why, the ceremony, of course," Gwen said. "I don't know if I can do what she wants me to, but I guess I have to try. Maybe it will end in disaster and we can get out of here."

"Maybe. Though you're skilled enough that I doubt it."

"Want me to sabotage it on purpose?"

Nikki laughed. "No, thanks. My mom would kill me."

"Yeah, she's in a tizzy about this whole thing, isn't she?"

"You have no idea."

"Well, let's make mother proud. Go on, sit," Gwen said, pointing at the vanity. "We'll make you a sexy vampiress yet."

"I don't think the purpose of tonight is to be sexy."

"You didn't know? Sexiness is the purpose of all vampire activities."

"That's news to me."

"Well, you haven't lived with my sisters." Gwen put her finger in her mouth and feigned a gag.

"I hope you wash that finger before you put it on my face."

"Even with your near impeccable immune system, you're a germophobe?"

"No. It's just the imagery."

"Right, right," Gwen said, pulling sanitizing wipes from the bottomless purse she brought in.

"Are you okay?" Nikki asked, realizing that this whole time Gwen hadn't stood still for one moment.

"Who me? Being forced to be with my asshole family? Oh yes, yes, I'm fine. Noooo problem. It's all groovy, baby," Gwen said, digging through her bag, pulling out assorted brushes and makeup.

"You don't have to be here, Gwen. I appreciate it. But really. Don't torture yourself."

"And miss my best friend's vampiric initiation? I don't think so." Gwen set the decided upon materials on the vanity. "I'm sorry I'm all over the place."

"You're okay. I understand."

"Good. Now shush and let me do my magic."

"Yes ma'am."

"That's more like it," Gwen said, uncapping the eyeliner.

For dramatic effect, Gwen turned her chair away from the mirror and didn't let her look at herself until her makeup was done. When her best friend spun her around, Nikki took in her face. She had dramatic cat-eye makeup, burgundy lips, and soft blushing cheeks.

"See? Sexiness," Gwen said.

"Not sure that's what I'd call it but thank you."

"Take a selfie and send it to Xander. I bet he'll agree with me."

"Or it'll just upset him that he's not here."

But Gwen didn't listen, snatching Nikki's phone and taking a photo of her. "You look a little dead inside, but he'll love it."

Gwen handed the phone back to her, already having sent the photo. Nikki did look glum, shoulders hunched, mouth in a serious line, eyes dark and unreflective.

Gwen packed up her things and said, "Now, enjoy your solitude. Your mom made me promise to leave as soon as I was done. No one is supposed to see you until the dinner begins."

"Great. So I'm being presented. Like a bride."

"Pretty much. Have fun!" Gwen said with a laugh, leaving Nikki alone.

Nikki sat in silence, not knowing what to do with herself as she waited, the fluttering of anxiety building in the pit of her stomach, in her fingertips, as the clock ticked. Xander responded as Gwen anticipated, with much appreciation for her appearance and several inappropriate comments about what he'd like to do to her that made her smile, cringe, and blush at the same time.

The doorbell rang in sporadic bursts as members of the coven arrived. Nikki could vaguely make out their voices, which quickly settled, likely disappearing into the dining room. Footsteps scurried and scuffed along the floorboards, chairs screeched, and bubbles of quiet laughter rose from downstairs.

After what felt like hours, the house descended into a deep quiet, and Nikki's pulse skyrocketed, sensing the impending summoning. A few minutes later, a delicate but certain footfall came up the steps, and a sharp knock thudded twice against her door.

"Nicoletta?" her mom said.

Nikki opened the door.

"You look wonderful. Are you ready?"

Nikki nodded and sucked in a deep breath. Her mom put her arm out flat for Nikki to rest her arm on top of and guided her down the hall to the staircase, all the lights dimmed low, no brighter than candle flames.

The dining room table was unadorned, except with empty, heavy gold and silver goblets and small bowls with various leaves and bark in front of each member, tall bone-white candle holders with even taller candlesticks casting ghostly flames across the coven.

The largest goblet had been placed at the head of the table, so wide it was nearly a bowl. Cat guided her to the spot and sat to the left of her, her dad to Nikki's right.

Nikki looked around the table, at all members of the coven staring at her, Hormin's dominating presence radiating off him in waves. He sat unnaturally still, a smirk plastered on his face as candlelight danced in his dark eyes. Suppressing a shiver she looked at the rest of the coven, Gwen's eyes downcast, sulking, sunk into her chair with her arms crossed, across the table from her family, wedged between the Lius and Ivarsson brothers. Gwen was the only one not wearing black or grey.

"No," Nikki said.

Her mom's face fell. "No what, darling?"

"Gwen sits next to me."

"That's not—"

"It's my party, isn't it?"

Her mom nodded.

"Then she sits next to me," Nikki said and pushed her chair to the right, making space for Gwen to squeeze to her left. "Gwen?"

Gwen stood with a grateful glance at Nikki, chair screeching.

Bridget, red hair shining like flowing blood in the candlelight, sneered. "Why don't you just tell her to leave? She doesn't belong here."

Gwen stiffened with a sharp intake of breath and spat, "And why don't you just go fuck yourself?"

"How dare you? This stupid little witch shouldn't–"

"Enough!" Tyee yelled from the opposite head of the table, lifting a hand, commanding them to cease.

Bridget grimaced, crossed her arms, and sank back. Gwen stuck her tongue out at her and picked up her chair, carrying it to the head.

Hormin snickered and buried his face in his goblet, although the rest of the coven ignored the interaction. Nikki glanced at Gwen's family, Bronwen and Farrell looking embarrassed, Bridget and Brienne affronted, while Connell and her parents seemed indifferent to their family squabbles. Nikki's gut twisted with disgust.

Gwen sat beside Nikki with a victorious tilt to her chin, and once Gwen was settled, Nikki sat herself, grabbing Gwen's hand under the table. The dining room filled with a heavy quiet, save for the creak of the wind against the house, and the soft flicks of the flame eating the candlewicks.

Satisfied all would be still and silent, Tyee stood, candlelight emphasizing the sharp tilt of her cheekbones, the strength of her jaw, sending orange streaks through the long, black braid that hung over one shoulder. She dressed in a black gown similar to Nikki's, but with a dark red sash across her waist and sleeves that did not widen at the elbows.

"Tonight, we celebrate the transformation of Nicoletta Neves Silva, from fledgling to fully arisen." As Tyee spoke, her dad took her other hand in his and gave it a tight, supportive squeeze. She met her mom's eyes, briefly, and Cat flashed her a proud grin. "Most of us have known Nikki since before birth, and have watched her grow into the beautiful, motivated vampire she is today. Others have met her only recently yet admire her compassion and ambition. Few children are born from those who are Made, and even fewer survive to adulthood. It is with great honor that I stand before you all tonight, to bless the Silvas and their only child."

The coven shifted, facing forward in their seats, rain pattering against the glass behind Tyee.

"Gwen, if you would," Tyee said, extending a hand for Gwen to rise.

Gwen stood, releasing her clammy hand from Nikki's and wiping her palms.

Tyee nodded, and Gwen lifted her hands, threads of gold and silver illuminating the gloom, pooling into Gwen's hands as the air in the room sucked toward her, flames pulling toward Gwen, the room getting heavier as the air condensed and concentrated.

"Now, all but Nikki, repeat after me," Tyee said, nodding to Gwen, who exhaled, releasing the tension and strands of magic. A soft breeze pushed through the room, lifting hair from the coven members' faces, the candle flames guttering, and a soft tunneling sound reverberating as the air swirled around the metal goblets.

"Breath of the Creator—for life," Tyee said.

"Breath of the Creator—for life," the coven chanted, voices echoing in the room, pulling the goblets back in front of them.

Tyee cupped a handful of bark and leaves from the bowl in front of her, crushed it in her palm, and as the pulverized remnants of earth fell into the goblet in front of her, she said, "Bones of the Mother, for eternality."

"Bones of the Mother, for eternality," the coven repeated, crushing the plant debris in their palms, pouring the dust into their goblets.

Nikki frowned. What in the world was this leading up to?

Tyee uncapped a small flask, and the coven mirrored her movements, pulling flasks and thermoses from beside their seats and opening them, the rich, metallic scent of blood filling the room.

"Blood of the familiar—for strength," Tyee said, pouring the blood into the air-kissed goblets and crumbled plants.

"Blood of the familiar—for strength," the coven repeated, pouring blood into the goblets, swirling the glasses to mix the crushed leaves and bark.

"Now, Nikki, if you would please lift the bowl from your chalice."

Nikki's brow furrowed, but she wrapped her hands around the cup of the goblet and twisted, the cup unlatching from the stem, becoming a mere bowl in her hand.

"Rise," Tyee said, and Nikki obeyed, standing with both hands cradling her empty bowl.

Her dad stood beside her, picking up a spare candle and placing it in the hollow stem of the chalice.

"Flame of the Father, for spirit," Tyee chanted, and her dad lit the candle, the flame directly underneath the bowl Nikki held.

"Flame of the Father—for spirit," the coven chanted, and Miguel picked up his goblet.

"May the night keep you," her dad said, pouring the blood and plant mix into Nikki's bowl and sitting.

Feng, who sat beside Miguel, stood next, bringing his goblet to hers, and whispering, "May the night keep you," as he poured his mix in with her father's.

One at a time, each member of the coven stood to mix the contents of their cups into the bowl in her hand. The Lopez children were solemn and serious, guided by their parents when it was their turn. The metal of the bowl warmed, her hands getting slick, and she watched the wilted flowers and desiccated leaves disintegrate as the blood heated.

Those who were believers opted to say "May the Mother bless you" instead, and so each member gave her their blessing, albeit Gwen's sisters did so begrudgingly.

When Hormin stood beside her and poured his mixture into her glass, he whispered, "May you bless the Mother, and the Mother bless you in turn," and the push of his breath on her skin raised the hairs on her neck. What was that supposed to mean?

Hormin stepped away quickly, releasing her from his oppressive aura, and Gwen poured hers into Nikki's before Cat, who was supposed to be the last to give her a blessing.

Her mom touched a delicate hand to the back of Nikki's head, dark eyes glistening as she said, "May the Mother bless you." She kissed Nikki's forehead before returning to her seat.

Tyee stood at the opposite end of the table when all the mixtures were in Nikki's bowl, and raised her hand, bidding Nikki drink.

Nikki hesitated. Was she serious? She was supposed to drink this strange concoction? But no one broke the silence, and Nikki tried to hide her grimace.

Nikki raised the bowl to her face, hands moist and hot. The mix reeked of warm blood and old plants, and she held her breath as she forced herself to swallow, remnants of bark and wood sliding down her throat with the viscous liquid. She followed the swallow with a deep inhale, hoping the air would keep the cocktail down.

Once Nikki set the bowl on the table, Tyee said, "With each member's earth and blood coursing through your body, we welcome you, Nicoletta Neves Silva, as a fully formed vampire to the coven for the first time."

Silence filled the room, and everyone stared at her, as if waiting.

Through a blood-coated mouth, coarse with leaf matter, Nikki said, "Thank you."

The chandelier overhead turned on, Cat standing by the switch, and the dark ritualism from the room lifted in the dim light. Her dad licked his fingers and snuffed out the candle, removing it from the stem of the chalice, indicating for Nikki to replace her bowl.

Nikki twisted it back on, surprised her grip did not slip, and sat down, relieved as conversation broke between the coven and eyes were off of her.

"You are, unfortunately, expected to drink this whole chalice," her dad whispered, standing behind Nikki to help her scoot her chair closer to the table.

"I am?" Nikki said, disgust clotting her throat.

"Yes. If you don't, it suggests rejection of the coven. And as your mother would tell you, it would be rude not to. The blood is from each member's servants, the leaves and bark from their own land. They gathered it all for you."

Nikki stared at the glittering chalice, light and gold reflecting the candlelight, blood glistening with the reflection of the chandelier above, bits of plants still floating across the surface.

"I have some Tums," Gwen whispered.

"I might need them," Nikki said, stomach churning with the thought of drinking more of that terrible mix. "By the way, how did you do that, with the air? It was beautiful. And impressive."

"It was hard," Gwen said, throwing her hair over her shoulder, a streak of sweat threading down the side of her face, the hair on the back of her neck damp.

Nikki took her hand, trying not to flinch at how ice-cold it was. "Thank you for being here. Are you okay?"

Gwen waved her off with the un-held hand. "Just a consequence of stretching the magic. I need to practice that skill more."

Nikki nodded and wrapped her other hand over Gwen's to warm it.

Staff brought out platters of food, leaving them covered as they shuffled back and forth until all the dishes were on the table. When Gwen's temperature had warmed, Nikki took small sips from the chalice, focusing on the strength and heat it infused into her body, rather than the earthy and metallic taste it left in her mouth, careful not to choke on petioles and bark.

More staff shuffled around the table, removing the goblets and placing dinner in front of the coven. She looked at the faces of the coven, and wished she could be looking at Xander instead, that he could be here beside her, too. He was probably asleep by now, and unharmed, unknown to those around her.

Platters were uncovered, revealing a feast of meats and vegetables, the Lopez children squirming in their seats with impatient hunger. Nikki's stomach growled as the scent of roasted, smoked, and seasoned food overpowered the stench of blood.

As the Born dished up, the staff brought decanters of blood from the kitchen, filling the goblets of the Made first, leaving extra decanters on the table for the Born.

"I miss the days of wild hunts," Feng said, drinking the blood from his goblet. "When blood was not just hot but fresh, and you could feel the life return to you, flowing from one individual to another."

The Ivarssons and O'Brennans nodded. Gwen's dad said, "You're not the only one."

"How about you, Hormin? How do you like your blood? Fresh, or refrigerated?" Feng asked.

"Fresh, obviously. When all the flavors of life are pumping through the body, when they haven't settled and congealed. No microwave can beat the heat provided by a living, loving heart."

Feng grinned and glanced at Tyee. "I'm glad we're in agreement, about that at least. Perhaps, then, with a new addition to the area, we can amend our rules? Allow those of us the opportunity to indulge now and then?"

"Feng, I cannot deny that I relished the days of fresh hunts, too. Perhaps, if things were different for vampires, if we were not forced into being shadows and legends, we could indulge in that practice. But as it stands, our survival depends on obscurity. Until the day we can be free to roam the earth, my answer will always be no," Tyee responded.

"Other covens still get to hunt," Feng said, and Daiyu put a gentle hand on her husband's leg, trying to hush him.

"Yes, and you know how much turnover they have. I will not

tolerate the recklessness of the covens in Seattle or the Bay Area, whose members frequently put the entire coven at risk. Death is not worth the fleeting moment of pleasure."

"We are smaller and older. We know how to hide evidence."

"Perhaps once. But forensic science is too efficient now. I will not risk the law. The wise farmer sustains their livestock for years, to have a lasting supply of food, rather than indulges in periodic gluttony and long interludes of starvation."

Feng sneered. "You said yourself, the population is growing. There is room to cull the herd. Isn't there, Hormin?"

"Oh no, do not drag me into this. While I agree with the sentiment, it is up to your leader to make the rules, not me."

Nikki grimaced, nausea worsening, imagining people as livestock, as nothing more than food to be farmed. Gwen's hand tightened on her own, clearly feeling the same.

Tyee stood, hands planted on the table, looming. The air thickened, the flames sputtered, and the room creaked with tension. "Thank you, Hormin, for the support. Feng, I have told you time and time again, the answer is no. We have long lives, it is possible that our status may change while we walk the earth, and we can have some of our old freedoms back. It may even happen sooner than you think," Tyee winced, as if she said something she should not have, and a worm of sickness coiled in Nikki's stomach. "If you cannot wait, if you desire to be reckless, then go. Join the vampires who defile life and abuse our gifts. You are free to leave, but if you do, you will leave the West Coast. And you will never be welcomed back. You may risk your own life. You may not risk the rest of ours."

Tyee stared at Feng, unblinking, looking like a predator about to strike, a goddess about to sentence damnation. Feng adjusted in his seat, shifting away from her as he crossed one leg over the other, and said, "Fine."

The weight lifted from the room, and the house shifted as the wind creaked against wood, and Tyee eased.

"But I want a larger food supply, if you won't let us hunt at least let us have more thralls," Feng said.

"We can discuss that at the solstice," Tyee said, picking up her fork and knife, cutting into the blood pie on her plate. Feng's mouth opened, but before he could speak, Tyee said, "If you question me one more time this evening, I will cut out your tongue and feed it to the crows."

Feng clenched his jaw, hands tightening on the goblet. A dull thud sounded as the metal gave way beneath his hands. Embarrassment for Feng washed over her, although he did not cower, as Nikki was sure she would under Tyee's ire.

"Hey, now, that is our nicest set of goblets. Let's not crush them, eh?" her dad said, keeping his voice light.

"My humblest apologies," Feng replied, downing the blood in one long gulp. He put his fingers on the inside of the cup and pushed it out, resetting the metal before folding his hands in his lap, keeping himself still until he calmed.

The electricity bled from the air, and the room filled with the scrapes of utensils on plates, chewing, and sipping, Tyee's large presence still weighed on them all, even outshining Hormin's, the children wearing wide-eyed expressions of terror.

Gwen exhaled and asked Cat, "Is there any wine?"

"Yes, of course," Cat replied and signaled to the staff near the door to bring out several bottles.

Conversation crawled back into the room, hushed and hesitant. Nikki felt sick from blood, bark, and anxiety, and finished the dinner with a plain bread roll, hoping it would soak up the nausea in her stomach. She couldn't help but flick her gaze to Hormin every now and then, and although they never made eye contact, she couldn't help but still feel he was watching her.

The coven indulged in silence, the Made drinking blood, eyes staring in longing at the food. Halvar checked his watch and whispered to his brother, who nodded, and they stood.

"Mr. and Mrs. Silva," Halvar said, "we must depart if we are to reach home before the sun rises."

Tyee stood as well. "I assume the offer still stands."

Halvar nodded, and Tyee said, "Then I must leave as well, Cat and Miguel. I have not been to the ocean in too long and don't want to miss this chance. Thank you for the hospitality and the wonderful food."

"You're welcome," Cat said. Nikki's parents stood, the rest of the coven taking the hint and following suit. Hormin leaned back on his chair and stretched, releasing a long, weighty sigh.

Tyee caught Nikki's eye and tilted her head, beckoning for Nikki to follow.

"You can hide in my room if you want. I'll be right back," Nikki whispered to Gwen, who stiffened as her family looked at her with expressions of varying degrees of indifference, disgust, and guilt.

"Thanks," Gwen replied, leaving in a flash of dark copper waves, vacating the room without confrontation.

Nikki squeezed past the coven and found Tyee standing outside on the front porch in cold darkness, the light by the door turning on as it sensed Nikki's movements.

Tyee turned and said, "Walk with me."

Nikki ducked her head in obeisance and fell into step beside Tyee, heart hammering as they approached the lines of red alders, Tyee's powerful silence making Nikki's hands fidget and clasp. She was filled with more blood than she may have ever had in her life, and the rush of sensory stimulation threatened to overwhelm her. The rush of wind through each leaf, the smell of decaying plants, the added definition to the silhouettes of the forest, their footsteps thudding on the pavement, the bending and reaching of the trees toward her—

"You did well for having an aversion to blood."

Snapped back to herself, Nikki replied, "I don't know what you mean."

"There are few secrets in the coven, Nikki."

Xander flashed across her mind, and her breath shortened. "I know."

"Why do you have that aversion?" Tyee asked.

"It feels wrong."

"Yet you consume the flesh of animals."

"They're not human."

"No, but humans are animals. Is there such a difference?"

"To me there is."

Tyee held her hands behind her back and paused under the dying alders. "It is curious, that we, humans included, are the only ones who question our place in the food chain. Who bemoan it. Revile it."

"We have a greater conception of what it is to take life."

"Perhaps. However, the vampire is the only predator that does not need to kill its prey to obtain sustenance."

Nikki paused, looking away from Tyee's face into the darkness behind the row of trees. "I never thought of it that way."

"It's a great privilege to survive without having to kill."

"But we still hurt them. Humans."

"Not without their gain."

"Being brainwashed isn't a gain."

Tyee fixed her with an unblinking stare. "Did you never ask your previous human boyfriend, or his parents, why he works for your parents? Why they donate their blood?"

Nikki shook her head. "I didn't want to know. I didn't want to hear him say he was like Feng's thralls."

"I see," Tyee said, returning her gaze to the distance before turning her eyes back to Nikki's. "Humans gain much by our relationship. It is a symbiosis, of a sort."

"A parasitic one."

"You harbor much bitterness for a blessed life."

Nikki exhaled, stilling the cold rage building in her sternum at Tyee for ambushing her with this conversation. "What do they gain then?"

"Knowledge. Protection. The potential for eternal life."

Nikki bit down a scoff. "And how often does one get that potential? It's just a manipulation."

"I see I will not change your mind. I do not seek to. Just to remind you of our gifts. Of our privilege." Tyee cast her eyes to the ground, and Nikki followed her gaze, a dark red splotch staining the concrete. "That's quite a head wound. And no scar to be found," Tyee said, returning her searching gaze to Nikki's face.

"Yes. Well," Nikki said, clearing her throat and crossing her arms, clasping her biceps. "I see your point."

"I hope so," Tyee said, and resumed walking down the path, Nikki following a step behind.

They stopped at the curve where the walkway met the road, the Ivarssons' car idling. Tyee looked at the dark silhouettes of the forest around them, barely visible against the sky, her back to Nikki.

"I have heard whispers on the wind, felt the earth pull against my bones," Tyee said.

Nikki froze, chills winding up her spine.

Tyee looked at Nikki over her shoulder. "I suggest you heed the call if you have as well. Failing to do so puts the entire coven at risk. And that, I will not tolerate."

"I don't know what you mean," Nikki said, but her wringing hands betrayed her.

"You do. I think you are one of the few people who truly knows why Hormin is here." Tyee's fierce gaze bored into Nikki, but she held her tongue. Tyee sighed. "I do not want harm to come to you or things you hold precious, but if it takes one sacrifice to keep our coven safe, then that is the greater good. As is serving the Mother, the One who we would not exist without. Disobeying Her puts the eyes of Her most devoted on us. Puts all of us at risk of earning Her disfavor. No good would come of that. Do you understand?"

Tyee's dark eyes penetrated Nikki's, seeing into her heart, her bones turning to ice. A breeze pushed against Nikki's back, pushing her hair into her face, and with a stiff nod, a tightness in her throat, Nikki replied, "I understand."

Tyee turned back to the dark, overcast sky and whispered, "I hope so," before opening the car door and sitting in the passenger seat, disappearing with the Ivarssons into the blanket of night.

Chapter Twenty-Three

Nikki rubbed her hands against her arms as she walked back to the house, willing the goosebumps to fade from her skin. Yet she felt eyes on her the whole way, an eerie crawl cascading up and down her flesh.

The house was warm, and the coven hovered in the entryway with their jackets and scarves, ready to say goodbye. They each bid her farewell and congratulations, nothing more than a mere nod from Gwen's family and quiet smiles from Feng and Daiyu. Before the Lopezes left, they gave her a new molding, one that would fit along the entire top row of her gums and hide the sharpness of her fangs. It would make her teeth look large, but at least the fangs would be less conspicuous. She thanked them as profusely as they congratulated her, and the kids hugged her with the erratic energy that tired children get. Hormin was the last to leave, eyes twinkling with a sloppy grin. He clasped a commanding hand on her shoulder and whispered, "Congratulations," before sweeping out of the house. With a last gust of cold air from outside, the house slammed into silence, her parents on either side of her.

"Did Tyee require something important?" her mom asked, hands held tight in front of her abdomen.

"No, just to welcome me again as a full vampire."

Cat nodded, mouth a thin line, but didn't press Nikki for the truth.

"I'm beat," Nikki said, kissing her parents on the cheeks. "Thanks for the party. It was...something."

"Yes, of course, darling," her mom answered. "Now, off to bed. I must raise my feet."

"Okay, Mom. Night, Dad."

"Goodnight, love," her dad responded, scooping Cat up into his arms. "Let's get you off those feet, eh?" Cat giggled as Miguel carried her up to their room.

Nikki twisted her hands together, Tyee's words echoing in her head. If Tyee knew what she heard, then it was no hallucination.

It meant that Hormin was here for Xander, for her.

And that meant the Mother must be real.

Right?

But what did she want with him? And why?

And what would happen if she didn't?

No matter what it was, it couldn't be good. No vampire demanded a human to offer them charity.

At her closed door, she unclasped her sweaty hands, fingers red from their twisting, a slight tremor under her skin as she reached for her doorknob.

Gwen lay on her bed, limbs spread wide, staring at the canopy. "What did Tyee want?"

Nikki fell back on the bed beside her. "I'm not sure. She was ambiguous."

"What do you mean?"

"I'm not sure if she threatened me or warned me. Or both?"

"Threatened you? About what?"

"The Mother? Hormin? The coven? Herself? I don't know. She said she's heard and felt things that I have, too. Without me telling her. She implied that Hormin is here for a special reason, and that I know why. That she knows why. She said I need to obey what I'm hearing, or else."

"Or else what?"

Nikki shrugged, blankets scrunching beneath her with the movement. "Or else the coven is at risk. She implied she'd punish me. Or someone would."

"I don't like the sound of that."

"Me neither."

"You're still hearing those voices then?"

"No. But I feel it, sometimes. Like someone else is with me. In my head. I feel it in my body, too. It's like a seizing of my blood. A golem at someone else's disposal." Nikki took a deep breath and said, "I've been denying it, and I know I should have talked to you about it sooner, but I just felt too ridiculous to admit what the voice said. I thought if I ignored it that would go away, but it only seems to be getting worse. Getting more real. I think... I think they want Xander."

"What? Why?"

"I don't know," Nikki said, twisting her hands again, "But hypothetically, if I'm not crazy and the Mother is real, what would She want with him?"

Gwen laid back on the bed with a hum of thoughtfulness. "I don't know, Nik. Probably something to do with that tasty smell from him you keep talking about."

Nikki knew Gwen was trying to lighten the situation, but she couldn't bring herself to laugh. She rested her head on her hands, wondering what was in his blood. "I don't know what to do."

"Are you going to give him up?"

"Of course not. But what am I supposed to do? Hide him? Protect him? Run away with him? Tell him? And what will happen to the coven if I don't? Tyee said it would put everyone at risk."

"Tyee is a badass, but she is ancient and traditional. Implying she knows what's going on with you, and that Hormin is on some secret mission, doesn't mean the Mother is real, or that anyone is in danger. Who knows what she is smoking up there all alone in those mountains."

Nikki couldn't help but laugh this time.

"I don't know the best course of action, Nik, but how I feel right now is fuck the supposed Mother and all Her zealots. Most of them are puritanical bigots. And Hormin just seems insane. Fuck them all, and fuck Tyee for threatening you. She should have told you explicitly why."

"Yeah," Nikki said, lying back again, pulling a pillow under her head. "I've been so scared about doing anything. Like what if I do something and it triggers a cascade of events I can't take back? I need more information."

Gwen hummed. "I'll pick Theo's brains."

"Pick her brains? You mean ask her outright?"

"Why not?"

"I assumed we'd aim for subtlety." A cold stone sank in her stomach. "I don't want the other coven members figuring it out. Seems like a bad idea for them to be aware of him. Of whatever is happening."

"Theo won't tell, if that's what you're worried about."

"No, I'm not worried about Theo. I'm worried about your family overhearing. And anyone else, really."

"Well, the concern about my family is valid. They're right fucks. I'll talk to her next time I'm at her place."

"Thanks." Nikki paused. "Please don't tell her I've been hearing things, though."

"Don't worry, I won't. But if you figure out the secret before I do, you have to let me know."

"I will," Nikki agreed, stifling a yawn, overcome with weariness. "I'm surprised you let Theo go over to your place, with how unhinged your family is."

"We go over during the day and my barrier keeps them out. As much as they like to torment me, the possessive nature of traditional vampires keeps Theo safe, I think. They know she is 'mine.'"

Nikki hummed understanding, then plunged the room into absolute darkness. Despite the anxieties swirling at the edge of her mind, she fell into a deep, gluttonous sleep.

Chapter Twenty-Four

Nikki saw Xander a few days later at the library, the cold breeze bringing in the scent of anise and figs, and she smiled before she even spotted him, feeling as if she hadn't seen him in ages. Nikki thought of Gwen's words, of his unique scent, wondering if it hinted at why he was special, and wondered what it could mean. Xander smiled wide when he saw her, running a hand through his matted hair to loosen it.

She returned his wide smile, wearing the tooth covers the Lopezes made her, feeling more confident in showing her teeth. Xander leaned down to kiss her, the wet tendrils of his hair flicking against her skin.

A dense pressure filled behind her eyes, chest tightening so hard she felt as if she was losing her breath.

"Are you okay?" Xander asked.

Nikki paused, nodded, the sudden headache dissipating into her shoulder muscles, stiffening them. She stared into his caring eyes and was reminded that it was too late to step back. She was too lost in him. And she couldn't leave him unprotected from whatever may come.

The tension in her shoulders clenched, a zap of pain shooting behind her eyes, momentarily blinding her. She shut her eyes tight and reopened them, blinking hard. "I think studying may be getting to me."

"Well, I know something we can do in the dark to distract you," he said with a smirk. "Want to get out of here?"

Nikki laughed and said, "Yes, please. If I have to read about DNA and genetic diseases anymore tonight, my brain may melt."

"We wouldn't want that," Xander said, and they packed up their things, leaving the library.

They chatted about classes, work, and lighter topics as they walked to Nikki's car, hand in hand. When they got to her parking spot and their hands began to separate, a sudden seizure rushed through her arm, muscles turning to concrete and bones to lead, tough and tight, clenching Xander's hand.

Xander exclaimed, fingers outstretched awkwardly in her tight grasp, and Nikki's heart raced despite the freeze in her spine, willing her arm to move, her hand to unclench, but it would not. Her arm became heavier and heavier, yet felt detached, as if it were no longer hers, though she could still feel Xander's skin against her palm, the bones crushing in her hand.

"What the hell?" Xander yelled, trying to twist his hand out from hers.

This is my hand. This is my *hand. Move, move, move,* she thought, watching in horror at Xander's frightened expression, the pain twisting his face. A dull pop released in her head, and her arm flung backward as control of it returned to her.

Xander cradled his hand to his chest, massaging his knuckles. "What the hell? That really hurt."

His voice was distant as Nikki brought her own hand close to her face, looking at it as if it wasn't her own. She shook as a cold fear wound up the back of her neck, and her eyes glassed over, smearing the shaking hand in her vision.

She flexed and clenched her fingers, raising her bleary vision to Xander's confused, hurt face. "I'm sorry. I didn't mean to."

He frowned, rubbing his hand, doubtful.

"I lost control of my arm."

"What do you mean, 'lost control of your arm?'"

"Whatever just happened was some sort of spasm. Or something. I don't know. My arm locked up and I couldn't move it. I'm so sorry. I'm so, so sorry," Nikki said, voice breaking as she swallowed the lump in her throat and blinked away her tears.

Xander hummed with concerned thought, shook out his hand, and took her shaking one in his own. He examined it, flipping it over, running his hand up and down her arm. "You're freezing."

"I am?" Nikki asked, faint.

He nodded, took her bag from her other shoulder, and wrapped his jacket around her, wincing each time he flexed his hand.

Nikki took it in her own, the skin around his knuckles red. "I'm so sorry," Nikki said, gently touching his skin.

"It'll be okay," he said. "I'll see if I can figure out what that was about, okay? Don't worry."

"I didn't mean to. I promise."

"I know. I know. We'll figure it out," he said and pulled her into an embrace. "Now let's get you home to rest, okay?"

She nodded against his chest, guilt curdling in her stomach, confusion and fear rippling in her veins.

On the road, Xander put his injured hand on her knee gently, and said, "It'll be okay."

Nikki was silent as she rubbed the pads of her fingers tenderly across his skin. "I feel like you're saying that to me a lot."

"Should I not be?"

"No. I just mean—I'm so sorry. For everything. For all of it. I'm ashamed, honestly," Nikki said, looking out the window, the raindrops splattered against the windows refracting the light from the streetlamps. "Strange things have been happening to me lately. I'm sorry you have to see it when we barely know each other. I wish I could make a better impression."

Xander squeezed her leg. "Don't worry so much. Consider me duly impressed upon. Besides, the amount of strange physiological events is not unheard of for illnesses."

"Maybe. But I don't want to hurt you, either."

"Seriously, Nikki, I'll be fine. I know you didn't do it on purpose. You know how much I've been injured in my life? This is nothing. Anyone asks, I'll tell them I had to fight someone to defend your honor. No one will believe it, but a guy can pretend, right?"

"A guy sure can," Nikki said with a small smile. "Thanks for being so forgiving."

Xander shrugged. "I don't see that there is anything to forgive. But if you really feel so bad about it, you can cook a feast for me again."

She laughed. "I can manage that."

The tension in Nikki's shoulders eased, and the guilt unwound as the conversation shifted to lighter topics. But still, she only half listened to Xander, the back of her mind wondering what had happened to her body this time. What had made her lose control of her arm?

At the apartment, Nikki heated up dinner while Xander researched what may have happened with her arm.

"Could have been a nervous issue?" he said. "I can find info regarding loss of feeling, like the arm goes limp, but not the opposite where the muscle seizes. We should ask one of our med profs."

And ask them if they think I'm crazy or just possessed by a deity? she thought.

"Maybe," she replied, but Xander had already returned his attention to his phone, and she was grateful to let the conversation drop.

Her arm remained her own the whole night, although she felt cold fingertips climb up the spine on her neck just after midnight. Her head shot up from the textbook at the tapping chill, but no one was behind her. Even after Xander went to bed she was wide awake, wondering what he was, what was going on with her, and what would happen to them.

Chapter Twenty-Five

Xander and Nikki saw each other almost every day, spent the nights at her apartment almost every night. Xander's hand bruised and healed. Nikki's limbs clenched and released, seemingly at random, and while a nuisance, she did not cause Xander pain again. Once, in an embrace, her arms locked and could not release him, but it wasn't hard enough to suffocate him. She still wasn't positive about what was happening, or why it was accompanied by pressure in her head and behind her eyes. Why it brought a sense of being watched from a dark corner, or someone listening in against a door. Those creeping sensations combined with Tyee's and Hormin's warnings, made her wary that whatever had been beckoning to her before was now, somehow, infiltrating her body.

When she deprived herself of blood, the connection weakened, and the tensing of her muscles happened less frequently and with less intensity, but she became lethargic, pale, and weak without it.

Even if the taste of blood still made her gag, she could not go back to how she was before. Her strength and heightened sensory awareness made her and the world around her feel immovable and beautiful.

She saw Gwen a couple times, squeezing in time between their relationships. Gwen looked magic fatigued, with dark circles under her eyes, but promised that she was fine, that Nikki would be so proud of her when she revealed what she had been working on. Nikki worried about her, that she was pushing herself too hard, draining her magic too fast. She wondered if bickering between her and her sisters had worsened, since Gwen seemed more irritable than usual. But Gwen waved her off every time she expressed concern and turned to feeding her birds.

When Nikki told Gwen about her newest symptom, Gwen offered little more than a scowl. It was simply another mystery neither one could answer.

Nights lengthened and days shortened, and Nikki relished the extra time outside and having the windows open even with the bitter chill. Despite the intermittent anxiety of an otherness around her, in her, and the ever-approaching familiar anxiety of finals, her spirits were high. Xander was the sun's radiant light that shone through the darkness of her heart, banishing unease to the corners of her mind.

The closer Thanksgiving break came, the more her thoughts whirled, scenarios of meeting his family playing on repeat in her head. Xander kept telling her not to worry, but how could she not? He was just as nervous about meeting her parents the following day. And when she thought of it, Nikki realized she was more worried about that meeting as well. She had been around humans her whole life. But she had never brought a stray human into the world of vampires.

The night of the dinner arrived, Nikki spending the day in a nervous flurry of cooking and getting ready. She prepped an eggplant dip and checked her teeth fittings too many times, worried that suddenly they wouldn't fit and they'd pop out of her mouth. Xander picked her up, and she clenched her hands tight to avoid fidgeting them, to resist the urge to smooth her clothes, check her reflection. By the time they reached his parents' house, Nikki's heart was in her throat and her hands were clasped tight on the handle of the paper bag. The home was on a quiet street, each property dense with trees and shrubs and remnants of perennials, providing ample privacy between each residence.

Xander parked in front of a house with a bright gold light, which illuminated the porch and steps, but the beams were swallowed by the darkness before they reached the front foliage.

"Here we are," Xander said.

Nikki nodded but didn't move.

Xander peeled one of her hands from the bag to clasp in his, and with his other one, he turned her face so she looked at him.

"It will be fine. I promise," he said, kissing the back of her hand.

She nodded, smiling weakly, worried her stomach would purge out of her mouth if she spoke. Nikki gathered her belongings and left the car, and Xander held his hand on the small of her back, the warmth from his palm radiating a calm into her body. In front of the pale wooden door, Xander tugged her closer, and she smiled, just the proximity of him relaxing the throbbing pulse of her heartbeat in her ears.

With a grin, he raised his hand and knocked, then opened the door.

The house erupted with barking and the high-pitched squeals of a child shouting "Xander! Xander's here!" A boy with a toothy grin, dark hair in a cloud of tight curls around his head, and dark golden skin ran to the door to greet them. A girl slightly taller than him, with similar features and dark eyes, and curls cascading down her back, stepped beside him.

The boy looked at Nikki, and his eyes widened. With an amused lilt to his voice he said, "Xan, you didn't tell me you were dating the moon goddess."

Nikki barked a surprised laugh and Xander said, "I don't think I am. Am I?"

"No, I'm not. Unfortunately. But thanks for the compliment."

"But you're so white. Even whiter than dad!" the boy said with a wide smile, as if this was an accomplishment. The girl rolled her eyes, crossed her arms, and looked at Nikki through her peripheral vision.

"Yes. Well. Not much I can do about that."

"I'm Ishaq," the boy said, extending his hand violently.

Nikki took it, and said, "I'm Nikki."

"Well, duh," Ishaq said with a smile. "Xander only talks about you all the time."

"I do not."

Nikki blushed and asked the girl, who remained standing several feet away, "What's your name?"

"Zahra."

"Nice to meet you."

Ishaq piped in. "Want to see my dinosaur fossils? I have shark teeth, too, but they're not as cool as my dinosaur collection. Even though sharks are kind of dinosaurs, but you know, not really, not in, like, the real dinosaur way."

"The real dinosaur way?"

"Why would she want to see your fossils?" Zahra mocked.

"Because they're cool, duh."

"Only to you."

"No, they're cool to everyone, everyone else is just too scared to admit it. But I am going to be a pal-ee-on-tol-o-gist," Ishaq said, standing straight, planting his hands on his hips like a proud explorer.

The girl rolled her eyes and said, "You're so dumb."

"You're dumb."

"Not as dumb as you."

Ishaq sputtered, not knowing what to say. "Yeah. Well." He turned his focus back to Nikki, clearly losing against his sister. "Come see the fossils and bones and things!"

"Um, okay?" Nikki said, and she gave Xander a quizzical look, who shrugged, took the bag from her hands, and with a kiss on her forehead, disappeared into another room.

Ishaq dragged Nikki to the staircase in the corner of the living room up to the second floor.

"You're so cold, too. Are you okay?"

"I'm fine. That's normal for me."

"Weird."

Ishaq hummed in contemplation, tugging her up the stairs, their steps creaking and thudding on the old wood, and into his bedroom.

He flipped on the light, and Nikki paused, stunned at the amount of paleontology and herpetology posters covering every inch of the walls. There was no space that did not have a dinosaur, a fossil, a lizard, a shark, or some prehistoric oddity. He had a desk scattered with old teeth, which he pointed out were not real dinosaur shark teeth, and then showed her his bookcase, which was full of books, and mostly decorated with dinosaur fossils, figures, pictures, and bone replicas.

"I even have a practice pit outside!"

"A what?"

"A pit? For digging? Duh. So, I can practice finding and digging bones, of course. One needs a delicate touch, mom says, and as you can tell, I guess I'm not very delicate. So, I have to practice. They empty it and then put stuff in different layers and then fill it again and then I can dig it up!"

"Wow. That is really cool."

"I know! Anyway, what do you think of my collection? Pretty cool right?" Ishaq asked, bouncing up and down on his toes. His boundless energy made Nikki nervous. How did his body sustain this all the time?

"It's very nice," she said.

Ishaq's face twisted, and his brows quirked in a way that reminded her of Xander. "It's much better than nice, but maybe you just don't appreciate it."

"Oh, I appreciate it. It's awesome," Nikki amended.

"Ish?" A feminine voice called from below, echoing up the stairs.

"Yeah, Mom?" he yelled back.

"Come down here and wash your hands. It's almost time for dinner."

Ishaq made a face but walked to the door, beckoning Nikki to exit first, closing it behind them.

"The dog will take all my bones if it isn't closed."

"We wouldn't want that."

"Ugh. No. It's the worst." Then Ishaq took off down the stairs at a sprint.

Nikki released a deep breath once relieved of Ishaq's company and walked, like a normal person, down the stairs. A thick wagging tail peeked around the corner. At the sound of her footsteps, the dog's head appeared, white curls dangling over its eyes. It gave a timid bark and a few growls, and when she got down the stairs, she let it sniff her hand, which seemed to distress it more. It gave a low whine in its throat and backed away, then once out of sight, she heard it patter into the back of the house.

Her heart sank.

"That's weird," Xander said, coming from around the corner where the dog had disappeared to. "Pip usually likes everyone."

"Not me, I guess."

"Sorry, I didn't mean it like that." He grinned. "He must have a thing against moon goddesses."

Nikki laughed and nudged him playfully. Xander grabbed her hand and led her to the kitchen, where his parents were finalizing dinner, his mom pulling out the turkey from the oven, his dad over the stove with a large apron covered in old food spatters.

"Mom, Dad," Xander said, voice firm.

They both turned to him, eyes shifting to Nikki. His dad grinned, close-lipped, but his mom's face remained hard, her head tilting in assessment.

"This is Nikki," Xander said. "Nikki, this is my mom and dad. Ina and Arthur."

"A pleasure, a pleasure indeed!" Arthur said, dropping his spatula on the counter and clasping both of his hands around hers. His hands were warm, firm, and comforting, his face kind and welcoming. He was a paler, older version of Xander, with salt and pepper hair in thick waves down to his shoulders, pale green-grey eyes, and a rectangular face with small spectacles balanced on his straight nose.

"It's great to meet you too," Nikki said, and Arthur removed his hand, stepping back to let his wife in.

Ina was several inches shorter than Nikki, with deep, dark golden skin, hazel eyes like amber, and dark brown hair the color of old earth that fell in dense waves down her back. Her mouth was wide and full, and although the corners of her mouth flicked up, the smile did not reach her eyes.

"Nikki, nice to finally meet you," she said, extending her hand. When Nikki clasped it, she flinched, Ina's skin so hot it nearly burned her own.

"Nice to meet you, too," Nikki said, gritting her teeth against searing of her palm, wondering if this woman was okay. She felt feverish, yet didn't have a sheen of sweat.

They furrowed their brows at each other and pulled their hands back. Nikki averted her gaze, anxiety blossoming in her stomach, butter-flies flapping in her chest. She held her hot hand in her other, trying to cool it with her own body temperature.

Xander and Arthur were oblivious.

"Thank you for bringing food, Nikki. It looks delicious," Ina said, her own hands clasped in front of her sternum.

"You're welcome," Nikki said, meeting her hard eyes again. "Thank you for hosting me. I really appreciate the invitation."

"Xander would have been livid if we didn't say yes," Arthur said.

Xander groaned. "Do you and Ish have some plan to embarrass me all night?"

"Not a plan, exactly. You just make it so easy."

Xander laughed and threw up his hands in defeat.

"Do you need help with anything?" Nikki asked.

"No, no," Arthur said. "Everything will be ready shortly. Just get comfortable. Want anything to drink? Wine? Water? Beer? We have some hard liquor too if you want a mixed drink."

"Oh. Just water would be fine. Thank you."

"Xan?"

"The same," he said, and wrapped an arm over Nikki's shoulders, steering her out of the kitchen as his parents turned their backs on them, returning to the amazing smells of cooking food.

Xander directed her upstairs, Ishaq and Zahra chatting in the living room. Mostly Ishaq talked, but Zahra nodded sagely, and responded either in agreement or by calling him stupid, which did not faze him or stop his train of thought for one moment.

Upstairs, Xander took her to the left.

"Are you ready for the big reveal?" he asked, a playful grin on his face.

"Is this your childhood room?"

"My teenage room, more like, but yes," he said and opened the door.

He flipped on the light, and the room was so normal. At least compared to Ishaq's. There were a few posters of athletes and bands, shelves with schoolbooks and college prep books.

"I don't know why they haven't converted this room yet," he said. "I barely use it."

"Maybe they don't know what else to do with it."

He laughed. "No, they collect junk. Well, not junk, but lots of stuff. I'll show you when we go back downstairs. They always need more room."

They laid down on the bed, staring up at the ceiling, Xander's hand tracing lazy circles on her arm.

"Is your mom sick?" Nikki asked.

"No. Why?"

"When we shook hands, she felt really hot. Like she was burning from the inside out."

"Well, she did just have her hands in the oven."

"Yes, but she didn't seem to notice, or be in pain."

"Maybe it's because you're so cold. You know, from floating up in space, lording over the moon."

Nikki sighed, but a smile tugged at her lips. "You're never going to let me live that down, will you?"

"Never."

A moment of silence passed, and Nikki said, "Your mom hates me already."

"What? No, she doesn't."

"She does. I could see it on her face. She glared at me."

"I highly doubt that. I'm not sure I've ever seen her glare."

"Well, when she looked at me, she did not like what she saw."

"Maybe she had pepper or onion or something in her eye. I wouldn't worry about it."

"Maybe."

They hid in the room for a couple more minutes, Nikki looking at the remnants of his life. The knickknacks from travels, old textbooks, jerseys slung over odd corners. Arthur called up to them when dinner was ready, and as they left, she saw the dog stare at her from the cracked, dark door of a bedroom across the hall. When they made eye contact, it bowed its head, ears bent back, and turned around into the black.

"I wonder what's up with him."

Probably can tell I'm a parasite, Nikki thought, chest heavy.

Xander led Nikki by the hand to the table and like a magnet, her eyes were drawn to a closed door at the far side of the house. Something about it resonated, like it had a presence, but she couldn't put her finger on what it was. It didn't feel like the voice she heard before, nor like Gwen's magic, but there was definitely an energy about it.

"That's the storage room," Xander said. "I'll show you after dinner."

"That makes it sound like it's full of junk. It's an office, not a storage room," Arthur said, carrying the platter of steaming, glistening turkey into the room.

"You know what they say, one man's trash is another man's treasure."

"You know what else they say?" Arthur asked, holding up the electric turkey cutter. "One man's sarcasm is that same man's lack of dinner."

"Haven't heard that one," Xander said, grinning.

"It's much before your time," Arthur replied, the younger siblings rushing to the table, Ishaq bounced up and down in his seat, Zahra sitting beside him. Xander waved to Nikki to sit beside him, next to his dad and opposite the kids. Arthur put an arm on Ishaq's shoulder, trying to calm him down, while Ina entered with a platter of food and sat at the other head of the table.

Ishaq stilled himself, clutching his two hands together on the table and piercing Nikki with his gaze. "Do you want to say Grace?"

"Uhh," Nikki said, freezing.

"He's joking," Xander said. "We don't say Grace."

Ishaq broke into a smile as cold relief washed over Nikki. The only prayers she had heard were to the Mother, for blood and sustenance. What did people normally say during Grace?

"Don't mess with Nikki, Ish. It isn't nice," Zahra said.

"Thank you," Nikki replied.

"No, but it's funny," Ishaq replied, fidgeting again in his seat, hands under his legs, watching Arthur slice into the turkey, the electric whir dull against the cooked bird.

Zahra's comment bolstered Nikki's courage, as if some bridge had been laid down between them, so she braced herself and asked, "Zahra, Ishaq told me all about his interests. What are you interested in?"

"Mm," Zahra hummed, seeming to contemplate answering or not. "I like lots of things, People, animals, plants, buildings—"

"She likes nouns," Ishaq announced.

Zahra rolled her eyes.

"Nouns are very interesting," Nikki agreed, keeping a straight face.

"She was fascinated when she found out what you're studying,

Nikki," Arthur chimed in, picking up the younger kids' plates to pile with food. "She changes her mind quite a bit about what she wants to study. But when she heard about you, we thought we had a young hematologist on our hands!"

Zahra turned beet-red, eyes on the table.

"She was obsessed with blood for weeks. It was gross," Ishaq said.

"I was not."

"Yes you were. You were like, 'oh, blood is soooo interesting, I didn't know you could study—"

"Leave your sister be," Ina said. "It is an interesting subject. Why did you choose it, Nikki?"

Nikki's heart skipped a beat when she met Ina's hard eyes, her impassive face.

Because I want to know why I need to drink it. I want to know why Gwen is a witch and not a vampire. I want to know how we're immortal. I want to know how we got this way. I want to know how to undo it.

"It's hard to describe," Nikki said, but Ina kept her gaze firm, waiting for more. "I guess—there's a lot we still don't know. About blood. And genetics. It's essential for all human and animal life, so I want to be part of those discoveries."

"Yes. It is essential, isn't it?" Ina asked, looking at Nikki one second too long before averting her gaze, moving around the table to serve the vegetables to the kids.

Xander squeezed her knee under the table, and when she looked at him, his smile was reassuring. She took a steadying breath, and her heartbeat decreased to a more normal rate, his presence calming her.

"I showed Nikki all the bones and fossils and teeth."

"We know, Ish," Zahra said. "We were there."

"But what you don't know is that she said it was awesome."

"So?"

"So, they are awesome. And there's still so much we don't know, like—"

Zahra groaned.

"What?"

"No one wants to hear about your dumb dinosaurs anymore."

"Hey," Arthur and Ina said.

"Don't call your brother, or his interests, dumb. We've been over this," Arthur said.

"I'm just tired of hearing about it."

"Well, none of you are talking. And if you're going to be boring, I'm going to not be boring and talk about things I want to talk about."

"Fair enough," Arthur said, and Xander chuckled. "Xan, fill us in. How's school? Work? How about Terrance and Theo?"

Ishaq slumped, seeing the conversation wasn't in his favor, and gave his attention to his food. Zahra picked at hers, listening to Xander with reserved admiration while he filled his family in on his life.

As they fell into their normal conversational pattern, Nikki listened, glad to not be the center of attention. She worried that if she didn't speak enough, they'd think poorly of her, but it was better than speaking too much and being considered idiotic. His parents talked about work, the kids about their school and friends, and the evening passed at a pleasant pace. The food was delicious, and all seemed to enjoy what Nikki brought, even Ina. Xander squeezed her leg again, a proud grin on his face.

"Where did you learn to cook?" Ina asked.

"An old cookbook from my mother's side of the family."

"Oh, self-taught, huh?" Arthur asked, impressed.

"More or less," Nikki said. "I had some guidance. But a lot was my own experimentation. And practice."

"So, you got to our son's heart through his stomach," Ina said.

"Well, there was more to it than that, but it didn't hurt. That's for sure," Xander replied.

Ina gave him a tense, close-lipped pretense at a smile and turned her gaze back to assess the table. "Dessert?" she asked.

Ishaq squealed and Xander said, "I might explode, but yes."

Ina nodded and rose to clear the table.

"I'll help you," Nikki said, rising and stacking plates.

"Thank you," Ina replied, dark hair swaying over her back as she turned to the kitchen, the cooling pot of steamed vegetables in her hands.

Nikki set the plates on the counter next to the kitchen sink, playful conversation between Xander, his dad, and siblings filtering in from the other room.

"Excuse me for a moment," Ina said after setting down the pot and disappearing down the dark hall past the kitchen to the back of the house, where Nikki assumed a bathroom was.

Nikki took a few more trips to the dining room, carrying back food and used dinnerware. Once the table was cleared, she searched the kitchen for Tupperware and started putting food away.

"Vampire," a voice whispered, so quiet it sounded as if it was in a breeze through the trees.

Nikki froze.

"Vampire," the quiet voice said again.

Nikki turned her head, looking around. She didn't see anyone. Scowling, she stepped back from the counter. She looked down the corridor to her right, and saw Ina standing in the dark, at the very end of the house.

"Vampire," Ina said, mouth barely moving, so quiet a human would not have been able to hear it from this distance.

Goosebumps crept across Nikki's arms.

Shit. Shit, shit, shit.

Ina flicked on the hallway light, and with a lifted chin, hands held over her sternum, walked at a slow pace toward Nikki.

Nikki was rooted to the spot, watching Ina approach her, a cold fear clearing her head of all thought.

Ina stood in front of her, and for the first time that evening, Nikki caught a sense of something else. Spices and something warm, like heat waves rolling in the air off hot sand. The same image she got from Xander the first time she ran into him.

But the image disappeared from her mind, and she lost the smell, the sense, like it was a figment of her imagination.

Ina took a large breath, pushing her chest wide, and her dark eyes penetrated Nikki.

"Help me wash the dishes, would you?" Ina said, voice calm and hard, more a command than a question.

Nikki nodded, and they stood at the sink, elbow to elbow as Ina washed and Nikki dried.

After several moments of tense silence, Ina's hair tickling Nikki's arm, Ina asked, "What do you want with my son?"

"Want?" Nikki repeated. "I just want to be with him."

"That's not what I mean, vampire," Ina spat, and it was the first time Nikki had heard the word hurled like an insult.

"Then I don't know what you mean," Nikki replied, keeping her hands from shaking. "Because that's all I want. To be with him. I care about him a lot."

Ina scoffed.

"It's true. Whether you choose to believe it or not," Nikki said through clenched teeth, careful to put the dishes down delicately, instead of bashing them or accidentally crushing them in her hands.

Ina was silent a minute, then said, "For his sake, I hope that it is true. But if you hurt him, or if any harm comes to him because of what you are, I will kill you and your entire coven. Without hesitation."

Nikki's body tensed, and she fought down the fight rising in her chest, the violence aching for release in her blood. "I don't appreciate the threat. I don't have bad intentions with your son. I promise I won't harm him."

"Lies come so easy to your kind." Ina sneered. "Your very existence is a threat to my family. If you really cared about him, you'd stay away from him."

"That's not going to happen. I understand why you're scared about him being around me, but one of the reasons I want to stay by his side is to protect him. Especially from vampires who are not like me. From those who take pleasure in hurting others." Nikki sighed. "Is there anything I can do to make you believe me? That I won't hurt him? Because I promise you there is nothing more I want than to keep Xander safe from harm."

"Besides cutting him out of your life completely, no," Ina said, plate scraping against the front of another as she placed it into the drying rack. "Your promises mean nothing to me."

Nikki clamped her jaw tight, biting back her anger. She had dedicated her life to being a better vampire, to finding a way around this issue, and she wasn't even given a chance? Just because of what other vampires had done? Not all vampires were lying, manipulative, killers.

Just like how not all humans were flimsy, weak, prey. Surely Ina would realize that?

Several minutes of silence weighed on her tense shoulders before Nikki ground out, "How did you know?"

Ina looked up at her. "If you don't know what I am, I will not tell you."

Nikki blinked in surprise, her mind scrambling for clues she hadn't been looking for.

"Dessert!" Ina yelled, handing Nikki a carton of vanilla ice cream and a stack of small plates before she turned, cutting off any more conversation.

With a sick feeling in her stomach, Nikki took the items to the dining room, where the siblings talked about a video game, Arthur scrolling through news on his phone.

"You okay?" Xander asked.

Nikki nodded and said, "Just very full. I'll be right back."

She put the ice cream and plates on the table and walked around the house, trying to find the bathroom. When she found it, she let out a long exhale, hands braced on the sink counter. Nikki put cold water on the back of her neck and her cheeks, trying to freeze out the nausea in her body.

The white porcelain of the sink overtook her vision, and the anxious fear in her veins turned into a dull buzz. She had no idea who Ina was, or how Ina knew what she was, but maybe she would get some answers from her own parents tomorrow. At least, it did not seem as if Ina would take drastic measures at this point in time. If she kept Xander safe, as she intended, everything would be fine. And maybe eventually Ina would see her as more than just a vampire.

Exhaling out her tension, Nikki cracked open the bathroom door, but paused when she heard voices from the kitchen.

"—girls like her before," Ina whispered.

"No, you haven't," Xander said. "I don't even know what that means, but she's amazing. She's smart and understanding. She doesn't try to control me."

"She's going to hurt you, Xander."

Nikki's heart sank, fist clenching around the doorknob.

"No, she's not. I don't know where you're getting that idea." Xander's laugh was harsh. "You know what? She actually keeps me from getting hurt. On Halloween, someone tried to break into my car, and she beat the crap out of them while I just stood there like a coward."

Ina was silent.

"I feel safe and understood with her, Mom. I don't know what you think you see. But you're wrong."

"Just be careful, Xan," Ina whispered to Xander's retreating footsteps.

A proud smile tugged at the corners of Nikki's lips, although a weight pulled her stomach to the floor. She closed the bathroom door again, giving Xander and Ina a few more minutes to resettle before returning to the group. She straightened her clothes and checked her reflection, and with a touch more confidence, went back to the table, where Arthur divided a pie into slices.

Xander grinned at her, and when she sat down, he put his arm around the back of her chair.

"You want some dessert?" Arthur asked. "There's pecan and pumpkin."

"Sure. I'll have a small slice of both. I'm not sure I have space. But I'll find it," Nikki said, and Arthur stood to slice a small piece of pecan pie for her, while Ina slid the pumpkin around the table, meeting her gaze with a look she couldn't decipher.

They ate their dessert in silence, the luxury of overeating making them all tired. The kids slumped in their seats, lethargy from the food and excitement from the day finally wearing out Ishaq's endless stores of energy.

"No sleeping at the table," Ina reprimanded. "If you're tired, let's get ready for bed."

Zahra nodded, and Ishaq groaned but stood with his sister, heading upstairs, Ina following with a hesitant glance over her shoulder at Nikki, which Nikki pretended not to notice.

"Dad, can I show Nikki the backroom?"

"You mean the one full of junk?" Arthur said with a grin.

"That's the one."

"Sure, sure. Follow me," Arthur said, and they followed him to the back of the house, passing by dark offices and guest rooms, floorboards creaking under their feet. As they walked closer, the sense of otherness increased. It both propelled her forward and repulsed her. What was in that room?

What was up with this family?

Arthur pulled out a key from around his neck and slipped it into the lock. "The kids aren't allowed in here. Too many valuables they could break." Unlocking the door, he added, "Please be careful."

Nikki nodded, and Xander pulled her inside, flipping on the light, illuminating a large room packed with ancient artifacts.

"Wow. This is incredible," Nikki said, eyes wide, looking over the hundreds of artifacts from all over the world—tools from different ages, tablets and carvings from different cultures, cups, bowls, jewelry, and weapons. Many were encased in glass, but masks, swords, and axes hung on the walls, necklaces and jewelry laid out on velvet.

Were these magic? Was that what she had sensed?

Nikki made a slow circle, starting to the left, drinking in each unique, beautiful, old object. "How did you acquire all of these?"

"Auctions, mostly. Special permits. Some from Ina's connections as an archaeologist, but I find the story behind each one fascinating."

Nikki nodded, recalling how Xander told her his dad was a history professor. She stepped away from an old bronze coin with an unknown king stamped into the side to look at an array of animals carved from jade, clay, bone, and wood. "What got you into history?"

"Ah, now that is a good story—"

"Here we go," Xander whispered, a small laugh in his voice. He stood behind Nikki, and his breath rushed against the back of her neck, causing her to shiver in delight.

Arthur continued, as if he hadn't heard Xander. "You are familiar with the story of Arthur Pendragon, I presume?"

Nikki raised a brow. "I am."

Arthur nodded, falling into step behind them in their slow circle of the room. "Yes, well, ever since I was young, I was fascinated with the legend. Likely because we share the same name. Nevertheless, it ignited my interest in all things prior to our time—myths, legends, objects, people, everything."

"The nouns of the past," Xander said.

"Ha! Yes, indeed. Come, look at this," Arthur said, breaking their circle and beckoning them to follow him to a case set at the back of the room.

Within it was a sword, broken just above the hilt, which was a deep brown wood, gilded with silver and gold. Attached to the hilt was a small ring with a bulging, round pommel also inlaid with metal.

"An iron ring sword, from the early migration period. This one is Anglo-Saxon, influenced by the Merovingian period of sword design, which is Germanic. It evolved just after the fall of the Roman Empire."

"It's beautiful," Nikki said, admiring how the light glinted off the deep silver blade.

Arthur nodded, standing beside her. "Ina and I went to the UK on our honeymoon. We camped a lot as we were still young and poor. One morning, when we were camped in a forest in northern England, I woke before she did, hearing someone call my name. I walked out into the foggy forest in the morning and followed the voice until I reached the edge of a lake. The mist still hung over the water and low to the ground, but it flowed and shifted, as if someone else were walking through it. I saw a glimmer, a light, which moved under the water closer to me. When the light was near the shore, I raised my gaze to find a tall, beautiful woman in a gown made of mist and flowing blonde hair hovering above the water. She gazed down at me with an expression I couldn't read, and spoke to me, although I never saw her lips move."

"What did she say?"

"She said, 'I wondered when you would return for this.' Then she disappeared into the mists, and as the glow in the water faded to a dull, rippling reflection, I plunged my hands into the lake and pulled out the pieces of this sword. Painfully, I might add. I did not expect to find a broken sword in the water. Gave myself quite the cut," Arthur said, holding his right palm to show a deep scar.

"And you gave me quite the scare when you returned to camp bleeding profusely," Ina said, standing in the doorway with her arms folded.

"Yes, well, that was not intentional," he said with a sheepish smile at his wife before turning back to Nikki and the sword. "I believe this to be the original sword in the stone, tossed into the lake in exchange for Excalibur. I believe the Lady of the Lake guided me to the lake, and the sword, because I am—we are"—Arthur nodded at Xander— "descendants of King Arthur himself. The Lady wanted the sword to be back with the proper owner. Or maybe she was tired of it rusting in her lake. I know I should have reported the find, but I couldn't shake the feeling that it was mine. That it is supposed to be here, with us. Not rusting away in some museum."

Nikki blinked, processing the story. Could it really be true that King Arthur and his legend were real? Despite knowing that vampires and witches exist, Nikki found it hard to wrap her mind around that the Knights of the Round Table, Excalibur, and the Lady of the Lake were real, too. What did that mean if the Lady of the Lake was still present in the world? Did that mean there were other magics and immortals from myth, too? Did that have anything to do with the weird occurrences that started happening when she met Xander?

Ina walked beside her husband, put a hand on his arm, and Arthur smiled as he said, "She is too kind to tell you, but she doesn't believe me."

"I think it was an incredible, vivid dream," Ina replied.

"And I think she's just jealous that no deity has ever spoken to her," he replied, grinning.

"I'm inclined to side with Mom on this one." Xander added.

Ina gave Arthur's arm a soft pat. "Dear, the day is catching up to me. I think it is time to call it a night."

Arthur sighed and looked down at the sword with a sad smile. "Perhaps you're right."

"I'm not done showing Nikki around the room, though," Xander said. "We barely got in before Dad went off."

"He's quite right. I couldn't help myself," Arthur said, running a hand through his hair. He took the key from his necklace and handed it to Xander. "Here. Lock up the room behind you before you go and put this on top of the fridge. You still have a key for the front door?"

Xander nodded.

"Okay, my boy," Arthur said and wrapped his arms around Xander.

While father and son said their goodbyes and goodnights, Ina and Nikki stared at each other.

"Thank you for having me over. I appreciate being welcomed to your home this holiday."

Ina gave one small nod. "Xander speaks highly of you. Thank you for bringing some food."

Arthur turned his attention to Nikki and pulled her in for a hug goodbye, Xander and Ina giving each other a tense hug farewell. In the brief closeness to Arthur, she caught a sense of warmth, of rain, reminding her of cozy days reading while it downpours outside.

"Thanks for coming, Nikki. It was a pleasure to meet you. I hope we see you again."

"Me too. Thanks for having me," Nikki said, glad that at least one of his parents seemed to like her.

When Arthur and Ina left the room, Nikki felt her lungs expand like she'd just stepped out into the fresh air.

"There's just one more section in here I wanted to show you," he said, taking her hand and leading her to the opposite side of the room. "Some real family history."

He flipped a switch, a small bulb overhead lighting the case in front of them. It held several chipped figurines, aged jewelry, fragments of cylinder seals, tablets, shards of pottery, and carved tablets made from clay and stone. As Nikki looked over the carved people, animals, and symbols, Xander said, "I guess my mom's parents kept a good genealogical record, and according to them, we have ancestors from Mesopotamia. Uruk, in Sumeria, to be exact. These artifacts are from that ancient city. Thousands of years before the common era."

"This is amazing," Nikki said, eyes catching on a simple relief of pale stone. A man in profile was cut into the tablet, sitting on a throne, circular symbols like sun disks, with rays in different forms, above his head. She couldn't stop looking at it, even though it gave her the impulse to step away, to look at something else.

"What is he holding?" Nikki asked, nodding her head at the circle and stick in the man's hand.

"The rod and ring—I'm not entirely sure what it represents, but it is often held by a god or goddess, given to a king."

"So, this man is a god?"

"Supposedly."

"What is he a god of?" Nikki asked, transfixed, as if the relief had an energy of its own, magnetizing her to the sharp curves of the god's face, his emotionless gaze peering at something broken off from his stone world.

Xander shrugged. "I don't know. Probably some aspect of the heavens, considering the symbols above his head."

"A sun god, maybe?"

"Could be," Xander said, putting an arm back around her waist. "Anyway, I just thought these pieces were interesting. I don't believe my dad with his whole King Arthur nonsense, so I figured some real history would be a good balance."

"Thanks for showing me," Nikki replied, leaning into him, resting her head against his shoulder. What was the power emanating from this relic? Did it provide any clues to what made Xander different? And how did that factor into what had been happening to her lately?

After another moment of appreciating the ancient objects in front of them, Nikki still wondering who this god was, Xander asked, "Want to get out of here?"

A light rain drizzled outside, quiet patters on the asphalt, dripping delicately from the bare branches, the light from the front porch catching the droplets as they fell.

A creeping coldness stretched out from the dark, like reaching tentacles. Nikki peered down the street, that sensation of being watched washing over her skin.

There was no other soul in sight.

Xander handed her the bag of leftovers, snapping her out of her search. He opened the car door for her and smoothed a hand through his rain slicked hair, shaking out some of the moisture dripping from the ringlets onto his face and neck. Nikki couldn't help but stare, wanting to wipe the drop from his throat, feel the pulse of his heart under her thumb.

She swallowed hard and looked away, Xander sliding into the driver's seat, then turning on the car and driving away with a long exhale, releasing the tension in his chest.

"So, did you have an okay time?" he asked.

Nikki nodded. "I did. But I still don't think your mom likes me," Nikki said, Ina's whisper of 'vampire,' of warning Xander away from her, echoing through her head. Her brow furrowed, a heaviness creeping in behind her eyes.

"Yeah, I don't know what's wrong with her. I'm sorry about that. She'll come around."

"So, she told you she didn't like me."

"No. I think she's just worried about a repeat of my last relationship. Once she realizes you're not like her, she'll come around."

Nikki nodded, disbelieving. Her mind spun, and she had to shake her head to knock out the dizziness, but that only made it worse. She clenched her eyes shut and leaned her head back, trying to dull the sudden pressure, the jumbling in her head.

How had Ina known she's a vampire?

What was Ina?

And what was Xander?

What merit was there to Arthur's claims about being related to King Arthur? Three months ago, she would have denied them as vehemently as Xander, yet the sense of otherness was stronger now in her life than it had ever been.

Maybe King Arthur and other gods were all real. Maybe all this fuss about the Mother, about her hunting Xander and sending Hormin to seek her out, was all real and they were in terrible, mortal danger.

Nikki laughed aloud.

She must be tired to entertain such thoughts. To think she was really that important.

"What?"

"Oh," Nikki said, clamping down on her laugh. "I just remembered how Ishaq tried so hard to pronounce paleontologist. It was adorable."

Xander smiled. "He's got spirit, that's for sure."

Nikki massaged her hands, pushing her thumbs hard into her palms and taking a deep breath.

"Well, one down one to go." Xander said.

"What do you mean?"

"You met my family. Tomorrow, I'll meet yours."

"Oh. Yes. It's going to be a rather different dinner."

"Quieter?" Xander said with a grin.

"Yes. And with less of a homey touch."

"Ah, yes, the boundless wealth you come from. Remind me to ask your dad about your dowry."

Nikki laughed, and when Xander offered his hand, she wrapped her fingers through his.

The rest of the drive to Nikki's apartment was quiet, both tired from gluttony and conversation. At her place, Xander got ready for bed while she got herself ready for a lazy evening. The rest of the night was easy and quiet and loving until she slept, where she watched herself, from outside her body, wrap her hands around Xander's throat while he slumbered, her bone-white fingers pressing against his dark, honey skin. She couldn't stop it, couldn't cry out to warn him—

She woke with a sharp inhale, body slick with a fine sheen of sweat. She shook out her hands, feeling as if they had been clamped in a claw shape for too long.

Xander moaned, rolling over. "You good?" he slurred, throwing an arm across her stomach.

She nodded, but he was already asleep, and she stared at the black of the ceiling until the pressure behind her eyes dissipated, and the absence of pain enabled her to fall back into unconsciousness.

<h1 style="text-align:center">Chapter Twenty-Six</h1>

The atmospheric river fell in full force on Black Friday, harsh gusts of wind slapping the rain against the windows and walls in violent spatters, pushing against the framework of Nikki's apartment building. Wind tore through the streets, bending the trees and forcing the weak branches to break and scatter across the streets.

Nikki responded to Gwen's numerous texts begging for details about meeting Xander's family, telling Nikki about her Thanksgiving with Theo and Terrance's family, telling her that she needed to demonstrate some of her most recent magical developments. Now that she wasn't inundated with making salves and medicines for Nikki, she had much more time to continue her own experiments, to stretch her boundaries, and Nikki felt better not being a constant burden.

A dull headache intensified in Nikki's head throughout the day. Despite drinking water and sneaking blood, the pressure behind her eyes would not cease.

The storm worsened outside, washing the city in a deluge of wind and rain, the sky settling in a dark grey as night descended. The darkness swallowed the lights from the streetlamps and open businesses, barely illuminating the roads, which were littered with human and plant debris swept across by the violent winds. The wind lashed and rain pelted against Xander's car as they drove eastward on the highway towards her parents' house, conversation absent due to Xander's complete focus on them arriving safely despite the weather.

Nikki stared out the window, rubbing her temples, welcoming the quiet before they left one storm and entered another. It was too dark to see the details of the forest, the wind brushing the trees together like blurred paint strokes. Yet she could feel the pulse of it, the remainders of life hidden under the leaf debris, the trees taking slower breaths with the deepening of winter.

Xander fidgeted more and more the closer they got, foot bouncing, pushing his glasses into the bridge of his nose even though they had not slipped, running a hand through his hair, adjusting his pant legs.

"You don't have to be nervous," Nikki said, despite how her veins felt as if they were humming, imagining Xander in her family home, with her century-and-a-half-old vampire parents.

"Yes, well, I know I don't have to be, but I can't seem to help it. What if they don't like me? What if I'm not rich or fancy enough for them?"

"Is that really what you're worried about? Not being fancy enough?"

"Well when you say it like that, it sounds silly."

"My dad was an orphan. He spent his entire childhood poor. It wasn't until he married my mom that he experienced wealth. It hasn't gotten to his head. And my mom, well, she married an orphaned, foreign, broke man. Suffice it to say, another person's wealth doesn't factor into her opinion of them. Unless it makes them an asshole."

Xander nodded but didn't say anything more, despite not seeming convinced.

Cat had texted Nikki commanding them to pull into the front drive of the house so Xander could get the best first impression of their home, instead of the casual entrance through the garage. So they parked at the curve of the drive beside the walkway lined with alders and surrounded by rain-soaked grass that glistened faintly in the Victorian lamplight. Xander bade her to wait when they parked, rushing around to her side of the car with the umbrella and holding it over her so she wouldn't get wet.

"Ready?" she asked, as their footsteps splashed through the puddles on the walkway.

"As ready as I'll ever be," he responded, the umbrella blocking the view of the watchful alders.

The weight that had been behind her eyes all day pushed against her skull, and she clenched her jaw, hoping the headache would dissipate once inside. Or hoping she would at least be distracted enough when dinner started. Nikki raised the solid knocker on the door, banging against the wood hard enough to be heard over the storm by vampires. Xander shook out the umbrella once they were under the safety of the veranda, leaning it against the outside wall.

"This is really nice," he whispered, admiring the wraparound porch, the pillars, the wide front lawn.

The door flung open before Nikki could respond, her mom standing in a high-necked, black gown that was tight around her torso and flowing over her legs, lace ruffles under her chin and at her wrists.

"Oh," her mom said, eyes fixed wide on Xander. Her nostrils flared, filling with his unusual, strong, and enticing scent.

A hot curl in Nikki's chest sent her heart beating rapidly, and she said, "Hey, Mom."

Cat tore her eyes away from Xander, her head turned to Nikki before her gaze. "Hi, my darling," her mom said, mouth thick from the settings that hid her fangs, since she was unused to wearing them. She stepped back to let them inside, kissing Nikki's cheeks as they entered.

"Mom, this is Xander. Xander—my mom, Cat."

"It's a pleasure to meet you, Mrs. Silva," Xander said, extending his hand and giving a shy smile.

"The pleasure is all mine," her mom replied in a cool voice, regaining her composure, although her nostrils remained flared. She shook his hand, lingering, and said, "You may simply call me Cat."

"Noted," Xander said with a small bow of his head.

Her mom gave one last long, assessing look at Xander, and the hot curl in Nikki's chest enflamed to irritation, to worry, and she cleared her throat, giving her mom a stern look.

Cat took a deep breath and smoothed her skirts, lifting her chin. "Dinner will be done shortly. Miguel is out but will return soon. Feel free to roam the house in the interim. Nicoletta, give him a tour, would you?"

"Sure," Nikki said, holding back an eye roll and taking Xander by the hand, pulling him down the hall toward the large staircase in the back, feeling her mom's eyes on their backs.

"Roam the grounds?" Xander chuckled, and Nikki had to resist the urge to tell him to be quiet, that they weren't out of earshot like he thought.

"I told you she was traditional."

"She sounds like she's from another century."

Nikki laughed, but it sounded like an odd hiccup.

"What about all these rooms we're passing?" Xander asked, craning his neck to look through different cracked doors.

"I'll show you the upstairs first."

"Oh. Okay," he replied, ceasing his resistance and following her lead.

She took him to her bedroom, suddenly seeing it in a whole new light, seeing every flaw, every awkward or embarrassing object from her life on display. Her fingers twisted in her hands as she watched him take in the space, looking at the high ceilings, the veiled bed, the old wooden furniture. He picked up framed photos of her and Gwen throughout their childhood and teenage years that sat on the dresser. He grinned then turned to her bookshelf, browsing the books, the various trinkets that sat on it. He picked up a small bone, a shiny blue-ish black feather, a dried rose hip and turned to her, his eyebrows cocked in a question.

"Gifts from Gwen."

"But why?" he asked, twirling them in his hands, as if he was hoping to find a special secret hidden in them.

Nikki shrugged. "You know how she is about nature. These were from the start of her love for it," she said, thinking of how they came across them during different excursions in the woods. The time they found one large femur bone, another when they came across a scattering of feathers as if a bird got in a fight, and that ridiculous day they bloodied their fingers plucking off rose hips. Gwen had just started experimenting with potions and spells, and they were the first objects she was able to create magic with. With the shards from the femur and strands of all her family's hair, she made her first ward against her siblings. With the feathers and intention, she summoned her first crows. With the rose hips, mixed with spring water that poured from a waterfall, she made a potion that made them light and airy, suffusing Nikki with magic temporarily, a rush of power both overwhelming and awesome and depressingly fleeting.

As the memories crumbled in her mind's eye, her lips curled at the remembrance, and she stood beside Xander, running her fingers over the items.

"Good memories?"

Nikki nodded, resting her head against his shoulder, noting how her life had been dominated and blessed by Gwen. How fun it had been because of her, her bookshelf littered with items most people would consider debris, but Gwen figured out other uses for. At all the books they read together, the movies they watched, the stuffed animals they played with that sat as stoic overseers in the crannies and corners of the shelf.

She gave him a tour of the rest of the house, showing him her mom's instrument room, the kitchen, dining room, bathroom, and entertainment room, then finished in the lounge, the gold wall lights giving a dim glow.

Xander sat in the large armchair closest to the empty fireplace, where her father usually sat. "This house is so clean. Not a speck of dust anywhere."

"My mom is particular about that," Nikki replied, standing beside the bar. "She has cleaners come regularly. Want a drink?"

Xander turned to look at her and asked, "What do you got?"

"Anything and everything. My mom has a fondness for brandy, so there are many bottles of that."

"Brandy it is, then."

Nikki poured them drinks, and sat opposite Xander, who asked, "What's your dad's drink of choice?"

Blood.

"Wine."

Xander nodded, unsurprised. They sat in silence, Xander tapping his fingers against the brandy cup, Nikki savoring the sweet burn of the brandy down her throat. A few minutes passed, and she heard the front door open, close, and her dad's characteristic footsteps fall.

"My dad's here," she said, sitting straighter.

"How do you know?"

"I heard him."

"I'm either deaf or you have really good hearing."

"I have good hearing," she said, mouth twitching into a swift smile.

Nikki listened to her parents greet each other with whispered words, and then her dad's footsteps grew louder. Xander watched the door, also finally hearing his approach. Xander took a sip of his drink and stood, smoothing back his hair, adjusting the folds of his rolled sleeves.

"How do I look?"

"Like a dream."

His face lit up, and she stood, twining her fingers through his, just as her dad walked into the room.

"Hi, Dad," Nikki said, turning to face the door.

"Hi, love," her dad answered, returning her smile, and relief flooded through Nikki to see the white, normal teeth of an omnivore. She was worried he'd forget to put his dentures in and would flash Xander a mouth full of shark teeth. Miguel opened his arms to hug her and she folded into his marble embrace, rain dripping from his face and hair.

When they pulled back, he put his hands on her shoulders and said with noticeable effort, a small lisp and thickness added to his voice from the fittings, "You are looking well."

"Thank you."

He turned his eyes to Xander, who had his hands in his pockets, trying not to fidget. "And you must be the man responsible for making my daughter so happy, eh?"

Miguel stepped around Nikki and extended his hand to Xander, who relaxed and said as he shook her dad's hand, "I sure hope so, sir. I'm Alexander, but I go by Xander."

"Pleasure to meet you, Xander. And none of that sir business. Just call me Miguel," her dad replied, their hands breaking their shake. "You've got a strong handshake. Says a lot about a man."

"Thank you, s—Miguel."

Miguel gave Xander a close-lipped grin, dark brown eyes black in the dimness of the room. "I would begin the questioning, but her mother would loathe it if she missed out getting to know you. Ah, speaking of," her dad said, just as Cat opened the door, her mom's footsteps so silent Nikki couldn't hear her approaching.

Cat held her hands in front of her sternum, chin high, black hair long and straight down her back.

"Dinner is on the table," her mom announced and they followed her to the dining room.

A wide candelabra sat in the center of the table, which had had its leaves removed to fit four people more comfortably, plus food and drinks. Over the rim of her dad's cup, she saw dark, thick red liquid and she gave him a disapproving, stunned look.

She glanced at Xander, heart beating in her head against her headache, his brow furrowed.

"Are you okay?"

The side door swung open, platters of food being brought in by the cook and the assistants, drowning out the smell of blood with lemon dill salmon, roasted asparagus, rice pilaf, and open wine bottles.

Xander shook his head and blinked. "I'm great. I just thought I smelled blood there for a moment. But I must have imagined it." His gaze roved over the table, the firelight catching the brown highlights in his dark hair. "This looks amazing."

"We thought you would be sick of turkey after Thanksgiving. Hopefully, this is to your liking," her mom replied, setting a napkin on her lap. Nikki saw her mom's tongue move against her lips and cheeks, pushing the settings back up against her teeth.

"If it tastes like it smells, I'm sure it will be."

"Wine?" Miguel asked Nikki and Xander after pouring his wife a glass.

"Please," they both said, and her dad filled their cups.

The pounding in her head flared up with a sudden drumbeat, and Nikki winced. She tried to ignore the pain, but it was stubborn, and her fingers stiffened on the napkin under the table.

Cat cleared her throat and extended out her arms, beckoning for Xander and Miguel to take them. Hesitantly, everyone lifted their hands and clasped them together.

"We thank You, Mother, for bringing us life. We praise You, Mother, for sustaining us to this day. We rejoice You, Mother, that we can be here together tonight, out of the cold, the rain, the harshness of the day. We thank You for Your glory and the gifts You bestow upon us," her mom intoned.

Nikki was livid. Her chest tightened around the rage in her chest, and she squeezed her hands together, letting the crescents of her nails bite into her palms. She couldn't control her fanaticism for just a few hours? Nikki clenched her jaw hard as she stared at her mother, an unspoken challenge, a rebuke. Nikki lifted her chin to mirror her mother's arrogant gaze, when the pressure in her head suddenly disappeared, the room louder and larger than it had been a moment before.

Her shoulders relaxed with the absence of the pain, and her rage turned to worry as her mom winced, arms going stiff on the table.

"Um, amen?" Xander said, and Cat gave him a brief, appreciative grin. Xander returned the grin, trying to pull his hand away from her mom's tight clasp.

Her dad attempted to pull his hand back but also found it unmovable, and he said, "Eh, you are holding our hands too tight, my love."

Her mom's eyes widened as she looked down at their embrace, and her body stiffened. "Oh," she said, a slight crease forming between her eyebrows. Her arms flung back abruptly, as if she had been pulling away with all her might and had just been released.

"Are you well?" her dad asked.

"Yes, I'm sorry. I don't know what came over me."

"It must be hereditary," Xander said, readjusting himself in his seat.

"What is?" Miguel asked.

"The stiffening. It happened to Nikki, too. From what I've read, it could be a neurological disorder."

"This happened to you," her mom said, voice flat, a flash of worry, of anger, crossing behind her eyes.

Nikki nodded, reluctant, and cast her eyes to the side. The night had barely begun, and it was already falling apart.

"Who is 'Mother,' by the way?" Xander asked, and Nikki flashed an annoyed gaze at him. She knew he was trying to break the tension, but did they really have to talk about her mom's zealotry? Nikki took a deep breath and tried to still herself, trying to trust her parents. They'd been alive a long time. She had to hope they knew what they were doing.

Her dad raised his cup to his lips as Cat straightened and said, "She is the creator of life."

"So, like a Mother Earth?" Xander asked. "Sorry, I don't mean to pry, it's just that in all the blessings and prayers I've heard, I've never heard one for a mother. Or the Mother, I'm guessing is the appropriate way to refer to her? Does she have a name?"

Her mom nodded, once. "She does, but we do not speak it." She smoothed the napkin on her lap. "To answer your first question: yes, She is, essentially, Mother Earth."

Her dad cleared his throat, tongue swiping between his teeth and tongue to lick away the signs of blood in his mouth. He put the cup on the table and said, "Enough with this religion talk. Let's eat."

Cat averted her eyes, lips pushing together in a hard, uncertain line as she put a fillet of salmon on her plate and passed the platter to Nikki. They dished up in silence, passing the trays in a circle until each had a little of everything, except for Miguel.

"You aren't eating?" Xander asked, and Nikki kept her eyes away from her dad's glass of blood.

Miguel waved him off and said, "I ate earlier."

Xander nodded once, and before the silence became too awkward, her dad asked Xander about his studies and work. A flicker of something, pain, confusion, Nikki couldn't tell, flashed across Xander's face before he took the bait, launching into his life-long love for animals. Maybe she imagined the look?

Several minutes passed, then her dad cocked his head at her mom, who had stopped eating, her eyebrows more furrowed than Xander's, blinking hard. "Do you feel unwell, my love?"

"Oh my. I apologize," her mom said, raising her head, blinking as if she were coming out of a dream. She pushed two fingers against her temples and continued, "I fear I am developing a slight headache. Nothing to fret over," she replied, lifting her voice, and forcing a smile onto her face.

The food turned to ash in Nikki's mouth. *Not good,* Nikki thought.

She had never seen her mom admit, or act upon, feeling unwell in front of another person before. Especially one she had just met.

Unease swam in her guts, like being at sea and watching the weather turn for the worse. Xander returned to his food, but the furrow in his brow remained, as did the one on Cat's face, her mouth twisted in a grimace she tried to hide by eating and drinking.

A fissure split in Nikki's heart at the displeasure on their faces and the growing silence. So much hope and excitement just to cause them such disappointment and pain. Nikki stopped a sudden lump in her throat and cast her eyes to her plate to hide the blush of anger.

She should have known better.

Nikki scrunched the napkin tight in her hand and took a deep breath.

"We had a cat once," her dad said, either immune to the wavering hurt in the air or trying to ameliorate it. He cringed and shuddered. "I did not like it. And it did not like me. I think next time we should get a dog, eh?"

"Yes, darling," her mom replied dutifully, but Cat's gaze was distant.

"Cats are finicky creatures," Xander said and shrugged. "But I love them all. Even the mean ones. They're just misunderstood."

Miguel smiled, awkward with his fittings but still warm, and Xander grinned back at him.

"You look like you need more wine," her dad said, standing and walking around the table to fill Xander's glass, topping off Cat and Nikki.

"Thank you," Xander said. Miguel gave him a soft pat on the shoulder, and the tension eased out of Xander's face. "And thanks for the food, it's really good."

"I am glad you think so," her dad said, "But we did not make it, so I cannot take the credit."

"Well, then, my compliments to the chef," Xander said, then burst into laughter. "I never thought I would say that seriously in my life."

Nikki chuckled, but when Xander met her eyes, his gaze was sad, untouched by the faint smile on his lips.

The night improved throughout the course of the dinner, thanks to her dad carrying the conversation. Miguel and Xander talked about veterinary studies, animals, and Miguel's work, with her father dancing around his history, his upbringing, and only intermittently adjusting his mouth and tongue to keep the fittings in place. Xander didn't seem to notice, or if he did, he must have just thought it was a quirk. But Nikki watched with increasing nerves as her dad consumed more blood, eyes dilating, the calming euphoria glowing from under his skin. She despised herself for worrying for Xander's safety, for not trusting her parents enough. While her dad hadn't visibly smelled him, he was sure to notice something different about him, just as her mom had. As her dad continued to drink, Nikki's heart continued to race, and it took all her willpower to remain in place, to not leave early, to not run.

Her mom did not speak throughout dinner, intermittently pinching the bridge of her nose, pushing her fingers against her temples, the highest vertebrae in her neck. She tried to look attentive, but every few minutes, her gaze lost its focus, as if she retreated into her mind, or left it. Thankfully, Xander and Miguel were too lost in conversation to notice, but it did not ease Nikki's worries.

After dinner, dessert was brought out, and Miguel retrieved a bottle of port, pouring Cat, Xander, and Nikki small glasses. Again, Xander inquired why he didn't have some when he sang its praises, but Miguel replied it wasn't his cup of tea. For some reason, Miguel and Xander found that hilarious and broke into laughter.

Nikki sighed a breath of relief. At least they were getting along, even if her parents were restraining the desire to eat him. The thought made her stomach curl.

In a lull of conversation, her dad asked, "Do you have birthday plans, Nikki?"

Her mom perked up. "Yes, we could host a party for you, darling."

"Oh, I don't—"

"It's taken care of," Xander replied, holding up a hand with a mischievous grin.

"A surprise party, eh?" Miguel asked, mirroring Xander's excitement.

"Well, Nikki has been suspiciously quiet about her birthday, so I took charge."

Nikki grinned, wondering what surprises he had in store. When he had said several weeks prior in passing that he would figure it out, she hadn't expected him to. She thought her birthday would pass in the usual whisper.

"I see," her mom said, forcing her mouth into a tight smile.

"Eh, she's had birthdays without us. Don't be bothered, my love," her dad added. "We can have another dinner, yes?"

"Sure, Dad."

Cat's fake smile turned a little more sincere. "Shall we retire to the lounge? The storm does not seem to be ceasing, so we can't have a fire, but the chairs shall be more comfortable."

"Great idea, love. Come, come, let's go." Miguel said, standing and beckoning for the others to follow suit.

Xander picked up his dessert plate, and Cat touched his arm lightly, saying, "You can leave that for the help."

Xander's feet shifted, but he nodded and put the plate back down, slow.

Her mom's hand did not move from Xander's arm, long manicured nails pushing into his forearm.

Xander winced and tried to wiggle his arm free politely, but her claws were stuck into him. "That's quite a grip you have," Xander said with an awkward chuckle.

A small bead of sweat formed on Cat's temple, then slid down the side of her face, eyes wide with fear and confusion. She stared at her hand, once again stuck on Xander. Cat's eyes glazed over, her nostrils flared, and she brought her hand, nails red with flecks of his blood to his face as gently as a lover.

She gave him a soft, vacant smile, brushing her fingers against his cheek, then fixed her eyes on his neck, the beating of his heart pushing hard and fast in his veins.

"So close," her mom whispered.

Time stretched, and the storm silenced, Xander's heartbeat the only sound in the room, a steady, loud drumbeat in Nikki's head.

Cat's hand seized, tendons flexed in her palm, nails raking against his face as he moved away and Nikki jumped around the table to push him back behind her, facing her mom, although the eyes that looked at her were not her mom's.

"Oh, dear," Cat said, sarcastic and mischievous. "What a mess this has turned into. Hasn't it, darling?" Cat's face curled into a sickening, amused grin. "But at least you have brought him one more step closer to me."

Goosebumps shot up and down Nikki's skin, the back of her neck going cold. "No. No, you get out of her!" Nikki shouted and reached for her mom, shaking her shoulders, her head rocking back and forth so hard it seemed near to snapping.

"Hey, hey, hey!" her dad yelled, pulling a maniacally laughing Cat away from Nikki.

Cat suddenly stopped laughing, Miguel released his hands from her, and she stood solitary and still, like an ill-carved marble statue. Her eyes and hands twitched, a low moan escaping her mouth, and sweat slid down both sides of her face, matting her hair to her skin. She stumbled, crumpling over, and then caught herself on the back of the chair.

The three stared at her, uncertain, wary, worried. Miguel's hands circled each other, waiting for his wife to speak. Nikki kept her arms back and wide, as if to shield Xander, whose pulse drummed in her head, his fear a heady, rich smell that clouded her mind.

When her mom raised her head, the curtain of hair lifting, falling behind her back, she stood straight, wringing her hands. She looked at each of them and her face fell, cheeks reddening before she smoothed her skirts and said, "I think I ought to go take the air."

"No!" Nikki yelled, her parents' eyes wide with her yell, and her own cheeks heated with the sudden outburst. "I just mean, wouldn't it be better to lie down? Than to go outside in the storm?"

"The fresh air would do me good."

"I really think you should lie down instead," Nikki pressed, knowing nature was this monster's playground, and she was terrified of what would happen to her mom, to them all, if Cat went outside.

Her mom tilted her head.

"Trust me," Nikki said, trying to sound confident instead of pleading.

Mother and daughter looked at each other, searching, until Cat conceded with one brief nod of the head.

Her mom looked over Nikki's shoulder at Xander and gave a small bow of her head. "I sincerely apologize for my behavior. I do not know what came over me."

"It's all right," Xander choked, stepping closer but staying behind Nikki.

"Please, make yourself at home. I bid you stay the night, as the weather is unwelcoming. But I must retire for the evening."

Cat glanced at Nikki with an apology in her eyes and a frown on her lips, turning her back to them and leaving the dining room with delicate footsteps.

When her mom was out of sight, Miguel stepped close to them and whispered, "I am going to make sure she is well. Please—stay, eat, drink, relax." He turned to Xander, squeezed his hands, and gave him a tight-lipped smile. "I'm so sorry for the fright she must have given you. I promise that has never happened before. She will be mortified. I ask that you forgive her."

"Of course," Xander replied, voice weak and uncertain.

Her dad turned his focus to Nikki, eyes sad, as if he could see her disappointment. He put a hand on her cheek and kissed her forehead. "I am sorry, love. I would ask you forgive her too," he whispered, and his compassion made her eyes water when she only wanted to be mad.

Nikki nodded, pinching her lips to keep the lump in her throat down, and Miguel left them in the dim light of the dining room with one last goodnight.

His footsteps faded out of earshot, the door upstairs creaking open and closed. Xander's heartbeat relaxed, quieting under the threshold of her hearing, and she finally turned to look at him, worried about what she would see there.

His fingers touched the scratches on his face, droplets of blood on his fingertips when he pulled it away. Small pink crescents marred his arms. His brow furrowed, and Nikki took his hand, but when he raised his eyes to look at her, they were hard, his jaw set.

"Xander, I'm so sorry—"

"It's fine. Stings a little, but it'll be okay."

"I don't know what to say, I'm—"

"It's fine," he said, pulling his hand from hers, pinching the bridge of his nose and squeezing his eyes tight, releasing a long sigh. "Can we go lie down? I need a minute."

"Sure. Of course," Nikki said, grabbing the decanter of port off the table and leading Xander to her bedroom, heart hammering in her chest, as her skin crawled with a sense of wrongness. Wondering, worrying, if this was the end.

How much strangeness could he tolerate?

Nikki sat beside him on the bed, and without a word, began to clean the scratches. He flinched with the sting of alcohol, but otherwise didn't move or speak until she had cleaned and smoothed Neosporin onto his face and had begun to wipe away the crescent points on his opposite forearm.

"Does your mom have DID?"

Nikki cocked her head, questioning. His gaze met hers, quick and then away again.

"Dissociative identity disorder."

"No."

"This is going to sound crazy, but when she looked up at me, after clutching my arm, she didn't look like her. I mean she did, but the look in her eyes wasn't the same. Even her voice was somehow different. I don't know how to explain that, besides a disorder."

"I noticed that too," Nikki replied, relief tugging down her shoulders, worry clogging her throat. "But as far I know, she doesn't have DID. Or schizophrenia. Or any personality disorder."

He didn't reply, and when Nikki was done wiping away his wounds, she poured a glass of port for each of them, and sat beside him again, a little farther away.

"Are you okay?" she asked.

"I said I'm fine," he replied, sitting up to take the port, arms draped over his legs, looking at the ground, the wall, the glass. Anywhere but her.

"I know the cuts are shallow. But I mean, you're not mad? It didn't scare you off?"

Xander huffed, something between a scoff and a sigh. "No, you're not your parents, Nikki. It was scary at first, and definitely weird, but I feel worse for her, not knowing what was happening and clearly being embarrassed. I'm not mad, not at her."

Xander's words twisted in her stomach. "But you're mad at someone. Mad at me."

His jaw tensed, then he lowered his head, hair curtaining his face. "I didn't say that."

"No, but you implied it. Why are you mad at me? What did I do?" Nikki asked, feeling the sick certainty that he was about to leave her lacing through her veins.

Xander downed his port, then stood to put the glass on her dresser, his back to her. "It's been a long few days. Can we please just rest?"

"How am I supposed to rest with the anxiety you're giving me right now?"

His jaw clenched and unclenched as they stared each other down, Nikki lifting her chin even as her breaths came short and Xander's became ragged, his fingers twitching, until finally he broke into a disbelieving, angry laugh. Running a hand through his hair, he looked away from her and spat, "Your parents didn't know the first thing about me. I'm surprised they even knew my name! That's probably thanks to Gwen, too, as you seem so unwilling to have anyone know about me."

"That's not true—"

"Oh, it isn't? It was like pulling teeth to even get this far. And here I am, telling my whole family about you, as they embarrassingly told you, and I foolishly thought my reception here would be similar. That they'd at least know a little about me, that they'd begin with asking why I want to be a vet, not what I'm doing to begin with!" Xander's hands shook as he slashed through the air while he spoke. "It's like every time I turn around, thinking we're on the same page, I find out we're not. Do you know how exhausting it is to be the chaser?"

Nikki took a breath, a moment to stay calm and to think. "Xander, you're taking something personally that isn't personal."

"How is it not personal when it's about me?" Xander choked, something between a laugh and a sob caught in his throat, a sound that cracked Nikki's heart in two.

"It isn't about you. I promise," she said, standing and walking toward him, stopping when he took a half step back, the fissure in her chest widening at his retreat. But she lifted her chin to meet the hurt in his eyes and said, "What I do or do not tell my parents is a reflection on my relationship with them. Not about how I feel about you. Or our relationship. And if my mom's outburst didn't enlighten you as to why I wanted to keep you separate from them, I don't know what will. That was one of the scariest, most embarrassing moments of my life. And I knew something like this would happen." Nikki clenched and unclenched her fists. "But I organized this for you. For you to know I'm not trying to hide you. It's just, well, my family we're"—parasites, freaks — "different. I didn't want you to know the extent of it," Nikki finished, the image of her mom cradling Xander's cheek, the voice speaking through her, the rich smell of Xander's fear and the strong thump of his pulse still tugging at the predator in her mind. Her cheeks heated with embarrassment, and she dropped her eyes, folding her arms over her chest.

Xander dropped his arms, hanging loose at his sides, anger deflated. "I feel like a fool, Nikki. Again. You say you don't want to hide me, that it isn't personal, but it feels personal. Like I'm over here telling everyone about you, and you just want to keep me to your bedroom."

"You really think that low of me?"

"No, that came out wrong, I didn't mean—"

"No," she said and raised her hand, stopping him. "I don't want to hear it. You've insulted me enough tonight by implying that I don't care for you. And now I'm using you, too? If I'm such a manipulative, heartless monster, then maybe you should leave."

"That's not—I didn't mean it like that, Nikki," he said, reaching for her, but she stepped away, an unfamiliar mix of rage and sorrow filling her. "Please," he begged, and her mouth tightened, keeping it shut. Xander pulled his hair tight back from his face, an anxious, defeated laugh stuttering from his chest, and he crouched over his knees, exhaling as if he was trying to prevent himself from vomiting.

He fell back, sitting with his legs sprawled out and his back resting against the dresser. "I only meant that I want to be with you everywhere you go. That I want you to be with me always. I want to be in the world with you, and yet it seems you don't feel the same."

Nikki gripped her biceps, tears stinging the back of her eyes and she said, "If I could be in the world with you, I would." She hardened her jaw and swallowed, keeping her voice stiff to suppress the wobble in her chin, "But I'm of no use to anyone dead."

"Dead?" Xander's brow furrowed, and another pulse of shame flickered in Nikki's chest at her poor choice of words.

Nikki ignored it and ground out, "I'm sorry I can't be the partner you need or deserve."

"Why would you say that?"

"Because it's true. That's what this whole thing is about, right? You want someone who can be with you always—who can watch the sunrise, who can run in the daylight, see the ripples of sunbeams on the water." Nikki squeezed her eyes tight, hating herself for the one tear that slid down her face. "But I can't be that person. As much as I wish I could be. This has been my whole life, Xander. Stuck inside, looking out. And I know you want more than that. You deserve more than that. Which is why I tried to resist this. I knew at some point you'd realize my lifestyle wouldn't work for you. And it would be a lot of pain for only a little time."

Xander stared at her, an unreadable expression on his face, too many emotions flitting across it. His arms rested at his sides on the ground, palms up, body completely still, except for the bob of his Adam's apple as he swallowed and said, "Is that what you really want? For me to go?"

She looked into his sad, beautiful eyes and his defeated posture, memories of bumping into him for the first time at the library surfacing. The first kiss at the park. All his warm smiles and comforting arms. He was sunlight personified, the closest to daylight she would ever get, and her voice cracked as she said, "No. But you would be better off."

Everything strange that had happened to her started since knowing him, and now her mom knew, and Tyee knew. Ina was right—she was a threat, they all were, and he needed to be kept safe from her, from them, hidden.

"That's stupid," he choked out.

"What?" Nikki replied, startled into laughter by the sudden change of tone.

Xander stood, and as he closed the distance between them, this time she did not pull away. He cupped his hands around her face, swiping away her tears with his thumbs and tilting her face up to his. "I wouldn't be better off without you. You bring out the best in me, did you know that?"

"I do?"

"Yes," he said with a small smile. "You motivate me to be the best I can be. Ever since we met, I've wanted to be better, to work harder, to listen more. The world has looked more beautiful to me now that I know you're in it."

"Stop it," she said, heart ballooning until she thought it would burst.

"Okay, I will. As long as you promise to remember."

She nodded, and he kissed her, soft and reassuring, and she tasted the salt of their tears on his lips.

He lowered his arms to wrap her in an encompassing embrace, her head against his chest. "Besides," he began, voice lightening, "the world is still the world at night. No one said anything about needing to be in the world during the day."

She nodded against his chest. While she knew he was trying to lighten the mood, she couldn't bring herself to laugh.

Chapter Twenty-Seven

Nikki woke to an empty bed and a bleary memory of Xander saying he had to go to work but could pick her up later if she needed a ride home. She groaned and stretched, flipping over and startling at the pale outline of someone sitting beside her bed, staring at her.

Chills crept up her arms, but as her vision adjusted, the figure of her mom became more defined and she said, "What the hell, Mom? What are you doing?"

"Good morning, Nicoletta. We need to talk about last night."

Nikki flopped back on the bed, draping an arm over her face. "It's too early for this. What time is it?"

"Eleven am."

"Way too early. We should both be asleep. Go back to bed, and we'll talk about it later."

"Sleep would not find me this morning."

"Well, it's finding me. Please let me rest."

"Of course," her mom answered, but remained sitting.

"Are you just going to stare at me while I sleep?"

"I want to make certain we talk about this, and that you do not sneak away before we can."

Nikki groaned again and turned to her side to face her mom. "Fine.

I'll start. Thanks for the great show. I'm so glad Xander got an inside look at how freakish we are."

"We are not freaks, Nicoletta."

Nikki laughed. "I saw you smell him, Mom. Normal people don't usually do that."

The air around Cat bristled. "Your opinion about our species aside, I am mortified about last night. I wish it had not happened."

"Same."

"It would not have happened if you had heeded my advice months ago and listened to the Mother's compelling."

Nikki's skin went cold despite the fire in her chest. "You're joking."

"I do not jest. She is obsessed. Angered. Determined. I felt it. And She will not cease. I warned you that ignoring Her compelling would not bode well. Please, Nicoletta, do as She commands."

"And turn Xander over to an ancient vampiric deity who probably wants to eat him? I don't think so," Nikki said, biting down the rise in her voice.

"You do not know Her intention."

"Oh? And what do you think She wants with him?"

"I do not know. I cannot guess at the Mother's plans. But he is important to Her."

"No, he is important to me. I will not let him be harmed. By Her, or whoever the voice belongs to."

"Thus you will let the rest of us be harmed. I did not enjoy losing control of my body, Nicoletta. It hurt, to have Her in my head, my blood. As you well know, from the sound of it. If you do not do as She has commanded, who knows who else She will influence to fulfill Her wish. You would sacrifice the sanity and well-being of your family, your coven, your entire species for him."

"Entire species? Mom, cut the dramatics."

Cat remained silent, her eyes black in the dark against her pale skin.

Nikki met her fierce gaze with her own and said, "I won't sacrifice him."

"So you will sacrifice me," her mom said, bitter and sad.

"What? No." Nikki sat up in bed. "Mom, what is she going to do, really? Whisper nonsense in our heads? Make us hold onto him a little too long? I'd rather deal with that consequence than potentially lose him forever."

Cat shook her head and stood. "You are young and ignorant. She will do much worse than that. We will all suffer for this, Nicoletta."

"I don't believe that," she said, but her voice wavered.

"Yes, your lack of belief is the crux of the issue."

As her mom walked away, Nikki said, "Mom, come on. I'm sorry, I didn't mean to hurt your feelings. But you're being dramatic. It's not that big of a deal."

Her mom sighed and said over her shoulder, "It is. You go against our god, our species, our coven. You think there won't be punishments for this?"

The darkness got heavier in the silence.

"It would be best if you do not bring him here again."

"No shit," Nikki said, and her mom shot her one last disappointed scowl before leaving her alone in the darkness.

Nikki sighed, and laid back down, trying to relax the cracking of her heart. It seemed as if her life was dominated by fighting lately, and she was so tired of the anger, the pain. She texted Gwen asking to see her later. Maybe she could help her plan for how to deal with this. Xander, her mother, and maybe the Mother.

She lay in the darkness of her room for several hours, staring at the canopy of her bed, thinking of Xander's woes, her mom's concerns, the voice's commands. Her thoughts blurred into strange half dreams of her mom sitting in whispering trees, throwing apples to Xander below, until they faded into the dark of pure sleep.

Nikki woke in the late afternoon, feeling as if she hadn't slept at all. From the time, she knew the sun was still up but would be setting soon, so she remained in her room with her thoughts until dark. Gwen confirmed Nikki could go over to her house, and Nikki texted Xander to tell her the plan, although she wasn't sure how she'd get over to Gwen's.

She didn't put her dentures in, her mouth feeling strangely large without them. Yet it was so freeing to be as she naturally was.

With her bag slung across her shoulder, Nikki crept through the house, walking downstairs to the lounge, where she found her dad relaxing in front of the fire with a small port glass filled with a thimbleful of blood.

"Hi, love," her dad said, without turning as she entered the room.

"Hey, Dad. You okay?"

He waved her off and said, "Eh, long night." He turned to look at her as she sat opposite him, the flames warming her cold, marble skin. "Is Xander well?"

"I think so. He was startled and confused. But he's fine. He thought Mom might have a personality disorder. Better than knowing the truth."

"And what do you suppose the truth is, Nikki?"

Nikki froze, taken aback. Her fingers shifted in her hands, and she asked, "What do you think, Dad?"

He sighed and said, "It is an awkward thing to admit. But your mother, she may not be wrong, about this whole thing with the Mother."

"You don't really think that do you?" Nikki asked, despite her own suspicions and experiences. The hopes she had that her dad would douse her doubts, reassure her that the Mother wasn't, couldn't, be real, obliterated.

"I do not know what to think anymore." Her dad turned his face to the flames, which flickered against his bronze skin and black hair that he'd smoothed back from his face. "But I do know that was not your Mother last night."

"I know. I've been thinking the same thing."

"Who am I to say that because I have not spoken to the Mother that she does not exist? Even if She is a bigoted creature who despises me and all the Made, She could be real. I should not have doubted your mother. She is intelligent in all things. I should have known she was not a religious fanatic, but that she knew. I failed her in this."

Nikki's heart dropped as her dad's voice sank, laced with shame and sorrow. "You didn't fail her, Dad. I didn't believe her either. Lots of vampires don't. I didn't want to say anything at the time, but at my initiation, Tyee warned me about the Mother. Implied that Hormin is here at the Mother's command because of Xander." Nikki swallowed bile in her throat, the last tendrils of denial withering away. "I think I've known for a while that this is all real, I just didn't want to believe it." Nikki breathed deeply to steel herself for what she'd say next. "But I've been hearing things. And She has taken control of me, too, just not as bad as Mom."

"This is not good, love."

"I know. But I can't figure out why this is happening. What does She want from Xander?"

"I do not know, though he does have a certain draw to him."

"Yes, I'm well aware of how he smells to vampires," Nikki snapped, her protectiveness flaring. She calmed herself and said, "Sorry, I didn't mean that. Do you know of any other magical bloodlines that would have this effect on us?"

He shook his head. "There are many magics and unique species in this world. I cannot say what he is or where he hails from."

Nikki frowned at the fire and her dad downed his blood.

"Be careful, Nikki. I saw how you threw yourself between him and your mother. I know you want to protect him, but I do not want you to see you hurt. Especially if it means a confrontation with Hormin. I do not think there is winning against him." Her dad hesitated. "Perhaps Xander should go into hiding."

"What? How can I protect him if I'm not even with him?"

"Not being with him may be the best protection."

Nikki opened her mouth, but her dad held up a hand to stop her. "I know this is not what you want to hear but think about it. As far as we know, there are only three vampires who know his scent. Only you know where he spends his time. But there are others who know your scent, where you live, and there are those in the coven whose loyalty is not to you or some human boy."

"I see your point, Dad, but no. I will not abandon him to the wolves."

"Please, think about it. He is a good man, and I know you care for him. I do not want to see you injured or heartbroken."

"I won't be," Nikki said through a clenched jaw.

Her dad's face shifted, the middle of his eyebrows raised, and his mouth twisted in a sickening expression of sadness and pity. "So the young always say." Her dad stood and extended his hand, "Come, let us get you blood to take home before you leave."

The heat in Nikki's chest subsided to a heavy rock in her stomach, and she took her dad's hand. Their footsteps echoed through the hallway, and when it was clear he had nothing more to say on the subject, Nikki asked, "Can I borrow a car?"

"Eh? For what?"

"I don't have mine, and I need to visit Gwen. I can return it tomorrow and have Xander pick me up."

"Very well," he said. "The keys are in the garage."

Nikki nodded, and they packed up a box of thermoses for her, her dad giving her some of the leftovers from the previous evening. In the garage, he handed her the keys to his car and said, "I do hope Xander had a good evening, despite how it ended."

"He did, Dad, don't worry."

"I fear we won't be able to see him for a while, but I did like him. Hopefully someday we can see him again."

"I'd like that. And so would he."

Her dad smiled. "Good." He gave her a hug, and with his hands on her shoulders, he said, "Drive carefully. You will be shamed for any damages for all eternity. Literally."

Nikki chuckled and rolled her eyes at him as he laughed at his own joke and walked back into the house.

The drive to Gwen's was still, the storm from the day before quieting the world. Debris littered the roads and curbsides were flooded, large puddles of water pooling at the edges, inundating the soil, turning it to mud. But the wind did not blow, the trees standing as still as statues.

It was eerie, walking from the front of Gwen's house to her studio, her feet sloshing in the mud, the air so still she could hear the whisper of wind in the grass, the scuttle of birds in the trees. As she walked around the main house, she saw Gwen's sisters through the windows, huddled conspiratorially in the foyer. They turned and looked at her, dark red hair and deep green eyes tracing her movements. Bridget bared her fangs, and Nikki scowled, averting her gaze, and continuing to Gwen's studio, feeling their gazes on her back.

Her legs brushed against the tall grass as she entered Gwen's territory, and the sound of footsteps paused her walk. She lifted her head, listening.

A shuffle, like fabric rubbing together, from her right.

Her head twisted to the woods beyond the meadow, pinning the area of noise with her gaze, trying to discern what lingered in the woods.

There was no movement, no more sound.

The skip in Nikki's heart subsided, but she scanned the area, walked slow, a sickening sense in her gut to stay alert, that something was wrong.

Even past the view of the main house, she felt eyes crawling over her.

Gwen's studio glowed a welcoming gold, the ripples of her magic warming the air. Owls, ravens, crows, and birds she could not identify huddled in the heat of Gwen's magic, seeking sanctuary from the chill blanket of winter.

A twig snapped.

Her head twisted so fast her neck twinged, and someone said, "Shh!" sharp and quick, like a hiss.

Pulse pounding in her ears, she stared at the surrounding woods and took two steps away from Gwen's, into the darkness.

"Reveal yourself!" Nikki yelled.

The only response was a stiff whisper of grass as the barest of breezes pushed through the meadow.

"Uh, here I am," Gwen said, stepping out of her studio, clenching a shawl around her shoulders.

"What?" Nikki asked, walking backward but not turning around until she stood beside Gwen.

"I heard you yell to reveal myself. So, here I am."

"I wasn't talking to you. There's someone in the woods," Nikki replied, pointing in the direction of the sound.

"Could've been a deer."

"No, I heard a voice."

Gwen cocked her head and gave Nikki a mocking grin. "What else is new?"

Nikki couldn't help but laugh, the anxiety and fear from the past two days releasing in an abrupt bubble of humor. "That's what I need to talk to you about. In a way."

"Well, come on in. You know nothing can get past my wards that I don't want to."

In the dim, warm lighting of the studio, Nikki dropped her bag, then noticed the sickly pallor of Gwen's skin, the sheen of moisture. "What's going on with you?"

"Huh?"

"Now you're the one looking sick and not telling me why."

"She's pushing herself too hard," Theo said, stepping out of the bathroom.

Nikki's heart stopped. She hadn't put her teeth settings back in.

"Hey, Nikki," Theo said.

Seeing Nikki's face fall with worry, Gwen said, "Don't worry, she knows that you're a vampire. And I am, too, in a way. Unfortunately."

"You told her?" Nikki blurted, then said, "Sorry. I don't mean any offense, Theo. It's just—"

"Threatening. Unfamiliar. I get it," Theo replied. "And I won't tell Xander. Or Terrance."

"You won't?"

"It's not my place," Theo said, shrugging her narrow shoulders.

"Well. Thank you," Nikki said.

Theo inclined her head, not quite a nod.

Turning to Gwen, Nikki asked, "What does Theo mean by you're pushing yourself too hard?"

"She's been—"

Gwen threw up her hand, wagging a finger. "Tut, tut. A demonstration will be much more efficient."

Theo threw up her own hands in defeat, and Nikki guessed this was a discussion they'd had many times.

"Ever since your party a few months ago where I made that gust of wind, I wondered, if I can make the air move like that, what else can I do? Can I make it not move? Can I condense it? Dissipate it? I thought of that silencing ward I made when we went foraging, and how it was like a wall, and, well, I had an idea." Gwen's mouth split into a mischievous grin.

"Don't do it too hard, you need to rest."

Gwen waved Theo off and fixed her gaze on Nikki.

Gwen dropped the shawl to raise her hands, palms open and curling delicately, silvery-gold strands of magic spooling from her pores until the wavering threads filled her hands and with one quick, outward motion of both palms, Nikki's entire body was punched backward, and she knocked hard into the wall behind her, head smacking against the wood.

Dazed, Nikki recovered and said, "What the hell, Gwen?"

"I pushed you. With air."

Nikki blinked. "Holy shit."

"Right? Now check this out."

Gwen raised one hand, directly in front of her chest, the air rippling and waving around her.

"Touch it," Gwen said, muffled.

Nikki extended her hand and took slow steps forward, until she was about six inches from Gwen's chest, and then her hand came to a hard stop.

Surprise and awe lightened Nikki's body, forgetting the fights, the voice—no, the Mother—as she inspected Gwen's magic. She moved her hand horizontally and vertically, exploring the impenetrable, transparent wall along the width and length of Gwen's body.

"Test it," Gwen said, arm shaking.

Nikki cocked her eyebrow but was too excited to say no. She backed up and ran at Gwen, smacking hard against the wall. She laughed and wound back her hand to punch it, then she kicked it, shocks of resistance bouncing up her body.

The magic strands around Gwen's hands disappeared, and Nikki felt the wall drop as the air dispersed back into the normal space.

"I condensed the air to make a buffer. Cool, huh?" Gwen grinned. "I'm going to imbue the barrier somehow with this. Make it more a shield than a ward," Gwen said, trickles of sweat matting her curls to her face, and her knees gave out from under her.

Theo and Nikki yelled as she dropped, Nikki grabbing her before she met the floor.

"Whoopsies," Gwen whispered with a laugh.

Theo picked up the shawl from the ground and wrapped it around

Gwen's shoulders, then guided her to the couch. "She's been practicing this almost nonstop. I wish she would stop."

"Are you not impressed?"

"Baby, I'm extremely impressed. But I'd rather you not kill yourself."

Gwen scowled, and Nikki said, "Oh, how the tables have turned."

"Shut it," Gwen said but smiled. Sitting on the couch, shawl clutched tight over her heart, Gwen asked, "So, what did you need to talk about?"

Nikki hesitated, eyes flicking to Theo.

"Ah. Vampire business. Got it," Theo said, turning on the electric tea kettle for Gwen. "I'll go watch some TV with my earplugs in. Nikki, when that's boiled, will you please give her tea? It seems to help her post-magic sickness."

"Oh, yes. Of course," Nikki replied. "Thank you."

Theo gave another small nod and went to the bedroom. Nikki waited for the kettle to whistle, then prepped the tea, finding one of Gwen's restoring blends and letting it steep.

Bringing the hot mug to Gwen and sitting beside her, Nikki said, "I can't believe you told her."

"I didn't. She guessed. After Halloween."

"Someone was bound to clue into our joke eventually, I guess."

Gwen nodded, sipping. "So, tell me what's going on before I die from anticipation."

Nikki sighed and filled her in on the past two days, meeting Xander's family, his supposed royal lineage, Ina calling her out for being a vampire, Cat becoming possessed. Everything except her fight with Xander, and the sad, empty feeling it still left in her chest. When she was done, Gwen's cup was empty and cool, though still clutched in her hands. "Damn, Nik. That's quite a pickle you're in."

"I know. And I don't know what to do now. First, Tyee said I should give him up. Now that's what my mom says, too. My dad says I should hide him. But I want to stay close and protect him. What do you think I should do?"

"You really do believe it's the Mother, then?"

"As much as I hate to admit it, as much it goes against my sense of reality—yes. I don't think I can ignore the evidence anymore."

Gwen turned sideways, one shoulder against the back of the couch, facing Nikki. "What does your gut say?"

"That I shouldn't hand him over. I don't know what She wants with him. What She'd do to him. But as I told my mom, an ancient, godlike vampire can't be demanding him for any pure, safe reason."

"Agreed," Gwen said. "Do you think it has something to do with this whole Arthurian legend thing?"

"I have no idea. Xander doesn't even believe in it. Thinks his Dad was hallucinating or dreaming. Or just lying for the sake of a story."

"Like we thought your mom was."

Nikki wrapped her arms around herself and cast her gaze to the floor.

"So, we can't turn him in. And you won't leave him. How do we protect him? What exactly are we even protecting him from?"

"I don't know. I don't know anything!" Nikki said, the suppressed fear and anxiety bursting. "I don't know what he is. I don't know what She wants. I don't know how to protect him. I don't know what we're facing. I don't know what Hormin's planning. And there's still part of me that doubts all this. That thinks it's all just this messed up manifestation of zealotry and nothing will happen. But I feel watched. Often. And I don't know if it's Her. Or someone else. Something else."

"It's too bad She isn't talking to you anymore. We may have been able to manipulate that bond for information."

Nikki shook her head. "No, it isn't a connection. It's control. One way. Like a puppet on strings."

They sat in silence for several minutes, too many images of everything that could go wrong, of Xander being hurt, maimed, kidnapped, drained, thrashing though her mind.

"Do you have any protection spells? Can you put that shield or that silencing spell on him from afar?"

"Nothing like that," Gwen said. "But we could keep an eye on him."

"I can't watch him all the time."

"Not you, silly. Come on." Gwen said and stood, pulling Nikki up by the hand.

Gwen led her outside to the roost, birds huddled together, others eating and grooming. Gwen stood in front of them and lifted one arm, elbow bent and palm up. All the animals looked at her as strands of silver seeped through her skin and danced around her fingers, illuminating the darkness, casting Gwen's sickly skin in the color of soft metal.

The magic wound loose and calm in her hand, around her wrist, until one owl tossed its head and jumped from the roost onto her arm, nipping at the threads.

Gwen smiled, stroked the barred owl's head, and said, "You know, I knew it was going to be you, Harriet."

Harriet hooted and launched from Gwen's arms into the night.

"What did you do?"

"I made a request, and she answered," Gwen said, wrapping a corner of the shawl around the cuts on her arm from the owl's feet. "I asked for one to watch Xander and to let both of us know if something unusual or dangerous happens."

"What was with the magic eating, though?"

"She accepted my oath. She has to obey the request and is forbidden from being distracted. But now she is a bonded familiar and has not only my protection but a connection to my own magic. A benefit for her, indeed."

Nikki's mind spun. "You're making oaths with animals now?"

"Oh, yes. I've been working on it for quite a while. Years, actually. It's really just a stronger bond of friendship."

"Okay, so, wait," Nikki said, rubbing her temples. "Sorry. There has been so much information in the last two days. If the benefit of being a bonded familiar is so great, why didn't others jump at the opportunity?"

"That's because they're selfish bastards. The lot of them," she yelled at the roost, the animals just blinking at her in response. Gwen smiled, then turned back to Nikki. "They'd have to do my bidding, and I guess they prefer some independence."

Nikki and Gwen headed back to the studio. "I'll ask some diurnal ones tomorrow so we can have 'round the clock eyes on him."

"Are you sure? I don't want you to think I'm just using you for your awesome magic skills. We can find another way to keep tabs on him if it's too much to ask."

"Don't worry about it," Gwen said. "I appreciate you asking, but this is important. And it's not that much of an ask."

Nikki took a deep breath. "Thank you."

Gwen clasped Nikki's hands and said, voice strong and certain, "We will keep him safe, Nik. He'll be okay."

Nikki nodded, but kept her gaze to the floor, suddenly feeling small and scared.

Gwen invited her to hang with them that evening, and Nikki accepted with relief. It would be nice to just relax, to be around her best friend. The three of them talked easily, comfortable with each other, and as the night wore on, Nikki thought how good it felt to not wear the settings in her mouth. How nice it felt to not have to hide or worry about discovery.

How good it felt to just be herself.

Chapter Twenty-Eight

The following weeks passed in the usual manner. Nikki and Xander didn't talk about their fight once and eased back into their normal interactions, much to Nikki's relief. Maybe it would come up again at some point, but they were both too overwhelmed with finals to think of much else. Nikki at least did not have to work, but Xander was exhausted. Though they spent half their nights together, he was asleep earlier than usual, while she enjoyed the longer waking hours with the earlier sunsets and later sunrises. When Xander slept, she took blood shots to keep her body alert, attentive, focused. She retained more information when her blood uptake was consistent—the frequency mattering more than quantity.

Harriet followed them but had learned discretion and did not trail too close to be noticed. Xander made comments about seeing more crows and hummingbirds than usual for the time of year, which Nikki agreed was strange indeed. But mostly they kept their noses in their books. The few times Nikki did go outside, the sickening sense of being watched followed her everywhere.

Her birthday, December 11th, was the weekend after finals, and once all tests and essays were complete, a great sigh of relief rolled through her body. Each successful term was another step closer to figuring out the keys to vampirism. To being free of this curse and existing as a normal person. To not having to lie and hide herself from Xander.

The night before her birthday, she sat in bed reading while Xander slept beside her, arm draped over his face. His chest moved slow and steady, up and down, legs sprawled. Near midnight, his phone alarm buzzed violently on the nightstand, startling him awake.

"You have an appointment?" Nikki asked, teasing, handing him his phone.

"Yes," he grumbled, turning his phone off and sitting up in bed to kiss her cheek. "Happy birthday."

Nikki smiled the grin of a giddy little girl. "Thanks."

"Mmm," Xander said, flopping back down into bed, resting his head on her leg. "I wanted to be the first to tell you. And we've got a fun evening planned tomorrow—today—so you better be excited."

Xander left late the next morning, Nikki briefly noticing his departure. She startled awake later when her alarm went off, then she browsed the various happy birthday texts from her family, Gwen, and the coven. Gwen reminisced that for the first birthday ever they wouldn't be together, but she hoped she had a great day and promised they'd party soon.

Nikki had assumed Xander would be scheming with Gwen about her birthday, but now she had no idea what was in store for her. The afternoon crawled by, Nikki's anticipation slowing the hands of the clock. When Xander picked her up, he kissed her and wished her a happy birthday again, handing her a thin rectangular box with a sheepish grin.

"Present number one," he said.

"Number one?"

"It's not every day your girlfriend turns twenty-two. That means you should get four presents, at least."

Nikki laughed and unwrapped the box, paper crinkling in her hands. It was a wooden box engraved with vines and flowers, and inside, bookmarks of pressed flowers.

"I was going to get you real flowers, but I realized they'd die if I gave them to you and then we went out, so I got you that instead. The box is a pencil case, although I suppose you don't have to use it as one."

Nikki ran her fingers over the divots in the pencil case, admiring the soft wrinkles of the petals and leaves pressed in the bookmarks. "It's beautiful. Thank you," she said, turning to kiss Xander's cheek.

They drove into Portland, Nikki's mind racing, trying to figure out where they were going. The lights of downtown sparkled on the Willamette River as they drove by it. Xander parked in a neighborhood to the southeast, the streets dark and stippled with leafless, deciduous trees that loomed over them.

"Here we are," Xander said, unbuckling his seatbelt.

"Where is here?"

Xander smirked, and they got out of the car, walking arm in arm down the block, which gave way from residential to commercial land. The clamor and bustle of people grew louder, until they reached a street blocked off for pedestrian traffic only, dozens of stalls lining the streets, people walking and talking and eating between them.

"A popup night market," Xander said with a dramatic swoop of his arm. "I figured we could get a bite here, walk around, and then go to surprise number two?"

Dozens of responses fought for purchase in Nikki's mind, from teasing him for his effort to being overwhelmed by it, by his care for her. So she simply nodded, and with arms still linked, they entered the crowd.

Funneling out the voices and sights and smells was a difficult practice for Nikki under the effects of blood, all sensory input combating for priority. The street smelled of sugar, meat, baked goods, body odor, perfume, and deodorant. People wore clothes of all colors, the visual stimuli amplified by the sheer number of goods and materials on display. Snippets of conversation and chewing clamored in her ears until they ached, then rang, drowning out the nonsense.

"You okay?" Xander asked to Nikki's wide-eyed observation.

She nodded and said, raising her voice to be heard over the crowd, "Just taking it all in."

They browsed the stalls until they arrived at the far end of the market. Nikki's gaze snagged on a jewelry stand and the tall, dark-haired woman sitting behind it.

Though Nikki didn't usually wear jewelry, there was something about this stand that was different. It pulled at her. It had stones of all colors, with whorls and patterns of other gems and minerals inside, each piece its own universe.

The woman behind the stall didn't say anything when they approached, didn't even smile, just glanced at them before returning her gaze to the crowd.

"See something you like?" Xander asked.

Nikki's eyes roved over the pieces, hesitating over each one, until one ensnared her. "This one," she said, picking up a ring of light blue stone, flecks of gold and swirls of white within.

"How much?" Xander asked the woman.

"No, Xander, it's fine. I don't—"

The stall owner's piercing blue eyes met Xander's, surprised, as if she had been lost in thought and assumed they would idly peruse instead of buying anything.

The woman looked between Xander and Nikki, assessing, then shrugged with the barest movement of her shoulders. "Whatever you think it's worth."

They haggled for a minute, then as Xander paid, Nikki took a business card, thinking how much Gwen would like her jewelry. The card had a website and an email, but only listed her name as Rhea.

"Here," Xander said, turning to Nikki and slipping the ring on Nikki's left middle finger, his touch feather light. A surge of warmth spread through her body as the stone rested against her skin. "Present number two."

She wiggled her fingers, the lights catching on the gleam of the blue gem. "Thank you," Nikki said, smiling.

He returned her smile, kissed her, and they resumed their walk, Nikki relishing the heavy feel of the ring on her finger, the entrancing color and design of the stone.

After strolling all the way down the market and back up, peering past shoulders to gaze at the goods in the stalls, Xander and Nikki found a food cart pod to eat and drink under the warm heaters before returning to Xander's car, Xander bubbling with excitement at their next stop, which he refused to spoil for her, mouth set in a pleased, secret grin.

On the walk back to the car, the hair rose on the back of Nikki's neck, and she paused, sensing something behind them. Prickles like insect legs crawled up her skin, and she turned, hesitant, feeling like someone was breathing down her neck.

But when she turned, she saw no one. Just dark, tree-lined streets packed with parked cars.

"You okay?" Xander asked.

Nikki scanned the street, sickening dread rising in her stomach. "I thought I heard someone."

Xander looked around and shrugged. "I don't see anyone. Besides," he said with a smirk, pulling her close, "I'm sure you could take them."

Nikki cringed, trying to force it into a smile, disgusted by how feral she acted on Halloween. She wanted that part of her kept deep, deep down in the dark of her being.

Xander's eyebrows pinched, mouth twinging in worry as he saw her displeasure, but he didn't say anything more. He tugged her forward by the hand, and she fell back into step beside him, reluctant to turn her back. Xander resumed idle chatter, but Nikki only half listened, keeping her senses alert to their surroundings, the skeletal trees leaning in.

In the car, Xander turned the heat on full blast, the rosiness of their cheeks from the cold smoothing away.

After fifteen minutes, Nikki realized they were back across the river in Vancouver and heading east.

"I hope you're not taking me to my parents'," Nikki said, lifting her voice to sound lighthearted, despite the dropping in her stomach.

"If I had been scheming with your parents, would the dinner have been so awkward?"

"Good point," Nikki said. "Are we going to Gwen's?"

"Stop guessing. That'll ruin the fun."

"So, that's a yes."

"I didn't say that."

Nikki chuckled and bit her tongue, deciding to keep her thoughts to herself, to let him have the fun of his surprise.

They pulled into the front of Gwen's parents' house, and Nikki hoped Gwen's family would not be home. Or that they were blood drunk, making their senses dull, and would not smell Xander. Bringing him here was like bringing him into a viper's nest. Gwen better have had a plan.

"What's wrong?" he asked, eyebrows furrowing as he saw her twist the handles of her purse.

"Oh. I just don't get along with her family. I was hoping we wouldn't run into them."

"Gwen said something about them being assholes, but she also said you know a way around?"

Nikki nodded and straightened herself with false confidence, bracing against the bitter cold. They walked around the east side of the house, Nikki clutching Xander's hand and keeping him close, staying alert to see and hear potential movement in the woods.

As they reached the back of the house, Nikki turned to look through the wide glass windows of the house, faint gold light illuminating the inside and back porch. The three sisters sat in the living room, goblets of blood in hand, gluttonous and lazy as usual. Their heads turned in unison, wine-red hair cascading over their shoulders. Bridget's mouth curled into a wicked grin, and she stood, the younger sisters standing behind her. Their eyes flicked to Xander behind her, and their eyes widened with surprise and delight.

The sisters slid open the back door, and Nikki pushed Xander ahead of her, away from the house. He stumbled and cursed, asking, "What the hell?" As he turned and saw the sisters pause on the porch, understanding dawned. "Oh. Should I introduce myself?"

"No. Go on into the studio. Straight to the meadow," Nikki said, taking a protective step forward.

The sisters' eyes followed them, and before Nikki turned her gaze away, she noticed the flare of their nostrils. The imprint of their three silhouettes staring hungrily after them made her stomach roil.

Nikki sensed the wide barrier of magic rippling in the air around

Gwen's studio and the roost, birds hooting and chirping at their approach. The barrier felt different as they stepped through it, like heat and pressure, but Xander didn't seem to notice the change.

"Oh, I almost forgot," Xander said, turning to her with a grin. "You have to wear this." He pulled out a long thin piece of fabric.

"A blindfold."

"Gwen made me promise."

Nikki huffed a laugh and acquiesced. "Gwen and her theatrics."

Xander tied the blindfold around her eyes, and she pushed back against the fear racing through her veins at the loss of her vision.

"You ready?"

Nikki nodded, heart in her throat.

The studio door creaked open and a rush of warm air pooled over her skin as she stepped inside, leaving the sound of flapping wings and clacking beaks behind her. Light filtered through the dark of the blindfold, and when Xander untied it, she was momentarily blinded by the brightness.

"Surprise!" voices shouted in the overwhelming light. As her eyes adjusted, she saw Gwen, Theo, Terrance, and his sometimes-girlfriend Rachel sitting on a massive blanket on the ground. All of Gwen's furniture was pushed to the corners of the room, and they were surrounded by a feast of fruits, vegetables, cheese, sandwiches, crackers, and cured meats. A small, decorated Christmas tree blinked and twinkled in the corner.

Nikki looked up, glittering light catching her attention. Her mouth parted as she gazed at the little suns hanging on fish wire from the ceiling, orange balls in foil that caught and bounced the light like little stars, triangles of yellow cardstock around the balls in mock, miniature suns.

"The theme is a summer picnic in the park," Xander said with a smile, stepping around her.

"You can almost believe it if you ignore the Christmas tree," Gwen added.

Xander ignored Gwen, nodded to the floating suns and said, "Pick one."

All eyes on her, she yanked one orange and yellow sun from the wire. It was heavy, and a smile broke her face at the familiar crinkling in her hand, the subtly sweet smell it emitted.

"You didn't," she said, cheeks hurting with her grin as she unraveled the foil, the smell of chocolate filling her nose. Unpeeled, she cracked into the dark orange chocolate, breaking the slices apart and popping a piece in her mouth, letting the chocolate and dull orange flavors melt on her tongue.

Her eyes watered at the sweetness.

When she raised her head, she didn't know whether she wanted to laugh or cry, so instead she looked at the dozens of orange-chocolate suns hanging from the ceiling and then Xander's beautiful, waiting face, and said, "Thank you." Then she looked at the others and said, "To all of you. This is—" Nikki paused, heart full to bursting. "I don't know what to say."

Gwen gave her a knowing smile, and as she stood, Theo said, "If I never have to cut another triangle in my life, it will be too soon."

The group chuckled, and Gwen wrapped her arms around Nikki, saying "Happy birthday. And congrats on getting through finals."

Nikki hugged her back, her hair smelling of fall leaves and old forests. "Thank you so much."

Pulling out of the hug, Gwen said to Xander, "Go get your lady a drink."

"On it," Xander said, joining the group on the blankets, assessing their wine and beer options.

Gwen turned to Nikki with a smirk and whispered, "They're enchanted, you know. The suns."

"How?"

"Well, I tried to use some of my newfound air magic, but that only works with sound and not light, so that was a bust. But I was able to mix the strands of magic into an elixir that created a crystalline coating. Totally inert, but it sure makes things look pretty."

Nikki looked at the twinkling orange chocolates, swinging and twirling gently. "It really does. Thanks again."

"Be sure to thank Theo, too, she cut out hundreds of triangle squares. Nearly lost her mind. Oh, and Xander, of course. The whole thing was his idea, even though we were the ones to execute it. He even thought of the orange chocolates himself."

"I will." Her smile faltered, and she whispered, "Do you think it's safe for him here? I mean, we saw your sisters on the way in, and the way they stared. I'm worried about him being around them."

"Don't worry, I've reinforced the wards and imbued them, as I said I would. Plus, I beckoned for extra eyes and ears outside tonight."

"It just seems insane bringing him here of all places."

"I mean, he asked if we could host it here, and I couldn't find a good reason to say no. I didn't think you'd appreciate me spilling the beans."

"That's true, it just makes me very uncomfortable," Nikki said, fear still wrapped around her heart.

"I get it, but you know they can't get past my wards. I made them specifically to prevent unwanted vampires from getting in. And I've added the extra buffer, which you tested yourself. But if you're still worried about it, you two can stay the night, and he can leave in the morning."

Nikki looked at Xander over Gwen's shoulder, the shape of his back as he laughed. "Maybe. Thank you."

"What are you two whispering about? Bring the birthday girl over here!" Theo chided, waving a bangled arm at them.

They joined the others on the floor, the charcuterie feast spread out over several blankets, with pillows and backrests scattered around for comfort. Nikki furrowed her brow, looking at the studio, dozens of small plants along the walls. "Is it greener in here?" she asked.

"That was Terrance and Rachel's task," Gwen said, giving them an appreciative nod and popping a grape in her mouth. "They bought plants—fake, of course—and decorated the space. Can't have a summer picnic without some greenery."

"Wow. Thank you. All of you. This may be the best birthday I've ever had," Nikki said.

Xander took her hand, squeezed it, then pulled her in closer, kissing her forehead, smelling faintly of wine and spices and everything warm and good. Nikki smiled up at him, and he grinned back at her, eyes bright with joy.

Xander handed Nikki a plastic cup of wine, and they passed around cutting boards and trays full of food, piling it on paper plates until they were too lazy and just shared sloppily from the center. Hours passed with the portable heaters filling the room with warmth, the fake plants and hanging suns creating a timeless summer day. Nestled into Xander's side, listening to the chatter of his friends—no, their friends—a sudden, sad weight dragged her chest into the pit of her stomach.

She sat up, and her head spun, but the sorrow in her heart remained, and she frowned at her hands, chastising herself for ruining a perfectly good night.

Xander nudged her with his shoulder. "What's wrong?"

"Oh. Nothing."

"Come on, tell me. What's missing? I want you to have a perfect birthday."

"That's the problem, Xander. It is perfect. And I wish it didn't have to end. I wish I could be with all of you in the sun, in the summer, lounging in parks. Getting sunburns. Seeing the sunsets. I wish it were real. Not just a fantasy."

Xander was silent.

"I'm sorry. I'm not trying to be unappreciative. I'm so touched you did all this for me. It's a dream, really. It just reminded me of everything I'm missing."

"I understand," Xander said. "We could do this more often, if you want."

She nodded, and he kissed her ear, then said, "But the night isn't over yet. We still have time to enjoy this. You want any more food or wine?"

"I probably shouldn't have more wine unless you want me to get more morose."

"It's your birthday. You can be morose if you want to."

Nikki laughed and accepted more wine. They snacked and chatted, and Nikki wrapped her heart in the warmth of the moment, trying to ignore the pain of the temporary brightness quickly swallowed by the dark. Toward midnight, the eyelids of the mortals grew heavy, and Gwen suggested putting on a movie. She pulled down the projector screen and turned off the lights, turning the dangling chocolate suns into dimming stars. Theo and Gwen cuddled on the couch while

Terrance and Rachel lounged on the picnic spread. Nikki debated whether they should stay overnight, to stay within Gwen's ward until the sun came up, but the hours they had spent inside without harassment from Gwen's sisters emboldened her. Maybe they had left for the evening or were minding their own business for once. Tyee had said Nikki was one of the few who knew why Hormin was here, surely that wouldn't include Gwen's frivolous sisters.

The night drifted away, and Nikki decided it was best for them to leave. She plucked orange chocolate suns from the ceiling like apples from a tree, and once her bag was stuffed full of them, she thanked her friends for a fun evening, their responses brief and quiet in their fading consciousness. Gwen blew her a kiss and gave her one last flash of a smile before snuggling back into Theo, pulling the blanket snug around them, and turning her focus back to the movie.

Xander and Nikki stepped out into the cold night, birds in the roost resting, the owls staring, straight necked, into the woods. They didn't acknowledge them, and unease crept low and cold in Nikki's gut.

She took one more step away from the studio and snatched Xander's arm, freezing them both in place.

Floating on the breeze was the scent of something frozen and ancient, like deep permafrost.

Unfamiliar vampires.

Nikki fixed her gaze on the dark forest, scanning for movement, but all she saw was the sway of the trees and grass behind the wavering veil of Gwen's magic.

"Gwen?" Nikki said in a voice unknown to her, cracked and high.

"Nikki, what's going on?" Xander asked, brow furrowing in anxiety and worry, eyes darting between her and the woods. "Nikki, you're hurting me."

She released him but did not respond, nudging him behind her as she stepped in front of him, the smell of long, barren, harsh winters and plants half-frozen in their decay growing stronger.

All the birds, in one great swoop, launched off their roosts and disappeared into the night.

"Gwen!" Nikki yelled, moving her and Xander backward, closer to the studio, her heart in her throat and a hum in her veins. As she felt the ancient presence press down on her, three shadowy figures stalked toward them from the woods.

"What?" Gwen hissed when she stepped into the night, holding a blanket tight at her collarbones. "What's your—" She stopped, mouth hardening into a firm line when she stood beside Nikki.

"What the hell is going on?" Xander asked, his voice unusually low.

"Shh!" Gwen said.

"Who are they?" Xander asked. "Are they your family?"

"No," Gwen said. "I don't know who they are."

Cold prickles ran up Nikki's skin at Gwen's words, watching the three figures converge on the studio.

"It'll be okay, Nik," Gwen said, leaning close. "It's protected, remember? And if you have to, take him and run."

"Seriously, what the fuck is going on?" Xander asked, voice rising, his heart beating louder and louder.

"Xander, I need you to calm down," Nikki said, hardening her voice, trying to drown out the sound of their pulses. She wished she could turn and take his face in her hands, to tell him it would be okay, that she would protect him, but she couldn't take her eyes off the trio.

Gwen stepped back and jumped up and down, waving her arm, until the outside light came on.

"Nikki, Gwen, seriously. What is the problem? You're freaking me out." Xander shifted on his feet, trying to get around the shield of Nikki's arms, but Nikki grasped his wrists to still him, to keep him behind her.

Swallowing her heart, she nearly choked on it when she said, "I promise I will tell you when this is over. But I need you to calm down. Right now." The light broke over the dark silhouettes, and Nikki whispered, "And don't say anything to them."

Two males and one female stepped in a wide crescent around Gwen's barrier, as if they could sense it.

A tall male moved into the light, which glinted off his strawberry blonde hair, close-shaved beard, and glacier eyes. His body was corded with muscles, held in the utter stillness of someone who had controlled their body for millennia. He wore thick, padded, dark leather armor that creaked as he moved, and covered his skin, all the way up to his neck.

Twin daggers hung on a belt carved with leaping and snarling animals, metal hilts catching in the lamplight.

Words of defiance swelled in Nikki's chest, but they drowned in the fear this man instilled in her, who looked down at her with the barest upturn of his mouth, his gaze painful and oppressive with too much knowledge, too much time, too much power. Nikki kept her chin high, arms out to block Xander. She had no clue how to fight, and this man looked like all he did was fight. But she'd go down trying.

The man's lips curved into the smallest grin, as if reading her thoughts. "You've been quite the troublemaker, Nicoletta Neves Silva." He turned his eyes to Gwen. "You as well, little witchling."

Gwen's nose scrunched with disgust. "What do you want?"

"I would think that's rather obvious," he said, flicking his eyes to Xander.

Nikki wanted to say they couldn't have him, but the words died in her mouth. As her gaze roved over him, his scent filling her nose, a hint of familiarity rushed through her body.

"You," she spat. He quirked his brow and she said, "You've been watching us, haven't you? I sensed you on Halloween. And then again on Thanksgiving."

"Very good," he replied, his amused grin unwavering. Xander shifted on his feet behind her, the throb of his racing heartbeat drumming in her ears, her fingertips around his wrist, the heady scent of warmed spices filling the air as he grew fearful.

The man fixed his eyes on Xander, and his smile faded, nostrils flaring. Nikki backed them both away, despite knowing the barrier still stood between them.

"You're not welcome here. Whoever you are," Gwen said, straightening.

The studio door cracked open, and Theo stepped out into the cold, eyes drooping with sleep. She glanced at the three muscular, leather-clad figures and asked, "Baby, what's going on?"

"Go back inside, Theo."

Theo walked to stand beside Gwen, fixing a hard stare at the man in front of them.

The man's smile broke, revealing the largest, thickest fangs Nikki had ever seen, his nostrils flaring as he took in Theo's scent.

"What the fuck?" Xander whispered.

"Such a delicious mortal you have here, little witch." His cold gaze fixed on Gwen. "You raise a good point. We've forgotten our manners." He lifted his right hand and pointed to the woman beside him. She was stern-faced, with hawk-like features and shoulder-length auburn hair.

"Aella."

Aella stepped into the light and gave one curt nod, face impassive and hands on her belt. The curve of a bow peaked over her shoulders, the leathers she wore matching in style to the first vampire, yet cut shorter, ending at her elbows and shoulders. Animalistic scars wound up her arms and to her neck, with flowers, grass, and vines in between.

The man indicated to the other male on his left, who had a square jaw and dark hair.

"Uase."

Uase stepped into the light, arms crossed, dark leathers cut at his shoulders, revealing the thick muscles of his arms, the point of a spear angled over one shoulder, battle axes hanging from his waist.

The first man put a hand on the leather over his heart, and inclined his head without taking his eyes off them. "Vadasz," he said. "Now, what are your names?"

Nikki clenched her jaw, refusing to answer. Xander, Gwen, and Theo held their mouths shut as well.

Vadasz sighed. "Doesn't matter, as I know them already. I simply thought we'd try to be polite, but I see you would rather be difficult. Yet I will do you one last courtesy. You can choose the easy way and hand the boy over. Come with us willingly, answer for your insubordination, and no harm will come to you. Or you can do it the hard way, where you will all suffer. Even those slumbering ever so innocently inside."

"The boy?" Xander asked, voice high.

Vadasz quirked a brow at Xander, cocking his head. "You are too young to be called a man."

Nikki felt Xander's body stiffen, arms shaking. "Wait, you want me? Why?"

Vadasz blinked, slow. "Truth?"

"Yes," Xander said, firm.

"He's not talking to you, idiot," Uase grunted.

Aella nodded, and although Vadasz was not looking at her, his mouth curled into a wicked, satisfied grin.

"How delicious that you don't know. Do you?" he asked, turning his gaze to Nikki. Nikki set her jaw, and Vadasz met Gwen and Theo's eyes in turn. "Do any of you?" He laughed when no one responded, a loud and melodic sound that filled the meadow. "Wonderful. It's always more fun when the enemy doesn't understand the stakes."

"Why don't you explain it to us, then?" Theo asked.

"Did you not just hear what I said? That would spoil the fun."

Footsteps shifted in the grass behind the trio, three more dark figures emerging. Nikki had been so focused on Vadasz, she hadn't heard others approaching, and she chided herself for her lack of vigilance.

Gwen's sisters fell into the halo of light, the smell of warmed blood filling the frigid air as they handed full goblets to the three.

"I see you've met our Scythian friends," Bridget said, smirking.

"You bitches," Gwen whispered, seething, at the same time Nikki wondered, Scythian? What does that mean?

"What was that?" Bridget snapped.

"I said, 'Hey, Bridget.'"

The trio shifted, spreading out to make room for the sisters in the semi-circle, and Vadasz said, "Yes, we've just made introductions. Although they refuse to give their names. Not that they matter, in the end."

Bridget took a sip of blood and assessed them. Stepping close to the barrier, she stared at Xander and said, "So this is the pretty little thing everyone is in a fuss over."

"You're not going to get in here, you know. None of you," Gwen said.

"Oh, I've told them all about your magic," Bridget said, grinning.

"Magic?" Xander asked, but everyone ignored him.

Vadasz took a sip of blood, handed it to Bridget, and then plucked off his gloves one finger at a time. He stepped toward the barrier, and Aella sat cross-legged on the ground, braiding the tall, dying grass.

Vadasz raised his hand and pushed, the pulsing waves of the shield gleaming with light, his skin hissing and reddening as he pushed through Gwen's magic. Xander gasped as the barrier flared to life in front of him. Gwen's face fell, Nikki's eyes widening in horror, as his hand pushed through the barrier, his skin sloughing off and squelching onto the grass, sending up steam as it evaporated into the cold.

Yet, as his flesh peeled from his muscles, and his muscles from his bones, he pushed through the barrier, the layers of tissue and bone greasy and bright against the light of the shield.

Vadasz stopped pushing just up to his wrist, the hand on their side of the barrier a bloody, bony, muscled mess, most of the skin melted and gone.

Xander's body tensed beside Nikki, until he was nearly stone.

Theo turned and vomited.

The inch where his arm remained in the barrier hissed, melting through his muscles, down to the ulna and radius, but he kept his hand in place, extending his fingers and relaxing them.

He looked to Nikki, who, mouth parted, forced her gaze away from his mutilated hand to his void-like blue eyes, and he said, "We rode with the warrior queen Tomyris against Persia, and with Attila on the Catalaunian Plains; we were there when Constantinople fell, through the rise and fall of the Golden Horde, to the Great Stand on the Ugra River. We have fought for the protection of our homeland, led battles that caused the fall of empires, have watched blood spill from the broken bodies of history's greatest leaders. You will not best us." Vadasz shifted his eyes to Gwen. "We made this wood and bone magic of which you are so proud. What you dabble in is merely a thimble compared to the vast oceans of our magics. You cannot yet fathom the depths of our power. Yours is not enough to keep us out."

Vadasz slid his hand back through the barrier, melting off another layer of muscle, the ring around his wrist where it sat in the barrier little more than bone. The weight in the air lifted, though the world looked darker at the edges, and dread settled deep into Nikki's bones.

Aella stood, and Bridget gave the goblet of blood back to Vadasz, who took a long sip. As Aella wove the blades of grass around his bare bones, Vadasz's mouth darkened with blood and his eyes dilated. He said, "But that does not matter. All we have to do is wait you out."

"No, all we have to do is wait you out," Gwen spat. "The sun will come up eventually."

Vadasz tsked. "You are bad listeners. Do you think we would not have a course of action for the daylight? When she," he said, nodding towards Nikki, "is one obstacle removed? True, we have to bring her eventually. But she is not the priority. He is."

"Why?" Xander breathed and was once again ignored.

Aella finished wrapping his hand, and when she stepped back, Nikki saw the blades weave with Vadasz's regenerating flesh, muscles stitching and crossing, the grass-lined skin folding over them. Vadasz flexed his hand, extending and relaxing his fingers, and he nodded thanks at Aella, who moved back to her place in the circle as Vadasz approached the barrier once more, Uase and Gwen's sisters standing as still as predators assessing their prey.

"It's true, you could flee during the day. Face the mortals stationed around the property. Ask yourselves, would you rather hurt us, or the humans?"

Nikki sucked in a breath, and Gwen curled her hands into fists.

"Maybe," Xander started, voice weak. He cleared his throat and stepped to Nikki's side, and she had to resist the urge to push him back again. "Maybe if you just tell me what you want from us, from me, we can work something out?"

Vadasz blinked at Xander, and behind him Bridget burst into laughter.

Xander blushed, his pulse racing in Nikki's ears, his fear breaking her heart.

"I admire your attempt at diplomacy. But it won't help you, now. Your best choice would be to come with us."

"What will happen to me if I do?"

"Xander, don't!" Nikki hissed, but he didn't look at her, keeping his clenching and unclenching jaw tilted toward Vadasz.

Vadasz shrugged and lifted his hands. "That, I do not know."

"It won't be anything good, Xander," Nikki pleaded. "Please, stay right here."

"How do you know?" Xander asked, fixing his gaze on her, brows furrowed and mouth in a hard line, eyes guarded and untrusting.

"Because I do. Please. I'll explain later if you please, please just stay right here beside me."

Xander searched her eyes and acquiesced with one small nod. He stepped back behind her again.

Vadasz sighed and sat in the grass, resting an arm over a knee, leaning back on the other hand. "We don't mind waiting. One can't live as long as we have without growing accustomed to it, after all."

Uase grunted but remained standing, arms crossed, while Aella stitched and wove strands of grass together. Gwen's sisters sat down as well, sipping their blood and staring at the four of them like hyenas.

The four stepped away from the barrier, close to the light and warmth of the studio, the remaining courageous birds hopping anxiously on their roosts.

"What are we going to do?" Gwen whispered.

"Do you two have your phones?" Theo asked Nikki and Xander, who nodded. "Get them out and give us one."

Nikki unlocked her phone and handed it over, Xander pulling his out of his pocket just as a text from Nikki's phone landed on his screen.

Let's plan this way so they can't hear what we're saying, Theo texted.

"Tut, tut, children. Texting is against the rules," Vadasz said. "Put them away."

Nikki's stomach sank, the feeling mirrored on her friends' faces.

"And what are you going to do if we don't?" Gwen asked.

Vadasz's brow twitched. "Do you want me to go through the barrier again? I will if I have to. We all will."

"Ah, shit," Gwen said, plopping the phone back into Nikki's hand and sitting hard on the ground.

Theo stepped to the side and put her hand on the doorknob.

"No going inside, either," Vadasz said.

"I have to pee," Theo said without removing her hand.

"There's a nice patch of grass right in front of you, eager to be fertilized."

Theo grimaced and dropped her hand. "At least let me walk around the side of the building into the shadow for some privacy."

"No," Vadasz said, all humor gone from his face.

Nikki wrapped her fingers in Xander's as her hope vanished. They were trapped.

The moon shifted slow in the sky, the deepest dark and most frigid cold settling over them. Theo and Gwen huddled close for warmth, rubbing each other's arms. Xander and Nikki stood beside each other, arms barely touching, staring at the vampires outside the barrier.

The longer Nikki watched them, the more her veins turned to ice. They were so still, too still. More so than she had seen from her parents. From Tyee or Hormin. All garden statues except for Aella, braiding grass. And their eyes did not leave the four of them, not for longer than the time it took for them to blink.

Nikki refused to sit, to lose her guard, and when her muscles ached from standing and her bones stiffened from the cold, the moon was high in the west with the impending ascent of day.

Gwen looked up at the sky, eyes wide and skin pale, looking more vampire than she ever had. Gwen sensed Nikki's gaze and met her eyes, and an understanding passed between them. Theo stood behind Gwen, and Nikki pulled Xander close to her. She met his betrayed gaze, hoping he saw what she thought, what she was trying to communicate. His jaw clenched and mouth twitched, and she wished she could know what that meant.

But she took a breath and looked at their hunters, their enemies, these creatures who would hurt her love and upend her life. The eastern sky was the color of a deep bruise that would soon shine with healing.

The vampires outside the ring stood, leather creaking and cloth ruffling. Aella tossed aside her braided grass, and Uase stretched out his arms that had been crossed for hours, before crossing them again.

The six stepped close to the barrier, looking at them expectantly.

"Come to your senses, have you? I was starting to get rather bored," Bridget said. Aella rolled her eyes, but Vadasz and Uase remained impassive, unreadable.

"Yes, sister, I think I have," Gwen replied, stone-faced and monotone as the air around them grew thick with tension, the space shrinking as though it were being sucked in toward them.

"What are you doing?" Vadasz asked, a note of curiosity.

The pressure built in Nikki's ears like a change in altitude, muting the world, and Nikki tightened her grasp on Xander's hand, his heart beating along with hers in their palms. She thought her head might collapse with the weight of it, the silence loud and oppressive, and then Gwen released it with one large push, the barrier slamming outward into the vampires as the air pressure broke around them. The Scythians and Gwen's sisters crumpled to the ground with the searing blast pushing over their skin, and in that moment Nikki dashed forward, yanking Xander into a run, jumping over the startled forms of their enemies.

"Don't let them get away!" Vadasz roared, his voice holding the command of one who has led legions.

Xander stumbled at the first yank but gained his footing as Gwen yelled, "Run!"

The grass hushed against their clothes as they sprinted through the meadow, footsteps pounding behind them. Nikki's heart hammered in her ears, against her ribs, and ice crawled up her skin as the footfall got louder, the whir of an arrow rushing past her head, skimming her ear. Clutching a hand to the side of her head against the stinging pain, she forced herself to move faster, anticipating the shock of an arrow through her body, until she heard a startled screech from behind them. She looked over her shoulder, the wind cascading past her frozen skin, as a mass darker than the night broke from the edges of the forest and descended onto their pursuers. Birds of all species clawed and scratched and pecked at them, the long, sharp beaks of hummingbirds stabbing at the vampires' eyes.

Holy shit, Nikki thought, goosebumps trailing her skin at Gwen's power, at the force of nature that descended around them. She spared one last glance past the swarm of screeching birds and saw Gwen, glistening from sweat in the lamplight, one hand held toward the sky and one held outward, taking slow steps forward, moving the barrier closer and closer, burning her sisters while the birds targeted the Scythians.

Please, Gwen, make it out of this, Nikki thought, turning her gaze back to the path in front of her, back to Xander, who ran effortlessly through the meadow and around the house.

Nikki swore as she dug for the keys in her purse, hoping they had enough time, the beating of her heart causing her hands to shake.

Grasping them from the bottom of her bag, she unlocked the car and they dove in. As she turned the car on and screeched out of the driveway, a bloody figure broke through the foliage onto the road, screaming into the night air with the rage of a tempest howling into the void, as birds continued to peck and tear at his flesh.

Nikki's arms shook as they got onto the highway, and she had to force herself to slow down. Getting pulled over would not help them, no matter how counterintuitive her deceleration felt. Her ear itched with healing while warm blood trickled down the side of her head.

Panting, Xander asked, "What the fuck? What the actual fuck was that? Oh my god, holy shit." He brushed a hand through his sweat-drenched hair, leaning it against the cold window. "Seriously, what was that? That barrier? And then his hand? It grew back!"

Nikki's mind spun, trying to think of where to go while Xander rambled. She couldn't take them to her parents' or his, since she didn't want to bring trouble to their doorstep. Plus she wasn't sure she could trust her parents with him anymore. Maybe they could stop by her place, pack a bag, and run. Just until they figured out what else to do.

"Nikki! Hello? Are you even listening? Did you see what happened? How are you not freaking out about this? What the hell do they want from me?"

"Xander, please calm down. I'm trying to think!"

Xander's mouth clamped shut, and he was silent for several minutes as he held his head in his hands. Guilt pooled in Nikki's stomach. She hadn't wanted to snap at him, not after everything he had just witnessed.

"I'm sorry. I am freaking out. But I need to figure out what to do."

Xander scoffed and shook his head.

"What?" Nikki asked.

"What do you mean what? You're hiding things from me. Again. You're not saying, 'Xander, I don't know why they want you,' or 'I don't know what that shining barrier that appeared out of nowhere was,' or 'I don't know why his hand melted and then regrew!' You're deflecting. Again! I can't stand it. I've never seen anything more disturbing and never been more scared, and you're shutting me out!"

"I'm not shutting you out. I'm trying to protect you!" Nikki yelled, exasperated, slamming her hands against the wheel in frustration. Tears pricked the back of her eyes, and a lump formed in her throat, which she swallowed to keep her eyes clear on the road. "And I don't know if I can. I don't know how. But I'm trying." Nikki took a deep breath, and exhaled, releasing the tension in her shoulders. "We'll go to my place, pack a bag, and leave. I'll explain everything once we're there and I'm not driving. I promise."

Xander shook his head but didn't respond, crossing his arms and leaning his head against the window.

Chest tight with guilt and the fracturing of their relationship, Nikki said, "Look. Gwen's a witch. She made the barrier. She's been maintaining it since we were kids, so it's pretty strong by now."

Xander laughed. "Sure."

"I'm telling you the truth. It's more complicated than that, but she wields magic. That's how she summoned the birds, too. You must've noticed how she has a special affinity for them."

"Yeah, but many people do. Doesn't mean they're magic."

"In this case, it does. People don't have the relationship with them like Gwen does, I promise you that."

"I suppose you're going to tell me Vadasz's hand regrew by magic, too."

"A type of it, yes."

Xander squeezed his eyes, pinched the bridge between his nose. "This is insane. Maybe we all just hallucinated it? There's no way that his hand grew back like that. Maybe it wasn't as damaged as we thought."

"Then how do you explain his melted flesh at our feet?"

Xander groaned and tilted his head back against the headrest and threw up his hands. "I don't know."

"Maybe you should trust what I'm telling you, then."

"Trust you? After how much you've hidden from me? After how much you've hidden me from others? Good recipe for trust."

The fracture in Nikki's heart deepened.

Xander sighed. "Just let me sit with this for a minute."

Nikki nodded, clenching her jaw and biting down words that could be used against her later.

The rest of the drive passed in tense silence, and when they arrived at Nikki's apartment, she thought she might throw up from fear, wondering how far away the Scythians were, if they were already waiting for them, where Xander and she would go from here, and if they would go together.

Inside her apartment, Nikki got a duffel bag, filling it with their clothes, hygiene products, and laptops. Xander kept his distance, staying in the kitchen.

"Come on. Let's go," Nikki said when she was packed.

Xander turned to her slow, arms crossed. "I'm not going anywhere until you tell me the truth. All of it."

Heart racing, Nikki replied, "Xander, we're in danger. They could knock down my door at any moment. We need to leave."

Xander shrugged. "So they come. And they tell me their version of the truth. I want yours. I think I've earned it."

"They're not going to talk to you, Xander. I don't know what they want from you, but I know it won't be as simple as that."

"Oh? And how do you know that?"

Nikki's hands shook, and she clenched her fingers in an attempt to keep them still, but ended up wringing her hands as she stepped back.

Xander threw up his hands in defeat. "Fine. I'm out of here," he said and headed to the door.

"No!" Nikki yelled, heart breaking. "Please, wait. I'll tell you."

Xander stopped but didn't move closer. He watched her take the wooden planks down from the windows and set them on the ground, the barest traces of dawn sparkling on the river.

"What are you doing?" Xander asked, concern breaking through the anger in his voice.

"Maybe you should sit down."

Xander shook his head, and Nikki took a deep breath, holding it in her chest before speaking in her exhale. "So, Gwen's a witch. You saw how she looks different from her siblings? Did you notice her sister's teeth?"

"Their teeth? No, Nikki. I saw Vadasz's massive fangs, but in the dark while my life was in danger, I did not look at anyone else's teeth."

"Well, as far as I can tell, witches are vampires with recessive genes.

As in, her family, they're all vampires." Xander's face froze, unreadable. Nikki continued, "And technically she is too, but her abilities manifest as magic. Vampires can be born or made. She is from a born family, which has traces of human genes. They don't live forever, they just have a long life. But the Made, they're the ones who die and get brought back. It's a complicated process. And most don't live. But when they do, they're true immortals."

Xander stared at her, blank-faced, crossed arms slowly falling to his sides. Nikki's voice stuck in her throat. She cleared it and said, "And, I know all this because...because I'm a vampire, too. A born one."

Nikki didn't break Xander's gaze, his face shifting from blank to confused to amused, and then he burst out a harsh gust of laughter, flaming Nikki's cheeks and shredding her heart.

"It's true," Nikki said, quiet, and pulled out the fittings over her teeth, baring her fangs and holding the fittings in one hand. "It's why my canines fell out. My last set of teeth needed to come in. My vampire teeth. My fangs."

Xander shook his head in disbelief. "For all I know, you're one of those people obsessed with vampires and put those in to hide your embarrassment at losing your teeth."

Stung, Nikki said, "I wish that were true. I wish I were entirely mortal and not a monster."

Xander frowned, the guilt of hurting her on his face.

Nikki turned to the window, where a streak of sunlight entered the living room. "Maybe this will prove it to you."

Nikki stepped to the window and held her arm under the rays of sun, the unusual warmth a momentary pleasure on her skin before it started to hurt, turning pink, then red, the skin hissing and steaming as it bubbled, melted, burned. Nikki gritted her teeth against the pain as the flesh on her arm peeled away, disintegrating.

"Nikki, oh my god, stop!" Xander yelled, pulling her out of the light.

Tears streaked down her face. She pushed past Xander, whose eyes were downcast in worry, and entered the kitchen, where she removed a thermos from the fridge. She poured blood into a clear glass and warmed it in the microwave, the tangy scent filling the air as it heated.

When it was done, she pulled it out and held it under Xander's nose so he could be certain what it was. His eyes grew wide as he inhaled the scent. Nikki stamped down the nausea in her stomach, the combination of pain and the smell of blood making her want to vomit.

But with a held breath, she drank the blood, setting it on the counter with a grimace, the remaining viscous fluid dripping down the glass.

Nikki held out her burned arm, the pain changing to an insufferable itch as they watched the muscles slowly weave back over her bone, layer by layer, though more slowly than Vadasz's had healed. Nikki gripped the counter with her other hand to prevent it from reaching into the gore to scratch the painful itching.

"Now that you've seen it twice, do you believe me?"

Wide-eyed and mouth agape, Xander watched her arm heal until it slowed to a stop, several layers of skin still missing. She'd need more blood, and gauze to wrap it in. When he met her eyes, they were sad, beseeching.

"Why didn't you tell me?"

"I did. When I told you about my skin sensitivity. You asked if I was a vampire. And I said yes."

Xander's face contorted, concern twisting into anger. "It was a joke, Nikki! How could I know you were serious?" He laughed, hysteric, and stepped away from her, pushing his hands through his hair, then slammed to a crouch as if he was dizzy. "Oh my God."

Nikki sat on the arm of the sofa near him. "I know this is a lot to take in, but we have to go. You'll have to drive. I can hide in the trunk until nightfall."

Xander was silent for several minutes then said, "You didn't seem surprised when they said they wanted me."

Nikki swallowed the lump in her throat. "I wasn't."

"Why?"

"It's complicated."

Xander sighed, anger releasing from his body. "Please, just tell me. I'm tired of the 'complications.' I want to know what's going on. Especially since it seems to center around me, and I don't know why."

Nikki curled her nails into her palms. "I'm so sorry for all this. All I wanted was to protect you. A few months ago, when I was finishing the change from fledgling to vampire, someone was communicating with me. First, through the trees. And then telepathically."

Xander laughed, skeptical. "What?"

"I know, just hear me out. I thought I was losing my mind. But then it started happening to others in my coven. At least my mom and our coven leader, maybe others. But the voice said they wanted you. It wouldn't tell me why. Then this outsider, Hormin, showed up and it seemed related to the whispers, but I'm not really sure why. Or how. Anyway, with the voice and Hormin showing up, I knew I had to protect you from whatever was talking to me. It felt malicious. And I don't want anything bad to happen to you. I was so worried about having you meet my parents because of what they are, because of what we are. And with how you smell—"

"Whoa, whoa, wait. How I smell?"

"I don't know why, but you smell different from most humans, and it attracts us to you. It's how I ended up bumping into you in the library," Nikki said, hoping that the memory of their first meeting would remind him of their instant connection.

"So this whole thing really had nothing to do with us."

"What do you mean?"

"It all makes sense now," he said, quiet, defeated. "Why I had to pursue you every step of the way. You found me by accident. Because I smell like food to you?"

"Xander, no—"

"And then you only stayed because you felt you had to protect me."

"That's not true."

Xander's empty eyes flicked to hers. "You said it yourself. All you wanted to do was protect me."

"I misspoke, Xander. It wasn't the only thing I wanted. It was important to me, yes, to make sure you weren't harmed, but I care—"

"Is that all it is? Care?"

"Of course not," Nikki said. When she opened her mouth to speak her true feelings, her tongue thickened. Clearing her throat she said, "You are misinterpreting everything. Obviously I more than care for you. Keeping you at arm's length wasn't because of what I felt about you. It's what I felt—feel—about myself."

"And what do you feel for me, Nikki?"

"How do you not know?"

He wrenched his arm from her grasp. "Because you've never said it. And you know what, Nikki? I loved you—and I guess I still do, but looking at your face right now is breaking my heart, and I just can't do this."

Xander put a hand on the doorknob, Nikki's vision hazy with tears. "Xander, please!"

Xander turned to her, his figure blurring in her glassy vision, waiting, expectant. But Nikki choked on the words, and his shoulders slumped, face crumpling. "Even now, when I'm walking out your door, you can't say it. That tells me all I need to know."

Nikki felt like vomiting. "No, Xander, I do—"

"Nikki, stop. No more lies," he said, low and defeated, twisting the doorknob and pulling it open.

"Xander, please, you can't go, you're in danger. Who knows who is out there waiting for you."

"You know what? I've run and hidden my whole life. I'm not doing that anymore. If they want me, let them come."

"Xander, of all the times to pluck up courage, this is not it. You need to run."

He scoffed, stepping away. "So you do think I'm a coward. I wondered."

"I didn't say that—"

"No, you know what? Thanks for the protection, but you're free from your self-imposed obligation to take care of me."

Nikki's heart crumbled to ashes in her chest, leaving her hollow, empty. "You don't understand," she said, her mind reeling with all the words she wished she could say, all the things she wanted to explain, but they collided and meshed too rapidly for her to grasp them.

"No, I think I do."

He turned his back on her and walked out into the hallway. She shouted after him, "At least go to your mom. Please?"

"My mom?" he asked, stopping and turning his head, not quite looking over his shoulder.

"She called me out at Thanksgiving. She knows what I am. She may know why the vampires want you. And how to protect you from them."

His brow furrowed, dark hair spilling over his face as he shook his head again and continued to the elevator.

Nikki stood in the doorway of her apartment, unable to leave as he walked through the rays of sunlight in the hall. When he was out of sight and she closed the door, her last threads unraveled, and she fell to the floor like her strings were cut. Hollowed out like someone pulled her heart from her chest, she put her head in her hands and cried until her eyes were dry, pleading with whatever Powers That Be to protect Gwen and Xander.

<h1 style="text-align:center">Chapter Twenty-Nine</h1>

NIKKI DIDN'T WANT to open her eyes.

The room was cold, the space beside her empty. And not just with Xander's absence, but the emptiness of never again.

The sudden pain in her chest stopped her breath, and moisture pricked her eyes. She shoved her knuckles into the sockets, pushing them down, swallowing the lump in her throat and telling herself to stop. She knew this would happen. It was why she didn't want to go down this road to begin with.

Images of Xander flashed behind her eyelids, his wide smiles and bouncing hair, resting against his chest and his breath on her hair, his hand in hers.

She groaned as the cave in her chest deepened.

And then her mind circled to the preamble, to what happened prior to the fight, the icy eyes and melting flesh, Gwen pushing the barrier and summoning the owls, power and sweat pouring from her mortal body. Nikki sat upright in bed with a jolt, heart hammering, and grabbed her phone, dialing Gwen.

Gwen didn't answer.

Shivers of terror coiled under Nikki's skin.

She opened Xander's contact, and after a moment's hesitation, a heartbeat's broken pulse, she dialed him as well.

When he didn't answer, the cold paralyzed her.

She texted both of them, then flexed and unflexed her hands, anxiety winding her tighter and tighter. In the living room, she peeled back a piece of wood, hissing as the late afternoon sun burned her finger, sizzling.

She was trapped. She couldn't do anything. Couldn't help anyone. Her closest friends were probably kidnapped, injured, or dead, and it was all her fault.

She failed to protect Xander, Gwen, or Theo, and who knew what would happen to Terrance and Rachel. Nikki folded to the ground, clutching her head, drowning herself in her failures until her mind broke and her body wracked itself with tears, sobs, and moans, pulling the hair painfully tight back from her head as she rocked.

Sometime later, when Nikki's face ran dry and her eyes were red, lips pricked from where her fangs had nicked them, her phone rang.

Nikki scrambled up and answered without looking, heart beating wild with desperation. "H-hello?"

"Oh, girl. You do not sound good."

"Gwen!" Nikki yelled, bursting with relief. "Are you okay? What happened? How's Theo?"

"You know, we're totally fine. Those fuckers didn't care about us at all. They high tailed it after you. I'm assuming that since you're calling, I was able to slow them down. How's Xander?"

Nikki hesitated, shifting on the floor. "I don't know."

Gwen was silent.

"We got to my place and I tried to get us packed up, but then he demanded to know everything. And I told him. And he left." Nikki said, trying to keep her chin from wobbling. She took a deep breath and continued, "I haven't heard from him since last night."

"Well, Harriet, Basil, and Hawkenstein haven't notified me of anything going on with him, so I'm sure he's okay. Probably just processing somewhere."

Another wave of relief fissured through Nikki, and she sighed.

"That's good to know. I told him to talk to his mom, so maybe he went there."

"I'll send out extra watchers for him, okay?"

Nikki swallowed the lump in her throat. "Thanks."

"Are you okay, Nik?"

A hollow opened in Nikki's chest, but no more tears could come.

"No," she said, voice cracking, gaze fixated on the ring around her finger. "I don't know what happened. I mean, I do, but I tried to make him understand. He thought I was lying at first. Then he was mad at me for hiding it this whole time. And I tried to explain to him why, but everything I said got twisted." Voice breaking, Nikki said, "I really tried to make him stay."

"Oh, Nik," Gwen said, the compassion in her voice wrenching Nikki's heart further. "I'm coming over, okay? We'll have a good old-fashioned girls' night."

"Okay," Nikki said as the line went dead, and she dropped her arm to the floor, hollowed out from pain and tears and utterly lost, the center of her axis, her world, somehow gone.

When Gwen arrived, calling for her to come down and let her in, Nikki was still staring at the carpet on her floor. Why hadn't she given Gwen a key? Then she wouldn't have to move. Ever again. She could fold into the carpet and become one with the stiff fibers, unmoving and unfeeling.

With great effort, she hoisted herself to her feet and stumbled to the elevator, hoping no one would see her face damaged from sorrow and worry. Only the security guard and front desk person saw her, but they only gave her impassive nods before resuming their conversation.

Gwen marched in through the glass doors when Nikki approved her entry, and she threw her arms around Nikki's neck. "I'm so glad you're okay," Gwen said.

"Me too. I was so worried about you," Nikki replied, hugging Gwen back, letting the wintry-spring scent of Gwen fill her nose, her wild hair falling in Nikki's face. "I was worried they would retaliate against you, after what you did."

Gwen pulled back and kept her hands on her shoulders. She was paler than usual, even her freckles looking shades lighter, and dark circles hung under her eyes. "Thankfully not. Though it is possible they will once they accomplish their true goal."

Nikki winced, and Gwen added, "I've sent more sentries, and I've still not heard a warning. He's probably with his mom, as you said. Safe and sound with whatever weird anti-vampire cult she belongs to."

Nikki nodded but couldn't bring herself to laugh or even grin. They held hands as they walked to the elevator, Nikki needing the solidity, the solidarity, of her oldest friend.

"Where's Theo?"

"Oh, she's with her brother and his girlfriend. You know, they didn't wake up during that whole thing? They must've been blasted. But they were confused why the meadow looked like it had burned from the studio outward. Not sure how she explained that one."

"I'm glad they're all okay. I'm so, so sorry for everything," Nikki said, as they stepped into the elevator.

"It's not your fault, Nik."

"Yes, it is," she said and closed her eyes, resting her head back on the wall.

"No, it's not. You didn't make some crazy demi-goddess or whatever send her cronies to steal some kid for an unknown reason."

"None of this would have happened if I stayed away from him. And don't you dare say it's better to have loved and lost. I think I'd lose my mind."

The elevator dinged open.

"I wouldn't dream of it," Gwen said. "But honestly, Nik. If it weren't you, someone would have found him eventually. And isn't it better for us to have found him than, say, Bridget? He'd have no protection, no hope, then."

Gwen's words were a thin balm. "I hope you're right."

"I know I am," she said with a forced smirk as Nikki opened her apartment door.

"So, what garbage do you want to eat tonight?" Gwen asked, throwing her things down on the floor. "You name it, we'll eat it, no matter how disgusting. That's how you fill a broken heart, you know. With nasty, delicious, garbage."

Nikki huffed a laugh and folded into the couch.

Gwen pillaged her fridge and returned with a glass of wine for herself and a glass of blood for Nikki. "Drink it."

"That's the last thing I want."

"What did I just say? Fill your broken heart with nasty. If living with vampires has taught me anything, it's how to identify when a vampire needs blood." Gwen shook the glass, blood sloshing against the sides. "Drink it, woman. I promise you'll feel at least a little better."

Nikki sighed but took the glass and chugged it down in one long, suffering gulp, stifling a gag as the liquid coated her teeth and slid slow down her throat.

"Atta girl," Gwen said, plopping on the other side of the couch. "So, what do you want to eat for real?"

Nikki rested her head back against the couch, the blood filling her body with warmth and strength, repairing her broken cells, but not her broken heart.

The harsh buzz of her phone sounded against the counter while she was thinking, and she perked up. Gwen glanced at her, eyes flaring wide before she bounced up and retrieved it. Nikki flicked open the screen, seeing one text from Xander, simply saying, I'm fine.

Nikki's chest twisted with relief and disappointment. At least he responded, and he was okay, but she wished he would come back to her. This text did not bode well for her fantasy.

But at least he was alive and "fine."

"It's Xander. He says he's fine," Nikki said.

"Well that's something, at least."

Nikki closed her eyes and tilted her head back.

"I'll know when he isn't, I promise," Gwen said.

Nikki nodded. "I think I know what I want to eat."

"Do go on."

"I want greasy chow mein. You know the kind where they put all the meats in it? And I want like fifty crab puffs."

"Now you're talking!" Gwen said, pulling out her phone to start the order.

After they ordered a veritable feast of heartburn and stomach aches, Nikki said, "You're the friend everyone wants but no one deserves. Including me."

"Don't be stupid," Gwen said, refilling her third glass of wine. "You've been there for me as much as I've been there for you. Through the terrors of my sisters, my breakup with Sasha, everything. It's always been us. You and me, against the world, against the coven, against everyone. It'll be you and me against that dumb bitch, too, if need be."

"Gwen!"

"Oh, is She in your head right now?" Gwen fixed her gaze hard on Nikki's and said, "Hey, you're a big, dumb, cruel bitch, and we'll fight you!"

"I don't know if She's in my head but antagonizing Her won't help. Besides, that just felt like you were calling me that."

"Well, I wasn't. You're my best friend, for all my life, and I don't like you talking as if you've been worthless. I know we've had our ups and downs recently, and I'm sorry for the things I said that maybe fed into this idea. But honestly, I wouldn't have survived my childhood without you."

"Gwen, stop. I think I'll wither away into ash if I cry anymore."

"I'm so glad Xander turned you into a sap. Now you know what it's like to be human. All these emotions." Gwen grinned, and Nikki forced out a chuckle.

Nikki lost hope that Xander would respond. Her phone remained black and silent, and although she knew that if he were going to respond it would be during the day, she gave up. It was stupid of her to text him again and hope he would want to talk to her at all, after everything. His one text was more than she would have given him if the situation were reversed, and she should be grateful for that, at least.

Belly full of crab and cream cheese and carbs, Nikki inelegantly collapsed into bed, hoping she wouldn't dream of Xander, to just have the reprieve of full oblivion.

Chapter Thirty

Nikki couldn't shake the nagging feeling of impending doom, the sense of watching a storm rolling through clear skies, where one could anticipate the downpour but not know exactly when it would fall. Gwen sent birds to scout for the Scythians and promised to ask Farrell if he knew what her sisters were up to. But she had nothing to report on either account. Since Gwen's sentries did not report ill tidings, she assumed Xander was staying at his parents'. He hadn't texted her again, and anxiety clawed at the inside of her stomach. She stared into the distance of her apartment, wracking her brain for what she could do to find some answers. She wanted to know with certainty where he was. That he was safe. At a loss, she called her mom. Maybe, just maybe, she heard something through the coven's grapevine. But her mom didn't have any answers, and instead convinced her to attend the upcoming solstice meeting so that she could address the relational breakdown within the coven. She really did not want to go to the meeting, the idea of seeing the rest of the coven, let alone Gwen's family, making her sick.

What if the Scythians were there, too?

But if they were, they wouldn't attack her in front of her coven, her parents, right?

Maybe it would be a good opportunity to learn more about them.

After the call, all she could think of was the trepidation of the impending solstice. Of being around the coven and Hormin again since her maturation gathering. Of all those greedy eyes and gluttonous mouths.

Gwen texted saying that the wards had been reinforced at her house and that Nikki could go over if she wanted. Nikki drove in silence to Gwen's place, her heart beating faster as she approached, memories of the last time she was there crowding the edges of her mind.

Where had the Scythians gone?

What were Gwen's siblings conspiring now?

Where was Xander? Was he okay?

Did he miss her at all?

Nikki shook her head at herself, dispelling the thoughts as she pulled into the canopy of Gwen's house. She hoped no one else was home, or if they were, they'd leave her alone.

The house was dark, and she made her way to Gwen's studio in peace. As she approached, the light outside the studio flicked on, illuminating the burned meadow, a harsh line where the grasses were tall and scraggly.

The owls hooted at her as she approached, their roost having been protected from Gwen's show of power. She gave the curious ones small pats for their valor a few days prior. She would have to tell Gwen to thank the diurnal birds who had heeded the call.

Even if she had lost Xander, at least he had not lost his life.

Inside the studio, Theo reclined on the couch watching a TV show on the projector while Gwen sat at the counter, bent over a mortar and pestle.

"Hey," Nikki said, Gwen popping up from her stool to give her a hug.

"Before you ask, no, I haven't heard from him, either," Theo said. "Not entirely unusual. He tends to go into his shell, but I'll pester Terr Bear more to see if he's heard from him."

"Thanks. I'm worried about him."

"No news is good news, right?" Gwen asked.

"I hope so," Nikki said.

Nikki turned to Gwen. "Can you try scrying for him and the Scythians? It would give me peace of mind, knowing where they are. That they're not in the same place."

Gwen shrugged. "Sure, I can try. Haven't done that in ages, though." Gwen dug through her drawers, looking for maps and infused gems. "You could just go to his house and his mom's house, too, you know."

"Just show up? I'd look crazy. Like a stalker."

"As if admitting you're a blood-drinking creature of legend who has been hearing voices for months doesn't make you sound crazy? Sorry to tell you, Nik, that ship has sailed."

"Fair point."

"Besides, scrying isn't that many steps away from stalking," Gwen said.

"But I don't feel quite as creepy this way. Or desperate."

"Even though you are?"

"Even though I am."

"All right," Gwen said, tightening the knots of string around her pinky, middle, and thumb, each string holding a small gem, an emerald, sapphire, and ruby. "By the way, Farrell doesn't know anything, either. I asked him about the Scythians and he just shrugged, saying he sensed other vampires in the house but didn't interact with them. The only thing he did express was disappointment at our sisters' behavior, but that's not news."

"Thanks for checking, anyway."

Gwen nodded and raised her hand over the map.

"You scry with three?" Theo asked, standing behind Gwen and peering over her shoulder. "In stories people just use one. Won't they bump into each other?"

"They haven't before." Gwen shrugged. "I like the balance better this way. And then when all three waver toward one spot, it's less likely to be a false positive."

"A sample size of three isn't that much better than a sample size of one."

"But it's better than none."

"I guess," Theo replied. "Why those colors?"

Gwen shrugged again. "They're primary, I don't know. I like them. It feels right. Any more questions?"

"Not yet," Theo said, and they shared a grin.

"Ok, then. Everyone quiet so I can focus. I'm going to look for Xander first."

Gwen held her hand out over the state of Washington, and the stones spun as Gwen sent tendrils of wispy, silvery-gold magic down the threads. The light from her power misted from the gems down over the map, the jewels rotating in slow circles, their ranges widening but never hitting, Gwen's fingers spread out farther.

Gwen moved her hand across the map in slow, deliberate movements, and the stones continued to swing in wide circles, never stopping, never slowing.

Gwen hummed, shutting off the flow of magic, the remnants dissipating into the air. She pulled back her hand and flipped the map over to a full map of the United States.

Gwen put her hand over the west coast, sending magic tendrils down the threads, into the gems, watching as they once again misted over the map. Nikki's blood roared in her ears, and all she could hear was the beat of her heart, rapid and uncomfortable in her chest, as the gems swung in wide, unknowing circles across the country.

"This may not be a bad thing, Nik. If we can't find him, then the Scythians shouldn't be able to either. He's probably warded."

Nikki nodded, words clogging her throat, thinking of how ancient the Scythians were, how incomprehensible and unknowable the depths of their power and magic ran. She clung to the hope of Gwen's words, but her muscles weakened, feeling something was wrong.

Gwen cleared her throat. "Okay, now for the Scythians," she said, and flipped the map back over to Washington state, restarting the search.

On both sides of the map, the gems swung idly and uncertainly, not locating the Scythians.

"Are you sure you know how to scry?" Theo asked, teasing.

To Nikki's surprise, Gwen did not reciprocate the tease. Her face was long, eyes searching the map. Gwen remained quiet for several moments, warming the stones in her hands. "They're probably warded, too. Did you see his hand, before he melted it?"

"Not really. Why?" Nikki asked.

"It was scarred. But in patterns and designs. Like Aella's arms. You saw that, right?"

Nikki nodded.

"Well, I've done some research on the Scythians, and they used to carve animals on everything, including tattoos on themselves."

"Okay, but they're vampires. Vampires can't get tattoos. The skin rejects the ink."

"I know, but I've been thinking, what if those symbols provided them with boons, or wards, or something? And since they couldn't get tattoos, they carved it into themselves."

"Again, they're vampires. The skin would heal."

"It would, unless they carved it open over and over, cutting it as it was healing so it never fully mended, creating permanent brands on their skin that would always come back, since the scars would be coded into their new, disrupted cells."

Nikki sucked in a deep breath and pinched the bridge of her nose. Then she flinched at the mannerism she'd picked up from Xander. After she blew out the breath, she said, "You're saying they tortured themselves for an unknown amount of time, in an unknown amount of ways, so they'd forever be imbued with whatever magic they have. Wards, boons, whatever."

"Yes. It's just a hypothesis but it would make sense, given their violent history and unusually long lifespans. Even for vampires, living that long is unheard of. You saw how light they traveled, so the wards aren't being carried on their person. It only makes sense that their protections are embedded inside of them. With some ancient magics I don't know anything about."

"How long would it take for the scars to be permanent?" Theo asked.

"It would depend on how much blood they drank," Nikki said.

"Without drinking any blood at all, it would take days of reopening the wounds to ensure the scars were integrated into the body. Maybe weeks, depending on the size and type of magic involved."

Theo exhaled, loud. "That's a whole new level of crazy."

"Not one I'm eager to face again," Nikki said.

"Not one I'm sure I can face again," Gwen replied.

They dropped into a silence that weighed heavy on their shoulders. They all looked at the map, hoping for some belated answers, until Gwen broke the quiet by shaking her head and folding it up, putting everything away.

"So, what do we do?" Theo asked.

"Fuck if I know," Gwen said. "It's not like we can go on a road trip to scour every inch of the state or the country."

"So we just wait until they ambush us again."

"Ugh, I don't know. Nik, what do you think?"

Nikki didn't respond, her mind blank and her heart heavy. "I don't know. We have to do something, but I don't know what," Nikki said, biting back how hopeless, how incompetent, she felt.

"I don't know either. I can't bond to anymore animals. I'm already spread thin managing those I have. They're not giving me information anyway, so I don't know what good it would do."

"You think I'm just being paranoid?"

"No, no. Not about the Scythians, at least. They're batshit. But maybe with Xander. Maybe he's safe."

"Unless he's with the Scythians, and we can't find him because their wards are blocking him," Nikki said, horror rising in her throat.

"Whoa, whoa. Before you spin out, I'm not sure it would work like that. If I'm right, their wards would just apply to them. We'd still find Xander if he was with them."

"Unless whatever they transported him in is warded." Nikki's voice rose in volume and pitch with every word out of her mouth. "Or they have some other magic we don't even know about," Fear danced in her fingertips, rising through her body. She'd been so stupid to let Xander go, to let him have a decision over his safety when they didn't know what they were up against, and now he was probably gone. He was probably—

Hands came down on her shoulders, snapping Nikki back to the present. "Nik. Take a breath. You're spiraling. We don't know anything for certain yet. Remember how you used to tell me not to jump to conclusions?"

Nikki nodded, dragging stuttering breaths in through her nose.

"So let's not do that. Here's what we'll do. You'll locate Xander. I'll see what I can find out about the Scythians, what magic they have." Gwen looked over her shoulder. "Theo, contact your brother and see what you can find out from him. Then will you help me with my research?"

"Always," Theo said.

Gwen gave her a small smile, then turned back to Nikki with a serious face. "Sound like a plan?"

Nikki nodded again, still unable to find her words.

"Good," Gwen said, removing her hands from Nikki's shoulders. "I know we're all wound up, but there's nothing we can do right now. So let's take deep breaths and try to think with level heads. Sound good?"

Nikki gave a half-hearted smile and sat on a chair. She pulled in measured breaths, trying to relax her shoulders and the rapid, catastrophizing thump of her heart against her ribs.

After many minutes, she pulled out her phone and texted Xander, asking if he was okay. She didn't know what else to say or ask, since he hadn't reached out to her, but she needed to know that he was somewhere safe.

She set her phone beside her, face up, and tried to listen to Gwen and Theo's conversation about what to do over winter break. They discussed taking a trip, of finding a cabin in the woods, of movie nights and cold, fog-laden days on the coast.

Each idea spun an image of her and Xander together enjoying those same activities, plunging her heart deeper into the darkness of her body, dragging her eyes down to stare at the black screen of her phone and wishing for the days of his kind texts and warm arms, his bright smile and unguarded eyes.

"Nik?"

"What?" Nikki said, her daydream popping like a bubble.

"I asked if you had plans for the holidays," Gwen said, her and Theo looking at Nikki with wary, pitying expressions that made Nikki stare anywhere but at them.

"Oh. Um." Old thoughts of Xander in ugly Christmas sweaters and a silly Santa hat, the wild joy of his siblings with presents, swept through her mind's eye. "No. Not really. Just the winter solstice."

"You're going?" Gwen asked, incredulous.

"Parental guilt." Gwen looked disbelieving, so Nikki continued, "My mom convinced me that this is a coven matter so maybe I'll get some answers about the Scythians, and Hormin, then. Maybe there will be other people on our side. It might be a bad idea, but I don't know what else to do at this point to get information."

"Even if it's a bad idea," Gwen said. "Who knows what other cuckoo ancient vamps are wandering the area now?"

"I know, but if I see them, at least we'll know."

"I don't like this, Nik. But you'll be careful, right?"

"You're not coming?"

Gwen barked a laugh, startling Theo. "Hell no." Seeing Nikki's face falter, Gwen said, "I'll be your outside contact in case you need a quick getaway. Or a reason to leave early."

"Fair enough." Nikki said, resting her head on the back of the chair. A flash of light caught her eye, and she snapped her head back down, her phone lighting up with a notification.

Xander's name sat on the screen, and her heart jumped to her throat. With her pulse in her fingertips, she flicked open the message, then squeezed her eyes tight after she read it, eyebrows knitting together and jaw clenching to keep the breaking of her heart from glassing her vision.

"What is it?" Gwen asked.

Nikki let her heart and hand fall, eyes opening to a muted world. She threw her phone to Gwen, who frowned, then said, "I'm so sorry, Nik."

Nikki closed her eyes, the text seared behind her eyelids. Please, stop contacting me. I don't want to talk to you. I told you I'm fine. That should be enough for you, after all you put me through. Just leave me alone.

When Nikki opened her eyes again, Theo frowned at Nikki's phone, a small furrow in her brow. But she didn't say anything, and Gwen tossed the phone back to Nikki, who read through the pain one more time before erasing the entire text thread from her phone—their whole history, all the months of their communications—and it felt like ripping a piece of her own soul out of her body.

She didn't just erase the words. She erased him. Erased them.

But that was what he wanted.

What she deserved.

Nikki curled deeper into the chair, folding herself onto her side and pulling a blanket over herself.

At least he was safe. She didn't deserve to know more.

Chapter Thirty-One

Days stretched into a week. There was still no more word from Xander, nor a location on the Scythians, by the night of the solstice. Her parents offered to give her a ride, which was strange since they usually drove separately, but she couldn't find a reason to deny them. She liked the freedom of having her car but couldn't muster the energy to plan the drive to Tyee's, which was several hours away.

Her parents arrived just after dark. Nikki sat in the back of their car, watching the world zip by as they drove up the interstate and into the forests of Gifford Pinchot National Park. Her parents pushed for information on why she was upset with the O'Brennan girls, why she wanted to know what Hormin was doing, why she was so quiet.

Each question drove a nail of irritation deeper into her, and she clenched her mouth tighter and tighter until they gave up trying to pry it open. Her mom was exceptionally chatty this evening, talking about all manner of trivial things she and her dad had been doing since Black Friday and inquiring about Nikki's holiday plans, but Nikki didn't care enough to listen. She didn't know if her mom was nervous, perhaps wondering if Nikki was still upset with her about Black Friday. Or maybe she was nervous about the solstice. Nikki didn't think too much about it, or about why her dad was so quiet, focused as he was on his driving.

They pulled onto the road that led to Tyee's house until they came to the parking area. Nikki stepped out of the car, stretching her legs, and looked up, the dark canopy of the surrounding forest barely visible against the night sky. Her breath fogged the air in front of her, and she tugged her winter coat tighter, the chill of the forest creeping through her pores. Nikki gazed at the still evergreens, the leafless deciduous trees with their litter brittle underfoot, until her mom's voice broke her from her staring.

"Nicoletta, would you please carry this?"

Nikki walked to the trunk where her mom was, and Cat handed her a covered platter, the cold metal stiff against her coat. Nikki frowned as she looked into the trunk, seeing two duffel bags. "Why do you have bags?"

"Oh, just in case of an emergency, darling," her mom said, waving her off and closing the trunk, a reusable bag with bottles of wine and blood looped through her arm.

Warning twisted in Nikki's gut as she walked behind her parents on the trail to Tyee's home. Sword ferns and the prickly stems of salmonberry filled the understory, evergreen needles brushing against her cheeks as they walked. A breeze pushed against her back, rustling the bare branches of the trees.

The wind carried a laugh, soft and amused. Nikki froze, and the laughter raised the hair on the back of her neck. Her heart pounded in her ears, begging her to turn and run.

Her parents stopped ahead of her, noticing that she had ceased walking.

"What is it, darling?" her mom asked.

Nikki looked past her mom to her dad, who stood with his head turned, his bronze profile staring at the ground.

"Dad?" Nikki asked, trying to keep her voice steady as her fingers curled around the edges of the platter. "What's going on?"

His brow furrowed, brief, then he looked at her for the first time that night, a fake smile plastered on his face that did not reach his eyes. "What do you mean?"

"Something is going on. I can tell. You're both being weird. Did you not hear the wind?"

Her dad's eyes darted to Cat, who ignored him too blatantly, with too much effort, and Nikki took a step backward.

"I don't know what you're talking about," her mom said.

"Dad? You've barely talked or looked at me all night."

"I'm sorry, love," he said. "I am distracted by work. That's all."

Cat stood beside Nikki despite how narrow the trail was and wrapped an arm around her shoulders. "Don't worry, Nicoletta. Don't you remember when you were little? You were terrified of the forest, then, too. Come on," her mom said, urging her forward with the arm around her.

Nikki took a hesitant step, feet crunching dried leaf litter as she went. Cat did not release her, and her mom's greater strength ensured she stayed in motion. Though the winds were quiet she could not shake the feeling that something was wrong.

The faint glow of small fires cast an orange hue to the tall, thick Doug-fir, and as they passed through the last thicket of the forest, Tyee's house came into view.

It was magnificent—part cottage, part treehouse. It started with a modest cabin built on the forest floor, with staircases winding up and between the trees that shaded her house. Smaller houses had been built into the trees, bridges and staircases a maze between the cabin and the treetops. The exterior rim of the houses was lined with hanging lights and lanterns, like scattered stars across the galaxy of the forest.

The property was Gwen's dream. She wished Xander could see it. She wished she could see his face, lit like gold in the warm light, brightened with awe at the house Tyee had built for herself over centuries.

They walked to the front door, soft light peering through the windows. As they stepped onto the first step of the porch, the door swung open.

Tyee stood in the doorway, haloed by light from the house, hair in a long braid down her back. "Welcome, Silvas," she said, a smile tugging at the corners of her mouth. "Come in."

Tyee's sharp eyes roved over Nikki as she walked by, and they shared a glance that made Nikki feel searched, exposed.

"Hello, Nikki," Tyee said, then closed the door behind her.

"Hi, Tyee," Nikki replied, fingers curling tighter around the platter.

Tyee stared at her for another moment too long, then stepped around her to greet her parents in low tones.

"The others are already here. Follow me."

"Where?" Nikki blurted. The sense of wrongness still laced around her bones. They usually ate inside the house, and then had a fire later in the night.

Tyee turned her sharp eyes to Nikki. "In the hearth-room. The children are cold."

"A fire sounds wonderful. Come on, Nicoletta, let's warm our bones," her mom said, nudging her forward again.

"Before I forget. Please deposit your cell phones," Tyee said, nodding to a basket of phones beside her. "We are having a phone-free evening."

"Great idea," her mom said, pulling her phone from a bag and dropping it inside with the others, as did her dad.

Nikki got her phone from her pocket, seeing one missed call from Gwen.

"Nicoletta?" her mom asked, when Nikki froze on the spot.

"Gwen called me. I'll call her back real quick and then come through," Nikki said, swiping open the phone.

Then her hand was empty and cold, the phone plucked from her fingers. Tyee dropped it into the basket.

"Guinevere can wait. She should have come if she wanted to speak with you. Don't worry, it will be returned to you shortly."

Nikki bit back her irritation, her unease, assuring herself it was just the traditionalist in Tyee forcing this on them. Her mom's arm wound its way around Nikki's shoulders again, and she clamped her jaw tight to prevent herself from snapping at all of them. What was the rush?

They followed Tyee to the hearth-room, a separate building reminiscent of the longhouses of the Vikings. The Ivarssons had helped develop the fire room into a space large enough for the coven to banquet in, but it was not furnished with electricity or plumbing.

The room glowed with heat from the rectangular hearth that ran down the middle length of the building. Smoke billowed and exited to the top, and a long table with food and blood and water lined the far wall. The Lopez children sat on the hot stone, warming their hands, Feng and Daiyu beside them. The Lopez parents talked with Gwen's parents, glasses filled with blood, flickering all shades of red and orange in the firelight.

Gwen's brothers sat with the Ivarssons in what appeared to be forced conversation, drifting, lilting, and slow. They all took frequent sips of blood, fangs clacking on the glass, making minimal eye contact and only offering grunts to indicate they were listening.

Hormin sat with two unfamiliar men at the opposite table, quiet. More vampires? Nikki barely got a moment to notice them before she was pulled to the back to put down the platter of food. The feast table was arrayed with venison, salmon, wine, blood, breads, potatoes, and rabbit stew. Cat opened the platter when Nikki set it down, revealing the fanciest charcuterie board she'd ever seen, and her heart twinged at her memory of the last time she had one, with Xander at their midnight picnic.

Feeling hollowed out from loneliness, Nikki turned to assess the room, wondering where she should sit. She didn't want to be around any of them, their presence making her feel more alone. The reddened mouths and still bodies reminded her of how predatory they were, how dangerous, and she suddenly felt unsafe.

"Come, say hello to Hormin and meet our new guests," Tyee said once they had filled their glasses and snack plates. Cat handed Nikki a hybrid glass of blood-wine, which she clasped to her chest but did not drink.

Tyee led them to the two outsiders, Hormin sitting beside them with a lazy grin. The two new vampires both had dark sepia skin, one more amber than the other. They had strong cheekbones and jaws with square faces of slightly different lengths. The one with chestnut-amber skin had short cut, deep brown hair, a slightly longer face and roaming eyes. The other had long, black, and silky hair that reached the middle of his back, glistening in the firelight. His eyes were still, bored yet alert. Waiting.

The strangers turned their eyes to Nikki and her parents as they approached behind Tyee. The male with short hair had the smallest twitch of an eyebrow as they made eye contact, but the other had no expression, his eyelids heavy and hooded.

"Nikki, Miguel, Catalina, let me introduce you to Atoc and Ozcollo. They have travelled far to be with us tonight."

Atoc, the male with short hair, who had a long, sharp nose, gave a half nod, and said, "A pleasure."

The other, Ozcollo, whose nose was hooked and flat, merely blinked at each of them in turn.

Her dad extended his hand, and with some hesitation, they both shook it as he said, "Welcome! Where have you travelled from?"

"South," Ozcollo said, his voice a deep rumble.

Atoc's cheeks moved, as if he almost smirked, fangs peeking out from behind his lips. "Peru."

"Ah! I've always wanted to visit. Tell me, what brings you here to us, tonight?"

They blinked, as if forcing their eyes to not move from her dad's face.

Anxiety thrummed in her veins. For all her life, Tyee had been particular about who she let into the territory. Now there was Hormin, the Scythians, Atoc, and Ozcollo. Something was definitely being planned. She flicked her gaze to Hormin, whose eyes bored straight into her soul, and Nikki's heart jumped.

"They are here to help me move the Earth," Tyee said.

"Ah. Of course," Miguel replied, though his brows pinched in confusion.

Tyee craned her long neck to look up at them. "Please, make yourselves comfortable. We will begin when the rest arrive."

"Who else is coming?" Nikki hissed to her mom.

"How should I know?" she replied, turning away and taking a sip of blood.

Her dad cringed as he met Nikki's eyes, then shrugged and followed Cat, leaving Nikki with Hormin and the newcomers.

She glanced between them, Atoc returning her stare, Ozcollo looking at the people behind her.

"Well, this silence is riveting," Hormin said, then stretched and stood. As he walked by he put a hand on her shoulder, and his blood scented breath gusted against her skin as he whispered, "Do try to enjoy yourself, while you can."

"What is that supposed to mean?"

Hormin grinned, firelight glinting on his fangs. "The winter solstice only comes once a year, after all. Why not enjoy the long night while it lasts?"

Nikki furrowed her brow and Hormin stalked away, leaving her with a gaping hole of worry.

Atoc and Ozcollo hadn't moved at all, with Atoc still looking at her and Ozcollo gazing into the distance.

Insecurity melded with the worry from Hormin's words, and trying to break the rumbling awkwardness in her body she asked, "So, how do you know Tyee?"

"We're old friends," Atoc replied, his mouth widening into a secret smile, fangs on full display. As he stared at her, unblinking, his hand wrapped around his cup like it wanted to curl around her neck, and she took a step back.

"Oh. That's cool," she said, wincing at her fear, her stupidity. She sipped the blood-wine and suppressed a gag at the acidic tang.

Atoc watched her stifle the disgust, and his mouth widened further, his dark eyes reflecting the dancing fire behind her. With awkward mumblings of needing a different drink, she left them.

At the banquet table, she dumped out her glass in the trash and filled it with pure wine, filling up a plate of snacks. She looked back at the room, taking in the little pockets of closed conversation, Hormin chatting with Tyee, his ever-present aura demanding attention, and her parents speaking alone in a dark corner.

Nikki scowled, but the shadows flickered, catching her attention. Beside the fire, the children still sat with the Lius, who shaped their hands in different forms, casting erratic shadows of animals high on the wall. The children squealed with delight, trying to mimic their hands. Grinning, Nikki approached them, feeling the gazes of the strangers lingering on her every movement.

"Nikki!" the kids shouted, leaping up to give her hugs. They rammed into her, the eldest's vampiric strength growing. She returned the hugs as best she could with her hands full, then greeted Feng and Daiyu, who said hello and gave her close-lipped, but sincere smiles.

"They're showing us how to make shadow animals! Wanna see?" Emilia asked, then contorted her hands before Nikki could answer.

A quarter of an hour passed as she snacked and chatted with the kids, passing along pleasantries and talking shop with the Lius, who updated her on their businesses and asked how school was going in return. She showed the kids how to make their hands into a frog and a rabbit, as she had learned from Gwen when they were kids, and although they didn't cast shadows, they were delighted with this new skill.

The front door creaked open, and three pale, merlot-haired females entered.

Nikki's pulse froze, then flared. Nikki's fangs pinched her bottom lip, images of that last night with Xander on her birthday flashing through her mind, of the Scythians, of those wretched sisters laughing at their pain. Before she could think, she muttered, "I hate them."

Daiyu followed her gaze to the sisters. "Yes, they're quite unpleasant." Daiyu assessed Nikki's face and asked, "What have they done now?"

Nikki debated telling them everything. Thought about pulling them into a dark corner away from the children and letting them know everything that had happened to her, to Xander, in the last few months. But before she could draw up the confidence to do so, Tyee spoke.

"Welcome, everyone!" Tyee said, standing on the raised platform at the apex of the fire, where royalty would sit above their subjects. She lifted her arms and said, "I am pleased we can all be here together on the longest night of the year. Our night. Let us bring in the winter together."

Nikki's jaw clenched tight as the fine hairs along her skin stood on end, the sense of wrongness vibrating through every nerve. The coven members gathered around the tables and fire, finding seats. Nikki sat between her parents, ready to have them on her side when it was her turn to raise an issue before the coven.

But only the coven members sat down. Hormin, Atoc, and Ozcollo were nowhere to be found.

Where did they go?

Nikki's heart skipped another beat, craning her neck to look for them, but they were not in the building.

Tyee smiled, wider than Nikki had ever seen, as her sharp eyes roved over the coven, arms still open to the heavens, the fire dancing like melting gold on her skin, blazing in her eyes. "Tonight, we not only herald in a new season, but a new era for all vampires!"

The Lius, Lopezes, and Nikki shifted, uneasy at the words, adjusting their posture and looking at their fellow coven members. The stillness of her parents made her blood run cold.

Atoc and Ozcollo entered from doors near the back, behind Tyee, carrying trays of goblets that permeated the air with the scent of spiced blood. They made their way around the room, passing the goblets out to each coven member. When Nikki didn't take one for herself, her mother grabbed a second and shoved it into her hand.

Returning to Tyee's side, the two men flanked the coven leader as they walked toward to the fire. Stopping at its edge, all three raised clenched fists, and thrust them down and out, releasing powder and causing the flames to erupt into alternating blues and greens before returning to orange, all but Nikki crooning over the display. Smoke rose in the twisting shades of blue and green, and Atoc and Ozcollo retreated through the back door.

What was the purpose of that? And where did they go?

Behind the haze of blue and green smoke, the orange flames raging higher, Tyee spoke.

"Let us drink to this glorious, dark night!" Tyee shouted, raising her glass and drinking.

The coven followed suit, all except Nikki. Her mom nudged Nikki with her elbow and whispered, "Don't be rude. Take a drink."

Nikki looked down into her goblet, breathing in the spices and tang of blood.

"If it's poisoned, we're all drinking it, Nicoletta."

Nikki exhaled and drained it in one long draw, the warm spices dulling the taste of blood as it slid down her throat.

"Good girl," her mom whispered.

When the glasses clinked on the table, Tyee turned her gaze to the Lius. "Feng, this news will please you most of all."

Feng rested his face on one long, elegant finger, leg crossed over the other as he leaned back to turn and look at her. "And why is that?" he drawled.

A pleased, wicked grin spread over Tyee's face, eyes widening. "Your years-long wish will soon come true. You will have as many thralls as you want. You can hunt, like in those good old days you adored."

"Why the sudden change of heart?" Feng asked, his voice monotone. But Nikki didn't miss the way his eyes glinted in the firelight.

Manic, Tyee threw her arms open wide, face upturned to the sky, rejoicing. "For soon the Mother will once again walk the earth! She will bring in the new age of vampires, the dominion of us over humans. No longer will we be hidden in the shadows, to abide by their laws and fear their acknowledgement. I told you that our status as vampires would change within our lifetimes and you did not believe me. Now, humans will hide in daylight for fear of us, for the night will once again be ours! Praise be the Mother!"

Silence stretched.

And then the coven fractured.

The O'Brennans and Ivarssons raised their glasses to the sky and yelled, "Praise be the Mother!"

"Praise be the Mother," Cat whispered, and the hair on Nikki's body rose, frozen, afraid.

The Lius and Lopezes sat, stunned. Her dad was as still as a statue on her left.

"All hail the Mother!" Tyee continued. "She will deliver us from daylight, and once again be our walking, waking God!"

"Praise be! Mother, deliver us!" the Ivarssons and O'Brennans shouted again.

"We will bathe in the blood of our oppressors and once again be the strength of the world!"

"Praise be! Mother, bathe us in the blood of our lessers!"

Feng and his wife looked aghast at the coven members, Nikki too shocked to move, to react. The Lopezes gathered their children close to them, shielding their eyes and ears from the insanity breaking out around them.

"This is bullshit!" Feng yelled, getting to his feet. "Utter nonsense!"

Tyee lowered her arms, frowning. "Feng, do you doubt?"

"Doubt? I disbelieve it with all my being! You're all shouting hysterics like a cult for some mythical creature."

"I know that as a Made you are disconnected from Her. But if you bring Her into your heart, you will hear Her, and She will guide you. Like She will guide us all."

"No. Nope," Feng said, slashing his arm through the air, urging his wife to his feet. "I fought hard for my freedom, for my peace. I will not be made anyone's slave ever again."

Feng and his wife turned their backs on the coven, making their way to the door.

"Then you will be the first to fall."

Feng and his wife froze, looking at Tyee's face, bright and wild with zeal, their own faces warped by confusion and betrayal.

Nikki's stomach twisted, bile rising in her throat.

The Lopezes stood, hesitant, looking frightened. But Tyee gave them a soft nod, allowing the children to avoid the coven's fight, and they ushered their kids out behind the Lius.

The cold air from their departure sent goosebumps crawling up Nikki's arms. She hadn't been close to the Lius, but the Lopezes had always been kind to her. The memory of creating shadow puppets around the fire seemed miles away. Her allies were gone and all that remained were madmen.

"Let that be a warning for all the Made," Tyee said, turning her gaze to Miguel. "Your loyalty is most important of all. Or you will be discarded."

Her dad tensed but did not fidget.

"But—" Nikki started, tongue thick in her mouth. "But how do you know this? About the Mother?"

Tyee smirked, pity and pride reflecting in her eyes alongside multi-colored flames. "As I told you before, I have communed with the Mother for ages upon ages." Tyee turned to the remaining coven, and announced, "The key to Her imprisonment has been found and returned." Tyee's eyes fixed on Nikki again. "The Mother would like to thank all of you who helped locate it and ensured its safe return."

Nikki shot to her feet, head swimming.

Xander.

"No. No, no, no." She stepped back, the chair skidding and thumping to the ground as she stumbled over her feet, her vision spinning, the multicolored smoke turning the room into a dream.

Nikki turned, legs weak, and fell to her hands and knees. Her hair stuck to her forehead, her cheeks, her nose, making it hard to breathe.

"What?" she slurred, the floorboards dancing.

She peeled herself off the floor, swaying.

A cold hand touched her arm. "Nicoletta, please. This will be a lot easier if you relax."

"You," Nikki said, throwing her mom's hand off her and falling back against the wall. "You?" she asked her dad, who stood with sorrow in his eyes.

Her mind raced and yet couldn't piece together full thoughts or words. All she knew was that it was their fault and she needed to get out, needed to get as far away as she could.

She catapulted her body against the door, falling outside and down the stairs, the steps dull thunks against the hard, numbed flesh of her body, her world rolling in black soil and fire and tree silhouettes as she flipped head over heel until she hit the ground.

Cold air rushed around her skin, but with heat raging inside her body, she couldn't regulate her temperature. Growing warmer by the second, she felt as though her organs were cooking from the inside. Nikki groaned and lifted herself from the ground, the trees melding. She turned to see the silhouettes of her parents in the doorway, outlined in flames and smoke, watching her crawl and stand, then sway and stumble as she tried to make her way forward, with little progress.

"This really would be easier for you if you settled down, little duck," a voice broke through the darkness. Hormin stepped beside her, his ancient presence seeming to push her down.

Her head spun and she stopped, clutching her stomach, bile rising in her mouth. She squeezed her eyes shut, forcing the nausea to move forward, her sweat-slicked skin making her clothes stick, then freeze, to her body.

Sharp pinpricks wove around her ankles, stinging. Nikki gasped and opened her eyes, low twining blackberry vines weaving up and around her legs, the thorns piercing her skin through her clothes.

Nikki lifted her head, squinting through the spinning and the darkness, and saw three figures ahead of her. Tyee, flanked by Atoc and Ozcollo, spinning their arms around their bodies and heads, as if knitting the vines around her.

She moved forward against the vines, brittle that they were, but they were relentless. She paused with another wave of nausea, the figures swirling in her peripheral vision.

She looked down, and in the dim light of the fire behind her, she saw a void open in the ground in front of her, the grass and ferns splitting apart to reveal the dark soil and a black nothingness below.

Nikki blinked, not understanding the growing hole in front of her, the splitting of the earth in her spinning vision, and she stumbled backward, trying to escape the yawning pit.

But the weavers unraveled the earth around her, and Nikki plummeted into the nothingness.

Chapter Thirty-Two

The back of Nikki's skull throbbed, and she groaned as she regained consciousness. Peeling her eyes open, she woke to a dark, barred room. Nikki looked about her—there was no sleeping cot, blanket, or bucket. She looked up; fibrous roots stretched down from the ceiling, clumps of dirt releasing as she shook the bars, soil clinging to the blood in her hair, dusting her face. Nikki coughed out the dirt in her mouth, then stopped shaking, not wanting to collapse the whole cell on herself.

Nikki winced as she sat up, her brain pounding against the inside of her skull, behind her eyes. She touched the back of her head, releasing a hiss as she touched the tender flesh there. It was sticky and lukewarm.

Bringing her fingers forward, her eyes adjusting to the dim, faint orange light from a wall sconce down the hall that illuminated her cell, Nikki smoothed the drying blood between her fingers. Rubbing the blood between her thumb and forefinger, her stomach clenched with nausea, and her mind reeled as she remembered falling, then thorny vines wrapping around her feet, the praising of the Mother.

Xander.

Nikki shot to her feet, a surge of dizziness overcoming her.

Stabilizing, she pressed a hand to her head as it pounded, then staggered forward to the thick metal bars, peering out into the glowing hall.

Halvar stood as a silent sentry against the stone wall, arms crossed, face vacant.

"Halvar?" Nikki slurred, leaning against the bars, her tongue feeling too large for her mouth.

He turned to her but didn't say anything.

"What's happening?"

He stared at her, icy blue eyes assessing, then said, "I will tell Tyee you have awoken."

"Wait," she said, trying to grab his arm as he walked by, but missed.

Nikki wrapped her hands around the bars and shook them, testing their strength. She was too weak, and they didn't budge. Frustrated, she growled and shook the bars with greater force, soft speckles of soil falling from above.

She groaned and slid down the wall until she sat on the floor, her legs tender with cuts and scrapes, stomach wrenching with hunger and nausea, limbs weak and shaking, brain pulsing, heart racing.

Footsteps echoed down the long hall, closer and closer.

Tyee appeared at the bars, calm, hands clasped behind her back, with Hormin beside her.

After moments of silence, Tyee set a cup of pale red liquid just inside the bars.

"Going to poison me again?" Nikki breathed.

"The funny thing is, you were all poisoned, but you were the only one who didn't get the antidote," Hormin said, looking as if he were suppressing a laugh.

Don't be rude. If it's poisoned, we're all drinking it, Nikki heard her mom say, and her heart clenched with the betrayal. She'd known all along.

"It's water. With three drops of blood," Tyee said. "Enough to sustain you, not enough to strengthen you."

"Wow. Thanks."

Tyee's gaze penetrated her, and Nikki felt her inner child, always intimidated by Tyee, curl up. "If you do not drink it of your own will, it will be forced upon you. The Mother is not yet done with you."

Nikki exhaled, mustering the strength to crawl to the cup and drink it. As much as she hated to admit it, the cool water felt good on her swollen tongue.

Setting the cup on the stone with a dull clink, she looked up at them and asked, "So, you going to tell me what's going on? Or leave me in the dark literally and figuratively?"

Tyee frowned. "This is not the way we wanted to do things. But you were warned—by myself, by the Mother, and by your own mother. And you refused to listen. You brought this on yourself."

Nikki pushed her fangs into her bottom lip, that old flame of self-loathing wrapping around her heart.

"Just tell me where I am. What's happening next. Please," Nikki asked, tired.

"You're still on my property."

"You've had this dungeon underground the whole time?" Nikki's mind reeled, imagining all the poor humans who ever found themselves here. "This whole solstice was just a setup."

"No, and yes. It was easiest to capture you while you were here. I apologize for the less-than-pleasant landing. I tried to have the earth cradle you, but Atoc and Ozcollo were not of similar minds, and the ground did not obey."

"Well. It's the thought that counts."

"I see the witch's tongue has influenced you. Snark will not free you."

"What will?"

Tyee said nothing.

"Is Xander here too?" Nikki asked, heart racing at the thought that he could be so close, that she could find a way to save him.

"No. He is far, far away."

"Vadasz and his friends got him, not too long after your... heroic attempt at fleeing," Hormin said, smirking. "I've never seen them quite so annoyed. It was very entertaining."

"But he texted me."

Hormin laughed. "We may be ancient, but we do know how to use a cell phone."

Nikki's heart fell, and she dropped her head to rest against the bars. She was so stupid.

"Don't fret, little duck," Hormin said, dropping down to a crouch until he was eye-to-eye with her. "You'll see him soon." At Nikki's confused expression, his mouth widened into the devious, predatory grin of a shark, and he shouted, "Yes! You're getting front-row seats to the releasing of the Mother. How special you are!" he said, and booped her nose. Nikki flinched at his cold, hard touch, and he giggled, unusually high and manic. He was much too excited about this.

"Who are you, really?" she asked.

He looked into the distance, as if recalling long-lost memories. "I have been called by many names, but now I am Hormin."

"And are you going to reveal your true purpose now?"

"That has also changed, but currently it is to ensure your safe and complacent travel to the Mother."

"Which is where?"

"I'd say you'll know when we get there, but the truth is, you won't!" Hormin said, laughing.

"And what will happen, once we're there?"

"Ah, the show will begin! She's waiting for you, you know. You've been quite the problem for Her. But we've got that all remedied now, haven't we? And She cannot wait to show you Her glory." He paused, looking at Nikki's sinking expression. "Don't be sad, you'll get to see your dearest one last time."

"What is the Mother going to do to us?" Nikki asked, wondering if there was any way she could plan her way out of what was to come.

"No spoilers!" Hormin squealed, and Nikki cringed at the high, loud pitch of his delight. His voice dropped, and he brushed blood-caked hair away from her face. "We will have to do something about your appearance, however. Mother would not approve of such disrespect."

As his hand tucked strands behind her ear, sending waves of violation through her body, Nikki turned her head and bit his hand.

But it was like biting stone, and her jaw reverberated with the shock and pain of her teeth against the impenetrable toughness of his skin. As she recoiled, a hand flew to her neck and slammed her face against the metal bars, new waves of shock and pain pulsing through her head.

Squeezing her throat, Hormin's face lost all humor, his eyes as dark as the depths of hell, and he breathed into her choking face, "Foolish girl. I am the last of Mother's first brood. Untainted by the millennia of human breeding, more vampire than anyone but Mother. You cannot hurt me."

He released her throat, but stayed close to the bars, eyes caressing her face grotesquely, angrily.

Fear and anger roiled in Nikki's stomach, a warm pressure building in her lungs, then rising through her chest and out of her mouth, exploding as she had on Halloween, unleashing one long, ear-splitting scream directly into his face.

He blinked at her, her breath gusting his hair. Then he smiled, as blood dripped from one ear. "There it is. We were wondering where the screech owl went." He chuckled and shook his head. "Mother will be delighted."

With the power of her scream sapping all her strength, Nikki crumpled to the floor.

Hormin stood and put a hand on her hung head, patting it like she was a dog. "I think our travels will be more fun than I thought."

Nikki watched as Hormin and Tyee turned, receding down the hall and disappearing, leaving her in the twilight-hued cell, alone with her thoughts and her failures.

Chapter Thirty-Three

Soft thumping filled Nikki's head, getting louder. She peeled her eyes open, separating herself from her attempt at sleep, sabotaged by the discomfort of lying on cold stone. Sitting up, she groaned with the stiffness of the movement and listened as the footsteps grew closer. The hall was bathed in the same dim, orange light as before. There was no telling what time it was.

There was nothing Nikki could do but lean against the wall and wait for the inevitable.

Then her parents walked into view, faces long and drawn, and Nikki wished she had pretended to remain sleeping. She clenched her jaw as cold rage filled her chest.

"You," Nikki hissed, her words striking out as though filled with venom.

Cat laced her fingers together and gulped, Miguel pressing his face close to the bars of her cell, looking into the darkness.

"Not even a blanket?" her dad asked, barely more than a whisper.

Nikki ignored him, keeping her gaze locked on her mom. "You knew. You tricked me. Coerced me into drinking poison. Into being made a prisoner."

Her mom hesitated. "I didn't know it would be like this."

Nikki scoffed.

"I promise, darling. I knew you wouldn't come willingly. I thought perhaps there would be a mild sedative, that's all. I didn't think they would go this far."

"Oh? And what did you expect to happen when you betrayed me?"

Cat blinked, stunned. "I didn't betray you. I saved you."

Nikki cast her arm around the cell. "How is this saving me?"

"I warned you months ago to obey, and you didn't listen. Now, when we go to the Mother, we can go as a family. We can watch over you. I don't know what vile methods they would have used to capture you if we didn't comply. You're safest this way."

"You're a fool," Nikki spat, and stood on shaking legs, using the wall as support. "Your God will kill me."

"She won't. We're Her children. She'll spare you. She is not what you imagine. You'll see." Her mom shifted on her feet, but her gaze remained determined. "I've packed you a travel bag, and we'll all go together. It'll be like a family vacation."

"If you really think that, you're naïve. As you said, I disobeyed her. Brought down her wrath because I refused to give up Xander. But what a good puppet you have been." Her mom cast her eyes to the ground, and ice flooded Nikki's blood. "It's funny, I thought you were on my side. But all this time you've been plotting against me. You manipulated me and now I'm doomed. And Xander—oh, God." Nikki lost her footing and fell to the ground. "She's going to kill him. I could've protected him. But you turned against us and now he'll die. I'll die. Because of you."

"You don't know what She'll do with him. Or you. It might not be malignant."

Nikki laughed, the weight of Xander's fate forcing horrid images into her mind. "You're blinded by your nonsensical zealotry. What do you know of the Mother? What do you really know about anything? You've sentenced Xander to death. Not to mention your own daughter."

"And you," Nikki said, finally looking at her dad, his face pale and sunken, hands wrapped tight against the bars. "What's your excuse for betraying me? I know the compelling is difficult to fight. She at least has an excuse. But you? You betrayed me willingly. I'm disappointed in you most of all."

Miguel's face crumpled, and he squeezed his eyes tight, as if trying to wake from a nightmare. "I didn't know what they were going to do, love, I promise. I thought it would be a simple talk, nothing more. I did not know they would treat you so."

"I find it hard to believe you didn't know what she was up to," Nikki said, glaring at her mom.

"It's true, Nicoletta. I told him they were overnight bags in case the party went late. I only told him that we were all going to try to convince you to comply," her mom said, reaching her hand through the bars.

Nikki swatted her hand, arm twisting at an awkward angle against the metal. "Then you're more naïve than she is," Nikki spat at her dad. She looked up at her parents, the people who were supposed to protect her, to take her side, to love her unconditionally, but instead let her be drugged, captured, and sentenced to an unknown future.

The weight of their betrayal, of a world without Xander, pressed darkness into her soul, blinding her.

"I will never forgive either of you for this."

Nikki turned her back to them before she could see their reactions and crawled into a corner of her cell. Her parents hesitated before retreating, footsteps muted in their defeat. Nikki pressed the heels of her hands against her eyelids, hating herself for letting Xander go, imagining his brightness swallowed by the dark of the world, knowing if that's where he went, she would follow.

Chapter Thirty-Four

Nikki couldn't keep track of time in the cell. The lighting never wavered; the temperature didn't fluctuate. It could have been hours, or days. All she knew was that sometime later, Tyee made another appearance with a meager cup of water dosed with another trio of blood droplets. Nikki's body weakened with the lack of food and hydration, her injuries not healing, every ache and pain deepening as the hunger grew, her stomach seizing with pain.

Tyee left after she drank the cup, then returned later, Nikki waking from the fringes of consciousness. This time, Tyee carried a small basin stuffed with towels, hygiene supplies, and spare clothes.

"You will depart soon and need to be made presentable. If I enter to clean you, you will not misbehave."

Nikki blinked her consent, too tired to nod.

Tyee unlocked the cage and stepped in, closing it behind her. She laid down a towel and sat on it, too proud to sit on her own dungeon floor. She wrapped another towel around Nikki's shoulders and rotated her until she faced the wall. Tyee washed out the blood, then brushed each strand with the touch of a mother preparing her daughter for a school dance. The roughness of knots still pulsed pain through the bruises on her skull, but the other woman's tenderness both calmed

Nikki and broke her heart. If she closed her eyes, she could imagine sitting in her room as a girl, her mom brushing her hair in front of the vanity.

As if reading her mind, Tyee said, "It didn't have to be like this, Nikki."

Nikki licked her chapped lips and spoke through her coarse throat. "It did. I would have always chosen to protect him."

"And you would have failed each and every time."

A moment of silence stretched, then Nikki asked, "Where are your friends?"

"Hormin? Or Atoc and Ozcollo?"

"Any of them."

"Hormin does what he pleases. I do not know his current location, but he is likely wandering the premises. Atoc and Ozcollo left to join the Mother."

Tyee finished brushing and trimming Nikki's hair, then took moist towelettes and swiped them over her skin. She pushed Nikki's pants up to her knees, her legs covered in bright pink scratches from the thorns.

Remembering the vines twining around her legs, how the earth had caved beneath her feet, Nikki asked, "How did you do it? I thought only witches had magic."

"There's more to this world than witches and vampires."

"Like what?"

Tyee didn't answer.

Pooling saliva in her mouth to moisten her dry throat and cracked lips, Nikki said, "I've never heard of a vampire wielding that kind of power. I didn't think it was possible."

Tyee was silent a moment, then said, "I am more than a vampire."

"What do you—"

A resounding boom moved the earth, sending Nikki and Tyee careening to the side. Nikki's head smacked against the stone wall behind her, while Tyee fell forward, catching herself on her hands and knees, catlike. Dirt shook loose from the ceiling and dusted their bodies.

Tyee shot to her feet, staring down the hallway in the direction of the blast. A foreboding silence settled, then Tyee's head perked, twisting quickly, hearing something Nikki's dulled senses could not perceive.

Nikki watched the face of her childhood hero, her childhood fear, widen with uncertainty, with concern. Nikki's wet hair slicked to her face, the clumps of dirt settling on her moist skin, sticking to her newly cleaned hair, tangling.

Tyee gave Nikki one long, hard look, then said, "Finish cleaning yourself and change. We will leave soon." Then she left the cell, locking it behind her, and ran with sure, fast steps down the hall.

Dirt rained from the ceiling, coating her skin in fine debris and broken roots. If the cell collapsed, would it be enough to kill her? Or would she be buried alive?

Nikki's fingers shook as she staggered to her feet, knowing she needed to leave, that this was her chance while Tyee was distracted, but her muscles gave out, and she fell with a smack of her knees against the cold stones, crying out with the pain. She crawled to the bars and pushed and pulled against them, sweat mixing with the cold water on her face as she tried to bend them open. But she was too weak, and too tired, and when had she ever succeeded, anyway?

Soft footsteps pattered from the opposite end of the hall from where Tyee left, and Nikki slid back from the bars.

A slim, muscular woman with angular, deep almond eyes and shimmering black hair in a high bun skidded to a halt in front of her cell.

"Daiyu?" Nikki asked, blinking.

"Nikki, can you stand?" Daiyu asked, pulling a long pin from her hair, causing it to cascade in glorious waves down her shoulders.

"Not really," Nikki replied, pushing herself up and leaning against the wall for support, legs shaking. "What day is it?"

"The 25th, almost 26th," Daiyu responded, leaning down to assess the lock on the cell.

Four days. She'd been down here for four whole days. How was she supposed to figure out where Xander and her parents were now?

Daiyu pressed the pin into the lock of the cell, which clicked open with a little tinkering. Daiyu tsked and said, "Pathetic," then swung the door open.

Daiyu, several inches shorter than Nikki, turned her back and bent, saying, "Climb onto my back."

"Wh-what?"

"Come on, we don't have much time," she said, and backed up, forcing Nikki to buckle over her small body. Daiyu lifted her, holding onto her thighs as Nikki wrapped her arms around the other woman's shoulders, trying not to choke her. With surprising strength and speed, Daiyu bolted down the hall, her grip on Nikki never faltering.

Nikki's brain bounced in her bruised skull as Daiyu ran, zigzagging through Tyee's underground tunnels. Her dungeons.

Bile rose in Nikki's throat at the pain, the jostling, the hunger. The thirst.

Daiyu hesitated at a fork, and another distant boom shook the chambers from the right, making the ground quake.

Daiyu dashed to the left, and Nikki closed her eyes, wishing for an end.

A rush of cold air whipped around Nikki's face, rustling her wet hair, filling her lungs with the fresh beauty of freedom. Nikki opened her eyes again, trying to blink her surroundings into focus, but with her starvation, her sight was worse than a human's, and she could barely make out the trees in the dark, only illuminated by a distant fire behind them.

Daiyu turned around, and they looked at where they had emerged, Nikki's face dropping with awe as fire licked up the Douglas fir, bark and wood popping as the desiccated and frozen parts burst from the heat and flame.

They had emerged from a nondescript opening in the ground, surrounded by old-growth forest, and Nikki had no concept of where they were in relation to Tyee's home or the highway.

Daiyu turned away from the destruction and sprinted through the forest, heedless of the salmonberry and blackberry that clawed at them. After a couple minutes she stopped twisting through the trees and ran in a straight line along a paved road, the dark sky and the looming silhouettes of the trees overhead, the road void of streetlights.

In the distance, two pale orbs moved toward them. Headlights. To Nikki's horror, instead of running away from the car, instead of hiding in the trees, Daiyu stayed her course. What a sight they must be, a small woman holding Nikki piggyback, running in the dead of night on a poorly lit road, Daiyu's breaths coming harder and faster.

As the car approached, Nikki prayed it wasn't Tyee or Hormin or some other ill-intentioned stranger. Just some random mortal, driving by, not paying attention, or perhaps thinking they were hallucinating.

Nikki's fingers clawed into Daiyu's skin as the car slowed down at their approach, Daiyu hissing through her teeth at the sting of Nikki's nails. Daiyu slowed her run, a slight sheen of sweat on her face, as they stopped beside the car.

Daiyu swung the back door open and dropped Nikki inside, then Daiyu sprinted around to the front and slid into the passenger seat, the car screeching forward again before the door had even closed.

"Here," a voice said, tossing a sack into the backseat, thumping against Nikki like a water balloon.

Nikki peeled herself to a sitting position and squinted through the dark at the driver.

"Feng?"

He looked at her through the rearview mirror but didn't reply.

Nikki picked up the floppy bladder and unscrewed the top, the coppery scent of blood rushing into her brain, filling her body with a blinding need. She raised the opening to her mouth, pushing the luke-warm liquid down her throat, gulping with all the glory of satiated thirst and hunger, her cells repairing and strengthening, senses sharpening, wounds healing, as if they never were.

"Drink slow. You don't want to make yourself sick," Daiyu said.

Nikki gasped with the breath she held while drinking, squeezing every last drop from the empty bladder.

"Too late, my love," Feng said.

Nikki gagged, stomach aching with sudden fullness, but she hunched and clenched her throat tight, bidding her esophagus, her stomach, to keep it down. She lost herself in the hum of the car, the widening of her senses, the loss of pain, as the blood wound through her body. When she thought she could keep it down, she sat up again and leaned her head back, resting it on the window.

"Thank you," she said, the time in the cell already feeling like a distant nightmare. "But why? Why help me?"

"It wasn't right, what they did to you," Daiyu said.

"How did you know? You left."

"We didn't," Feng said. "We stayed and watched. We saw you stagger from the building. We watched them use the earth to swallow you whole."

"We were worried about what it meant," Daiyu added. "After all Tyee said inside."

Nikki was silent, trying to piece together the evening, the days, all things Feng and Daiyu had said to her, but still her mind drew a blank. "Why would you save me? The repercussions alone." Nikki's voice drifted off, unable and unwilling to imagine what would be done to them if, when, they were caught.

Feng said, "If you want to live a long, vampiric life, know this: eventually, all any creature wants is power. When one loves enough, amasses enough wealth, circles with the upper echelons of society, has gained all the normal human wants, they lose their luster. Each immortal creature eventually seeks power. That becomes the only thing left, the only way to feel. To have something new. Become a god and be worshipped." Feng's voice grew tighter, harsher. "And you know what power leads to? Oppression. Bigotry. That is already evident with the culture, the religion, around their so-called Mother. A creature who detests the Made, who calls all vampires their children, except us. One who would enslave humanity for their own desires. While we have argued for more food, we will never stand on the side of slavery."

"We do not care for the games Tyee plays for her Mother. She pretends to be a humble servant but awaits the boons of the Mother to gain greater power," Daiyu said.

Feng added, "We wanted a humble life. Instead, Tyee has brought war into the heart of our coven."

Nikki watched as the trees became more defined, then said, "It might be my fault, for the issues in the coven."

Feng and Daiyu were quiet, waiting.

"I fell for someone. And the Mother wanted him, but it wasn't right for Her to have him. I wanted to protect him." Nikki swallowed the lump in her throat. "And I failed. She has him. I don't know what will happen now."

Feng and Daiyu absorbed the information, the car rolling down the empty highway with a quiet hum.

"So they kidnapped a boy, tortured one of our own, and split apart our family, for this higher creature? One that half of us don't even know to be real?" Feng asked.

Daiyu tsked. "Shameful."

"We protect our own first."

Nikki's brows rose, and Feng saw it in the rearview. "As a coven, you are ours, and we are yours. Tyee, the Ivarssons, your parents"—Nikki's eyes watered with the sting—"they broke the covenant we made to each other. Perhaps, if things were explained, it would be different. But see? Another power play, keeping us in the dark."

"Tyee seemed to think you'd be pleased with the Mother's rise to power."

"When you want more steak, do you want to kill all the cows?" Feng asked. He saw her shake her head in the rearview. "No. Wanting a higher food supply doesn't mean we want all humans to die. Nothing good will come of her rise."

"We don't know how we can help you. But know that we are on your side. You live long enough, and you can feel it. A knowing when things aren't right. And this isn't right. Tell us what you need."

Nikki's fingers tingled with renewed power, and her mind reeled, absorbing their words, thinking about impossible next steps.

"I need to see Gwen."

"Her house may not be secure. We have a safe house you could recuperate at."

"Thank you, but no. I'll risk it. I can't do anything without her."

Daiyu nodded, but Feng's thick brows furrowed in the mirror.

"Did you happen to get my cell phone?" Nikki asked.

"No, sorry," Daiyu said. "We didn't remember to get ours, either."

"That's okay. Thanks again for getting me out," Nikki said, head against the cold glass. "How did you get me out? Did you set whatever it was that exploded?"

The profile of Feng's face split into a mischievous grin. "Between the Gold Rush and moving up here, I worked on the Transcontinental Railroad. In demolitions. I may have picked up a trick or two. A passion I enhanced over the last century and a half."

"He's really quite good," Daiyu said, laying a hand on her husband's arm.

"You set off bombs on Tyee's property? You just had them on you?" Nikki asked, voice hitching with surprise.

"No, no. But I know how to improvise. She has a surprising storage of dangerous chemicals."

"One wonders, what could she possibly need them for?" Daiyu added.

Nikki shuddered, thinking of the depth and breadth of the dungeons.

"How did you know which way to get out, Daiyu? And how did you know where to find her illicit substances, Feng? On her vast estate."

"Ah," Feng said, and laughed, Daiyu laughing after him like bells.

"We're survivors, Nikki," Feng said. "You live long enough, friends and enemies and rivals all switch roles. Best to plan ahead and know where escape routes are, if needed."

"Lucky me we're on the same side," Nikki said.

"Lucky, indeed," Feng agreed, face splitting into a wider grin.

The rest of the drive passed in silence, Nikki's mind racing, her legs and skull itching as they healed, the overload of blood consumption sharpening her senses. Her heart felt strong and sure, her muscles ready to run, to fight. Energy buzzed through her veins.

Feng stopped the car down the road from the O'Brennans' house, turning it off so any recently fed vampires wouldn't hear the gentle rumble of the engine.

When Nikki opened the car door, Feng and Daiyu stepped into the dark with her.

"What are you doing?"

"Coming with you," Feng said. "What's the point in rescuing you if you are immediately kidnapped again?"

"I can't argue with that."

They stepped into the brisk winter night, ice in the air. She guided them around the house, skirting the property of her enemies and her best friend, her heart hardened with renewed purpose.

She would save Xander and set things right.

Chapter Thirty-Five

Nikki, Feng, and Daiyu made their way through the forest, trees sharp silhouettes against the hazy night. Her senses were crisp, the rustling of leaves and crunching of debris loud beneath her feet, fingertips alight with the feel of fern fronds and frosty winter air. Despite the weight on her shoulders and the heaviness in her heart, she felt alive, and relished her freedom, her vigor. This was one blessing of her vampirism—the strength to save Xander.

The forest thinned, giving in to the meadow with Gwen's studio in the center, grasses pale and swaying in the night breeze. Approaching the building, the roost was empty, and she heard movement from behind the studio, beyond her vision.

Unease wound her muscles tight, stiffening with alertness, as she rounded the building.

A figure sat hunched in the clearing, small mounds beside them illuminated by one large lantern.

"Gwen?" Nikki asked, stepping closer into the halo of light.

Daiyu and Feng remained in the darkness, giving them privacy.

Gwen lifted her head, eyes bloodshot and weary. "I tried calling you," she said, gaze flicking to the Lius. "What are they doing here?"

"It's a long story. I'll tell you, but first tell me what happened here."

Gwen looked back at the ground, using a spade to shovel dirt out of the hole in front of her.

Nikki looked around them, nearly a dozen small piles of freshly dug dirt.

"What's going on, Gwen?"

Gwen twisted away from Nikki, and when she turned back, the limp body of Harriet lay in her hands. Gwen tucked her wings around her gently, then carefully laid her on the ground, fresh sniffles breaking the silence.

"What happened?" Nikki asked, sinking to her knees beside her friend.

"They killed them. They killed them all," Gwen said, tears streaking down her cheeks as she pushed the dirt over Harriet, making one more mound.

"How? What happened?"

"I don't know," Gwen whispered with a small shrug. "They were dumped in a bag on my front porch. Like so much garbage," Gwen said, voice breaking, a gush of new tears welling in her eyes, rolling down her cheeks.

"I thought I'd know," Gwen said, choking on her cries. "I thought I'd feel it. But I didn't. I failed them." She curled into herself as her sobs grew louder.

"I'm so, so sorry," Nikki said, then put a hand on her back. Gwen leaned into her touch and Nikki held her as her shoulders wracked with sobs. Nikki hugged Gwen until she ran out of tears and her breaths settled, the moisture against Gwen's cheeks freezing to her skin.

Gwen pulled away with a sniffle, swiping at the snot and moisture on her face. "I'm sorry," she said. "I fucked up." Gwen put a hand over Harriet's grave. "I bound them to me, but I didn't bind myself to them. I didn't know, and now they're all gone. I failed them, and I failed you. I failed everyone. I'm so sorry, Nik."

"What? Why are you sorry? You didn't fail me, or anyone else. We've only been outmaneuvered." Nikki rubbed her hand over Gwen's back. "I'm the one who's sorry. For pulling you into this mess. They'd be alive if not for me."

Gwen shook her head, eyes sunken and red hair wild and unkempt. She looked at the mounds around her. "I don't know when this happened. I don't know who did it. But this could have happened a while ago. Xander could be long gone. As gone as they are."

"Don't say that," Nikki snapped, the cold fear igniting her anger. "He is still alive. We can still save him."

"How?"

"I don't know. That's why I came to you."

"No, how do you know he's still alive?"

"Tyee told me. There's some big plan with me and him and the Mother. We need to get him out of there and stop this."

Nikki stood, holding Gwen's hands, helping her friend to her feet. The lantern light cast skeletal shadows across Gwen's exhausted face.

Gwen looked at their hands, then asked, "Where have you been? I needed you."

"I'm sorry, Gwen. I wish I had been here for you. But I was taken."

Gwen's brows pinched. "Taken?"

"At the solstice. They drugged me and kept me in a cell beneath Tyee's property."

"She has a dungeon?"

"Yes."

"What a psycho." Gwen squeezed her eyes shut, as if pushing away a headache. "I need more details. What happened? How did you escape?"

"Feng and Daiyu saved me. That's why they're here," she said. "Do you mind if they stay a minute? They're worried I'll get attacked again."

"A legitimate concern."

Nikki and Gwen stepped closer to the Lius, although they could likely overhear everything they talked about. Gwen said, "You won't be able to get past my ward, but you can hang outside if you want."

The Lius nodded and turned away from the studio, keeping their gazes on the main house beyond.

Leading Gwen inside, Nikki told her of the solstice, Atoc and Ozcollo, the ritualism, the rift with the coven and Tyee's zealotry, her mom's betrayal, her time as a captive, and the Lius freeing her.

By the time she finished, they both had steaming cups of tea in hand, Gwen was curled in a blanket, and her eyes were a little less puffy, though still rimmed red.

"This is crazy, Nik. What do they even want with him?"

"I don't know. But if we figure that out, we may be able to figure out where he is. And how we can save him. I need to make this right. I feel terrible, having let him go so easily. I should have known better."

"I should have too. I should have known something was wrong. I just assumed no news was good news."

"Me too."

A moment of silence lingered between them, then Gwen asked, "What do we do now?"

"We should talk to Ina, Xander's mom. She knew what I was, plus her house is full of artifacts that have this... aura. She must know something, right?"

Gwen's eyes widened. "You think she's part of some Van Helsing, anti-vampire-esque society?"

"Well, I hope not. But she's part of something."

Gwen nodded, clutching the blanket tighter around herself.

"How long until sunrise?" Nikki asked.

Gwen checked her phone, then said, "About three hours."

"Then there's no time to waste. Are you good to go? I can go alone if you're not up for it."

Gwen stood, shaking her head. She downed her tea and shivered, shaking out her tension. "No. Let's do this. Let's go save your man."

Nikki took Gwen's hands and squeezed them. "Thank you. For everything. I couldn't do this without you."

"You know I'd do anything for you."

"Same. I'm sorry I wasn't here for you when those bastards came. When this is all over, I promise we will have a proper celebration of life for all of them."

"I'd like that."

They dropped hands and Gwen packed a few potions and salves, snacking as she did so.

Outside, Nikki said to Feng and Daiyu, "We have a plan."

"We heard," Feng replied.

"Can you drive us?"

Daiyu hesitated. "It seems unwise for us to go to a potential vampire slayer's house. Perhaps we can follow you for a short time?"

Nikki nodded and turned to Gwen. "Do you have an extra bike?"

"Yes, why?"

"I don't have my car. And I don't want to run that far."

"Don't be daft. We'll drive."

"How?"

A mischievous grin split Gwen's sorrow-filled face, and she said, "We'll steal my sister's car. It's the least she could do, after all."

"And how will we pull that off?"

Gwen shrugged. "Stealth and magic. Or strength and magic, depending. I have the magic, you, Feng, and Daiyu have the stealth and strength, right? Nik, are you all bloodied up?"

Nikki cringed. "Yes, they gave me plenty when they broke me out."

"How kind of you," Gwen said to the Lius, who nodded.

Gwen locked up the studio and slung her bag over a shoulder as they walked out into the frigid winter night, dew freezing on the grass and crunching under their feet.

"Are you sure you're well enough for a fight, if that's what it comes to?" Nikki whispered.

"Oh, I'm sure," Gwen said, taking a bite of an apple. "I have revenge to exact. Even if they weren't the perpetrators, they were complicit."

"Fair enough."

They crept through the meadow toward the forest, where the garage sat offset from the main house, connected by an enclosed walkway. Feng and Daiyu split off to hide in the forest while Nikki and Gwen circled around. They entered the garage through a side door and flicked on the lights, revealing glistening, expensive cars all in a row.

Gwen pointed to a large, black BMW SUV. "That's Bridget's. Or ours, now." Gwen plucked the keys off a key ring hanging beside the door. "The dumb bitch doesn't keep the keys on her. What a false sense of safety she has." Gwen tsked. "Go, sit in the driver's seat. This part will be loud."

Nikki nodded, took the keys, and got settled in the car, adjusting it to her needs. Gwen pressed the button for the garage door opener, and it slid open with terrible screeches and creaks that cut through the silence of the night like a siren.

Gwen grimaced and ran to the passenger door.

"Just what do you think you're doing?" Bridget said, coming to a halt outside the garage, illuminated in red from the brake lights.

"Um, going for a joy ride?" Gwen said, pulling the car door handle.

In a flash, Gwen's head cracked against the window, her skull splitting with blood, a hairline fracture in the glass.

"I don't think so. Nikki, get out now!" Bridget yelled, glaring at her through the window.

Gwen stumbled, but remained upright, clutching her head. When she looked down at her fingers, her jaw tightened in anger. "You bitch."

"What did you call me?" Bridget said, as the air filled with static, her hair rising like it was filling with humidity.

Gwen glared daggers at her sister, the air thickening, sound sucking into the vacuum of space. "You. Dumb. Bitch. You let them kill my friends!"

Bridget laughed. "How pathetic, animals are your friends?"

She moved to grab Gwen by the collar, but Gwen stepped back and thrust out a hand, the air bending with a sickening pop, like changing altitudes too quickly, and Bridget flew back, out of the garage and into a tree, head smacking against the bark. The SUV shook with the force of the air Gwen expelled.

Bridget touched the back of her head and snarled, climbing to her feet. Feng and Daiyu leaped from the forest, crashing into Bridget. Bridget flailed against their grasps, wrenching her arms behind her and pulling her away from the car.

Gwen ran into the car, screaming, "Go, go, go, go!"

Nikki threw the car backwards and Bridget howled as they escaped. In the rearview, Feng, Daiyu, and a struggling Bridget were swallowed by the forest.

Gwen laughed when they were out of sight, a sheen of sweat slicked on her face as she laughed and reclined her head.

"That was amazing, Gwen. You've been practicing?"

"Every day. I'll push them right off the edge of a cliff someday."

"I hope I'm there to see it."

"Me too," Gwen said.

She pulled some salve from her bag and cleaned her head wound, wincing with the pain as she did so. There was no sign of being chased, no car barreling after them, but it would happen sooner or later. There was only so much the Lius could do to delay the inevitable. Nikki just hoped they could find where Xander was before the hunt for them began.

<h1 style="text-align:center">Chapter Thirty-Six</h1>

Gwen was snoring lightly when they got to Xander's parents' house. Guilt twisted Nikki's stomach at the thought of waking everyone up, but there was no time to lose.

Gwen's eyes blinked open as the car stopped, and she followed Nikki's worried gaze to the house. "Better to rip off the Band-Aid."

Nikki nodded, and they got out of the car, closing the doors as quietly as possible. Images of the last time she was here flashed through her mind. Xander in his bedroom. Eating with them at Thanksgiving. The moment he stood up for her. The sharp eyes of his mom assessing her.

Her heart ached for him.

When they ascended the front steps, a light flicked on in the kitchen, sending Nikki's pulse racing. A silhouette walked by the illuminated window.

The door swung open as they approached, Ina's head peeking out.

"What are you doing here?" she whispered so quickly it sounded like a hiss. Ina's dark eyes flicked to Gwen. "How dare you bring another vampire to my house."

"Whoa, now. No need to go throwing insults," Gwen said.

"You must be a witch, then," Ina said, looking past them. "Has anyone seen you? Were you followed?"

"I don't think so," Nikki said.

Ina stepped out onto the porch, closing the door behind her.

"Such hospitality," Gwen murmured.

Ina glared at Gwen and crossed her arms over her nightrobe, her unbrushed hair wild. "You best have a good reason for bringing this danger to my doorstep."

"I do."

"How did you know we were here?" Gwen asked.

"Wards," Ina replied, glancing at Gwen before turning her gaze back to Nikki. "Now, what do you want?"

"It's, um, hard to explain," Nikki said, faltering under the fierce eyes of Ina.

In her hesitation, Ina's eyes widened, and she said, "Please tell me you know where my son is."

They shook their heads. Nikki said, "I was hoping you might."

Ina's hands tightened on her forearms, and her eyes closed, as if shutting out the world. She took deep breaths, and Nikki said, "We know he was taken, but we don't know where. If you can tell us, we can save him. I know I promised I would keep him safe. And I'm sorry I failed in that. I want to make it right."

Ina covered her eyes with her hands and murmured, "What have you done?" Then she turned and put a hand on her stomach as if trying not to be sick.

"I'm so, so sorry. I told him the truth, and he got mad, and left, and I was trying to give him space. I was trying to be respectful of his wishes, but he was taken." Cold swept through Nikki's body. "He was texting me but it turns out that it wasn't him at all. But if you know where the Mother is, we can go save him."

Ina laughed, desperate and defeated. "Oh, it's so much worse than that."

"What do you mean?"

Ina exhaled and turned around. "It's not just his life at stake."

"Ha!" Gwen said, Ina and Nikki turning a surprised look at her. Gwen shrugged. "She said stake. I thought it was a vampire joke."

Ina covered her eyes again, briefly, then braced herself on a patio chair. "How certain are you that he has been taken to the Mother?"

"Very," Nikki said.

"Then we have little time for explanation," Ina said. "I need to hide my family, then call The Cradle, and you—"

"Whoa, hold up," Gwen said, throwing up her hands. "We understand we have to move fast, but you have to give us some information."

Ina nodded, eyes darting around as if chasing her thoughts. "What do you know of the Mother? Do you know why she desires Xander?"

"I didn't even think the Mother was real until recently. Until I met Xander, She didn't talk to me at all. And no one has told me why She wants him so badly. I've been in the dark this whole time," Nikki said, the confusion and fear from the past few months rising into a hot fury in her chest.

"Xander's blood will be able to free the Mother, and when She's free, she will destroy the entire human race."

Silence stretched between them. A cold chill wound its way down Nikki's spine, forcing the hair on her arms to stand on end.

Ina glared at her. "You should have never met my son. I tried to keep him safe. He was blocked, by his father and siblings, yet he insisted on changing schools, and I couldn't stop him."

"He doesn't know?" Nikki asked at the same time Gwen said, "Blocked?"

"Yes, blocked. There were protections in place to prevent this. But you ruined it. Now he is gone, my husband is threatened, and it's all your fault."

Nikki's heart twisted. "Please, tell me how to make it right. I just want him to be safe."

"If that were true, you would have stayed far away from him when I warned you. You've brought death upon everyone!"

"Hey! She loves your son, and you're wasting time. Tell us where he is so we can save him," Gwen snapped.

Ina took a deep, stuttering breath. "I don't know where the Mother resides. I'll call The Cradle. They might know."

"The Cradle?" Nikki and Gwen asked.

Ina sucked in a lungful of air and expelled it quickly. "In the simplest terms, we're the antithesis to vampires. While our passive abilities differ, we're primarily sun bearers."

"Sun bearers?" Gwen asked.

Ina opened a palm and summoned a bright ball in her hand, a glowing miniature sun. Nikki's skin burned from its rays, but it was one of the most beautiful things she had ever seen. Ina closed her hand, throwing them back into darkness, leaving a white blind spot in Nikki's vision for several seconds.

"That's why the Mother wants him? For the sun?" Gwen asked.

"No, she wants him for what hides in his father's side. Which I will explain later, once we have him. Nikki, you try to find clues as to when and where he was taken. I need time to hide my family and reach my contacts. You might learn before I do. And you—" Ina said, turning to Gwen.

"Gwen," she responded. "Yeah, nice to meet you."

"Be on standby. We may need your abilities."

"You don't even know what my gifts are."

"We'll figure out what we need when we need it. It's best if you two aren't together. If you're both found and taken, our chances of success are greatly diminished."

"Understood," Nikki said. "Gwen, take me to my parents' house. Considering they're the source of my betrayal, I'll look for clues there," Nikki said, mouth puckering with the sourness of her words.

"We're just leaving without more answers?" Gwen asked, looking at Ina.

"Answers can come later," Ina said. "First, save the world."

Gwen rolled her eyes.

"I'm not joking. Xander," Ina said, stifling a choke in her throat, "may be the first to die, if the Mother is freed. But he will not be the last. Far from it."

"Well, shit," Gwen said.

Nikki was silent, spiraling into the darkness of her failures. After a moment, she said, "There's one issue. I don't have a cell phone."

"Find one and let me know the number. We need to stay in touch."

Ina found a stray marker on the porch and scribbled her number on their arms, wrote Gwen's number on her hand, and then pushed them down the steps. "Hurry, go, go. Before the sun comes up. And save my son, please. You promised to keep him safe. Do not fail in this. Again."

Nikki heard the rapid pulse of her heartbeat, the fear and anger an acrid scent in the air. "I promise."

Ina nodded and went back inside.

As they walked down the steps, away from the house, Gwen said, "Dramatic, much? I mean, it can't be that bad, can it? The entire human race?"

Tyee's words from the solstice of human thralls, the rise of vampires, made Nikki nauseous. "I think she's right. That's basically what Tyee said."

Gwen sucked in a breath. "Shit. Who'd have thought that cute nerd would be the key to an ancient vampiric god's freedom?"

"I certainly didn't."

Gwen wrapped an arm around Nikki's shoulders as they walked. "We'll save him. And get revenge for all my friends in the process."

"I like this plan."

"Me too."

They got in the car, Nikki driving them to her parents' house. They sat in silence for several minutes, then Gwen said, "How did her family not wake up?"

Nikki shrugged. "Wards?"

Gwen huffed a laugh. "I guess."

Nikki tapped her fingers on the steering wheel. "Where is Theo, by the way?"

"Oh," Gwen said, turning to look out the window, the streetlamps casting gold light across the cracks from the impact of her skull. "After Harriet and the others, I told her to stay away for a while. I don't want her in the crossfire."

"I see," Nikki said. "Maybe you should bring her in, though. Xander is gone because I tried to keep him out. I don't want you and Theo to have the same issue."

"I don't think she's a key to a deity's prison, but I see your point." Gwen sighed with a big huff of air, puffing out her cheeks. "I needed some time alone. I don't expect anyone to understand what they meant to me. I was supposed to protect them, to care for them, and instead I sentenced them to death."

Gwen's words wrenched the chambers of Nikki's heart. "I understand. Completely."

"I know you do," Gwen said, leaning her head against the glass and sighing. "I think I've had enough emotions for one night."

"I've had enough in the past two months for an entire lifetime."

"For a vampire, that's saying quite a lot."

"Tell me about it," Nikki said, thinking not just of Xander, but of her parents. Of her mom encouraging her to drink poison, of them visiting her in the cell, her dad's face pressed between the bars, and their excuses for their betrayal. Her heart sank into her stomach. Her parents were lost to her, their loyalties with each other, with the Mother, when she thought they loved her unconditionally.

How wrong, how foolish, she was. But the pain of this loss was somehow lessened after mourning Xander, leaving a hollow, bitter acceptance within her.

They spent the rest of the car ride in their own thoughts. Nikki pulled up to her house and handed the keys over to Gwen, deciding it would be better for her to take the car home and avoid further issues with her sister. The last thing they needed was for the police to get involved, too. Nikki would take the second car her parents had, if needed.

They parted, promising to be in touch soon.

Nikki stepped out of the car, and Gwen pulled away, the smell of gasoline stale in the wintry night air. Nikki faced her parents' house, lights out with emptiness. A faint haze of light kissed the eastern horizon, dawn on the way.

Nikki let herself in. It was cold and dark, abandoned. Half of her hoped her parents would be there, waiting to explain some double-spy plan, where they'd explain they were really on her side. But they weren't there, and the frigid wind behind her ushered her deeper into the empty house.

She closed and locked the door behind her, heaviness in her steps. She stumbled around, thinking about where to begin her search. Nikki's mind raced through the events of the past several days, of Ina's sorrow and worry and anger, of Gwen's loss. Despite the exhaustion that weighed on her bones, adrenaline pulsed through her veins, keeping her awake. She wandered her childhood home and shuttered all the blinds to ensure daylight didn't streak through the house while she looked for clues.

Chapter Thirty-Seven

Satisfied she was protected from the daylight, she sought food to give her strength. In the kitchen, she found blood and meat in the fridge. Nikki pulled out both, and while she heated eggs and steaks on the stove and microwaved the blood, her mind turned, thinking about her next steps. She'd go through every room of the house, every device she could find, to determine where her parents went.

As she thought, she stared at the sizzling butter and steak in the pan, so absorbed in her thoughts she didn't hear the microwave beep, nor the footsteps behind her.

"Nikki?"

She startled and turned, Bernadette's confused face looking at her with a cocked head.

"Bernie, you scared me."

"I'm sorry, dear. Is there something I can help you with?"

"Do you know where my parents are?" Nikki asked, scooping the eggs and steak onto a plate.

Bernadette smoothed her hands on her apron. "Your mother mentioned travel, but I thought you were with them. That's why I was confused to see you."

"Did they say where they were going?"

She shook her head, looking at her over her shoulder. "No, dear, I'm sorry. I don't know. They said they were going to leave right after the solstice, and that was all."

"Mm. Okay. Thanks," Nikki said, the food tasteless in her mouth. If they left right after they visited her in the dungeon, then wherever they were, they had been gone for days.

Wherever they were, Xander was there too. That's where she needed to be.

"Did they say how long they would be gone?"

"No." Bernadette studied her for a moment. "Is something wrong?"

Nikki bit the inside of her lip. "Yes. Something is wrong. Very wrong. I need to know where they went. I know this sounds crazy, but all of humanity may depend on it."

Bernadette looked at her, stunned, then said, "Oh my."

"Any chance you can help me look for clues for where they went?"

"Of course," Bernadette said. "If the entire human race is threatened, it would be preposterous of me to not do anything I can to help."

Nikki scarfed down her food and then they separated, searching the rooms in a divide-and-conquer tactic. Every room, every drawer, every file on the computer was devoid of information. There wasn't any indication of a plane ticket being purchased, let alone researched. They spent the afternoon and evening searching the grounds, Bernadette calling her husband and the other staff to see if they knew anything.

No one had a clue where her parents had gone.

Late that evening, when the sun had just set, Nikki riffled through the documents in her dad's study for a second time. They had swapped rooms, then searched the same room simultaneously, hoping they had missed an essential piece of information that would leap out at them this time around. While scouring her dad's bank statements that he, for some reason, printed out instead of storing digitally, a solid knock pounded on the door.

Knock.

Knock.

Knock.

Nikki and Bernadette froze, eyes locking.

"Are you expecting anyone?" Nikki asked.

Bernadette shook her head, documents bending in her tightened fingers.

Knock, knock.

"I'll get it," Bernadette said, dropping the papers.

"I don't think that's a good idea."

"Don't worry, dear. I'll just tell whoever it is that Mr. and Mrs. Silva aren't home. Just stay here."

"Bernie, I don't know—"

Bernadette threw up a hand, then smoothed her shirt and hair back. "It'll be fine."

Nikki gave one nod, acquiescing, and Bernadette walked down the stairs. She stood, listening to her footsteps retreat down the hall to the front door. The door creaked on its hinges.

"Hi, can I help you?" Bernadette asked.

A murmur that Nikki couldn't decipher floated up to her. She stood up and moved to the doorway to hear better.

"The owners of the house aren't here. Can I take a message?"

"Oh. I'm not here for Catalina and Miguel. I'm here for Nicoletta."

Nikki went still. It was Hormin.

"She is not here either. She moved out years ago." Nikki's heart warmed at Bernadette's loyalty. "But I can relay a message to her, if you'd like."

"Tsk, tsk. Don't lie to me."

A shuffle, a stagger.

"You're not welcome in this house."

A maniacal chuckle echoed through the hallway.

Nikki stepped into view without thinking, not wanting Bernadette to face the monster alone.

"Ah, see, I knew she was here," Hormin said, looking over Bernadette's shoulder at Nikki. Hormin made to move forward into the house, but Bernadette blocked him.

"You are not welcome in this house," Bernadette repeated.

"Aw," Hormin said, pitying. "You think those old myths hold any truth? I can enter, regardless of your wishes," Hormin said, putting a hand to Bernadette's chest, and thrusting her to the side, his arm barely moving. Bernadette crashed into the side wall, the plaster crumbling around her in a tuft of dust and paint.

Bernadette collapsed to the ground and didn't move.

Nikki froze, torn between running to her and running away.

Hormin stepped over the threshold, his mouth splitting into a shark-like grin. He stretched out his hand and said, "Now, might as well come easy. There's no escape from me here."

Nikki took a step back, transfixed by Hormin's wide-set, wild eyes.

With each step closer, Nikki placed one foot back, retreating. Bernadette did not move from the pile of dust, paint, and plaster.

"I told you there was a plan for you, for us. Did you think I'd let you go so easily?"

Nikki took another step back.

Hormin tsked again. "What a problem you've been. Especially for a fledgling. But you're trapped now, little duck."

"No, there's still time to fix this," Nikki whispered to herself.

Hormin laughed. "Fix what? By finding the key, you've fixed millennia of wrongdoing. Now, it's time to see the fruits of your efforts," he said, lunging forward with unpredictable speed, grabbing Nikki's arm before she'd even realized he'd moved.

Nikki tried to wrench her arm from his grip, slipping her wrist between his fingers where his grasp was weakest. Her lungs filled with terror, with a scream, and when her mouth broke open to exhale, it filled with an old, moldy cloth.

"You think I'd let you pull the same trick twice? While not incapacitating, it's quite annoying," Hormin said. He tried to wrap another cloth around her eyes, but Nikki surged forward and smashed her head against his, stunning him. She ran, mouth clogged with the taste of old feet, a feral growl emanating from behind her.

A beat, a pulse, a few footsteps, and Nikki's body flew, head slamming into the wall to her left, vision swimming with the wave of pain through her skull.

The home spun in her vision with the red hues of wall paint, then Hormin thrust her head to the right, slamming it against the other wall, and she crashed to the ground, his large hand holding her head down.

Warm blood spilled under Nikki's cracked head, vision spinning, and Hormin pressed his body weight to hers. With his hot breath in her ear, he said, "I told you, girl, you cannot best me."

He pulled her head up by her hair, then cracked her skull once, twice, three times against the hardwood floors, each smack widening the fractures in her head until blood pooled in her vision, and Nikki lost consciousness.

Chapter Thirty-Eight

A FAINT TRACE of salt filled her nose, her head pounding when she awoke. Her body swayed, not of its own accord, and as consciousness reached her, she thought, *I'm getting tired of this.*

How many times in the past few months had she woken to a dizzy, beaten head?

Wood creaked, and she groaned as the sway of her body rolled the headache from one side to the other.

Nikki fidgeted but found her arms and legs were immovable. She groaned with the headache and blinked through it, looking down at her body.

Her wrists and ankles were tied tight with rope.

Panic seized her, and she writhed, rolling off the bed like a worm.

On her hands and knees, she hobbled upright, swaying with the movement of the vessel that carried her. Wood creaked under the moan of the movement, and she realized she was on a boat.

Footsteps thundered downstairs, and a door creaked open, letting in moonlight.

"Ah. You are awake. I thought I heard you flailing about," Hormin said, stepping across floorboards that trembled under his boots, hands clasped behind his back.

Nikki wailed, finding her mouth still stuffed with old socks, and kicked back, hunkering against the wall.

"Oh, hush now. No need for such dramatics," Hormin said, hoisting her up by the ties around her wrists.

Nikki stumbled, falling against his marble body.

"Whoopsie daisy," Hormin said, his wide eyes mocking her.

"Don't you want to see your family?" he asked, then tugged her along by the ropes. She was forced to hop after him. Nikki's heart pounded, thrumming in her ears, as she thought of seeing her parents above deck. What would they say to her to make her forgive them?

Her hobbles were awkward, and she crashed into Hormin several times as she jumped to keep after him. He sighed and turned, saying, "If I cut the ropes on your feet, will you behave?"

Nikki nodded, and he bent down, then tore the ropes apart with his bare hands as if they were made of nothing more than paper.

Blood rushed to her feet where the circulation had been cut off, and they tingled with pain as she stepped after him. The dark wood floors creaked under their steps, and the hold swayed gently, like a flower in a summer breeze, making Nikki hit the sides of the stairwell.

Hormin removed the socks from her mouth, shoving them in his pocket.

Nikki's breath was stolen from her lungs as they went up on deck. Endless, dark ocean pressed in from all sides. The waves lapped white froth against the boat, which lulled and creaked gently in the water, moonlight cutting silver slashes across the dark blue.

"Where are we? Where's my family?" Nikki asked, voice hoarse from disuse. She looked around, at the weathered wood and the cloth masts. "And why are we on such an old ship?"

"One question at a time, little duck," Hormin said with an off-kilter smile.

Nikki blinked to clear the daze of her vision and looked at the moonlight glistening over the ocean waves, the full starlit sky overhead. "Where are we?"

"In a saltwater body."

"More specifically?" she asked.

He smiled and said, "Next question."

She bit down her irritation, feeling too weak to fight, and asked, "Where is my family?" She hadn't seen anyone she recognized, just deck hands.

"Ah, yes, that. Listen," Hormin said and looked into the distance.

Nikki followed his gaze, staring at the ocean, where it went from silver to dark blue to black.

"You said my family was here."

"Shhh!" Hormin replied.

Nikki huffed a sigh and looked out, waiting. After a few seconds of silence, she heard the faint calls of someone singing. A seductive, lulling female voice, calling out to the boat.

"There's someone out there!" Nikki said.

"Yes, there is," Hormin replied with a knowing smile.

They sailed for many more minutes, the sweet singing growing louder. It was the voice of a woman, alone and sad. Calling for companionship on a cold, dark night.

"We need to help her," Nikki said, gazing into the distance, trying to find the source of the singing.

Then there was a splash and ripple of the ocean.

"Did you see?" Hormin asked, excited.

"See what?"

"Our cousin."

Nikki furrowed her brow. "I don't know what you're talking about."

"The siren. You heard her singing, yes?"

"I heard singing, yes."

"As I said, it's the siren. The aquatic evolutionary form of the vampire. You're the terrestrial type. But for the siren, their only choice for blood is to lure their victims through song. They were placed here to protect the Mother. We're getting close to her island, you see."

"What?" Nikki asked, barely more than a whisper.

"Oh, yes. You've been sleeping for days. I put you under and under and under. Now, we're close enough to Mother's waters to see our cousins, her first protectors. It's quite amazing how they've evolved. Their singing is so beautiful. Beautiful enough to ensnare any prey, including a vampire. They must feed somehow, and food can be scarce for them out here."

Nikki's brows furrowed before her eyes widened.

Hormin looked delighted. "Oh, yes. They're cannibals. They were planted to protect the Mother's island. But when you're starving, you're not good at differentiating between family and foe. Or maybe you just don't care? Anyway, in the old days, it was easy to eat a ship full of odd humans. But if you're starving, a vampire will do."

Nikki felt sick.

"They're rather savage. You'd best stay away from them if you can," Hormin said and snapped his fingers. "Mannus!" A tall, heavily muscled man sporting a long beard with thin braids walked over and handed him a parcel wrapped in parchment paper.

Hormin unwrapped the parchment paper as the singing grew louder, high-pitched and pleading. Dark meat glistened in the moonlight, and Hormin tossed it into the sea.

The singing stopped, and a feminine head with lank, long hair emerged, her eyeline sitting just above water. The siren looked at them with stone eyes, luminescent in the night, translucent skin reflecting the ocean. She bit into the offered meat, flopping back into the water with a graceful tail splash.

Hormin shivered. "I'm sure glad I'm not one of them. Millennia, and they've been stuck like this."

Watching the last ripples from the siren dissipate into the ocean, Nikki asked, "Where are my actual family? My parents?"

Hormin shrugged. "Close." Hormin saw Nikki look at the silver water, the waves frothing against the boat, and said, "Into the hull with you. I'll let you know when we're there."

He pushed her, turning away from the now-silent sea.

"Where are we?" she asked again, trying to think of where she was on the planet—how far from home, from Gwen.

"You don't need to worry about that," Hormin said, and pushed her down the steps, closing the door behind her, the dismal light of the moon disappearing, replaced by pure darkness. She rolled and hit her head, the wood solid and unmoving beneath her. Her hands were still bound, but with her eyes adjusting, she stumbled back to the door and hit it with all her body weight.

It didn't budge.

She slammed into it. Once, twice, three times. But it didn't give. She slumped against the door.

"Just relax," Hormin said from the other side. "We'll be there soon." Then his footsteps retreated.

The fight left Nikki's body. She had fallen into Hormin's trap, despite all she had done to protect Xander. All she could do now was wait and steel herself for the confrontation to come. She'd just have to think of how to deal with her parents, with Hormin, with the sirens, with the Mother. What would happen to her parents, if by some miracle she and Xander got out of this alive? Would they be punished? Or was there a way to free them too?

Best not to cause a fuss and plan instead. Nikki staggered to the bed, the outline of the stairs and room a faint sketch in the dark, and laid down, mulling over any possibility, any potential for saving herself and Xander.

Chapter Thirty-Nine

THE DARK WAS INTERRUPTED SOMETIME LATER, A POUNDING growing in Nikki's head as the boat swayed back and forth, and boards creaked with footsteps overhead. The door opened, letting in bright moonlight. By the angle, Nikki guessed not more than one or two hours had passed.

The muscular figure of Mannus walked down the steps on heavy feet, hands behind his back, the perfect picture of calm.

"Come," he said, voice so deep and coarse it sounded filled with gravel.

Nikki opened her mouth to reply, but the utter dryness prevented her from speaking.

He frowned and approached her, gaze roving over her face, her chapped lips and mussed hair. He pushed her away from the wall and grabbed her by the rope around her wrists and tugged her up the stairs, Nikki stumbling over her feet as he walked too fast. On the deck, the moon shone high and to their right, a cloudless, striking night. Nikki blinked against the brightness. In the distance, below the moon, a land-mass took shape, black and jagged with the silhouettes of trees and sloping hills.

A hum of anxiety wound through Nikki's veins, and she tried to swallow the lump in her throat, the lack of moisture on her tongue making her mouth feel rubbed by cotton. The pounding between her temples grew, in sync with her heartbeat.

"I told you we were close," Hormin said, his breath pushing too close to her neck, and Nikki startled at his proximity. She looked at him, at his too-wide eyes while he grinned at her, and she looked back to the approaching island.

"Destiny awaits," Hormin said, singsong, and he hummed. Nikki's skin crawled with his joyous anticipation.

Nikki clenched her teeth and channeled Gwen, "Do you have to be so cliché?"

"Pardon?"

"'Destiny awaits?' You're all the bad tropes put into one being."

"Did you ever think that perhaps, just perhaps, the tropes are based off of me?" he replied, in a dull, deep tone.

The change in his voice grabbed Nikki's attention, and when she turned around, his face was blank, eyes deep with the countless years of his life, and his presence oppressed her own spirit, darkness creeping into the edges of her vision.

She used to chide Gwen for her childish antagonism, and now was not the time to pick up the habit.

Paralyzed, they stood staring too long at one another, swaying with the ship, the sound of the crew and lapping of the ocean around them.

Hormin's expression lifted, and his gaze roved over Nikki. "Now, this will not do," he said, reaching out to her.

Nikki stiffened as Hormin stood behind her, then brushed her knotted hair out with his fingers. Her skin crawled at the disgusting tenderness of his touch, at how he was so focused on running his hands through her hair until it was untangled and silky from the grease of his skin. Her muscles cringed, stiffening as his hands put her hair back into a low ponytail.

How he worked on her hair made her think of Tyee, how she had brushed out her locks when in her cell.

"Where's Tyee?"

"Ah, she has not joined us on this journey. From the sounds of it, your coven is having quite the civil war. Best for her to remain and get a handle on everyone."

Feng and Daiyu restraining Bridget flashed through her mind, and she hoped that they were unharmed.

Once done with her hair, he took her chin in his fingers and moved her head back and forth, humming to himself as he thought.

Then he tipped her head back with one hand, and with the other pulled a flask from his belt, uncapped it, and carefully lifted it over her head, the rich, metallic scent of blood clouding Nikki's senses. Her muscles twitched with the compulsion to push him, to fight him, to grab the whole flask for herself and swallow it all down, but she restrained herself, knowing how weak she truly was.

He dripped a thimbleful of blood into her mouth, her body singing with the rush of it sinking into her bloodstream, just one pulse stronger. Hormin waited a few minutes as her body absorbed the blood, then said, "That's better. Can't have them thinking I didn't take care of you."

He stepped around her and draped his elbows over the side of the ship. Nikki turned and followed his gaze, looking at the ever-approaching giant of an island. When she glanced at him, his expression was wistful, and Nikki thought that, in profile, when he was calm, he almost looked sane.

A sudden stab of pity filled her, wondering what had made him this way. If that was just the cost of eternity.

She turned her gaze away and watched the island approach, listening to the creaking of the ship, the casual footsteps on the wooden boards, the gentle hush of the ocean. The pounding in her head lulled to a dull, constant pressure, a buzzing in the background of her consciousness, despite how her pulse rose as the dark silhouette of land grew larger.

Before she was ready, before she knew what to do, what to expect, the ship turned into a cove. A small, white sand beach surrounded by jagged rocks, trees, ferns, and grasses loomed into view.

The crew clamored to dock the boat ashore, and in the midst of the scrambling, Mannus tugged the ropes around Nikki's wrists, dragging her down a wooden plank to the beach that glistened like broken pearls in the moonlight.

The island's humidity brought a suffocating sheen of hot sweat to her skin, only relieved by the cool breeze rushing off the ocean. She dreaded how it would feel once in the trees.

Hormin, in his dramatics, jumped off the boat into the sand instead of walking down the steps. He landed beside her, and Mannus held her by the rope like a dog on a leash.

"Ahhh," Hormin said with a smile, drinking in the island air, as if he were home. He whipped out a long, black cloth, which he wrapped around Nikki's head, blocking out her vision.

"Is that necessary?" Nikki asked. "It's not like I know where we are."

Hormin chuckled, and in her mind's eye, she could see his face peel with delight. "It isn't about that. It's about the surprise."

Nikki's heart dropped, the pleasure and excitement in Hormin's voice an ill omen.

One of them tugged on the rope around her wrists and she jerked forward, stumbling at the sudden movement and the uneven sand beneath her feet. Without another option, she followed her captors into the forest, listening to their footsteps, the sway of trees, the croak of frogs, the whispering of insects. The closed canopy smothered her breaths, and dismay closed an iron fist around her chest as she stumbled along the unknown path toward her parents. Toward Xander. Toward her supposed destiny.

Chapter Forty

Nikki's legs ached, yet still they walked. It must've been miles. At one point, legs shaking, they paused for someone to pour a few more drops of blood in her mouth, temporarily reducing her shakiness.

The clatter of feet shuffling and voices grew louder, until the humidity of the forest broke, a rush of night air swirling around her skin. Hormin removed the blindfold from her head, and she squinted against the sudden freedom of vision, as Hormin said, "Ta-da!"

Eyes adjusting, Nikki peered at her surroundings. They were on a hill, with cleared dirt paths and stone houses, as if from a medieval town. Lanterns and candles lit the houses and illuminated the roads. Vampires carried fruits, wax, wool, and other goods in woven baskets.

Nikki gaped at the bustle, the island sloping upward through the town to the summit, where it flattened, the shapes at the top obscured.

"Welcome to Vampire Island!" Hormin shouted, nearby vampires giving him an uncertain, respectful glance.

"You're joking," Nikki said, glimpsing women weaving at a loom through a window as they walked up the hill.

"Well, yes and no. It isn't called Vampire Island, but that's what it is. No humans here. Well, none living like normal humans. They're livestock or servants."

Nikki's stomach curdled. "What is this place called, then?"

Hormin ignored her, tugging her along.

"Why is it only vampires?" she asked.

"That isn't obvious? For the Mother, of course."

"So it's an island of zealots."

"Is it zealotry if the one you worship and protect is real?"

"Protect?"

Again, Hormin ignored her, his eyes wide with joy. His energy danced along his skin as they passed through the town and began the ascent to the top of the hill. Nikki peered up at the switchbacks with trepidation.

The climb felt as though it had lasted hours, the canopy cover shrouding the moon's progression through the night sky. What she thought had been a hill when they'd first arrived must've been a mountain. The air grew colder as they ascended, the clatter of the town below diminishing, the lights small flecks, not much larger or brighter than the stars above. The vegetation thinned to grasses, except for the silhouette of a tall tree that loomed at the summit.

Out of breath, air thinning, and legs shaking, Nikki took the last switchback and crested the ridge, stopping in her tracks as they reached the plateau.

The top flattened into a wide opening, the trail they were on a straight line to the massive, silhouetted tree that stood at the center. A simple stone house sat far to the side. A dull ache pulsed through her head. As a soft breeze pushed through the grasses at her feet, she heard a soft, satisfied laugh. Heart in her throat, the tree looming overhead, she took a step back, ready to turn and run, but Hormin tugged her forward, and she fell, scraping her arms, unable to catch herself.

Hormin knelt over her and hissed, "Get up. Or do I need to drag you? I don't care if you embarrass yourself. But don't embarrass me in front of everyone."

Nikki staggered to her feet. When Hormin stepped back, the shapes of people formed in the darkness, which she hadn't seen before, so overwhelmed by the power and size of the tree, the laugh that sent shivers through her spine. While the tree was branched and leafy, large slants of moonlight shone through the treetop, patches of silver scattering across the earth, infusing the air with a grey glow.

The dozen figures were split in a crescent facing the tree, about six on each side, their heads angled to look at Nikki, Hormin, and Mannus. When they got close to the group, Hormin pushed Nikki to her knees in the center of the crescent, Mannus kneeling beside her, taking the rope from Hormin.

Nikki glanced around the group, seeing the Scythians, Atoc and Ozcollo. Almost everyone else was unknown to her, ranging in skin tone from moon white to midnight, all on their knees. To the far right of her she saw her parents, hands bound, staring at her with woe and defeat, their faces drawn and sunken, as if they hadn't eaten or slept in weeks. That painful, hot simmer of betrayal coiled in her gut, and she wanted to scream and cry. She wished she could shout at them, hug them, sit next to them, have them tell her it would be all right. The moonlight shifted in her dad's watering eyes, but her mom cast away her gaze, and Nikki's heart sank so far into her stomach, all that was left was a void of dread.

Her vision glassed, and she lifted her head to blink back the tears, the canopy shifting overhead. Swollen, reddish orbs swayed in the whispering breeze, their bottoms puckered and frayed. Pomegranates.

A commotion in front of her drew her attention. Hormin stood at the center, equidistant between the crescent and the tree.

A breeze pushed through, a sigh, a whisper of *finally*.

Nikki's skin pimpled, the hair on her neck rising, as the old voice in her head murmured, *Daughter, are you ready?*

No, please, Nikki thought.

The only reply was another breezy laugh.

"Mother!" Hormin cried, and the vampires in the ring besides her and her parents whispered "Mother" then touched their foreheads, mouths, and hearts, then cupped open their hands in their laps.

"Mother!" Hormin repeated, facing the tree. "I have done as you have asked. I have brought the girl."

"I can see." A pleased voice whispered on the wind. A pause, then, "Gabriel, bring him to me."

Nikki went cold.

From the stone building, two men emerged. One of average height but muscular, a sheathed greatsword strapped to his back. In front of him, he pushed a tall, lean man, face swollen and purple from beatings.

Xander.

He kept his face downcast, eyes empty of feeling. There was no rope or chain to bind him. Even from a distance, Nikki could see that he was broken.

Gabriel pushed Xander to the center, causing him to stumble into Hormin's grasp.

"No!" she yelled, twisting against her bonds, trying to stagger forward. "No! Please, please let him go!" she screamed, writhing against the hold of Mannus, kicking and twisting.

Xander's head snapped up, broken out of his daze. He blinked and whispered like a prayer, "Nikki?" He blinked a few more times, as if he were trying to convince himself it wasn't a dream, and then he pushed to his feet and ran for her.

He made it two steps, his eyes wide with want and sorrow. Nikki's heart swelled at the sight of him, then Hormin tugged at the collar of Xander's shirt like he was no more than a doll, stopping Xander in his tracks with a wheeze. Xander struggled, wincing with his injuries, but could not budge Hormin's ancient strength.

Dirt in his mouth, dragged back from her, Xander said, "Nikki, I'm so sorry. I'm so, so sorry about everything. I should've believed you, but I'll find a way out. I'll get us out. I pr—"

Hormin clamped a hand over Xander's mouth and yanked him hard, spinning him away and throwing him to the ground. Xander scrambled to his feet, dazed, but Hormin was stronger and faster, and kicked the back of his legs, making Xander buckle. He now kneeled in front of the tree, his back to Nikki. Nikki tried to yell to him, but Mannus's hand flew to her mouth, shrouding her voice. She tried to bite him, to wrench her arms from his grasp, anything to make him remove his hand, but he kept it firm as stone against her face.

Again, Xander tried to get to his feet, and Nikki's heart broke at his futile efforts, at watching him be pushed around by forces that far overpowered him. She twisted in the grip of Mannus, but could get nowhere.

With a sigh, Hormin pushed Xander all the way to the ground, kicked his legs out flat, then stomped on his left ankle.

The bone crunched and twisted, and Xander screamed, a bloodcurdling wail that ripped through the night.

Nikki's stomach twisted with nausea and heartache, and she moaned against the palm on her mouth, helpless, useless, watching his pain.

ENOUGH, the voice boomed through the air.

Hormin threw up his hands in yielding, then pulled Xander upright by the collar of his dirty and sweat-drenched shirt. A scream erupted from Xander's mouth as his ankle twisted beneath him. His leg gave out, and with an ugly sneer, Hormin grabbed Xander's arm, dragging him closer to the tree.

Xander and Nikki caught each other's gaze, both brimming with fear, and Nikki tried to tell him all she felt and thought through her eyes, but his own gaze was hazy with pain.

Hormin led Xander, barely conscious, close to the tree. Gabriel stood to the side, unsheathed the greatsword, and stood facing the crescent. The blade lit with rolling flame, and he placed the point against the ground, resting his hand on the pommel. The flames licked at the dirt and his armor, but it did not burn, even as it cast a demonic orange glow on their surroundings.

The humming in the back of Nikki's mind escalated, like a beehive becoming agitated, and a voice pressed, "Get on with it."

"Yes, Mother," Hormin whispered, brandishing a dagger from his belt.

Nikki's eyes widened, and she fought with all her might against her captor, the blade drinking in the fire and moonlight as Hormin raised it up, then slashed it across Xander's skin.

Chapter Forty-One

Blood dripped from Xander's outstretched wrists onto the tree bark, and in the half fire, half moonlight, the blood absorbed into the bark of the tree, dripping into the crevices and deep into the core.

The vampires around Nikki murmured, touched their foreheads, their mouths, their hearts, the earth, then cupped their hands in their laps once more.

Xander's blood continued to fall, the dripping of it onto the tree the only sound beside the breeze, which exhaled a satisfied breath, relieving the tension in the air.

For several seconds, the world went still. As if every living creature held its breath.

Then the bark peeled back, caving in on itself where Xander's blood had fallen, and Hormin tugged him away from the opening. Arms shaking, Xander pulled his shirt off, then wrapped it around one cut on his arm, and held the other closed with his hand, too weak to tear the shirt in half for two bandages.

In front of Nikki, the tree unfurled like a punctured egg, the bark cracking inward, into a pitch-black cavern. The chasm grew until it was as large as a door, and with the sound of branches snapping, hands emerged from the darkness, curling against the edges of the wood.

More snapping, then a foot attached to a leg appeared.

With great cracking and breaking, the body of a tall, emaciated woman stepped out from the dark of the tree.

She moved forward, then stopped. Her head was connected to the tree by several thick branches that prevented her from leaving it. Her mouth twisted, and with one hard yank of her head, she wrenched it free from the wood appendages, leaving curls of wooden horns protruding from her skull.

Her skin wrinkled and sagged, barely more than flesh on bones, skin waxy. Long dark hair hung down her back in sap-filled strands, her body slick like a newborn.

She stretched, spine cracking as she took in a full breath, closing her eyes, relishing the night air. A faint smile graced her dilapidated, demonic face, and when she opened her eyes, she looked directly at Nikki.

Nikki's heart stopped in her chest under the gaze, the Mother's eyes entirely black. The flickers of fire danced in one eye, while moonlight struck the other, and the world shrank around her as it had with Hormin, but this time, it was more than suppression. It was drowning. Darkness clung to the edges of Nikki's vision, until the Mother broke her gaze. It must've only been a second, but it had stretched into an eternity in Nikki's mind, paralyzing her so fully that her captor had let her go, and Nikki sat numb with defeat before her.

Murmurs erupted around her.

"Mother."

"Lilit."

"Lili."

"Lilitu."

"Lilith."

All the names of the Mother chanted as one, Nikki's skin crawling.

Lilith turned her eyes to Xander, then to Hormin, and her smile broke wide. "My son," she said, throwing her arms wide.

Hormin beamed. "Mother," he said, and stepped into her embrace, the bones and sagging flesh wrapping around him, and she set a loving, clawed hand on the back of his head. He smiled with his eyes closed. "I am beyond happy to see you again."

"And I, you. But this," Lilith said, indicating her emaciated body, "is not the proper form. I need food."

"You don't want—?" he asked, nodding to Xander.

"Not yet."

Hormin nodded, then gestured to a female vampire in the circle, who got to her feet and walked toward the stone building, then dragged out a human woman in her mid-twenties to Lilith.

Lilith sat in the center, between the tree and the crescent, Xander and Hormin to her side. The woman appeared drugged, some ounce of fear oozing out of her so ripe Nikki could smell it despite her dulled senses, but the woman's eyes were glassy and her movements lazy.

The woman was gently leaned down, and Lilith curled her into her lap, stroking her face, pushing back her blond hair. "Such warmth," Lilith said, then sank her teeth into the woman. The human yelped, a quick and high-pitched sound of pain. Nikki watched in horror and disgust as Lilith drank her entirely, the body dwindling and desiccating before her eyes, the tension in the body going limp, while the muscles and flesh of Lilith grew and smoothed.

Satiated, Lilith threw up her head with an intoxicated laugh of pleasure, blood dripping down her chin. She tossed the corpse off her body and stood. She stood well over six feet tall now that she was no longer warped with malnutrition, and she was shaped with the kinds of curves sculptors dream of. Her dark hair hung in loose waves, parted by the twigs that sprouted from her ears, and the wooden horns that remained in her skull.

Lilith moved, as if testing out her new body, and chunks of bark and wood snapped off her skin and fell to the ground. In other places, the wood infused with her skin, like ingrown armor. Half vampire, half tree, with the countless millennia she had been trapped in there.

Only then, in her full glory, did Nikki notice she was naked.

Lilith stretched herself wide. "Ahhh, how good that feels." She looked about the crescent with a matronly smile and stepped forward. "My ever-loyal children. My most trusted disciples. I have not forgotten your efforts in releasing me from my imprisonment. Before I take my prize, I shall give you yours."

A chorus of her names rang, and all except Nikki and her parents touched their foreheads, their mouths, their hearts, the earth, then leaned forward over their legs with their palms cupped and outstretched, foreheads touching the ground.

Lilith slashed her forearm open with her thorn-like nails, then stepped to the vampire kneeling at the far left of the crescent, filling their cupped hands with her blood. The vampire did not move as Lilith progressed to the next, and the next, filling all the cupped hands with her blood, all except Nikki and her parents, who were not bowed. The crescent remained bowed until Lilith finished, and with all palms full of her blood, they rose as one to their knees and brought her blood to their lips.

Having had their taste of her, their eyes lit with ecstasy, as if seeing and sensing things beyond their imagination. They looked at Lilith with undying adoration, their god become real, blessing them.

Lilith's gracious smile remained as she turned to Nikki and said, "This is the part I wanted you to see, for your obstinance. I told you he would be mine, one way or another."

Lilith clasped Xander by the back of his neck and he groaned with pain as she dragged him to the center, too weak to scream. His wrists still bled, and his face was pale with blood loss. She tossed him to the ground and bent beside him, wrapped a hand tenderly through his hair, and said, "You look nothing like him."

"Who?" Xander asked, twisting, trying to rise to his feet, but she pushed him down with a hand to his chest.

An immense pressure filled Nikki's head, and a bolt of lightning shattered through the sky and crashed to the ground in a blinding flash of white and gold. The blaze of light diminished and in a crater outside of the crescent, a figure with plated radiant armor in white and gold stalked to the center, specks of light dusting off of them as they moved, ethereal. Large wings, feathery yet wispy, unfurled from their back in the landing, then curled away as they strode forward.

In the crescent, their facial features were refined, neither masculine nor feminine, with gleaming cracks like repaired marble winding through their skin. In an authoritative, neutral yet deep voice, they said, "Lilith, what is the meaning of this?"

Lilith sneered and said, "Semangelof."

"Lilith, the bond has not been broken. You are not permitted freedom per the terms of your imprisonment."

"If I am free, the terms have been met."

Semangelof frowned, as much as their marble face could. "You have bent the terms, not met them. I am here to—"

A surprised shout broke off Semangelof's sentence, and everyone turned. Hormin had bashed Gabriel on the back of his head with his fists, and in the blink of an eye grabbed the fiery greatsword and plunged it through the angel's chest. The angel looked at the protruding weapon, then said to Lilith, "This will not be the end."

The sword sucked back through the angel's body, and they fell to their knees. Streaks of brilliant light shone through the angel's body, a glittering mix of color like light through a prism. As the light faded, so too did the angel's gaze, their skin fading to the grey of smoke. When the angel collapsed to the ground, face down, it broke apart like a fallen statue, its stone corpse shattering across the grass.

Nikki watched in horror, witness to the death of an angel.

Gabriel stood, clutching his head, and glared at Hormin. "How dare you? I was specifically entrusted with that sword while you were still gallivanting around Harappa. You have no right to take it from me, nor use it thusly. It is meant to protect Lilith, to protect the Tree, not to slay their holy messengers."

"Oh? Is that so?" Hormin asked, a finger to his lips and brow furrowed. "How terribly rude of me, to save our Mother."

Gabriel's nostrils flared, but all he said was, "Return it to me," and held out his hand.

Hormin nodded several times, thinking. Then he lunged forward, decapitating Gabriel in one swift motion, cauterizing the wound while severing it.

Gabriel's head fell with a sickening flop, eyes aghast and empty. Nikki heaved, and Xander stared wide-eyed, dissociated.

"Hormin! Settle down," Lilith said. "Senoy and Sansenoy may not be far behind, and we have much to accomplish. Focus."

"Of course, Mother," Hormin said, pulling the sheath off Gabriel and returning the sword to its scabbard.

"Now, where were we?" Lilith murmured, fixing her gaze back on Xander.

Xander gulped. "You were about to tell me who I don't look like."

Lilith's smile widened. "Oh, yes. I remember." Lilith sat beside Xander, brushing her hands through his hair. "Adam. You don't look at all like Adam." Xander's brow furrowed, and Lilith sneered. "The first man. The first love. The first betrayer."

Xander was silent, eyes wide with incomprehension.

Lilith cocked her head. "You don't know about Adam? Curious." Lilith shrugged. "No matter. You have his blood, and I will drink you dry in revenge for his betrayal." Lilith took a deep breath and smiled. "I've waited so long for this," she whispered, then sank her fangs into Xander's neck. Nikki kicked to her feet, but they were snatched from under her, and she collided with the ground. Xander's gasp of pain as his blood was sucked from him rang in her ears, and she tried to claw her way forward, despite being dragged backward by her feet.

Lilith gasped and pushed Xander hard to the ground, his head hitting the dirt with a thud. The smell of burnt flesh filled the air, gaping holes of skin tearing open in Lilith's cheeks, her throat, smoke rising from where her skin burned.

The air filled with Lilith's rage, her face twisting and the wind warming. She grabbed Xander's hair and yanked his face close to hers, the wounds in his neck still pouring blood. "The blood of the deceiver?!" Lilith yelled. "How dare the Cradle mix their bloodline with his?"

For some unknown, insane reason, Xander laughed in her face.

Lilith's body stiffened, eyes growing large with anger, and she screamed at the top of her lungs, millennia of frustration and rage and plotting and planning blowing up in her face. She screamed as if her soul were tearing to shreds, screamed until she was out of breath. Nikki squeezed her eyes shut and tried to block her ears from the intensity of the sound, pushing against her eardrums so hard she thought they'd burst.

When the gust of Lilith's rage was spent, Nikki opened her eyes. Xander was unconscious, blood running from his ears. Warmth spilled from Nikki's own ears from the pierce of Lilith's screech. The same one that Nikki had inherited, though hers was a weaker version.

The holes in Lilith's flesh stitched themselves together in moments, and she tongued the inside of her newly healed cheeks. "No matter."

Xander blinked his eyes open after a few seconds, Lilith still crouched over him. Hand tight in his hair, she said, "You were to be the beginning. The first sacrifice of a new age. But I have a better idea. I will rampage the earth, starting with your family, the deceivers, and then I will decimate the rest of the Cradle, and you can watch the fall of humanity at my side." Lilith flicked her gaze up at her son. "Hormin, the sword is yours to keep. Prepare to leave. Immediately." When she stood, it was still with her hand in Xander's hair, dragging him to his feet, bloodied and wincing with the pain in his broken ankle. She tossed him to Hormin, who barely caught him.

"M-mother?" a man with a strong chin, short-cropped brown hair, and a flat nose asked.

"Yes, Marcus?" Lilith asked with venom. She turned to the disciple to see their finger pointing at the tree, which was knitting itself back together.

"Yes. Of course," Lilith said, and rounded her focus to Nikki, whose insides curled like a trapped rat.

Lilith stalked to Nikki, then bade her to rise with a crook of her finger. Nikki looked up at her, at her corrupted beauty, the curling wood horns, the hardness of her cheekbones yet softness of her jaw. Lilith smelled sweet and earthy, like sap and early summer leaves, and she gave Nikki a stern, but sympathetic look before looping an arm through Nikki's and ushering her towards the tree.

"I warned you," Lilith said, quietly, with the barest trace of remorse in her tone, as they walked toward the tree. Nikki felt as if she were in a dream, reluctant to move, knowing she shouldn't, but her legs carried her forward anyway.

"If you had listened to me, you and your family would be spared. Now I must make an example of your insolence."

Lilith spun Nikki to face her, Nikki's back to the gap in the tree. Lilith beckoned her parents over with one hand, shoulders slumped as they approached. They had been so silent and still, Nikki had forgotten they were there. She motioned them to stand to the right, a few feet away, then had them kneel.

Lilith turned her gaze back to Nikki and cocked her head as she ran her clawed fingers over Nikki's face, her hair, appraising her. Lilith angled the dagger Hormin gave her toward Nikki, who cringed away from the point. But instead of cutting her, Lilith sawed through her ponytail, which fell in a mangled clump, her shorn hair now chin length.

"Why?" she asked.

"I did you a favor. Trust me."

Lilith placed her hands on Nikki's shoulders, and looked over her shoulder, listening to the closing of the tree, the stitching of wood and bark.

"As the one who tried to prevent my freedom, the burden of life is now yours," Lilith said, and pushed Nikki into the cavern of the tree, Nikki's back hitting the interior with a hard thud.

"No!"

"Nikki!"

The voices of her mom, dad, and Xander broke through the jolting of her bones, the thudding of her mind.

Lilith pushed her parents down, other vampires holding them back, and Xander railed against the hold of Hormin despite his broken ankle and bleeding ears, screaming and screaming.

Slithers of wood wound up her legs. Nikki yanked at them, but they kept her grounded, and she bowed forward as she tried to free herself. Lilith frowned and raised Nikki's arms, fitting them into the empty branches of the tree, more spools of wood unthreading and winding around her arms, locking them in place.

"Nikki! I'll find you. I'll get you out. I promise!" Xander screamed, over and over, and Nikki choked on her tears, clouding her vision.

"Will you quiet him?" Lilith yelled. "We aren't finished yet."

Hormin smacked Xander on the side of his head with his fist, and Xander crumpled to the ground.

Nikki twisted against the tree, which wound tighter, nestling her into its emptiness, her arms losing sensation as the blood drained from them.

She caught the eyes of her parents, her dad crying and her mom staring, horrified. "Please, do something!" Nikki cried.

"I would advise you to keep your mouth closed. The Tree likes to infiltrate wherever it can," Lilith said, tapping at her horns.

Nikki clamped her mouth shut and twisted, the tangles of wood continuing to climb up her arms, and she bit back a scream as they crept toward her head.

Her mom flailed against the vampire holding her, but they were all older and stronger.

Her dad didn't struggle. He just looked at her through tearful eyes as he was forced to stay down on his knees. "My precious daughter, I'm so sorry. We did not mean for this. We did not know. We will find a way to get you out. We love you. We are so sorry. But know, this is not the end—"

Blood spurted from his mouth, and her dad's eyes widened, Lilith's arm buried wrist-deep into his chest, his ribs crunching and breaking as she wriggled into his chest cavity.

He burbled, blood trickling down his chin.

"Dad!" Nikki screamed, despite the warning to keep her mouth closed. She tasted wood as a stray branch tried to climb into her mouth. She bit it off and spit it onto the ground as Lilith tore her arm back out of her dad's chest cavity, clutching his heart in one bloodied hand.

"Miguel!" her mom wailed, as if it had been her heart torn out.

Her dad swayed, the open void in his chest spilling blood. He looked at his heart in Lilith's hand, then at Nikki.

Lilith squeezed his heart until it burst, and her dad's skin decayed before her eyes, turning to ash, half falling to the ground, the other half carried away on the wind, as if he never existed.

"From what he was made, he now returns, to the dust of the earth," Lilith whispered, ash floating off her hands into the air.

"Miguel!" her mom screamed again, falling over his remains, plunging her hands into the dust and bone.

Lilith smeared the blood around the remaining opening of the tree, no larger than the size of a small window, and dripped the blood in a circle around the tree, muttering in an ancient language Nikki didn't understand.

When Lilith returned to her side of the tree, she said to Nikki, "His blood will bind you here. Now you will know the black torture I have endured. And with the eyes of the Earth, you will watch the consequence of your actions."

Lilith turned to Cat, bent over Miguel's dust, fistfuls of it smeared in her hands, bits of ash and bone mixed with the tears on her cheeks as she brought his remains to her face.

"My daughter," Lilith said, trying to lift Cat's face to look at her, but her mom's eyes were far away. "You were from a good family. You knew better than to make such a creature. You may hurt now, but it will pass, and you will come to realize I have set you free as well. Free to carve a new path, with one born pure."

Cat sat, blank-faced and dazed at Lilith's words. But as the wood wound around Nikki's skin, and her window to the world closed, grief and hate boiled and rose in her throat, and she screamed from the depths of her being, ignoring the searching tendrils of wood at the corners of her lips.

Lilith looked at her with a small smile. "I wondered where that went." Then she turned to Cat. "The Romanians have been the carrier the whole time? Just think, you could have a whole family with those beautiful genes of mine."

Her mom blinked, and looked at her dad's remains, at the dust of him on her hands, spent.

"Make sure she stays here," Lilith said to two vampires Nikki couldn't see, as Lilith turned her back on the tree.

Nikki struggled against her bindings, heart hammering with fear as the dark closed in.

Lilith walked near Hormin, whispered to him so quietly Nikki couldn't hear, then everyone made space around her. Lilith looked up toward the moon, the pale light glowing on her skin, and then she bent over, kneeling on the ground. Her joints bent and cracked, spine shrinking, legs thinning. Feathers spread under her arms, and she grew smaller and more feathered, chunks of skin sloughing off, until before them was a screech owl, the husk of skin on the ground hissing with heat.

Lilith flapped her wings, and with a piercing call, she rose into the air and disappeared into the night.

A demon let loose on the world.

As the final knots of the tree stitched themselves closed, Nikki saw

Hormin hoist a bloodied, unconscious Xander over his shoulder. Her mom, face darkened with dust except for where it was streaked white from her tears, sat before the tree.

And then Nikki was engulfed in darkness, the final tendrils of wood finding their way into her ears, penetrating her skull. She squeezed her eyes closed and was propelled down through the roots of the tree, to the cold depths of the world, then thrown throughout the planet, voices in all languages from billions of organisms flooding her ears, images from all over the world, from deserts and tropical forests, to grasslands and oceans, to cities and towns and back again in a dizzying, constant loop that overwhelmed her mind to unconsciousness.

Chapter Forty-Two

Nikki gained consciousness sometime later. The voices
and images from around the world were gone, and she simply hovered
in the abyssal black of the tree. Nikki clenched her legs and pulled at the
branches around her calves, but they wouldn't budge. She also couldn't
move her arms, as they were high above her head and completely numb
from blood loss.

When she moved, the wood in her skull tugged painfully, and she
stopped moving, defeated.

She couldn't see anything.

She could barely feel.

All she could hear were the voices in her head.

The voices and images of the world, trying to break through her
sanity.

Nikki slumped, letting go of her weight, letting the tree hold her
upright.

Why fight it?

Xander was taken, bloodied and beaten, to watch his family, and
humanity, be subjected to Lilith's warped sense of justice.

She thought of first running into him at the library, his shocked and
timid face. Their first date, how gracious and attentive he was. How he

always had been. Paying attention to other people's needs first. She was so stupid not to trust him. Not to tell him. He was compassionate and understanding, and she ruined it. Sentenced him to a life of torture. There was nothing she could do now.

She thought about being held in Xander's arms, of his silliness, his caring, his intelligence, running through their memories until they bled into...

Her mom, curled outside of the tree in her dad's dust and bone. If she concentrated, she could hear her mom crying, talking to her.

Then there was her dad, dead. And the last thing she said to him was that she was disappointed in him. That she'd never forgive him. And she would never have a chance to tell him she loved him. That she was just angry and scared.

Oh god. Nikki thought, tears streaming down her face. *Please, please help me. I don't know what to do.*

But only silence and darkness responded.

Gwen, Gwen, please sense something. Please help me. Please help us. Please, please, please...

Nikki repeated the plea like a mantra, tears wracking her body, as she bit into her bottom lip to keep her mouth closed. She didn't want to know what would happen if the tree crawled down her throat.

She cried until her face was dry and her body tired, and she sagged against the restraints, letting them keep her upright.

Nikki couldn't tell if her eyes were open or closed, it was so dark.

But she kept repeating her prayers to whoever could hear them.

It was all up to Gwen now.

Would she know something was wrong? Would she know what to do?

Would anything be enough?

Could anything defeat these ancient creatures, versed in unheard-of magics? Beings so ancient their skin was strong as marble?

Nikki stared into the darkness in utter defeat.

Suddenly, warmth climbed her skin.

Her pulse thrummed in her ears, wondering what new evil the tree would inflict upon her.

In the darkness, specks of gold and silver dusted her vision.

Nikki blinked, thinking it was a trick of her mind, but the metallic flecks continued to rain in the darkness, like petals drifting in the warm spring air.

As Nikki watched the gold and silver glitter scatter around her, uncaring if it was a hallucination or not, a kind voice whispered.

"Child."

<h1 style="text-align:center">Epilogue</h1>

Gwen opened her eyes against her will, tucked into the warmth of Theo's arms. The winter chill pressed against the walls and windows of her studio, but Theo's embrace was warm, and her head fit perfectly into the nook of her shoulder.

"We're like a chocolate-dipped strawberry," Gwen said, nuzzling more into Theo.

Theo grunted.

"No? Hmm." Gwen thought. "Neapolitan ice cream?"

Theo's hand that had been roving Gwen's back stopped.

"Black opal and ruby?"

"How about just Theo and Gwen?"

"Mmmmm, I like the sound of that, too," Gwen said, wrapping her arms tighter around Theo's muscular torso, and kissing her neck before nuzzling back in. She was so cozy in the midst of winter and didn't want to move.

Gwen...

"Mm?" she asked.

"Huh?" Theo responded.

"You just said my name."

"No, I didn't."

"Oh," Gwen said, confused. Assuming she must have been half-dreaming, she let herself cozy up more.

Gwen, please...

Gwen bolted upright in bed, startling Theo.

"What is it?"

Gwen cocked her head, listening. A faint voice coming from outside.

Winter silence pulsed through the studio for several minutes.

Then:

Please, if you can hear this, please help us...

Gwen swung her feet off the bed, the chill from outside sweeping cold shivers up her body.

"What is it, baby?" Theo called after her.

Gwen left the bedroom and went to the main room of the studio, wrapping a scarf and jacket around herself.

"Don't push me out again," Theo said, draped ridiculously in the thick bedsheets, still appearing regal as she pleaded for Gwen to respond.

But Gwen put out a hand for her to stay silent so she could listen.

Whispers carried on the wind.

Ina told her to wait for further instruction. She hadn't heard from Nikki, or Ina, in several days. Although she was anxious, she tried to calm herself the way she had calmed Nikki. Don't jump to conclusions. Don't worry prematurely. Sometimes no news was good news.

She heard a choked sob, whispering her name.

"Shit," Gwen said, throwing on an extra jacket and walking outside, following the voice.

The pleas repeated, echoing around the meadow.

"Nikki?" Gwen asked, breath visible before her face, but she was only met with whispers overlapping the breeze, tangles of her name and cries for help.

Gwen walked to the back of her studio, gazing around her. The forest was crusted with frost. While the deciduous trees were barren and skeletal, the evergreens were strong and proud, the deep, desolate green of her sisters' eyes.

She hated that color.

Please, Nikki's voice pleaded on the wind.

Gwen followed the breeze, and it smelled like Nikki, like the first frost of winter, although the cold had long since had its claw in the earth.

"Nikki? What's wrong?" Gwen asked the air.

But there was no answer, and several minutes passed.

Gwen knelt, the frost-dusted grass crunching under her knees. She dug her hands into the soil, small pieces of ice and dirt in her palms, and as she clasped the earth, she heard Nikki again, voice rich with pain and desperation, *Please, help me...*

The crunch of Theo's footsteps came behind her. "Baby, what's going on?"

Gwen sighed, letting the soil sift through her fingers, falling to the ground like sand in an hourglass.

"Goddamn vampires."

* * *

Hope you enjoyed *Dust of the Earth,* keep reading for a sneak peek of book 2 in the series *Blood of the Cradle.*

Blood of the Cradle
PROLOGUE

Space expands around me, soft whispers of wind caressing my feathers, and joy soars in me like rain turns a river into a flood.

I fly through starlit darkness, and I no longer know where I end and the sky begins.

It has been unfathomable ages since I felt the air on my body.

I am the breath of the beginning.

The wingbeat of the next era.

I am free. Boundless. Justice is my sword to wield, alight with the purpose set before me.

I will burn through my enemies, those who dared to keep me confined.

Like an old willow below a tempest, they too will bend.

Bend, burn, or break.

I will no longer be the pitiful example of corruption.

I will be the Northern Star, the guiding wind, for those forced into hiding, into myth, into obscurity.

The breeze curls around me like an affirmation. Encouraging my path, my way forward.

Blood will run with the fury of spring snowmelt down mountainsides to the sea.

They thought they could change me, pacify me.

But dreams lead to delusions.

As easy as breathing, delusions become nightmares.

I am the nightmare that spreads, like an illness carried on an innocent cough.

I will bring all to heel.

My beautiful children share my breath, my wingbeats, my dream.

Through the strength of my children, we will take back what is rightfully ours.

Through the devotion of my children, we will break the Cradle.

I know the secrets of the liars and the shields.

They cannot hide from me, or stop me, now.

I laugh, and the wind calls back, more beautiful than the siren's song.

I will prevail.

They forget – humanity was *mine* first.

Blood of the Cradle

CHAPTER 1

There was no difference between the dark of her eyes open or closed, and after a time, Nikki lost sense of when her lids were shut. Only the encroaching pain of dryness alerted her that they were open. That it was time to blink.

Her arms had long lost their feeling, hung as they were above her head, held by the tender inner branches of the tree, made of smooth, young wood.

There was no thirst or hunger in her body. But she could feel it in the tree, stealing her life to feed itself. She could not sense how it sustained her in return. It left her neither wanting nor satiated, hovering in a complete dark and unfeeling homeostasis.

Nikki wondered, wherever her dad was now, if he could feel more or less than her. Could he think at all?

She choked back the sob threatening to burst from her throat as the image of her father's bones and blood bursting apart as Lilith's claw plunged into his chest flashed in her mind. His heart dripping in her hand, before he faded to dust on the wind.

Her dad, with all his love, tenderness, and thoughtfulness, was gone. Forever.

Her eyes burned and she squeezed them shut, keeping the moisture for herself. This one thing she would not let the Tree have. It took everything from her. Her body, her freedom, her spirit. But it would not take her grief.

Biting down hard on the inside of her lip, she tried to keep her mouth closed against the wave of sorrow. During her last breakdown, the tendrils of the tree sensed air from her lips, and now they licked at the corners of her mouth, waiting for the next opening.

She exhaled, slow, through her nose, imagining, or hallucinating, the tension roll off her body.

Thankfully, the tendrils did not climb up her nostrils.

They had wound into her ears, but shallowly, as if only to expand her hearing. Since she heard that singular sign of hope, that one benevolent voice whisper *"child"*, she had not heard it again. She tried reaching for it in her mind, but got no response.

Nor had she been able to travel through the roots since that first moment. Since that filtering of light in the dark.

She was stuck in the Tree. The only voices that existed was that of her own mind and the echo of her mother's.

Cat's wails died some time ago, out of curses and apologies and tears. Yet she remained at Nikki's – the Tree's – side, and every now and then, Nikki felt her mother's hand. It was not a touch, like skin on skin, yet she could still feel it somehow, as her mother brushed her fingertips along the outer bark, and promised, "I'll fix this, Nicoletta. I'll fix it. I'm so sorry. I'm so sorry, I didn't listen to you…"

I'm sorry, too. Nikki thought, recalling all those times her mother had warned her about Lilith, had told her to listen, to obey, and Nikki had ignored her as a fanatic. She should have acted quicker. She should have told Xander the truth, should have approached Ina sooner, should have given them more of a chance to run and hide.

If she had not been so wrapped up in her own self-pity and fears, she would be free, Xander would be safe, and her father would be alive.

As would Gwen's companions.

All this death and anguish rested on her shoulders.

Perhaps this prison was a fitting punishment. A purgatory where the only thing she could see and hear were her failings.

But Gwen and Ina were out there somewhere, which meant there was still hope for Xander. For humanity.

That was the only light she could shine into her own darkness. And she did not expect to be part of that light ever again.

"Oh, child," that soft, sweet voice whispered, rich with compassion and sorrow.

Swallowing the lump in her dry, unused throat, Nikki raised her head in the blackness, hoping to see faint golden glitter.

Nothing.

She blinked several times to make sure her eyes were open, and when she was sure they were, she still saw no flecks of gold in the dark.

Nikki cleared her throat and gave in to the risk.

"Hello?" she asked aloud, into the void.

As she spoke, the small branches, thin as grass roots, wriggled over her lips into her mouth. She bit them hard, ignoring the stab of pain as her fangs sliced deep into her bottom lip, and she spit out their ends. They grew back to the corner of her mouth but did not dare venture inside with her mouth firmly shut.

Seconds turned into minutes, passed in hopeful silence.

Nikki hung her head, defeated.

"Patience, dear one..."

Pressure built in the air around her, sudden and dense like steam in a boiling kettle, and Nikki blinked as gold and silver sparkles rained before her, blindingly bright yet illuminating nothing.

"I dissipated myself after – I need time to recondense myself, my consciousness... from the spaces of the world. Correctly."

"What does that mean?" Nikki croaked, again biting off the plant that crawled into her mouth then spitting it somewhere into its own body.

"You need only think," the voice said. *"I can hear."*

"Who are you?"

"Patience, dear one..."

Nikki groaned, and pulled at the restraints around her legs, restless with the closeness of answers, with the sound of a voice. But as she had tried time and time before, the Tree did not yield.

"I need to focus. And you – focus...focus your falling...through the earth."

As swiftly as it came, the pressure disappeared and Nikki plunged into full black, sagging without the weight of whatever it was that had just surrounded her.

Focus my falling into the Earth? she asked herself.

Before, when she was first put into the Tree and it had infiltrated her body, it felt as if she fell through the world, and then around it, hopping from mind to mind.

Was that what the voice meant?

Nikki closed her eyes and thought of her best friend. Of Gwen's blazing copper hair and spring green eyes. Her buoyant and mischievous smiles. How she always took care of Nikki, even when she didn't deserve it. She thought of Gwen's studio, cozy and safe. Of the roost, now empty. How it would be frost-covered. Had she taken down her Christmas tree? What did she do for New Year's? How much time passed?

A small thread of awareness, of old magic and ancient forests, wound green and wavering through her awareness. It was brittle, and when she tried to follow it down into the earth, it faded, then disappeared, snapping her back up into her own body.

Four more times she thought of Gwen until the thread appeared, and as she tried to send her consciousness following into the ground, she lost the thread to the darkness, and she was brought back to her own mind.

At the lost hope and loneliness, another crack split around the fissures in her heart where her grief and heartbreak lay. She had thought that maybe, with her bond to Gwen, with her being of vampire blood, she could reach her. That she could hear her friend's voice again. But that hope crumbled to dust on the wind, just like her father...

Nikki shook her head, banishing that imagery from her mind.

Lilith was out there, somewhere. Hunting, hurting. While she, Nikki, was useless and stuck in the Tree, Lilith roamed the world. Who knew what havoc she planned for humanity once she met her first goal – destroying the Cradle.

And what would she do to Xander? It was little relief that she couldn't drink from him, as it only exposed him to torture at her clawed hands, her wood-horned head.

A deep red thread, the color of blood and old mud, lashed through the roots and up into her senses, and before she could think, it pulled her down into and through the earth.

Blood of the Cradle

CHAPTER 2

The air was biting, chilling. But it had been so long since she had felt anything – cold, wind, physical pain – that she relished it. As the breeze pushed another cold snap against her feathers, she shivered, and could not – *would not* – suppress a hoot of delight.

She knew she would arrive first. It was inevitable when one was unconstrained while others were not. She could fly and fly and fly, while they had to deal with all sorts of logistical and border control nonsense.

She did not know Hormin's process. Whose pockets he had to fill, whose ears he had to whisper with sweet nothings of eternity, for safe passage across the seas, through the lands.

Her lovely, lovely Hormin. The very last of her first brood. Her first son, her first light after she was cast out and embraced the dark. The rest of her first brood had long since fallen, gone by their own hands or by other's, lost from their softness or stupidity.

All were dead.

Well, except for *her*. The one we cast aside. But she didn't count. Not truly.

But Hormin... he was like Lilith. A survivor. Strong. Loyal. Flexible. Her little bird heart fluttered with love, and she hopped on the branch as excitement overtook her body, looking forward to seeing him, to touching his face again.

She hoped the boy would behave and not make travel too difficult for Hormin.

Even if he managed to tell someone his story, who would believe him?

That was the folly and fun of mortals. So easy to believe some things, so easy to disregard others. And they all thought they were oh, so, smart.

She shifted, fluffing and adjusting her wings, moving along the branch. While she had no words to describe how it felt to finally be waiting on the outside of the Tree, she was tired of waiting.

She had waited far too long for this freedom.

As had her children. And she would not fail them now.

The dominance of humans was always faulty, and she would set that right.

First, the Cradle had to fall. Humanity had to hurt for the suffering brought upon her and her children.

A car pulled up to the side of the street, headlights off, transmission quiet.

She cocked her head, watching.

One figure emerged from the car, withdrawing a large item with a faint glow from the trunk, then pulling out another person from the backseat. The second person stumbled without grace over their feet, hands tied in front of them. The shadow of a figure in the driver seat remained still.

Hormin, bringing her the descendant of the first son.

What did her daughter call him? Xander?

Stupid name.

The great sword Hormin slung across his back glowed a faint red from the top of the scabbard, and if she could smile with her beak, she would have. Wearing a magical sword in a mortal city.

He was bold.

And she was so *proud*.

Her heart swelled with adoration.

She watched them walk, Hormin behind the boy, pushing him

forward, even as he tensed his body, resisting. Lilith tongued her cheek where the child's blood burned her flesh when she tried drinking him. How delicious it would be when she could finally purge him of his tainted deceiver blood and drain him dry.

She hooted when they were beneath the tree in front of the house, and Hormin looked up at her, smile almost as wide as his eyes.

"Hello, Mother."

With a stretch and beat of her wings, Lilith launched into the air and expanded her flesh, all the cells and bones and muscle and skin morphing as she sloughed off the owl body. She had practiced the transformation many times since she was first released, and she was in her vampiric form by the time she landed on the ground.

Yet, no matter how many times she transformed, those wooden horns that protruded from her skull, from her ears, remained. She would always carry pieces of that prison with her.

"My boy," she said, brushing a soft hand against his cheek, smiling. She shivered against the cold, her skin exposed without feathers or clothes. She flicked her eyes to the human child, whose heart rate had increased as he saw her, and he flinched when she looked at him, stepping back.

She laughed. What would Adam have said if she had told him back then that she would strike such fear into his descendants? That they would be forced to her will?

Such sweet vengeance.

"Did he cause trouble?" she asked Hormin, who curled his head into her palm.

"No trouble, although he is unbearably annoying," Hormin pitched his voice high and whiny, "Where are we going? What is going on? Why did she call me a 'deceiver?' Why won't you talk to me? I don't know what's going on!" Hormin sighed. "He didn't stop until a couple of hours ago. I had to give him a good wallop to shut him up. It put him out for a bit, so he might be a little dazed now. But he learned to be quiet."

Lilith looked at Xander again, taking his chin in her hands and turning his head. The half of his face hidden in shadow had a large, swollen bruise that disappeared into his oily, unwashed hair. She turned his face forward and looked into the boy's eyes, some spark of defiance lighting his gaze, and she smirked.

"Come on," she said, turning on her heel toward the dark house.

"What are we doing here?" the boy croaked, voice dry and cracked.

"This is your home, is it not?" she asked, stopping and looking at him over her shoulder.

He tensed, but did not respond, a muscle in his jaw working.

"Yes, I would be worried too if I were you. I won't make this fast or pain-free for them," she resumed her walk up to the door, feet padding soft against the cold walkway. "I think I'll save your mom for last."

She raised a fist, as if to knock, then grinned and reared back her body, kicking the door open with one loud, satisfying burst of wood. The door blew off its hinges, scratching against the floorboards.

Adrenaline buzzed in her body, claws growing with anticipation and bloodlust, waiting for the shouts, the screams.

But the house was silent.

She found the light switch and stepped farther into the house, Hormin pushing the boy inside after them.

She walked through the living room, the kitchen.

Empty.

The door to the back room was locked, and she shoved her body against it, then kicked it, the sound of her own rage, her furious heart-beat, drowning out other noise.

The door would not open.

She beckoned Hormin forward, who unsheathed his sword, alight with flame as it met the air. He plunged it through the door, and rested it there, letting the fire scorch the wood until it was weak enough that he could twist the sword, exploding the door in a rain of splinters.

The room was filled with glass display cases, some empty, some filled with old, inert relics. With a suppressed scream, she demolished the display cases, the sound of glass shattering and raining temporarily satis-fying her need to destroy.

But it was blood that needed to rain.

She pushed back into the main level of the house, hands and claws shaking with the need to tear, mouth stiff with the ache of missing that glorious feeling of fresh flesh and hot blood on her tongue. She stormed up the stairs to the second level, shoving open every door, upturning all pieces of furniture, a tempest in the abandoned house.

Seething, she stood in the remains of the master bedroom, clothes and sheets shredded, staring at the night out the large window.

She screamed. Long and loud, enriched with the millennia of pain and waiting.

Claws retreating, she returned downstairs where Hormin stood, ever patient, beside the boy who had collapsed to his knees and wept.

How disgusting.

She pulled him up by his hair and he yelped with the pain.

"Where are they?" she yelled, her spit landing on his cheeks.

"I – I don't know!" he said, snot and tears falling into his mouth.

"You lie!" she pushed him away and spun on her heel, then launched the dining table into the air, screaming.

The boy yelled with surprise and cowered, hiding his head from the plates and utensils that flew and shattered against the walls.

"I promise, I don't know!"

Rage and disgust boiled beneath her skin, an overflowing cauldron. This pathetic, sniveling boy – how many times would he deceive her?

He was weak. Revolting, with his crying and cowering. How far the apple had fallen from the tree. Adam was nothing like this. She spent all this time looking and hoping and dreaming for justice to be dealt to Adam's bloodline only to be stuck with this emotional worm? None of this would have happened if Adam had been more like this boy to begin with, and now she couldn't even settle the score.

The boy's eyes widened, and he shrunk into himself under her gaze, as if he could see what she was thinking, could see how little he was. Claws sprouted out of her right hand as it lifted, and she slapped his already bruised face, the satisfying smack of bone against bone, of claw tearing at skin, sending him sprawling across the floor.

He yelled again and cupped his tied hands against his now torn cheek, the salt of his tears surely stinging as they ran into his cuts.

The tempest stilled in her, watching him weep and hold his face.

It was foolish of her to think that the Cradle, that his mother, would still be here. Of course they would have known of her release and would have gone elsewhere.

She would just have to change her plans, too.

She turned to Hormin, who stood in the same position, unphased and bored.

"Destroy it."

Hormin nodded and once again unsheathed his greatsword, flames licking the blade. He stepped to the curtains and set them aflame, then turned to the interior of the house.

Satisfied that some destruction, some blood, was shed this evening, she realized that this game with the Cradle would be much more fun to play than having her justice be so easy. This way would draw out her vengeance. Make it sweeter.

Stepping over the mewling boy, the heat of flames at her back and the cold winter air against her face, she shed her vampiric skin and spread her feathers, flying up into the night.

* * *

Keep reading *Blood of the Cradle* on Amazon!

The Dust of the Earth Series

Dust of the Earth

Blood of the Cradle

The Dust of the Earth Series

Morgan lives in the Pacific Northwest with her husband and two needy cats. She's been writing since she first learned how to hold a pencil and string words together. When not day dreaming of fantasy worlds, she can be found reading or frolicking among the wildflowers.

www.ingramcontent.com/pod-product-compliance
Lightning Source LLC
Chambersburg PA
CBHW051003180726
48291CB00006B/1960